By the same author

One Little Room

". . . they shall behold the land that is very far off.
S fhada an gladeth bho lochodha."

From a Barkerville tombstone. The Gaelic translates as "(who) long have been kept from home."

Muckle Annie

Jan Webster

Heywood Books

© Jan Webster 1985

First published in Great Britain 1985
by Robert Hale Ltd

ISBN 1 85481 007 3

This edition published 1989 by
Heywood Books Ltd.,
55 Clissold Crescent
London N16 9AR

Printed in Great Britain by
Cox & Wyman Ltd, Reading

This book is sold subject to the condition that
it shall not, by way of trade or otherwise,
be lent, resold, hired out, or otherwise circulated
without the publisher's prior consent in any
form of binding or cover other than that
in which it is published and without a similar
condition including this condition being imposed
on the subsequent purchaser.

Preface

When men sought gold in the Cariboo in the adventurous years from the late 1850s onwards, the few women who accompanied them had to be mettlesome. They might be dancing girls from Germany or San Francisco, servant lasses from Scotland, farm girls from Northumberland or 'Celestials' from China. They saw fortunes come and go, men die of cold, fever or accident but like Jenny Allen from Fifeshire, on whose death all the flags in Barkerville were hung at half-mast, they learned to be nurse, confidante and friend; or like Bella Hodgkinson, supported their partners in hard times by taking in washing or performing other menial tasks. ('Why don't you sleep?' Bella's husband would demand, as the rattle of boilers and the swish of tubs disturbed his rest, and when poor worn-out Bella died he had 'Sleep, Bella, Sleep' carved on her tombstone).

Katie, Gerda and 'strapping, rattling hizzies' like the Kangaroo danced for the men in the saloons with names like the Go-at Them and the Fashion, while ladies from the Flowery Kingdom (China) were bartered and sold and one was reportedly 'highly elated' when her 'charms and fascinations' went for all of 700 dollars.

In the hard, hell-for-leather atmosphere where drinking and gambling were the norm, tragedy stalked with a long shadow. A Mrs. Hetherington, known as the 'Scotch Lassie' because of her Gaelic lilt, left her drunken husband only to be murdered in her cabin while she herself was in 'a high state of intoxication.' And perhaps most poignant of all,

Sophie Cameron was with her husband John when he made one of the richest strikes ever, only to die of the mountain fever before he could buy her so much as a new ribbon for her bonnet. The grief-stricken husband had her coffin taken to Victoria in a gruesome trip that lasted 36 days in 40-below weather, then not content to let her be, had her despatched to Panama before she finally came to rest in Cornwall, Ontario.

The brave and the broken, the hurdy girl and the sturdy wife, peopled these few pages of Cariboo history, while New Caledonia became British Columbia and British Columbia ceased to be a colony and joined instead the great new Dominion of Canada.

This is a tribute to those pioneers and all who came after them and especially a reminder that womanhood then as now is about loving and giving and not always counting the cost.

Part One

1

"Wipe your feet, lassie."

The hatchet-faced parlourmaid indicated Annie's boots with a look that said she'd never seen the like.

"The maister says go into the dinin' room and he'll deal wi' you." She gave the girl a firm and spiteful push. Annie shuffled forward in her late father's footwear. He'd been a slender man with small feet so in the beginning the boots had been wearable. But by now the laces were in shreds, the toes had curled and separated from the soles in front, so that they were very caricatures of boots, boots all but ready to give up claim to the name. All that could be said for them was they were better than nothing in the cold Glasgow spring, especially when she remembered to make insoles out of newspaper.

Coming into the warmth, her nose began to run like a burn and the hoast on her chest loosed its tightness so that she coughed with a sore, fierce persistence. Her chapped hands stung and her chilblains nipped and burned, but she could feel the warmth of the great house fold itself about her like a big down quilt, one she wanted to give herself up to, one she could sink into and emerge from again as one newborn.

She'd never been further indoors than the scullery before: the cook fed her scraps at the jawbox, making her stand over it so that crumbs fell into the sink. Now as she moved forward, drawing her raggedy shawl about her shoulders in an automatic gesture, she was all but transfixed by the magnificence of the big square hall with its red Turkish carpeting, gilt-framed pictures and enormous, loud-ticking grandfather clock.

Rare smells assailed her – bacon, fresh baps and something else, deliciously strange and exotic, that set the juices running in her mouth and made her pass a dry tongue over her chapped lips.

"Is that The Miscreant?" She stood at the morning-room door, shaking with fear at the timbre of the voice. All she could see beyond was the huge, frock-coated back of the man at the white-clothed table, and the folds of rough, red skin on the half-turned face. Not knowing what a Miscreant was, she could not answer. Transfixed somewhere between terror and amazement, she gazed at the well-furnished breakfast table and at something hubble-bubbling at the far end of it.

The big man turned impatiently and catching her look of bemusement said scornfully "Have you never seen a coffee percolator before?" He indicated to the servant that she should pour him another cup, which she did with an exaggerated stylish deference that set up a little quiver of unexpected disdainful amusement somewhere deep in Annie's mind. The woman then backed away against the chiffonier, terrified she would be dismissed before she saw this chit get what was coming to her. Fancy shouting at Miss Nana, the youngest and certainly the most spoiled of the Henderson bairns and all for running up and down the front door steps before they'd dried. Who did this cross-eyed pauper think she was?

The big man rose and warmed his back at the blazing grate, his look indicating Annie should come no further than the threshold. It was well-known he'd risen from nothing himself. It didn't mean he liked to be too close to the smell or sight of poverty. As a good Christian, he performed his charitable works and went twice to the kirk on Sundays. But the likes of this lassie brought back too much that was painful, unbearable, making him think the world and its stench would never be remedied, no matter how hard one worked or prayed. There was an irremediable stratum in society that could not be breached or mended. That would not help itself by being deferential to its betters but sank lower and lower into its own base ingratitude.

'You ken you have sinned.' He gazed at the girl distastefully, his mind already on the day's work ahead, irked by the fact his wife was sickly and still abed and he had to take on matters of domestic discipline that were surely beneath him. "You have taken the Lord's name in vain."

"Not in vain." Somehow Annie's voice found its protest. Maybe it was hunger that made her bold and the knowledge that nothing from that well-laden table would find its way down her thrapple. "I said 'Lord help us,' that was all. I had scrubbed and rubbing-stoned that step till it was white as the driven snow and then that wee besom Nana deliberately ran up and down it with her muddy feet."

"*Miss* Nana. You stole food from the kitchen. Miss Nana saw you."

"It was stale."

"You know what the Good Book says. 'Thou shalt not steal.' You're in need of a lesson, my lassie. You're not only a thief and a foul-mouthed sinner. I can see you're impudent with it."

"I want my wages."

"For your cheek, you'll get devil a penny. There's plenty will scrub steps and be civil with it. If you are to prosper, you must learn your place. Go home and ponder what I've said. It's for your own good. I don't want to see the likes of you round here again. You are dismissed."

The parlourmaid gave a little hiss of satisfaction, like water on the hob. Henderson the locomotive-maker, whose engines went all over the world in this year of 1863, felt himself momentarily almost burning up under the sudden furious glare of the girl on the threshold. What a strange-looking creature she was, he acknowledged, with her tangle of dark red curls and odd, skelly-eyed glower.

"I don't go till I get paid." The boots took up a solid stance.

"Aye, but you'll go," he said, amusedly. "I'll give you two seconds to get out of here, or I'll throw you out." He felt a spasm of near-mirth at the pathetic insolence of this bundle of rage and fury, pitting herself against his power and authority. He looked towards the parlourmaid as he said, "What is it they call her? Muckle Annie?" The woman joined him in ready sycophantic laughter. "How did you come by a name like that?" He made indulgent shooing movements and began to close the heavy mahogany door in Annie's face.

One of the disgraceful boots stopped his action.

"I'm not telling the likes of you how I got my name. For the likes of you –" Annie stared at the maidservant so that she was also included – "I have only got this." And gathering up what little spit was available to her she delivered it on the tessellated floor in front of Henderson the engine-maker with all the venom she could summon.

Outraged man and woman both sprang forward to lay hands on her but she was away on the dreadful boots, speeding through the hall and out of the front door before they could stop her. She was halfway down the drive, tripping over the split soles, weeping and half-laughing, before her momentum slowed.

She wasn't sorry for what she'd done. She *hadn't* sworn at that spoiled brat Nana. She had said, "Great suffering lamentable," but she'd only mentioned God the once, when Nana had deliberately run up and down the steps for the sixth time, giggling and defiant, and she had indeed required the Deity's help to stop her half-murdering the child on the spot. Just for once, the difference between Nana's well-fed insouciance and her own cold and hunger had been too much to bear.

Her mother would kill her if she knew about the spitting. That was a gesture for tinkers and gipsies. Maybe they felt all the time as she felt then – powerless, feeble, with no other way to express a terrified contempt.

She felt inside her bodice. Good job she'd had the foresight to tuck a couple of treacle scones down there, squashed and crumpled though they must be now. She didn't like stealing food, but they all did it, the whole army of assorted domestics at the Henderson mansion, hiding titbits on shelves, behind clocks and ornaments, anywhere the mistress wouldn't think of looking. If you were hungry you hadn't much option. Her mother would be angry about the wages, though. Annie began to weep with a desolate despair at the injustice of it. That was money already earned. How dare he? How dare he look at her like that as though she were *nothing*. She kicked at the wrought-iron gates as she went out, in howling frustration, until she realized the cracked boots were no protection for her dirty feet.

She thought it imprudent to go home at the moment. Maybe ever. She left the big grey-stoned house behind her and took to the fields, coming at last to a bridge and a little burn. Springburn, they called the area. Famed already all over the world for its steam locomotives. The water in the burns here ran milk-white to ink-black, with red and green and yellow in between. She remembered her mother telling her what it had once been like, before the distillers and dyers had fouled every stream that ran with their chemical waste. God had probably not intended this, she thought. She would have given a lot there and then for a drink of fresh, clean, unpolluted spring water. Instead she curled herself in the lee of the stone bridge and picked absently at a portion of crumbley treacle scone, tasting salt tears where there should have been butter.

Muckle Annie. So even he had heard about it, the nickname that had dogged her life since infancy. And all her own doing. Some elderly relative, looking down at her aged two, had expressed doubts even then about her comeliness. "I doubt she'll no' amount to muckle." And she'd upped and said, "I will. I will. I be Muckle Annie." And then as her

surname was McIlvanney it had become a childish taunt;
"Muckle Annie
Muckle-vanney."

It didn't greatly matter. Glasgow folk were great ones for nick-names. A man who kept bees was Bumbee Jock. A woman who dragged a crippled foot Trail-the-Bauchle. Another with too-long skirts the Draiggled Petticoat. People got named after their favourite songs or drinks or obsessions.

But the laconic amusement in the man Henderson's voice, meant to deny the last shreds of her inner dignity, had wounded unbearably. Some day, she would command respect from the likes of him and that contemptible maidservant who ran after him like a cur. She would have fine pale-grey boots and a different dress for each day of the week, even different ones for morning and afternoon. She would no longer squint or have to go around without drawers, the hacks on her cold-purpled hands would heal up and she'd go about in a carriage being kind to people. She would show him! She'd show them all.

For once, the day-dreams were no comfort at all. There was no getting away from the stark reality that her meagre wages were all that had stood between her own and her mother's starvation. She looked back to the time when they had both had good piecework from the mills, meat on the table and even something to put on the plate in the kirk on Sundays. But since the start of the American Civil War, the cotton was rotting on those faraway Southern plantations; the mills, the print stops and the dyeworks of Glasgow were all paying off.

It was beneath her to go out scrubbing steps – as her mother kept reminding her, she was off 'good folks,' – but even that job had been better than nothing. Now she should die unless something turned up. It wasn't so far-fetched. Women were dying on the streets of Glasgow every day God sent. She looked heavenwards and spoke out loud:

"Oh, God, help me. I'm sorry if I've been self-willed and

selfish. But help me. I'll try to be good."

"You don't really think He hears you, do you?"

She jumped up as though scalded. She had been shouting her desperate prayer to the wind, thinking the nearest human being was miles away. Now behind and above her, peering down from the parapet of the little bridge, was a young man of about her own age, which was 17, tall, well-favoured, fair-haired. Something about him suggested he might have been travelling and sleeping rough. She certainly had never seen him before. She rose on shaking legs and glowered at him furiously.

"You shouldn't have been listening."

"How could I help it? I should think the craws heard you. I should think the cuddy in the field over there heard you. Is something bad the matter?"

She began to walk away. "Never you mind. It's none of your business."

She hadn't expected to throw him off immediately, but when he first hung back obediently and then began to make what she saw were limping tracks in the opposite direction, something made her stop and call after him, scathingly, "*You* look like the one who's in trouble. Come a long way, have you?"

They stood, like two combatants in a duel, sizing each other up. There was something about him that discomfited her, a look close to fear or desperation, a loneliness. Yet his clothes, though dirty and rumpled, were good, he had the straight and slender bearing of someone who had spent more time with books than in hard manual labour. She was aware of the uneven, insistent thump of her pulse and knew it for what it was – the unnecessary, flustering commotion that overcame it occasionally when she was confronted with a handsome male.

He limped back towards her and she saw he was thin, that there were grubby purple shadows under his very blue eyes, where an unsettling pleading expression was now in evidence.

"I didn't mean to alarm you."

"You didn't, exactly."

"I just thought you sounded as if you could do with some help."

She half-smiled then. "And you were the one to give it to me?" Her contemptuous look at his dusty clothes indicated the unlikelihood of that.

"What happened?" he pressed. Somehow they were back in the lee of the bridge, she sitting with her skirts spread, he beside her, hunkered back on his heels.

"I lost my job. Such as it was. The master owes me money and he wouldn't give me a penny of it – him with all the money in the world." She began to weep, more from fury than out of pity for herself. " 'To them that hath, shall be given.' It's what the Bible says. Can you make sense o' that? For I cannot."

"I've got money."

"I'm too good for scrubbing stairs, anyway. I can read and write. I'm as smart as any of them at the big house. They think because you're poor –" She stopped, his words percolating her anger. "You have money? You don't look as though you have a bean to your name."

He took several coins from his pocket and held them towards her.

"Bring me some food and I'll pay you for the service." He began to talk rapidly, jerking his head towards a decrepit stone bothy in the nearby field. "I'm sleeping over there –"

"You hiding?" A kind of terror crept over her.

"I have to hide."

"Why?"

"I did something I shouldn't have done and now my brother's getting me a passage to the Cariboo. I have to lie low till then."

"Why here?"

"I got lost. But it's as good as anywhere."

"What did you do?" For some reason, she whispered.

"I can't tell you. What's your name?"

"My name is Annie Margaret McIlvanney. What's yours?"

"Hector James Mennock. I'm from Inverary – you know, the place Rabbie said had nothing but Highland pride, and Highland scab and hunger."

She nodded. "I know Burns back to front. I told you I can read. Can you?"

He nodded. "Of course."

"Are you a scholar o' some kind?"

"As the laird's sons, we all had learning." He gazed at her and said again, pleadingly, "Look, can you get me some food? I'm starving. My foot's been hurting – I cut it on a sharp stone in a ditch. Take the money –" he pushed some into her palm – "keep something for yourself, but bring me back some bread and cheese, scones, potted head, anything. And some ointment for the festering cut on my foot. Don't tell anybody about me, though. Promise, Annie Margaret McIlvanney."

She looked down at the coins in her hand. She could take enough to soften the blow when she told her mother what had happened that morning. It was a temptation. But she knew nothing about this desperate creature before her. He could be a murderer, or out to have her honour, for no one would hear her scream for help.

On the other hand, he had learning. And she had a hunger for that that was worse sometimes than the hunger for food. To know. To understand.

She wavered. "Take the money, anyway," he said.

She looked up slowly then and into the face it was already becoming alarmingly familiar, as though it had been imprinted on her mind since time began. Something, some trust wove itself between her and the shivering, cauldrife* man, in front of her, subtly altering what she had been up till then and would be in the days ahead. It was as though she took a great leap of commitment in that silent, vibrant

---

* Chilled.

moment when his cold hand touched hers.

"Wait here. I'll bring something for your foot." She stood up resolutely. "I'll come back after the Four Hours." At his look of perplexity she explained, "When we've had our tea." Her mother, whose grand-uncle had been one of the tobacco barons who'd started the tea-drinking ritual in the afternoon, still liked to use the old expression. When you had come down in the world the small refinements mattered.

A great, shivering sigh shook his frame.

"I'll be waiting for you," he said.

* * *

The grassy plateau where they sat in the lee of the bridge was now quite flattened by their feet and bodies. He had dragged a large, flat boulder from the stream for her to sit on. It was almost, she thought whimsically, like a little house, the kind she had made with her playmates when she was a child, transformed by the strength of her imagination into a place of magic and release.

"So," she said, "you struck this man and he went down and hit his head and never moved after. And his brothers took him away. But how do you know you killed him?"

"I don't know for absolute certain. Except he looked dead to me. He looked as if he'd never move again and blood was trickling from his temple."

"What was his name?"

"His name was Colin Macandrew. As if I will ever forget it."

"And you fought him for your brother Rab?"

"Because Rab had been half-killed by him the week before."

"And what was the fight about that time?"

"I don't know for sure. Some gambling debt."

"But you say it's gone on a long time, this quarrel between your family and the MacAndrews. Is it one of those feuds they talk about, that the Highlands are full of? Like the Campbells against the Macdonalds –"

"They did us out of our inheritance."

"But you said your father *had* to give them the land, to settle a debt of honour. Do they all gamble and fight, your family?"

"They call us the Fighting Mennocks."

"It's no title to boast of."

"There's Kenneth and Andrew and Rab – Robert – and me. We are the Fighting Mennocks. Strike one and you strike us all."

"And they – Kenneth and Andrew and Rab – are all free, while you have to flee the country. The youngest and the best."

"Why do you say I'm the best?"

"Because the others are older and should know better than to involve you in their drunken brawls."

"But I may have killed a man." His voice broke in the desolation of despair.

He got up and walked alongside the stream, throwing pebbles into its busy, rushing progress. For the second time now she had brought him food. Soon he would have to press on to the pub at the Broomielaw where Rab had promised the money for his passage would be waiting and the *Lizzie Shaw* ready for the journey round the Cape. He did not wish to embark till the last moment, or be seen at the Broomielaw, in case the MacAndrews who had Glasgow cousins by the dozen got wind of his plans. But suddenly he didn't want to think or talk about his departure. Suddenly it was much more important to keep Annie with him for a bit longer. He had been uncommonly glad when that small figure had trudged across the field half an hour earlier, with food and drink tied up in a spotted handkerchief. Why else would he have spilled everything out?

He went back to her now. "Come for a walk," he said. "The bluebells are out further up here. It was strange. I went out when it was dark last night and I smelled them before I saw them. All glimmering in the moonlight."

"You should have been resting that foot."

"The bread poultice you made last time drew out the poisons. It's easier."

She was pleased. "It was the baking soda did it." She fell into step beside him.

She had told her mother she was out looking for work. Lying easily for the first time in her life.

His boney hand caught hers, held it fast as they walked. She felt as though her spirit were tugging, tugging, wanting to be off into the peerless blue sky where the laverock was piping its disembodied song.

"Oh, Hector Mennock, the bluebells!" She stopped as they rounded the river path and were suddenly confronted by a woodland area, mainly of silver birch, interlaced as far as the eye could see with a wavering tide of declamatory blue. It wasn't the blue of the sky, or sea, but of some new element invented there and then for their enchantment, deep, strange and inviting. Annie disengaged her hand and ran into the flowers headlong, picking them right and left till she had a great sheaf of them. Then, turning and seeing him watching her with a strange, indulgent look, she threw them into the air and let them land all over him, so that he had to pick them from her hair and she from his. The sharp, sappy smell escaped from the stems and mingled with other mossy, leafy fragrances.

"I think this is paradise!" she cried. "And all for nothing! Better than the penny geggy! Better than books!"

He caught hold of her then, a little shyly, but with no intention of letting her go. The fierceness of his gaze alarmed her. He wound one of her dark red curls round a forefinger. Their stares were more eloquent, more informative, than any words.

"Ah, don't," she pleaded. She cast down her eyes, unbearably conscious as always of her strange squinting aspect. His finger gently closed the lid over the poor left eye. Savagely she pushed his hand away.

"I like it," he said. "It gives you a look of serious purpose."

"I'm skelly," she said. "I'm ringle-eyed. Go on, laugh at me. Laugh at Muckle Annie. That's what they call me, you know. It nearly rhymes with McIlvanney."

"What does it matter what they call you? The way I see you, you're proud and beautiful. You walk with your head up. It was the prettiest sight I ever saw, you coming across the fields to me this morning."

"Let me go," she said more gently.

"I don't want to. Bonnie Annie. Muckle Annie."

He had never kissed a girl in his life before. He did not know where the expertise came from, but he knew just how to do it, how to come down gently on her lips, to coax a yielding from her stiff little back. They drew apart, then came together again, till her face was within a hair's breadth of his and their breath mingled. But there was no escaping her pitiful distrust that still lingered.

"As God is my witness, Annie, I never meant to kill him," he burst out. "I've always fought fair and square. The stone he hit his head on was hidden by a tuft of grass."

"If you repent, the Lord will forgive you."

"But do you?"

"It's not for me to say."

He tore away from her violently, making a harsh, sobbing sound.

"Soon I'll be miles away from you anyhow. I'll put the seas between us. Will that please you?"

It was her turn for gentleness. She put her hand on his shoulder. "Why should you carry all the blame for your feuding family? I know in my bones you're not a wicked man."

"Annie, is that true?" His eyes raked her face.

"All I'm afeared of is you going away."

"It doesn't mean we'll never see each other again. I couldn't bear that."

"Do you mean that?"

"Yes, I do."

There was no way now they could keep apart. They fell down among the bluebells and with a wild, violent tenderness kissed and held and touched each other. To Annie, it felt like the whole beginning of a new way of life, a way she struggled to define through the lightning and thunder of her emotions. She was half-becoming Hector, she was giving everything of herself, emotionally, with an abandon that was half-terrifying, half the most wonderful sensation she had ever experienced. There was no going back on this road: she was her mother's child no more.

When they sat up, dazed, transformed by kisses, she said in a wondering voice, "So this is the way of it."

"What way?"

"The way of loving a person."

He gave her his beautiful smile, that she had never seen properly before. Always before it had been a fearful, anxious boy in front of her. Now it was a face full of volatile emotion, suffused with happiness, a dreamer's face, one she had dimly discerned in her own night imaginings, the idealisation of all her longing.

"This is the way," he said softly, "that the world was, before there were run-down mills, and poverty, and fights, and running away. This is how God first made it and you and me are Adam and Eve."

"I think I knew it," she said. "Before I came here today, there was this feeling –" she held her stomach – "down here. A waiting."

He pushed her down and pushing up her skirts found the taut little drum of her abdomen with his hand. He kissed her again. "When you kiss me," he said, soberly, "I am not on my own any more. Do you know what that means to me? I've been an outcast, even to myself."

She moved from under him and then over him with a slippery ease, allowing the full weight of her slender frame to come down on his, to sink on to him like a coverlet.

"When I cover you," she said, "it is so nobody can ever

get you, or hurt you. It's my way of loving a person."

He pressed her to him till it hurt. "And this," he said, into her hair, her bluebell-smelling hair, "is mine."

* * *

"No better than a whore," her mother cried. "Aye, Nellie Curran saw you. Looking for work, were you? If that's what they call work, then I'm a Dutchman."

"I love him," she said.

Lizzie MacIlvanney's sigh came from the depths of her being. "If it weren't for your sister and her good man, we'd be starving," she said simply. "And all you can talk about is some lad you picked up, like some common street-walker."

"It isn't like that."

"I don't wish to know what it's like. All I know is you'll see him no more. I'll take care of that."

"I have to see him, Mother."

They stared at each other from either side of the dull hearth. The mother saw a child who was changing before her eyes into a desperate-eyed woman, full of sharp, preoccupied movement yet only half-intent on anything that was said to her. The girl saw her hollow-eyed parent, skin yellow as parchment, trying to exercise the authority she scarcely had the strength to summon any more. She loved this parent, would do anything for her; had excused the drinking which had clouded their lives ever since her father had died; but was now prepared to defy her, to pay any mad price, to see Hector just once more before he sailed from the Broomielaw.

"Can you not remember what it was like for you and my father?" Annie appealed. "You always said he only had to whistle! My Hector is a laird's son –"

"*My* Hector! You'll not have your sorrows to seek, my lassie, if you go on like this. Why is it I've never set eyes on him?"

"He's shy!" She wasn't prepared to tell her mother everything. She had presented Hector as someone who had lost his way on a visit to an aunt before embarking for the Colonies and who was living with said aunt in some suitably vague area between Springburn and the Broomielaw.

Lizzie McIlvanney could feel parental caution trickle away. To be sure, the prospect of Annie having a love affair and marriage like her older sister Mysie was not one she had seriously entertained. The child was so odd, with her strange, hypnotic looks, her sharp intelligence, her forceful, argumentative nature. It had always appeared likely she would frighten men away. Now here was one, from all accounts well set-up, handsome, who was caught up in the age-old dance of desire with her wilful younger child and the signs were all that it was the real thing, nothing half-baked, but the kind of experience she'd had herself, with her half-Irish charmer.

It was little enough she'd been able to give Annie and now part of her was yielding, was saying she should let the girl go forward into the unknown, find out what it was like to have a great life-enhancing experience – even if it meant risking a sadness later on. She sighed again, from her cross-slippered feet.

"Mammie? Just once more? Can I go and see him? Please?"

* * *

She wore black pumps and white stockings. She was very conscious of this as she made her way towards the bridge and kept holding up her skirts so that she could see them, entranced by the daintiness of her feet out of the horrible boots.

After her mother's reluctant concession, the rest had been easy. Her sister Mysie had lent her the pumps and stockings, on condition that she never returned home again if she got so much as a mark on them, and her friend Nellie Curran, out of contrition for clyping on her to her mother, had been persuaded to lend her the white petticoat and the blue ribbon for her hair.

"You look beautiful," Hector said, respectfully. He had too cleaned himself up, washing in the burn.

"So do you."

"You're not supposed to say men look beautiful," he corrected her wryly.

"But you do to me."

"Then that's all right then." He grinned.

"Oh, Hector, I can't let you go to the Cariboo." She had made up her mind not to weep, and here she was with the tears coursing down her face. "You might be drowned going round the Horn, or frozen to death when you get to the Colonies."

"I've survived a week in a freezing bothy."

"Don't joke!"

"There is no help for it."

"Then I'll come after you. Somehow I'll come out and join you."

"That's what I've been thinking since I last saw you. I've been doing a lot of thinking since then. I wish I could take you with me, but I can't think of any way to raise your passage. Maybe in any case it's best I go ahead, because I know it's rough in the goldfields, no place for a woman."

"I'll raise the passage money somehow."

Their arms were wound tightly round each other's waists as they stood at the little bridge where they had first met.

"If I can strike gold," he said, with deadly earnestness, "and there is no reason why I should not, they do all the time, we'll buy a farm and have cattle, sheep, corn and horses."

"Yes." She could see the colour of the horses' manes and the corn growing high on the prairie, like a sea of yellow ribbons.

"Listen," he said, disengaging his arm and searching for a small sharp stone with which to draw a map. "If you can only get to Victoria, then try to make your way to Richfield Lower Town. I think they're starting to call it Barkerville now, after the man who struck it rich there. Anyway, it's half-civilized, you'll be safe there. Travel in the company of women or clergy. When you get there, go to the *Last Chance Saloon*. It's run by my second cousin Hamish Maclennan. I'll leave a message there letting you know where I've gone and when I reckon to be back. Don't go beyond Barkerville – it gets really rough then. Sit tight and I'll come to you."

"Yes." The breath was snared in her chest.

"It's a lot to ask of you."

"I've told you. I will come. I mean it."

"We'll be married. I wish there was something I could give you –"

"I've thought of that." She delved into an old pouch at her waist. "Look – two halves of an old penny. I found them in a drawer. I think they were my parents'. Look, they have holes you can put cord through. Let's wear them round our necks till we meet again. When we're rich we can have them polished and put on chains."

While he examined his half, she said in a low, tense voice, "Did you mean it, Hector? About getting married?"

"I never meant anything more in my life. Surely you know that."

"Well, then, it's easy," she said relievedly. "Why do you think I came here today, with white stockings and a starched petticoat? So I could be your bride."

As his jaw fell open, she waved a hand at the fields around them. "With the trees and birds for congregation."

"What do you mean?"

"We'll marry over running water, in the old Scots way, like Burns and Highland Mary."

She led him down to the burn, picking her way carefully round the clumps of yellow broom and jumped on to a boulder in the middle of the stream.

"You stay on the bank," she commanded, "but reach out and hold my hands. All we need is what we say to each other. We're one person, Hector. We don't need a church."

He did not answer. His gaze burned into her face as though he would cease to make sense of the world if he turned away.

"Now," she started, "I, Annie Margaret McIlvanney, spinster of this parish, do love you, Hector Charles Mennock, with all my heart and all my soul and all my might. And do swear by Almighty God to be true to you all my days." She stopped, her breath unaccountably caught and added, "Now you."

"I, Hector Charles Mennock –" He stopped, getting a safer purchase between bank and boulder the better to hold her steady, but then went on: "– do love you, Annie Margaret, Muckle Annie, more than the world and everything in it."

"And do swear to be true to me always."

"Thus do I swear, till the hills fall down."

"To be true."

"To be true."

She jumped back into his arms and an irresistible childish mirth took over both of them.

"If anybody saw us!" She was suddenly stricken by practicality.

"We must be a bit mad."

"But a good madness."

The laughter did not last long. She had brought a sketchy meal, which they ate in solemn silence and at the end of it she said, "Now we belong together forever. No seas can alter it. Time can make no change." When he reached to hold her, she was weeping, saying, "I can't live without you. I can't let you go."

"Tonight," he said. "Tonight I sail. Come, you know there is no help for it. You said you would be brave."

She shook the tears from her eyes then and spread her shawl for them to lie on. He took the yellow dust from buttercups and laid it on her cheeks, saying it was a fairy charm for sadness. "I'll tell you many Highland tales," he promised, "when you come to me in the Cariboo."

She held him as though she were protecting him from the seas that would buffet the *Lizzie Shaw*. And when he gently undid her bodice and his eyes looked wonderingly at her nakedness, when his lips touched her flesh with a delicacy and a reverence that shook her like winds shaking a field of barley, she knew glory and exultation. She wanted to fly up in the air like the laverock, to shake into fragments in the sun like the urgent water sparkling in the burn.

"It's like I'm new-born," she said afterwards, lying against his chest. "It's like I'm whole for the first time in my life. Mind you wait, out there. Mind you love nobody else." And she laughed as she warned him, for she knew it was impossible it would ever be like this for him with anyone else, any more than it would be for her.

2

"I don't know what to make of you," said Lizzie McIlvanney vexedly. "Since that Hielan' adventurer has slung his hook, you're no' the same lassie. You don't eat enough to keep a sparrow alive and I know well enough you cry yourself to sleep every night. All for a waster you'll never see again."

"I'll see him." Annie sat on a three-legged stool in front of the miserable fire and her determination was concrete, hardened by the predictable course of the argument they had been having over and over again. "He's no waster. I'm promised to him. We've made a vow. In our eyes and the eyes of the Lord, we're man and wife. It's Scots law and it's called irregular marriage – declaration de praesenti – Nellie Curran told me about it – her brother's a lawyer."

Annie turned her clever, squinting gaze on her parent and not for the first time Lizzie felt discomfited. For a penny scholar, this one could argue the hind legs off a donkey.

Reading and writing had been second nature to her.

"Married but no' kirkit! How many times do I have to tell you that as far as I'm concerned, and I'm the one who gave you birth, you're no man's wife till the minister has called the banns and conducted the ceremony. The kirk is the kirk and the Lord will not be mocked. For all you know, this waster may have tried out these airy trysts and promises on every lass he meets –"

"It was *my* idea."

Her mother ignored her and went on, "As a way to get a lass to give him what he wants. Be thankful you're not with bairn –"

"I wouldn't care if I was! It would be his bairn, to hold in my arms till I see him again." She was off into another storm of weeping and her mother said in pale exasperation, "You'll greet yourself into a decline." She rose and put her hand on her daughter's hair. "Have you thought," she said in a voice that was at once more tender and more resigned, "of how you could have kept a bairn if you'd had one? Lassie, we're dying o' hunger in the streets. No' so much as a shirt to sew! No' just one lassie out of work, but thousands. Selling themselves to get a bite to eat."

"Well, come to the Colonies with me."

"I'll see my time out here. Scotland's good enough for me. And it should be good enough for you."

"How is it good enough, if you starve?"

They were back to the same old impasse. Lizzie McIlvanney could see no way of impressing on her wayward girl the rank impossibility of her dreams of emigration. Supposing she got to the Colonies, how could she find this man she was so taken up with? Annie had an answer to that, too. She was to go to a place called Barkerville, in the Cariboo, and there in a saloon called the *Last Chance* there would be a message from Hector Mennock if he wasn't in the vicinity himself.

But how would she get from Victoria to Barkerville? She didn't know. One thing at a time. All that concerned her was getting the money for her passage, preferably the way Hector had gone, but failing that, a seven-guinea steerage by *Anchor Line* steamship to Quebec or Montreal and she'd get over the Rockies somehow. Others had done it. And if she couldn't get it, she'd be a stowaway. It did not bear thinking of the treatment she'd get if that happened. Waves of fright and apprehension passed through the mother's body. There was no saying what Annie might do to get the money. Ever since infancy, her strong-minded younger daughter had always found ways and means of getting her own way.

The mother felt a wry, irresistible smile rise inside her, that in its way hurt more than tears. She's got spirit, the girl, she thought, and she got it from me. They could never put me down, either. She herself had been raised by a great-aunt and uncle who had never been able to forget the wealth that had come into the family through the tobacco trade but been dissipated by spendthrift and feckless sons. All she'd learned from *them* was a taste for elegant clothes and tea drunk at the Four Hours. The former had been useful when her husband died and she and her daughters had been able to take on piece-work for the fashion mills. She wasn't able to think of the latter without remembering the red cloaks, the cocked hats, the arrogant swanking demeanour and gold-headed canes, with which her elderly male relatives tried to preserve their dwindling standards and the cruelty of the women towards the poor little scodgies who were all they had left to remind them of finer days.

She thought: Glasgow now, what is it without cotton and tobacco? She had sold everything she could sell and now it was hand-to-hand every day, with sometimes nothing but a slice of cloutie dumpling brought home from the big house where Annie scrubbed. Her husband had been a poor provider – a silver-tongued rascal. She was thankful Mysie her elder child was married to a decent man and lived nearby, but could take little from her, not when the girl had three fledgling mouths forever agape and another due to set up its fearful, squawking cries of hunger in a three-month.

Lizzie McIlvanney, not for the first time, did not know which way to turn. Always at the back of her mind were the scenes she had witnessed in the centre of Glasgow last time she had been there: girls younger than her seventeen-year-old Annie standing on corners, hands on hips, lewd invitation written all over their faces. Others, less spirited, dying – yes, she'd actually seen them expiring – in close mouths and spirit shop doorways.

It won't happen to my Annie, she thought ragingly, and it so easily could after I'm gone, there might be nothing else for her, and her in this desperate mood. So maybe, risky though it was, she should let her go to the Colonies. She had prayed to the Lord and increasingly it seemed He was pressing this answer on her. It would take Annie away from the filth and degradation that Glasgow had come to mean and even if this Hector Mennock never showed his face again, there would be jobs the girl could take, work on a farm, that would be hard, certainly, but at least healthy and away from temptation. There was one possibility she had not mentioned to Annie, because it had taken till now even to contemplate it with any seriousness. The last time she had been to kirk, and it had been without Annie because of the terrible boots, she had heard the minister mention a scheme to help poor but honest girls find a new start in the Colonies.

It seemed that out in New Caledonia, now to be called British Columbia according to the Reverend Barrie, there were far more men than women. Six thousands men in the gold-fields were wifeless. The Bishop and Lord Mayor of London, had already arranged to send out some orphans, widows and other suitable English females and the Reverend Barrie did not see why Scots lassies should not also be considered, for after all many of the men out there were from north of the border, and he was open to names and recommendations. The passage would be free and everything would be done to settle the girls once there.

Lizzie felt very worn, very tired. Her dead husband Willie rose in her thoughts, so like Annie, so clever in argument, so stubborn, almost as though he were trying to influence her in some way. Once again she prayed and Willie and the Lord, it seemed, both came up with the same answer. She could not leave her child to die in a whisky shop doorway or some cold tenement stairhead. Let her follow her heart. She felt a tearing inside her, that was like the rending of the two lives that had been so close till now. Annie must follow her destiny and with her mother's blessing, which would be a shield and support to her in the days to come.

She waited till Annie had gone to a temporary scrubbing job the next day before she rose from her chair and dressed herself in shawl and bonnet. She seldom got further than her own street these days, to do a little careful shopping; she felt so ill, but today she had to get to the manse.

The minister was the only man who could help her. Pray God that he would, that all the girls for the so-called bride ship had not been picked, for time was getting short.

* * *

"You'll go in the bride ship," said her mother. "That's what they're calling it, but there'll be other passengers, too, although you'll not be allowed to mix with them. You'll keep yourselves to yourselves.

"The kirk will pay your passage but you must keep an eye on the minister's niece, Effie Cameron, for she's none too strong. She's going out to wed her lad, who's started to farm on Salt Spring Island. When you get to Victoria, there will be connections to help you. There will be decent men, known to the kirk, who might be looking for a wife."

"It wouldn't apply to me," said Annie, "because of course I'm going out to Hector." She threw her arms round her mother's neck and hugged her so savagely they both almost fell to the floor. "But I'll wed him in church as soon as I can, that I promise you, Maw, if it'll please you."

"Annie," her mother remonstrated, drawing her round to face her. "You must listen to me. Hector Mennock is someone you may never see again. The minister's told me what it can be like in the Cariboo. Diggers can set off on false trails and never be heard of again. The cold or the mountain fever can kill them, or they get into murderous brawls. And he's not one to keep out of trouble, as we know."

"But he'll take care, for my sake," said Annie, looking so pitiable her mother almost relented. But she had a duty to make Annie face up to the realities of her situation. "You may get to Victoria, and then Barkerville, but never see him again," she insisted. "You may have to take a job on a farm, housekeeping for some girny* old man. But there will be chances there to better yourself. Why else would I let you go? There's nothing for you here, lass. I want something better for you than hodden grey and porridge all your life."

Some shadow in the mother's face made the girl burst into wild weeping. "Should I not go, Maw? Should I stay with you? You will stay with our Mysie if you're not well, won't you? And I'll send for you the minute I can. I'll send money –"

"The minister has said he will get me enough piece-work to see me through. And he'll send me a lodger." Lizzie tried to sound full of practical sense but her voice unaccountably wavered.

Annie stared sharply into her mother's face. The possibility that her mother was not capable of a strong, independent life of her own was one that had not seriously entered her mind until now. But now there was a something, an unconscious message, that she knew from her mother's stubborn, misty, removed glare she was not permitted to pick up or talk about. It was something she had to respect.

So she said, more soberly, "You can always be sure I'll remember the lessons you taught me, Maw."

"To respect yourself," said Lizzie adamantly, "so that

---

* bad-tempered.

others will respect you."

"To let no one tramp on me, but stick up for my rights."

"To be fair to those that employ you and give a fair day's work for a fair day's pay."

Annie gave her parent a sideways grin that was like storm-water with a rainbow lightening over it. "I'm Muckle Annie, after all," she joked, to cheer her up. "Who dare meddle with me?"

Alec Howie, married to her sister Mysie, had a battered dogcart he used for transporting smaller items of carpentry to his customers. He had put a plaid in it to soften the seat for Lizzie McIlvanney and had brought the whole family to the Broomielaw to see Annie depart. He was a soft-natured, gentle man who could scarcely bear to witness the scene in front of the sail-and-steam ship, the *Maggie Love Campbell*. The expression *the poorest of the poor* would not shift itself from his mind. Some of the passengers were young families who had made heroic efforts to appear clean and well-doing, but their poverty showed in the women's pale, strained faces and the whippet thinness of the men. There were some young married couples, not yet embarked on families, the girls clinging to weeping parents, the men sharing gulps of whisky with brothers or peers. Predominant were single men aged anything from fourteen to forty, some bloodshot and hungover, a few defiantly ragged, nearly all sharing a desperate impatience to get on board and get away from heaven knew what. Among the motley, one or two prosperous passengers stood out, men with hard faces and gold watch-chains and the look of hardened travellers, the women over-dressed and nervously peremptory about their luggage.

And as for the thirty or so 'brides' themselves, Alec thought they were like no young wives-to-be he had ever seen. Pale and hungered almost to a girl, they nearly all carried their pathetic belongings wrapped up in a sheet. He knew in Annie's case she carried a feather pillow, a petticoat or two and oatmeal, potatoes, scones plus a few greased eggs to augment what might well be a very spartan diet, especially near journey's end. Cheap labour for desperate farmers and gold-miners, some would end up wives and mothers, some as scodgies and some no better than they should be. His mother-in-law had been assured of Captain Bonamy's probity, but Alec's mind stirred with tales of captains who'd procured girls for the male passengers and evil doctors too drunk and ignorant to care for those who took sick. In the bad old days sometimes only half the passengers survived. Those days were over, surely? They'd had the Reverend Barrie's word for it. As for Annie, what would become of her? She looked small, young but so bursting with expectation it made his eyes water. He could not imagine that auburn head cast down or held at anything other than that proud and challenging angle.

An undemonstrative, inarticulate man, he went over to her now and held her against his chest. "Take care of yourself," he murmured roughly. And at this display of untoward emotion from such an unexpected source, Annie was momentarily non-plussed, but she pecked his cheek and patted his back and quickly commenced a game of keek-a-bo with the children, in case anyone should suspect her of giving way and to allow the immense lump in her throat time to dissolve.

The ship lay alongside the wharf like a talisman to which all eyes were dragged back time and again, in mingled fascination and dread. A mixed cargo, victuals, livestock – pigs, sheep, cows, fowls – and water barrels were being stowed aboard before the passengers were allowed to embark. They could only imagine as yet the dank berths they had been told about, the coarse pinewood shelves they would lie upon a mere inch more than two feet apart. They glimpsed the captain, a legendary figure from the West Highlands, his cap at a rakish angle. Someone nearby imparted the information: "That's Captain Bonamy. There'll be no mutinies or clapping in irons wi' him. His crew think he's God." Annie felt it would be no great hardship if she and the other girls were kept amidships away from at least some of their fellow-passengers. If there was cholera and fever they would be less likely to catch it. She resolved to swab her piece of deck daily with vinegar, to try to organise the girls into 'messes' of ten or so, as the Reverend Barrie had suggested, with a leader to make sure things were kept clean and tidy, so that food was taken to the galley to be cooked and the washing up was done afterwards. She would not be averse to taking prayers and Bible readings, to teaching the odd bit of reading and writing if called upon to do so, or to organising sewing bees and concerts. At the prospect of something practical to do, and of being important, she cheered up slightly. A picture of the immensity of the journey ahead was persistently presenting itself to her mind's eye, and of waves battering at the screw-propellered vessel as in the illustrations she'd seen in books lent by the minister's wife. It looked solid enough, the ship, the captain wore his cap at a jaunty angle, but the masts and spars creaked their own insistent warnings in the cracking Clyde wind.

There was a temporary diversion as someone dropped a basket containing hens and the fowls escaped all over the quayside, squawking and flapping in terror. A small, dishevelled piper with an empurpled face began to march up and down on the cobbles, playing Highland airs. It was Mysie now who clasped her sister, imploring her not to forget them.

"I'll be coming back one day," Annie promised her. "On a visit." Mysie's mournful face reflected her silent rejection of the likelihood of this. And as it was coming nearer, the dreaded moment when she would have to say her final farewell to her mother, Annie welcomed the bustling late arrival on the quay of the Reverend Barrie, with a pale stringy girl in a dipping black crinoline and black bonnet whom he lost no time in introducing as his niece Effie.

"Miss Cameron has been in frail health," he told Annie. "But she is going to where there will be fine open spaces and fresh air. I look to you, Miss McIlvanney, to keep her spirits up. She has recently been bereaved of her maternal parent."

Annie took the bloodless-looking hand extended to her and gazed into rather beautiful but inscrutable mole-brown eyes. Effie Morrison listened to her uncle's effusions with an expression that lacked all enthusiasm, to say the least of it. From time to time she gave a small, worn cough. Annie hoped it didn't signify the consumption.

The minister had brought with him a carpet-bag from which he now produced handsome volumes of the Old and New Testaments, which he handed to each girl in turn. Then holding up a hand for attention, he abjured them not to forget their native land, its beauty, its poets and its history. "You are taking a portion of that land with you," he declaimed, while a dewdrop wandered to the tip of his cold nose and fell unheeded down his dusty coat.

Looking round the coaldust blackened quay and sniffing the doubtful odours from the black-running river, Annie had the unworthy thought that it was a good job it wasn't the portion they stood on. And then, with alarming suddenness, passengers were being urged to hasten up the gangplanks, the small piper had stopped playing and was beating his frozen hands across his chest, the last fowl had been rounded up and the lamentations from those who found it all too hard to bear were carried off by the freshening wind.

Annie saw nobody then but her mother. Smelled nothing then but the dear familiar mother smell from shawl and hair. Felt nothing but the mingling of their tears and murmured words. She did not know how she managed to tear herself away, but somehow she stumbled with her belongings up the endless gangplank, somehow she fought forward for a place at the ship's rail so that she could see the small cameo of her family for the last time. The wind was cold, so cold it almost blistered her face.

Alec Howie gently touched his mother-in-law's shoulder. "Coming?" She nodded without seeing him. She could not believe the *Maggie Love Campbell* was passing from her sight, that the small fading figure, waving, waving, was the last she would see of her child.

In an act of magnificent courage she threw up her head and took the little girls, her grandchildren, by the hand as they walked back towards the dogcart. The lassie was gone. It was not a moment too soon. The lump that Lizzie McIlvanney had felt in her groin was getting larger, the act of pretending to normality, harder.

But she felt more comfortable now in the face of her own mortality. She had set Annie free, to let her spirit soar where it liked, like the laverock you could still hear in Springburn, but never at this sad place of departure, the Broomielaw.

Annie's first days at sea were greatly taken up with trying to carry out what she saw as her duties towards Effie Cameron. Not easy, for first Miss Cameron was prolongedly and repeatedly seasick and when she had recovered she began to make it plain she wished to associate with as few people as possible on board. She did not wish to share confidences and she took her bird-like meals in private, even if it meant standing, somewhat ridiculously, plate in hand, at the rail of the ship with her back to the others. She had a tiny private cabin.

It was as though her handsome crinoline set her apart, for the other girls could not run to such grandeur but made do with petticoats gathered as full as possible.

Annie was put out but did not allow it to spoil the rare adventurous quality of those early days. Apart from some initial queasiness, she had not been sick, but had adapted to shipboard life as though she'd been a sailor all her days. Everyone had been a bit subdued in the beginning and there were quarrels over the allocation and preparation of food and sleeping accommodation. But the sea air and sunshine worked wonders on slum-pale complexions and overwrought tempers, so that the girls began to form little circles of friendship and to realise co-operation was better than argument.

She missed her mother and Mysie desperately but when she looked down at the racing dark sea under the *Maggie Love Campbell* all she thought about was how every dip and thrust took her nearer to Hector. His presence, his voice, his promises, his touch, filled her mind. How amazed he would be at the speed with which she'd engineered a passage! She fantasised about his progress in the Cariboo, saw him strike gold and make for the saloon owned by the cousin in Barkerville, only to find her sitting there awaiting him. With such prospects she was like someone spellbound, protected alike from all doubt and fear.

She could not desert the ill-tempered Effie, for no one else would have anything to do with her. She had promised the Reverend she would try and keep up the other girl's spirits. You had to make allowances for people who were not in the best of health and Effie had that cough and suspicious hectic rosiness Annie had seen before in the tenements and must also be feeling the loss of her parents.

"Why are you so *cheerful?*" Effie demanded querulously on the fifth day, when heavier seas began to whip up and it looked as though a storm was threatened.

"Why are you so down-at-the-mouth?" Annie countered, amazed at her own temerity. She squatted down beside the pale-faced Effie and drew a plaid about her thin shoulders. "If you'd make friends with the others, it would help to pass the time for you."

"They are a somewhat low lot, are they not? I have no wish to be contaminated by their loose morals."

"Loose morals? They're mostly good girls, fresh out of service. The widows could not be more respectable." Annie sounded hurt, for she felt she was being categorised along with the others.

For the first time she saw a gleam of malicious satisfaction in Effie Morrison's eyes and had to fight to prevent her dedication turning to dislike.

"They live in pathetic ignorance," Effie went on. "They have no idea what is in store for us, going round the Horn. We may all perish. And if we survive that, the typhus'll get us before Canada does. I hate the sea. I fear it."

"Then why did you consent to come?" Annie's astonishment was genuine.

"You cannot think I had any option?" demanded Effie. "Any more than my poor Donald had? Scotland doesn't want us any more. We have had to take Destitution Road."

"What's that?"

"Destitution Road?" Effie permitted herself a thin-lipped smile. "It is the road to Ullapool, where the lairds used to herd their tenants on to the coffin ships – or any other road that leads to ships like this."

"I am sure things are not so bad as you make out. Captain Bonamy has the trust of your uncle. And you must not talk of herding –"

"But herding it was!" Effie insisted. "The people were *herded* off the island of Lewis – more than two thousand of them – and I've heard of a Colonel Gordon who *herded* his cottars on South Uist and Barra on to ships that took them to Quebec, where they were dependent on local charity for a crust of bread. They had *nothing*!"

Annie slipped her arm round the girl's thin shoulders.

"If things are as bad as that in the old country, we're better off out of it!" she joked. "And don't be afraid of the Horn! Captain Bonamy has made the journey many a time. He says it will take no more than a three-month. What's a storm at sea to a sailor like the captain? I've heard it said it's meat and drink to him. You've got to put your faith in the Lord –"

"What faith?"

"You mean –?"

"I mean mine is at present a very thin and watery faith."

"But your uncle is a minister!"

"Which may have much to do with it."

Annie pondered this riposte when she lay in her hard but not uncomfortable bunk that night. The storm had passed, the sea was calm, from a distance she could hear someone play *Cha till mi tuille* – We Shall Return No More – on the pibroch, a sound so poignant it felt as though her blood had changed to water. She had thought Glasgow bad enough, but it seemed the Highlands were in an even worse state. Oh Scotland, she thought, and wept. She had not known till then how much she loved her country.

The next day Effie lay in her bunk looking pale and wan, still queasy after the heaving of the ship the day before. Annie brought her some gruel and suggested she should remain where she was and try and get some sleep. But Effie gripped her wrist with surprising firmness and said, "Stay and talk. My thoughts are bad companions. Did you hear the piper play last night?"

Annie nodded. " 'We shall return no more,' " said Effie. "It is the tune my Donald plays. It is our requiem."

"Try not to upset yourself," said Annie.

Effie turned her face away brusquely, then with a tormented voice, full of anguish, cried, "It is death for the Highlands, the end of the Gaels. We know it, all of us."

"There is hardship in the Lowlands, too," Annie protested.

"Have the Lowlanders to be prised off the ground they lie on and carried bodily on to the ships? The women fainting and falling down the while? The Lowlands have not been rack-rented like our people." She gave a great, raging, wailing cry, beyond comfort. "I never wanted to leave my country. Nor did Donald. Now we shall never see each other again. I know in my heart I shall never make dry land."

Annie thought she might have to fetch the ship's doctor. Something was troubling Effie, something she could not define. She had seen him once, the doctor, a pale, scrawny, preoccupied young man she'd been told was paying for his emigration by his services to the passengers. But she made one last effort to try and comfort Effie, by putting her arms round her and rocking her silently, as she might do one of Mysie's bairns. Presently, as Effie's wild racking sobs subsided, she fell back on her pillow and eventually into a spent, exhausted sleep. Annie loosed her arm from under the sleeping girl and went in search of her own dinner. She was ravenously hungry and wolfed down a plate of potatoes and mutton, greasy though the latter was, with relish.

When she returned to see Effie, the girl was sitting up in her bunk, looking subdued but less deathly pale.

"You have been kind to me," Effie acknowledged. "Heaven knows, I don't deserve it." And the big, mole-brown eyes filled up with tears.

"That's as may be," said Annie.

"The difference between us," said Effie, "is that you don't complain. You have nothing but what you stand up in, but your spirit is so strong."

"I only have to think of Hector," said Annie fervently, "and I can take anything that comes along. One day we shall have our farm and seven children. I have made up my mind it is to be seven. Four boys and three girls."

Effie smiled tentatively and put out a hand which Annie took. That day an emotional bond was forged between the two young women. Annie began to talk yearningly, compulsively, of the day she would meet up again with Hector; of the hard times that had come upon her mother and her and her wish to better herself, to read more books and acquire more knowledge; of her determination to go back to Glasgow one day as a fine lady and confront the likes of Henderson, the locomotive-maker, her late employer, with her grandeur.

It seemed to ease some deep disquiet in Effie to talk over and over again about what had happened to Donald and Annie began to build up a mental picture of an angry and ambitious young man, deeply wronged like so many others by the ridding of their crofts.

"He was brought up in his grandfather's tradition of naming each sheep at the lambing and bringing them in to shelter each night after the milking," Effie explained, one night when her mood appeared more tender than ever before. "They thought because of the Biblical association every sheep was blessed, no matter how starved its poor flanks.

"But the Big Sheep, the Cheviots, brought in by the new landlords, they didn't need that kind of care. They were that strong, that hardy, they looked after themselves. Then when the laird Charles Mennock sold the croft from under him, Donald didn't know where to turn. He'd never thought it would happen to him. He had total loyalty to his chief. He would have laid down his life for him. In return, all he wanted was his land – not possession, just the right of occupation – we called it a kindness; but it was no kindness in the end. To know you are no longer wanted can break a man's heart, you know. His heart and his spirit. That's what's happened all over the north."

"Mennock?" Annie tried to keep her voice as normal as possible, but her heart had given a great alarmed leap in her breast. "Did you say the laird's name was Mennock?"

"Yes. Why do you ask?"

"No reason. It sounds a bit – unusual, that's all."

Effie nodded. "They commanded great loyalty, him and his sons – the four Fighting Mennocks – charmers and wasters all. The old laird maintained he would never have sold out to the Englishman had it not been for the gambling debts owed by his sons, but he was as bad as any of them."

Annie's heart had given another great leap of alarm and perturbation. She wanted to cry out immediately, "You are talking about my Hector. *He* was not like the others. He gave his birthright for his brother."

But caution silenced her immediately. She realised that she had never mentioned Hector's surname to Effie and now resolved never to do so, or to concoct a false one if necessary.

It was clear that Effie, having lived in Glasgow with her uncle for the past few months, was not privy to the latest piece of scandal involving the Fighting Mennocks – namely, Hector's disastrous fight with Colin Macandrew.

"You are quiet," Effie stated. "I am sorry if my discourse bores you."

Annie had noticed how quickly the other girl took offence. But her main concern was in keeping her face averted until the telltale redness over the mention of the Mennocks had died down. She could not bear to hear ill of anything connected with Hector. She did not want to think of the burden he carried in his soul – the knowledge he might have killed a man, albeit without intending it.

"Are you all right?" Effie persisted.

"Of course," said Annie, with great animation. "Right as rain. Now if I fetch you a dish of tea, do you think you could take it?"

"I might," Effie conceded. "But my bitterness chokes me the while."

* * *

As the *Maggie Love Campbell* rode the vast seas between the homeland and Cape Horn, Annie became an unofficial spokesman for 'the brides' whenever they had any matter to raise with the captain or other members of the crew.

The captain made it clear he was pleased with the behaviour of the young women, who in the main had stuck to the regulations laid down at the start – that they would not mingle with other passengers, that they would keep their quarters clean and do what they could to organise their own divertissement. Perhaps it was in response to these efforts that he suggested the girls should hold a dance and he would get the mate and the doctor to provide the music, the mate being adept on the penny whistle and the doctor a reasonable hand with the fiddle. No male passengers, mind, just a few jigs and strathspeys or whatever between the lassies, to help keep their spirits up.

Annie had a job to persuade Effie to take part. "You don't have to dance," she urged her. "Just come and watch." And at last Effie agreed, worried about her status but sick to death of the cramped conditions in her tiny cabin.

Annie introduced her to Pheemie from Blantyre, Wilma from Lesmahagow, Lizzie from Coatbridge and the good-natured girls did their best to persuade her to take the deck. Effie shook her head. She sat near the little doctor, Alec Comrie, watching his fingers fly over the strings of his fiddle, thinking how young he looked, desperately young and unfinished, yet Annie had reported to her that he'd won all the prizes at the university. Trust Annie. When the doctor needed an unofficial nurse-assistant, she was the one he turned to. Annie had reported with some satisfaction that he found her quick on the uptake.

'The brides' had taken up the social challenge and were as prettily turned out as they could manage in the circumstances. Those with best dresses wore them, while the others had taken trouble to dress hair or bodice with bits of lace and ribbons or silk flowers. The dances deteriorated into a whirl of elbows and feet after a while, each set of four or eight making up its own variations, but it was all good-natured if strenuous and amused some of the other passengers peering down from the upper deck.

Effie did not demur when eventually Annie and another girl pulled her up to join in a circle while they sedately danced 'In and out the dusty bluebells.' Soon her face was as rosy as the rest, her features as animated. The captain sent down some cordial and the musicians rested while, laughing and chatting, the girls collapsed in breathless heaps. A cool little breeze fanned hot brows and for a time the solid old hulk which had ploughed so many seas could have been a pleasure palace, alive with laughter and chatter and the soft murmur of confidence and reminiscence.

Annie could never remember afterwards when the ship began to buck and heave. The cool breeze certainly turned somewhat suddenly into a snapping wind, sending the girls scuttling for shawls and shelter. By the time darkness fell, rain was lashing the decks and a gale making a fearsome noise in the rigging. They had had a touch of rough weather before, but never a storm like this. Dishes flew from tables, chairs overturned, bunks callously disbursed themselves of their occupants.

She took it on herself to reassure a near-hysterical Effie, but for the first time on the journey felt the touch of real fear herself. All they could do was hang on to whichever bunk or surface offered itself, get up off the deck whenever a particular roll or heave was manifested and swallow the neat tots of brandy providentially sent down by the first mate with words of reassurance that the storm would soon blow itself out.

Through the long night Annie recorded episodes as if from nightmare – pigs, a cow and luggage washed overboard, deck seats smashed up like cheap firewood, the crash of broken rigging, the purple faces of crew as they did their best to carry out their duties. Even farce intervened – Pheemie's chamberpot shot from under her bunk, through the door and overboard. Through it all, there was this thin screaming sound from Effie, as with clothes plastered to her skin, she retched and vomited and retched again.

As dawn broke, the mate's reassurance at last proved valid. The storm had indeed blown itself out and the *Maggie Love Campbell* rode serene, sunlit waters, wearing the slightly ashamed and drunken mien of a duchess who has been on the razzle and still has all her clothing askew.

Effie was in an alarming state of exhaustion.

"We must get you out of these soaking clothes," Annie exhorted her. "Else you're going to die of a chill."

"Leave me," said Effie, through clenched teeth, but Annie ignored her and began to strip her wringing-wet crinoline from her body. Effie gave a convulsive movement and pushed her away. "Get out," she screamed. "Don't touch me." She gave another convulsive heave accompanied by a scream that tore at Annie's eardrums. With a final massive tug Annie relieved her of the dripping crinoline.

"We have to change your underclothes, too, right down to the skin," she urged, then stopped, unable to believe the evidence of her eyes. Underneath the soaking petticoats lay the gently curving protruberance of Effie's abdomen. She was with bairn!

The crinoline had hidden it, of course, and Annie remembered with a suddenly relevant clarity how Effie had always lain in her bunk with her bedclothes drawn up to her chin and never permitted entry to her cabin till she was fully dressed or undressed. That seasickness – it hadn't all been due to the sea!

"Oh, Effie!" she remonstrated, gently. Effie, with all her mealy-mouthed talk about the rough morals of the other 'brides' who accompanied them!

"*I'm having it*," Effie screamed at her. There was nothing refined now about her voice. It was rough and vibrant with pain and terror. "What'll I do, Annie? Tell me what to do?"

A resolute calm had descended on Annie. She tried to bring to mind what had happened during Mysie's confinements. The last had arrived before the howdie could be fetched and she had tied the infant's cord. But with the first – and she trusted it was Effie's first – it could take time. She dragged a warm cover from Effie's tin trunk and covered the shivering mother-to-be.

"You'll be all right," she said, with a conviction she was far from feeling. "The bairn'll not make its entry for a while yet. Lie back and rest. I'll fetch the doctor."

"That manikin! I'll not have him near me. I've heard about ship's doctors. They kill more than they cure. Promise me, Annie. Just you."

"Calm yourself. That's better. Now tell me, how far are you gone?"

"An eight-month."

"You were cutting it fine!"

"My uncle thought I would make it to Donald before it happened."

"Your uncle? The minister? He knew about it?"

"Why else do you think they got rid of me? As if they could have this kind of scandal at the manse!"

All manner of things fell into place now in Annie's mind. Effie's bitterness, her lapsing faith. Her mother had often spoken of this unforgiving strain in the Scots character – "Man's inhumanity to man Makes countless thousands mourn." The lines from Burns came unbidden. Terrified, forsaken, consumptive, pregnant, no wonder Effie had proved a difficult companion.

3

"God damn you, Donald Arrochar! God damn the Fighting Mennocks and all who belong to them! O, God damn my whited sepulchre of an uncle for sending me away!"

Effie's head was tossing from side to side on her narrow bunk, a stream of blistering invective flowing involuntarily from her lips. To Annie's alarmed gaze, it seemed as though Effie had retreated into her private hell where she only recognised her own private demons. The eyes that occasionally met hers made no sign of recognition. The noise she had been making had brought the other girls crowding round the door of the tiny cabin. By telling them she was delirious with what might be a catching fever, Annie had got rid of all of them save the observant Pheemie and Lizzie. They had not been slow to take in the truth of the situation. It was Pheemie who said now, "I don't care what her wish is. I'm going for the wee doctor." And she stumped off purposefully while Annie pushed back the last of her scruples.

Alec Comrie took in the situation in one hasty disillusioned glance. Sending Pheemie and Lizzie for hot water and clean rags, he quickly and reassuringly examined Effie.

"Now then. Big breaths, that's better. You are going to be fine, Miss Morrison. Your friend and I will make sure of that."

What a bedside manner, Annie thought. The slight, boyish figure had a natural authority and command. Whatever else he was, this wasn't the degraded, drunken lout of popular legend. Never once during the next frightening hours did the cool, dedicated expertise falter. By his voice and touch he talked Effie into a calmer state so that when the contractions became stronger she held his arm and pushed with a will.

But the child did not seem to wish to make its journey into the world. Poor Effie's pallor became ghastly; sweat matted her hair and ran from her brow despite Annie's mopping. Once, Alec Comrie's eyes met Annie's and the message was: I fear she may not make it.

"Oh, Effie, dear, don't give up." Annie held Effie's hand and gazed down at her pleadingly. "Donald is waiting for you, you and the baby."

For answer, Effie gave a great cry and from her parted legs the infant at last made his hasty, spontaneous way, struggling, crying, empurpled, the embodiment, Annie thought fancifully, of all Effie's rage and protest. Holding it by the legs, skilfully clearing its mouth and eyes with thumb and forefinger, Alec Comrie pronounced it a lusty enough lad.

"I want him called Aeneas," said Effie, before she fell into an exhausted sleep.

"Aeneas," repeated Annie, holding the little creature in her arms and smiling. He wore a look of stern disapprobation and a feathery coxcomb of dark hair, and did not have much in the way of finger-nails, the result, Alec Comrie pointed out, of a slightly premature arrival.

"He'll be right enough," he said. "But of the mother I am not so sure."

Annie's head flew up.

"She is in the last stages of consumption, poor soul. Let us do what we can to be kind to her."

They put the baby to his mother's breast and for the next few days Annie refused to acknowledge the finality behind the young doctor's words. Effie was happier than Annie had ever seen her, be it with a bright, febrile contentment that lapsed frequently into exhaustion and sleep.

"Will she never get to Canada?" Annie pressed the doctor.

He shook his head. "Nor can the child," he said sombrely. "There is no wet nurse aboard to save him."

The end, when it came, was bright with haemorrhage and horror and coped with single-handedly by Alec Comrie, who gave the baby into Annie's care.

"You're not going to die, wee one," she said distractedly. "Your poor mother knew the New World was not for her. But for you it will be so, for I'll take you to your father."

Alec Comrie shook his head. "We can try him with goat's milk," he said. "But he needs to suckle and has scarcely learned how."

"My sister hand-reared her youngest," said Annie defiantly.

"More by luck than good guidance, I should think. We've no bubby-pots or feeders aboard."

"But there must be *some* way."

"I leave that to you and your friends. I have a casualty to see to, fallen from the yard-arm."

'The brides' clustered round Annie and the baby with offers of advice.

"Soak some biscuit with milk and let him suck it through a rag," suggested Pheemie ingeniously.

"He's too young for pap," argued Lizzie. "Maybe once he's a three-month he could manage it."

"If only we had a caoutchouc teat, we could tie it on to a bottle from the pharmacy."

"We could tie a rag round the neck of a bottle and let him suck that."

"Or cut the thumb from a chamois glove and pierce it with holes –"

In the end, they tried out a number of eccentric measures. The baby did not take kindly to any of them, nor to the nanny-goat's milk offered from the spoon or cup. But Annie persevered with a single-minded determination until driven by the baby's weakening, hungry cries she took him again to Dr. Comrie.

He looked down at the mewling infant dispassionately, then shook his head.

"I have told you the chances of hand-rearing him are poor. Even in ideal conditions they are not great. And the conditions here are far from ideal."

"You can't just let him die." She pushed her face under his and said with a challenging fury, "You're a doctor. Do *something*."

His pale skin reddened, but he parted the baby's shawls and examined him. Aeneas drew up his legs, screwed his face as though to cry but instead, as though fascinated by the strange observant visage above him, gave a good-natured coo and waved his tiny hands.

"Yes, old chap. We'll have to do what we can for you," said Alec Comrie resolvedly. To Annie he said, with reluctant inspiration, "I suppose we could ask the captain to put out a message to the passengers at large, asking if any of them might have a feeder in her luggage. It's an outside chance –"

As it happened, a Mrs. Carmichael, providentially taking out a "Little Pet" feeder to her sister in Vancouver, consented to let Annie have it on condition she tried to replace it with something similar when they reached port.

Jubilantly Annie took the bottle to show Alec Comrie, but he regarded it sceptically. It was banjo-shaped with a sentimental verse addressed to the infant on the front and inside a long rubber tube with a teat on the end. "A murder bottle," he pronounced.

Annie's jaw fell.

"How do you propose to keep it clean?" demanded Dr. Comrie.

"With a feather."

He indicated to her to put the sleeping infant in his bunk and gestured to her to sit by him at his desk.

"You said to me a little time ago 'You're a doctor, aren't you?' and you said it jeeringly."

"No," she protested, "I didn't mean —"

"Being a doctor doesn't just mean binding up wounds and handing out physic. It means keeping up with the latest scientific thinking." At her questioning look he went on quickly "And the latest scientific thinking is that you get fermentation, putrifaction of organic matter where air does not reach." He picked up the baby feeder. "As in this long poisonous tube."

At her air of mystification his passion to explain grew. "A surgeon in Glasgow, a Londoner, Lister by name, is at this very time investigating how micro-organisms in the air we breathe can cause suppuration in wounds. But I go further. I'm convinced they can also cause disease."

"In the air we breath?" Annie could not conceal her alarm. "What are micro – what you called them? What do they look like?"

"I didn't name them. A Frenchman called Louis Pasteur did. Micro-organisms. Infusoria. They look lop-sided. And they're too small to see. But they can cause milk to go sour. My belief is they can kill hand-reared infants."

"Are they smaller than fleas?"

He grinned. "Much smaller. You can see them through a microscope. One day I'll show you."

"Too small to kill?"

"Aha. Annie McIlvanney, you do not miss the point. That's what I like about you. When I studied in France, I came across various theories whereby the development of organisms can be prevented. If you heat wine, for example, you can stop it fermenting —"

"So if you heated milk, it might stop it going off."

"We'll try it," he said. "We'll boil and then cool the milk we give Aeneas. We'll boil the bottle and the tube between feeds. We will see if we can prevent the diarrhoea that kills them off so relentlessly."

Annie was fascinated by the ideas that Alec Comrie tried

to put across to her. She wrote down the word micro-organism over and over till it was engraved in her mind. (She had started to keep an account of her journey, in any case, which she hoped one day to send to her mother.) She pestered Alec to let her see his notes and although most of it went over her head she began to have a glimmer of what some of his scientific studies were about. When they met up to discuss Aeneas's feeds he fed her a laywoman's version of some of the other studies he was pursuing, such as what he called the mind-body, or psycho-somatic, illnesses. He had this dream, he said, of a universally available medical service such as was already available – to Scotland's eternal credit – at Edinburgh Royal Infirmary. To Annie it was heady stuff although when she tried explaining some of it to her friends they countered with suggestions of Godfrey's Cordial for the baby and some brandy in his bottle if he refused to sleep. They were deeply suspicious of Alec and his new-fangled notions. But the baby, as though he sensed that the 'Little Pet' was his last chance of survival, took to it with a will, sucking hungrily and it was not long before his skinny frame began to fill out in a satisfactory manner and his good-natured gummy smiles found many friends.

In Effie's tin trunk Annie found a quantity of baby clothes and these were rapidly supplemented by hastily stitched and knitted items from the other girls. The baby, in fact, was a somewhat welcome diversion at this stage of the weary journey and there was no lack of willing arms to nurse him.

Captain Bonamy sent for Annie to ask her what should be done about poor Effie's burial. He favoured consigning her coffin to the waves, but Annie was horrified. "She hated the sea," she protested. "Can the coffin not remain till we reach Victoria?"

The captain seemed uneasy, not admitting to superstitious reservations among the crew. If he did not give in to their demands to get rid of the body, he could start up the mutinous anger that was always there beneath the surface.

He had no stomach for putting men in irons. After some thought he suggested a compromise: that they should put in at the Falkland Islands, reached before they went round Cape Horn and find a burial space there. They might also be able to replenish some of the livestock lost in the storm. It was not what Annie wanted, but she had not the authority to overrule the captain and at least Effie's resting-place would be on terra firma.

The port of Stanley in East Falkland was a bleak enough place, cold, misty, unwelcoming. The ship's piper played *We Shall Return No More* as Effie's coffin was carried to its resting place and a brief service read over her grave. Annie was to remember the Falkland Islands as a place of no comfort, uneasy ghosts seeming to wait in its hills, some unacknowledged threat in its chill shrouding mists.

But once the funeral was over, her mourning for Effie was superseded by concern for Aeneas, referred to by everybody as The Wean. How was she to get him to his father? Would Donald Arrocher come to Victoria from Salt Spring to meet the bride ship or was he in ignorance of Effie's plans? Effie had never made that clear. It was going to make getting to Barkerville that much harder, but it never occurred to Annie not to take responsibility for the child.

He was a winning rogue, quickly knowing when it was her arms that held him. She was less and less inclined to share his nursing with the others and he, in turn, would only take his bottle when it was she who offered it.

'You'll get that attached to him, you'll not want to part with him,' Pheemie warned.

"I'll part with him when the right time comes," said Annie stoutly. And that would be when she personally laid the baby in his father's arms.

Cape Horn lived up to its reputation with squalls and storms. Annie woke one night to find the baby fallen underneath their shared bunk, but sound asleep, so well swaddled he had probably felt nothing when he fell. Even when the ship was on even keel between storms she found herself walking with a round, rolling gait, her hands forever ready with a kind of newly-developed grasping suction movement to hold on desperately to rail, wall, or whatever was handy. Her whole body ached with cold and wet and tension, which were soon forgotten in the moments of desperate fear when the ship rolled and tossed and dived and seemed sometimes as though it would never come up from the glassy waves. At one point the engines packed up and the *Maggie Love Campbell* rolled helplessly in the trough of waves while the crew fought to raise her sails. There were cheers next day for the oil-grimed engineer who somehow got the engines going again. The journey went on forever. When the weather permitted it, the girls took to their bunks and slept. Games, songs, reading and other pastimes were forgotten in the sheer awful tedium of keeping warm, of crossing off the interminable days, of willing survival from the chill, the wet, the sickness and the sapping apathy.

Alec Comrie was kept busy in the small cabin he called the ship's infirmary. Storm injuries, sickness, lung complaints called for his constant attention, but as he told Annie when she took Pheemie to him with a stomach complaint, all he cared about was that cholera and typhus should not invade the decks. They had the cold to thank for that – if also for the two deaths from lung disease in patients who had been ill-advised to attempt the journey in the first place.

One night, in weariness, and leaving the infirmary with the baby after a busy stint, Annie looked down at the sleeping infant and wept her first reactive tears for her dead friend, Effie.

"I wonder what'll become of him?" She looked imploringly at Alec Comrie. "Will his father want him? How can a man bring up a bairn?"

Comrie poured her a tot of brandy. "Drink this," he ordered. "You're tired out. Maybe the answer is, you should stay with the father and bring up the child. You seem attached to it."

He had his back to her and there was a note in his voice

she did not understand. A note which suggested she should do no such thing.

"I am going out to my man," she said deliberately.

"*Your man?* You wear no wedding ring."

He whirled round, the boyish blue eyes incredulous and – could it be? – betrayed?

"We took our vows over running water. It is the same to me as being wed in the kirk."

"You told me nothing of this."

"You never asked me."

He sat down abruptly, his hands rubbing his knees distractedly.

"I have been let down by a woman once before –"

"But –" she protested.

"I should know better. I had made up my mind you should come with me, if you could give up the child. I'll need a housekeeper, but one with intelligence, not some slut who cannot take instruction."

"I am sorry," said Annie, "but housekeeping for you was furthest from my mind."

"I was supposed to wed my cousin." He gave her another furious stare, "and she went off with another, a big bubbley-jock returned from being a tea-planter in India. I wish him well of her. She had a tongue that would cut cloots."

"You didn't love her, then?"

"She made it impossible for me to stay in Glasgow. I felt what she did most keenly."

He got up and moved away, as though it were important to put distance between them.

"Understand. I have one passion," he said, in a low voice, "and that is medicine. It will always come first. I don't know if there's room for more. But I need the support of a sensible woman. She needn't have looks. They don't matter. She must have wit and tenacity and the ability to learn. In that event, I could see me getting quite fond of her. Within certain limits."

Annie began to feel a certain sympathy for the female cousin.

"Well, I'm not for you," she said, easing the baby on to her shoulder, where he stirred like a sleepy kitten. "I am spoken for. I am as dedicated to my man as you are to your medicine."

He put a hand boldly on her free shoulder and gazed down at her tear-stained face. "I could mend that eye for you."

"Hector says it gives me a look of serious purpose."

"Does he?" He relaxed slightly and gave a glimmer of a smile. "There might be something in what he says. But whatever, you'd be better off with me."

"The answer is no. But I have to thank you for asking me."

She was to remember the pleading, blue-eyed gaze, like burning ice, at intervals throughout the rest of her life. There was no doubting Alec Comrie's cleverness, seducing in itself.

If she'd had another life, to run concurrently with her present one, then she might have dedicated it to him, his books and his medicine. She might have shared his passion. But she had just the one life and it was complicated enough already, her worries about what was going to happen to The Wean confusing the plans she wished to make to get to Barkerville as quickly as possible.

Captain Bonamy, once the Cape was safely rounded, rallied his passengers in general to subscribe to a fund for the baby and gave it to Annie, in case the search for the father ran into costs she could not meet. Indeed, in the weeks to come the baby became the sentimental focus of much attention and Annie's devotion to it the object of universal admiration. Anything, anything was welcome as diversion, as with smoother seas plain and simple tedium took over. Food was growing disgustingly stale and weevily, bunks malodorous, the crew surly, supplies dwindling, appetites longing for freshness and change.

Fresh trade winds filled the ship's sails as it entered the Pacific and gave the tired old engines a rest. The *Maggie Love Campbell* put in briefly at San Francisco, but besides being anxious to complete the journey, Captain Bonamy was uneasy about the girls going ashore and allowed them only the briefest, chaperoned sight of the Californian city – in case they were tempted to stay ashore, as indeed some of the male passengers were.

And then at last after 17,000 miles and 102 days, they reached Esquimault on Vancouver Island and were ferried to nearby Victoria. Annie saw a wooden town almost totally hemmed in by forest.

A tremulous Pheemie observed she had quite forgotten what trees looked like. "There's wolves and Indians in *there*," said a crewman, helping them ashore. As for Annie, her feet went all over the place on dry land, but she left the *Maggie Love Campbell* with all the speed she could muster, and never a backward glance. Anything was preferable to another day aboard ship.

* * *

"Miss McIlvanney, will you step in here?"

The minister's wife was small, bustling, in black from head to foot and there was no brooking the note of cool authority.

Annie sat down in the chair indicated and joggled the baby on her knee. The office was housed in the barracks where the brides were living temporarily, until they were fixed up with their new positions. There had been no lack of interest in the neighbourhood, many of whose males had found urgent business near the quay when the ship put in with its female cargo. A local wag had been heard to say that the event had sent sales of men's apparel soaring up into unprecedented heights and caused a heavy strain on the water supplies.

But some of the initial euphoria was wearing off. It had been fun, if tiring, washing travel-stained clothes in the big, steaming tubs the local ladies had laid out for them on the barrack lawns and being interviewed by the newspaper reporters. The speeches of welcome, well-meaning but ponderous, had caused Annie, Pheemie and Lizzie agonies of suppressed giggles. But now the two others had been placed, Pheemie as housekeeper to a widowed farmer with connubial intent and Lizzie to a baker's family bursting with marriageable sons, and Mrs. Ogilvie, the minister's wife, was determined to get Annie's future sorted out also. By a steady sucking-in of breath she was indicating this was no straightforward matter.

"The infant, Miss McIlvanney, that is the stumbling block. I feel that in the circumstances, the best thing would be to place him in an orphan institution where he might be wet-nursed and we could then bend our minds to finding a suitable post for your good self."

"I have said," Annie insisted patiently, "that I will not be parted from him. I am taking him to his father on Salt Spring Island."

"And *I* have indicated," said Mrs. Ogilvie, testily, "that we do not consider Salt Spring a safe destination for one of our ladies, never mind a helpless infant child. There are Indians, who still fight and scalp each other –"

"But they leave the newcomers alone, so long as no one starts shooting at them. So I've been told."

"I know nothing of Mr. Donald Arrochar. At least, remain here until I can send someone to find out about him. I cannot help thinking, Miss McIlvanney, you would be best advised to take up the munificent offer from Dr. Comrie, who is prepared to rent a domicile here if you will housekeep for him –"

They had been over the ground in similar vein before. Mrs. Ogilvie could see by the rebellious downward cast of Annie's profile that she was getting nowhere. She said with barely-constrained annoyance, "I undertook to your sponsor, the Reverend Barrie and your mother, that you would be found a post in Victoria."

"My mother knows I want to get to the Cariboo."

"She hoped we would dissuade you. I intend to do all I can to dissuade you. There will come an end to your welcome here. Soon the barracks will be closed down and girls who have not settled a position will find themselves at the mercy of Fate. Please think on what I've told you and pray to the good Lord for counsel."

Annie walked back to the dormitory, gently rocking the grizzling baby and fighting down feelings of anger at everybody's interference in her plans. Especially Alec Comrie. It was he who, calling daily on the excuse of keeping a check on the baby's health, had bolstered up Mrs. Ogilvie's fear of the journey to Salt Spring Island.

Annie herself had lost no time in finding out how that journey could be made. There were sloops and schooners but as they were few in number the quickest way seemed to be by canoe, paddled by one of the aforesaid Indians. Most of the island settlers, she had discovered, used the Indians now to take their tobacco and fruit and vegetables to the market in Victoria. If only she could find someone to share the journey there. She did not fancy being quite alone with an Indian, but perhaps she should risk it. She could see the orphanage doors closing on poor little Aeneas if she didn't take action soon.

In the afternoon, when the sun came out, she wrapped the baby in a shawl and took him down to the quay to take the air.

Victoria, expanding as fast as building labour would allow, bustled with prosperity. She checked on larger vessels which might be going out to Salt Spring but drew another blank. Then, cautiously, her heart beating like a drum, she approached an Indian she had seen tie up a canoe the previous day and who now sat on a capstan, idly watching the human traffic on the quay.

'You know Salt Spring Island?'

At first he chose not to answer so she repeated the question. The man, who might have been anything between thirty and fifty, turned an expressionless face on her and said, "Steea. Island called Steea. Mean Island of Fire. Belong my people."

Annie nodded nervously. "Whatever you say. I want to go and see man there, Donald Arrochar." She watched, but the mask-like face gave nothing away. "You take me and baby? I pay."

"Annie McIlvanney, what are you up to?" Annie spun guiltily round on her heel and found Alec Comrie gazing at her, red-faced. "Are you making arrangements with this man to go to Donald Arrochar? Despite all the warnings you've been given?"

"And did you follow me here?" she demanded furiously.

"I saw you from my guest-room window. I deduced you were up to no good."

"You are not my keeper, Dr. Comrie."

"It is clear you need one, just the same."

"I *have* to go," she hissed at him desperately. "They will take Aeneas away from me soon. Can't you understand?"

"All right. All right." He turned to the waiting Indian. "You take this woman, the child and me to Salt Spring Island?"

"When you go?"

"Tomorrow?"

The Indian nodded.

"You mean," cried Annie, "that you'll actually come with us? Oh, Dr. Comrie, Alec, I can never thank you enough."

"They say it's a beautiful enough place," he said diffidently. "I might as well come and see for myself."

"Take three days," said the Indian. "Bring food."

* * *

Annie trailed her hand in the water. The midday sun on the third day was blissfully warm and the baby slept. They had kept his boiled milk cold by sealing it up in a tin box and trailing it in the water. Steea – in some ways she preferred the Indian name and used it always in her mind – was coming ever closer. She was thankful to be coming to the end of the painful intimacies enforced on the canoe, but it was amazing what a bucket, good balance, and discretion could encompass. She had grown fond of Alec Comrie, who, treating the expedition like a trip down the Clyde at home, had behaved like a schoolboy on holiday. Beneath his learning he was as young and callow as a ploughboy, she thought, and the insight made her warm to him as though to a brother. A younger brother.

By careful interrogation, they had gleaned a little of what the island was like. Apart from whites and Hawaiians, black Kentuckians were settling there. Jim White Bull indicated there were plenty of trout and bass in the blue lakes, wild cress and mushrooms for the picking all over the place.

Raccoon and otter played on the beaches and the small black bear came down from the hills to steal fruit from the settlers' gardens. Annie thought now that it sounded like paradise and as she looked the island seemed to shimmer through the mist and sunlight like a hallucination, pink and pearl and green. Something in her rose to worship it, something savage and uncivilised, untamed like the Indian. She was glad she had come here, glad that she'd dodged the worthy Ogilvies and trusted her instinct. As though he'd sensed her surge of exultation, Alec said from a half-prone position, "It would be pleasant to stay here forever."

The canoe grounded on a delightful, small, pebbley beach, which ran into woods of tall Douglas firs, pine and red cedar. The Indian led them to a path that skirted the woods, which they pursued in silence for about half a mile until the trees cleared, revealing green pastures that rolled up a hill and, on top of the hill, what looked like a half-finished timber residence.

"Donald Arrochar," the Indian affirmed.

"You take me to him?" Annie's heart had begun to race away from her. She edged, with a nervous look up the hill, Aeneas up on her shoulder. Jim White Bull shook his head, "You pay me," he said. "I go back Vancouver Island bloody quick."

"I can't go alone," said Annie, quailing.

Alec Comrie met her gaze squarely. "*You* said you'd take the bairn to his father. It's best you go alone."

He placed a finger under the baby's chin. "I concede I am sorry to part with you both."

"A fine friend you are," she argued.

"Look, I'm going back to Victoria with our guide here. What else did you think? This has been a diversion, but I have to get back, find a place to practise and get down to doctoring. I couldn't earn my corn here. You've made our situation clear enough. We are acquaintances, ships that pass in the night. No more."

Annie swallowed. "Fair enough," she allowed.

"I'll wait here till you get to the house. If you don't come out and wave a white cloth within the hour, I'll know you've been made welcome. From then on, it's up to you."

"Yes." She had a sudden, mad urge to cling to him, beg him to stay, but by coming here with her he had already done all she had a right to expect.

"I hope," she said lamely, "you find a good place to doctor in. Will you stay in Victoria?"

"Depends," he said brusquely. "I might take the Cariboo Road and see what transpires among the diggers."

"Well, take care." She planted a chaste kiss on his cheek and without further ado began her march up the hill. To Jim White Bull she indicated he could leave her trunk – or rather Effie's, which she had acquired – on the edge of the wood, to be picked up later.

When she was out of earshot, he said her name. "Annie. Annie McIlvanney." He stood for longer than the hour, till the Indian began to make clear his restlessness. Then with no indication from Annie he turned and made resolutely for the canoe. They might make the return journey more quickly, with the load lightened. He thought of his books and his scientific instruments, of the many areas open to his exploring mind. Medicine wasn't a bad mistress. As for Annie, she had merely confirmed in him the unreliability of the female. It was better not to depend too much on any of them ...

* * *

The cabin had been planned on a generous scale, but only one half appeared to be finished, giving it a spectral, uneasy air despite the solidity of the cedar logs on the completed side. Hens and chickens pecked and clucked in and around it and from rough outbuildings came the snort and grunt of pigs. To the right there appeared to be a stretch of young orchard, with what she was to learn later were plum trees and Bing cherry.

"We'll not starve here, Aeneas," she said. Her arms and back ached abominably with the carrying of him but her courage suddenly flooded back and she gave the iron knocker on the rough door a mighty thud with her free arm. No reply. She peered in at the window. A big expanse of living-room revealed itself with a wood stove in the centre, some roughhewn furniture, a bearskin rug and cooking utensils. Newspaper and sacking had been used to line the walls, obviously to keep out cold. No human occupant. She trod resolutely to the back of the house. With what appeared to be a U-shaped tree trunk with spikes along the sides, pulled by a yoke of oxen, a black-haired man was turning over the rough earth as though his life depended on it. The crude plough was doing a good job of dragging out roots and heaving over the rich soil.

Annie could not walk the baby over the soft turned earth, but still the man was not aware of her presence. "I am here," she called. "Mr. Donald Arrochar, is it?" At last some awareness on the oxen's part conveyed itself to the man and he turned towards her. With deliberation he finished the furrow. Then slowly he came towards her. No mistake. Donald Arrochar for sure. Dark-browed, forbidding of expression. Not unhandsome. He walked till he was right in front of her and still said nothing, merely raised a pair of uncompromising eyebrows.

"Can we sit down somewhere?" She was suddenly weary, on the verge of dropping. He led her in through the back door and indicated a chair. Still without word he poured her some coffee from a pot on the stove. She drank it thankfully. Aeneas stirred and indicated with little fretful cries that he too needed a drink.

"What brings you here with a child?" said Donald Arrochar at last. He said "Chilt" with the soft Gaelic intonation she had noticed in Effie. "Are you looking for work?"

She put down the drinking mug. "The child, Mr. Arrochar, is yours." She had been practicing in her mind how to tell him, relishing the drama of the moment, but she might as well have said "Pass the butter, Mr. Arrochar." He stared at her uncomprehendingly. She went on swiftly, "I came over from Scotland on the *Maggie Love Campbell* with your intended bride, Miss Effie Morrison. She died, Mr. Arrochar and is buried on the Falkland Isles. She died after giving birth to Aeneas here and it was her wish I should bring him to you."

The silence seemed to go on forever. What had she done, Annie wondered frantically, landing up alone with this strange, taciturn man.

"I am not surprised," he said at last. "I have been dreaming that a messenger would come to me from Effie, only I never saw its face. I have had a dream of islands." His voice shook. She looked at his hands and they were hard, coarse, calloused, covered in cuts. They made her feel worse than the look on his face. "I have the second sight," he said.

"The baby," she said, inadequately, "would you like to hold him? I have had job enough hand-rearing him but here on the farm with fresh milk and eggs maybe he will start to thrive better."

He looked down at the child reluctantly. "How can I be sure he's mine? This could be some tale you've made up to get free board and lodgings for the pair of you."

She whitened. "I have some of Effie's things in the trunk. You'll just have to believe me. Would I have come all this way, risking Indians and water, for nothing? Have sense, man."

He touched the child's cheek. "I never thought to have a son."

"He's like you." The truth was self-evident. The baby's hair and eyes were darkening, he had the same lean skull and thin, determined mouth. Aeneas mewed irritably.

"Was it bad for Effie?" he demanded, without seeing her eyes.

She said gently, "It wasn't the bairn who killed her, it was the consumption."

At last his look focused on her, seeing her properly for the first time.

"You look very young. If you did what you said you did for Effie, then I thank you. How are you called?"

"Annie McIlvanney. From Springburn, Glasgow. I have come to the colonies to be with my man."

"You are married?"

She blushed. "Good as. We took vows we mean to keep."

"What does that mean?"

"We haven't been kirkit. Wed in the kirk."

"You've come a long way, Annie McIlvanney. Can you pluck a chicken?"

"I can have a try," she said, through her fatigue. "But first, is there a cow or goat that will give fresh milk for the bairn? I am worried about him. He is going off his feed."

And she looked down at Aeneas, realising it was the first time her unconscious worries about him had expressed themselves. He was unusually quiet and good. On the canoe he had not fed much and had slept a good deal. Now his little face appeared to her to be growing somehow waxen. And a healthy baby should never be too good.

4

"She was not happy about the journey from the start. If she had been, she might have borne it better." Annie came to the end of her recital concerning Effie and looked carefully at the big man seated on the other side of the stove. A whiteness about the sucked-in jaws spoke its own story of his suffering.

"I didn't know about the child on the way."

"Had you no suspicions about the condition you left her in?"

His head came up quickly at the slight tartness in her voice. His glance did not meet hers. "That was between me and her. In loving kindness on her part, the night I left."

She said more gently, remembering Hector and the woods full of bluebells: "I don't think she regretted it. But she regretted the circumstances that parted you both from Scotland."

"Can you stay and care for the child? I can use you on the farm. There is a Scots hired hand, a poor enough creature parted from his speech –"

"I have explained. I came 17,000 miles to be with my own man. With Hector. I have to find my way to Barkerville, where I hope there is a message for me from him." She had to remind herself never to reveal Hector's surname. What would Donald Arrochar say if he knew her lover came from the family who had caused his disinheritance?

"It's hopeless, a woman setting out on the Cariboo Road. The engineers are still working on it. The roads are so bad they've even tried bad-breathed camels on them, for transporting goods. You'll never survive."

"I have a way of surviving."

"I can't look after the child. He will have to go back to

Victoria, to an orphanage." He watched her closely with his dark, brooding face.

"You can't let that happen. Is there no local woman?"

"I know of nobody. The child knows you. You are as good as a mother to him."

To her chagrin, Annie felt the tears course down her cheeks. Donald Arrochar spoke no less than the truth. If she had given birth to Aeneas, she could not have felt closer to him. To leave him behind was going to be like a little death. "I suppose I have no choice. But I can't stay for long. You must make other arrangements."

"If you stay, I'll make a privy up among that thicket of trees, no more than twenty yards from the house. With its own path," offered Donald Arrochar.

"I am not staying for long," Annie said emphatically.

"I will make it, just the same. I will get the hired man to help me."

That night, as though he knew the question-mark hanging over his future, Aeneas cried most of the night. The next morning his little face was damp and hot and he refused his feed. His stools were frequent and watery. "He has diarrhoea," Annie told his father anxiously. "I can only think the cow's milk does not agree with him. Do you know someone who has a goat? It's goat's milk that he's used to."

He sent the hired man to see if he could borrow or buy a goat. Annie looked at the poor man curiously. He had his own rough cabin separate from the house, his own pig and chickens. "He is a solitary," Donald explained. "He hates company, because of his mangled speech." Annie could see the man's left arm was only of half-use to him, the fingers curled into the palm. She had a delicacy about enquiring about people's disabilities. She smiled at the man and got a brief recognition. "I call him Mac," said Donald.

Mac returned after several hours leading a bleating nanny-goat heavy with milk, indicating with gestures that a sea-journey by rowing had been necessary.

"He's been to the man who keeps Goat Island," Donald

explained.

But Aeneas was beyond taking anything from the "Little Pet," even the fresh goat's milk. He turned his face away from everything offered, even the cooled water from a little Apostle spoon. His cries grew weaker and weaker.

Annie sat up all night with him, Donald Arrochar a shadowy figure by the stove, watching them both and an anxious Mac coming in from time to time, to put some wood on and offer silent sympathy. She rocked the baby in her arms, she crooned little half-forgotten tunes from her own childhood to him. At one point, she handed him to his father and the big man walked up and down with solemn, dedicated pace, incongruously gentle. Annie remembered Alec Comrie's word: "They seldom pass the four and a half month mark." The fear was filling her heart that poor little Aeneas would not even reach that.

"Do not distress yourself," said Donald Arrochar to her, as dawn at last filtered a pale light through the tops of the blanket-draped windows and she turned an agonised face towards him. "You have done all you can." But his expression matched her own.

"I won't give in," vowed Annie. "I brought him round Cape Horn. I smuggled him here from Victoria. I can't give in." She looked at Aeneas. It was as though overnight he had grown light in her arms, the weight of nothing at all, or a candle-flame. Soon the little flame would go out altogether. But in desperation she tried him again with a little watered milk sweetened with molasses and with a drop or two of brandy. At last the baby slept, his face sheet-white and tranquil as though already taken over by death. With dread crawling over her bones, she rose with a last, wild, weary purpose and said to Donald Arrochar, "I am going to find him a wet nurse."

"It's too late." He held her arm.

"It's not!" she screamed at him, sobbing.

"Where will you go?"

"I don't know. Anywhere. Can't you suggest a place?"

"There's some Kentucky farmers have a cabin over the hill. They're the nearest." He lifted a shotgun off the wall and handed it to her. At her stunned expression he said, "Take it. You go nowhere without it, understand? Jim White Bull and his tribe might decide on a raid at any time. You *never* shoot to kill or wound, unless to save your life. Shooting can start off a massacre."

Mac came to the top of the hill with her, to indicate where the Kentuckians' cabin lay, to keep a look-out for Indians and escort her back. She did not mind his silent company, but marauding Indians were the least of her worries. Aeneas filled her heart and mind with tremulous terror. Mac led her over the hill path that ran away from the shoreline, scanning the horizon for Indian activity. When he was satisfied it was safe, he indicated she could go on down into the valley.

At last in the warming sun she came to a clearing where the Kentuckians were going about their early tasks. She stood gaping at her first non-whites, trying to remember what she had heard about slaves coming here to escape the American Civil War, about them taking the brunt of the Indians' fury over what they regarded as *their* island. It looked as though this particular family was well enough established now. She could hear a man's deep, pleasant voice, singing. The log cabin was large, well-built, solid, like the nearby barns and the impressive-looking fences. A little girl came up to the fence and stared at her wide-eyed.

"Is your mother in?" Annie asked her. Her lips were dry.

"Ma-a-a!" screeched the child, not moving.

A round-faced, chubby black woman dressed in fresh ginghams came out from the open cabin door and approached Annie with unabashed curiosity and not a little hostility.

"What are you doin' round here?"

"Visiting," said Annie briefly. "With Donald Arrochar."

"The man on the hill?"

"Yes."

"You come over the sea, too?"

"A long, long way." The woman's image receded from her in a mist: her legs trembled with weariness.

The black woman's face softened, she opened the gate and ushered Annie through. "You like a drink of water?"

Annie barely managed to nod. Inside the cabin, seated on a stool, she began to feel a little better. She smiled at the little girl who had followed them in and said, "That's a bonnie little girl you have there. I have had the sad task of bringing Mr. Arrochar his infant son. The mother died on the voyage."

"Lawks!" The woman clucked sympathetically. "You stay and look after the child?"

Annie put a hand to her face and found it wet.

"What's the matter?" asked the black woman concernedly.

"The baby is dying. My only chance is to find a wet-nurse for him. I came here to see if you might know of somebody –"

"Bring him to me."

"Do you mean that?" Annie's head came up sharply.

"I share what I've got." The woman, laughing easily, indicated her own baby, about a year old, sound asleep on a cushion on the floor, a kitten curled up nearby. "I done it for the white bosses on the plantation, 'fore my husband bought me out. They never had no complaints."

"My name is Miss Annie McIlvanney," said Annie. "What is yours?"

"Henriette. Hetty for short. Hetty Laboucher."

"Hetty, will you come with me? There is no time to lose."

The man who had been singing was briefly introduced as Hetty's husband, Joe, who promised to mind the children till his wife got back from the Arrochar farm. To Annie the journey back seemed shorter but that was perhaps because hope gave her feet wings.

"How is he?" she asked Donald immediately. He shook his head.

Annie picked the baby up and shook him gently. His little face was still the same ghastly waxen colour, the odour of sour milk and sickness rose from his clothes. The dark eyelashes barely flickered; the wasted limbs jerked momentarily then were still.

Hetty Laboucher took the infant and with expert hands divested him of some of his swaddling. "Get warm water," she instructed shortly. She bathed the little face and hands then with great tenderness put him to her breast. The child moved, snuggled instinctively and weakly drew at the nipple. Annie could scarcely bear to look. She led Donald out of doors and suggested he should get on with some work. She drew deep breaths of air herself, like someone coming up out of a dark tunnel.

Hetty stayed till nearly sundown, by which time agreement had been reached that she would keep Aeneas at her own farm for a three-month, by which time he might be strong enough for cup-feeding. Annie would go down each day to help her and meantime Donald would look around for a dependable woman to come in and care for the baby when Hetty and Annie had performed their stint.

They were not out of the wood as far as Aeneas was concerned for several days, but after a couple of weeks the change in him was remarkable. Donald arranged to pay the Labouchers by lending Mac to help with the fruit-picking later on and by promising to help at their next building bee, when they hoped to erect a cabin for Joe's brother Cuthbert. It was how they did things on the island, Hetty explained. She hoped Annie would be around when they feasted after the cabin was built. Last time they'd roasted a whole cow stuffed with venison.

"It just like the Promised Land," Hetty reiterated, though her big warm voice hardened with remembered griefs when she told Annie what it had been like getting there, all those months overland by covered wagon, every kind of attack from Indians to typhus. Her parents and a child had died. But every day now they breathed the heady air of freedom.

"But what about the Indians?" Annie asked.

"They didn't like us," Hetty admitted. "Specially us Negroes. They've done killings, but mostly of each other.

But then, they've lived here a long time. All the paths and tracks are Indian paths. They know what roots to eat and what plants are good medicine."

"They got camps on the island?"

"The Cowichans got camps. My Joe seen them with scalps hung up round. They go wandering round the place, raiding for fruit when they feel like it. You got to watch out for the Lamalcha band – they the worst. Don't you never light your candles at night, 'fore you put up your blankets. You get an arrow in your back."

At Annie's saucer-eyed look Hetty gave her warm, easy laugh. "Sakes alive, child, don't look like that. They mostly kill each other. There's bad killing on the beach when the Haidas or the Bella-Bella come in on their canoes from the north to look for scalps or slaves. The settlers are all right so long as they keep their heads and don't shoot. Better let them make off with food than kill even one, for they never give up till they get their revenge. You scared?"

"Not me."

"Nor me. Not any more. We came here the month of the shooting stars, August 1857, and even though I was scared of the wolves and the cougars and the Indians and all, I knew it was a good omen."

"You didn't come because of the war, then?"

"No, we came before it, because we wanted freedom. Ain't no Indians going to take it away from us now, I tell you. Here we're all equal. But you got to be careful, all the time. Keep your gun beside you, even when you're cooking. That's all."

As the baby grew stronger and healthier – and always, at Donald's insistence, with her shotgun over her shoulder – Annie took time to explore the island. In some ways she would be sorry to leave it so soon for every day she found something else to entrance her, things she noted in her writing book. Sometimes she surprised otter, mink or raccoon on the beach, or saw wild pigs rooting in the marshes. Black Tail deer crossed her vision on their way to the deer parks hidden among the tree-clad hills and sometimes on those hills she saw elk. Once she had been sure she saw a small black bear in the orchard, raiding the early fruit.

But it was the wild birds she loved best, the quail and pheasant and grouse and ducks and sea-birds, so beautiful in their colour and variety, and Hetty identified for her the bald eagle piping high in the sky and the swooping sparrow hawk. Nature at home in Scotland had come to mean to her those spoiled burns with their chemical waste and the sweet but invisible laverock. Here Nature triumphed in all her profusion and something in Annie responded with a great hungering need to see it all, to watch and marvel and wonder.

"Look," she would say to Aeneas, pointing out birds, flowers, even frogs and insects. And they would crow and laugh together, with Donald Arrochar looking bleakly on as she filled the baby's hands with flowers.

She was not convinced he had taken to the baby. Perhaps he still had doubts about his own paternity, perhaps it was just that the work on the farm tired him out so much he had little energy left to play with the baby when she brought him out from Hetty's to visit. He did not ignore Aeneas: it was just that there seemed to Annie to be a cool waiting dourness in his manner that was worse than rejection. In her worst moments, cuddling Aeneas, knowing her love for him growing stronger day by day, she did not know how she would be able to leave the child with his own father.

And there was the paid hand, Mac, with whom she had established a reasonable enough relationship. She tried hard to understand his broken tortured sounds, but felt for him in his embarrassment. He was fond of Aeneas, making little clucking noises that the baby enjoyed. But she felt he was a man always on the brink of breaking out: indeed, he sometimes did, drinking too much, behaving in a threatening way towards callers, breaking up his tacky cabin and then not looking anyone in the eye for days.

Muckle Annie

She was sorry for him but did not trust him. Sometimes, as she picked wild mushrooms or paddled, solitary, on the beach, she would see him raise his back from his labours to watch her and the action lifted the hair on the back of her neck. A silent man and a violent man – were these the kind of companions she wanted for Aeneas? More and more, she was thinking of Aeneas as *hers*.

His apparent rejection of Aeneas complicated Annie's feelings towards Donald Arrochar. After his initial questioning attitude – and she admitted it must have been a shock for him when she turned up with the baby in her arms – he had been just and even considerate in his dealings with her.

He had provided her with privacy at night by stretching two blankets across a rope in a corner of the cabin, behind which was her little truckle bed. He had told her he would pay her a fee for her labours and named a monthly sum that seemed generous. (She was glad about the money, for the funds she had had for Aeneas had been swallowed up by paying the Indian to bring them to the island and she would need every penny to get from Victoria to Barkerville and to buy a few warm clothes for the journey.) She asked Donald to hold the money for her till it was time to leave and so she would not be tempted to spend any of it in the one local store.

She saw in fact that Donald Arrochar hated talking about her departure, that he was perhaps hoping she would settle down indefinitely. Despite the firmness and formality of her approach, her frequent references to Hector and getting to Barkerville, he behaved as though she *belonged* to Salt Spring Island and the farm. It was not so much in things she said as thing left unsaid, in looks and attitudes and the way he chimed into her moods as though they were something far more intimate than employer and housekeeper. As though they were man and wife.

She knew she was guilty of collusion in some of this. She found herself watching him from the cabin door, acknowledging that he was graceful in all his working movements, a man at home with his toil. Even splitting logs he was good to watch, his lean powerful arms bringing the axe dead centre, the wood falling away cleanly, the pile growing. He never wasted energy. She liked the way he looked, his hard, disciplined body and she liked his will to make the farm work, to get it together from nothing. From their talk, she knew he was of a studious, contemplative nature, full of Highland superstitions but also of a quick, intuitive intelligence. He studied the curative nature of plants and sometimes before bedtime amused her by relating ancient cures as practised by his kinsfolk. When she made bannocks, he told her to make a hole in them to prevent the fairies from taking them, his eyebrows raised to elicit her amusement but something in his expression telling her he half-believed it. She knew it was dangerous for her to get to like him too much, for him to oust Hector, even temporarily, in some of her fancyings. Dangerous to ache for contact, intimacy.

Her moodiness grew. If she had not brought Aeneas to Salt Spring, she would have reached Barkerville long ago and would know whether Hector had struck it rich yet in the gold-fields. The thought of him idling in his cousin's saloon while he waited for her appalled her, as much as the fear that he would take off into the wilds for further prospecting if she took too long to turn up. They might keep missing each other altogether and their beautiful dream get frayed at the edges. She had done a bad thing, coming here. Yet what else could she have done? Left Aeneas in an orphanage? She wept at the very thought. Yet would it have been any harder than leaving him here, with a father who had little thought for him?

Aeneas was in her mind one night as she climbed into bed. He was growing fast, getting strong, eating fish and chicken meat and beginning to drink quite well from the cup. Although Hetty wanted to wet nurse him till he was at least toddling, Annie felt he could be brought home now to stay, to get to know his father. If she could get him settled in, with a new housekeeper, then perhaps she would be able to finalise her plans for leaving. The air was getting colder. It would be best to travel while the weather was still her ally.

As though in response to her thoughts of winter, she heard something she had never heard before. An unearthly howl, followed by an eerie, blood-curdling scream. Grey wolves and cougar in the hills, maybe the nearby hills. An atavistic terror took hold of her, making her think of books she had read with illustrations of wolves with eyes that glowed an unearthly green and fangs dripping with blood. Hetty had told her tales of cougar hanging over babies' cribs, of them making off with young animals. She began to shake and gave an involuntary cry.

"It's all right. They're miles away." Donald spoke from the other side of the blankets. He had not yet retired, but had been sitting in front of the stove, reading by the light of a candle. She got out of her bed and put a shawl over her nightgown, driven to join him by the stove by her chittering terror.

"How do you know? They could be on the hill –"

"They sound much worse than they are. The wolves would be more afraid of you than you of them."

"It's such an awful sound. It curdles my blood."

He laughed, but said on a gentler note "Nothing will happen to you. I will take care of that. Stop your chittering. I'll get you a toddy."

He put a little whisky in a mug and stirred in hot water from the stove. She sipped it slowly, feeling the beating of her heart quieten, her limbs stop their jerking.

"I must get away from here," she said.

"Is it so terrible? I thought you liked it. The flowers and the birds –"

"There are a lot of things here I'm frightened of."

"Such as?"

"Wolves and cougar."

"And what else?"

"You." The word, spat out almost involuntarily, surprised even her. He put down his toddy mug and gazed at her in simulated shock.

"Me? Why should you be afraid of me?"

"I'm afraid you'll never take to your child, that you will keep me here by hook or by crook to care for him, because you know I love him like my own."

"I own I would like you to stay."

"You will not so much as admit I have a right to go. I have a man to go to."

"You don't know what you're undertaking," he said straight-forwardly. "The Cariboo is a wild place, full of wild men, gamblers, drinkers, men who'd kill for a shilling. If you ask me, I don't think you will ever see your Hector again. What sort of a man was he, to ask you to make this journey on your own in the first place?"

"He's a better man than you'll ever be!" she answered swiftly.

"You're young," he went on relentlessly. "Young and daft. You think some silly vows you took before you were out of your swaddling clothes should bind you to some loon forever."

She was shaking again, this time with fury.

"You think it was just him? It was my idea, too. *I* made up my mind to join *him*. *I* am a person."

"You're a mere girl, a child."

"I am not a mere anything. Do you know what they call me at home? They call me Muckle Annie. I've never been known to give in once I make my mind up. I'm terrible determined. Terrible. And I'll get to the Cariboo if it kills me."

He took a poker and raked the stove. From her stool, she watched him and saw with a leap of pure pleasure that she had discomfited him, that emotions he had not bargained for, perhaps had not even known he possessed, were fighting for expression.

"Do you know how lonely it is here?" he burst out. "How

hard I've had to work? How desperate it was in the beginning?"

"That's your lookout."

"When you came I thought you would be trouble. But instead I got my food cooked for me, my hens looked after, a hundred and one jobs taken off my back."

"Well, you knew it would only be for a while." Her tone was more conciliatory. She smoothed the nightgown over her knee, noting almost with detachment that her fingers were trembling lightly.

"Can you blame me for wanting you to stay? Apart from anything else, I like the look of you. I like to hear your young voice, your laugh. It's very pleasant. It makes the whole place come alive for me in a way it never did before. The whole place. The house, the orchard, the fields. If I can look up and see you're there."

"You shouldn't say these things to me."

"I am only telling you the way it is. Could you not consider staying? The place is a paradise – deer, grouse, pheasant – I can walk out of here and they're there for the taking. Tobacco, barley, apples, pears, Italian prunes – the ground'll grow anything."

"But the Indians. The wolves –"

"The Indians will settle down. Indians, Negroes, whites, we'll all grow rich together. Aeneas can go to the black teacher's school. Did you know about him, the Negro teacher who works for nothing? This is a good place, Annie, full of good people. How can you think of exchanging it for the Cariboo?"

"Because," she said steadily, "Hector is there."

He said, "Come here to me."

"I will not." But she went. When their hands touched it was as though an electric current went through her. She looked down into his face and saw the pleading there. He pressed his head into her shoulder and although she kept her back stiff, she could feel a softening go on all through her body.

"Kiss me, Annie."

"I won't." But she did. His lips were hard and firm, her own tentative and guilty. He made a murmuring sound and slid his hand underneath her nightgown. With a sob she drew back and brought her hand crashing across the side of his face, seeing shock mortify his features as she staggered back towards her blanketed corner. She felt under the thrown-back covers for her shotgun and sat on the edge of the bed with it between her knees.

"No," she said, frantically, "Donald, no."

He tore the blankets down and threw them on the floor.

"You want it," he said. "As bad as I do."

"I'll kill you if you come any nearer. I mean it."

"Put the gun away," he said, contemptuously. "I would never force my attentions on a lass who didn't want it."

"Did you force them on poor Effie? She never approved of that side of things. She told me."

"What a woman says and what a woman does can be two different things."

"Not with me."

He laughed at last, at the sight of her sitting there with her tousled hair and scarlet face and the gun at the ready. Carefully he put the blankets up again, then parted them and smiled at her.

"You kissed me," he taunted her. "That was something."

"It is all you'll get."

The next day she saw the Indian.

She had risen to another peerless morning following the cold of the night before. The Island began to cast its inexorable spell, as, wolves and cougar all but forgotten, she looked out on the white hens clucking contentedly under the orchard trees. *Her* hens. He had said so. He had said so many things, things that had reverberated in her mind last night as she had lain wide-eyed and sleepless. She turned away almost angrily from the scene before her. The spell of the island had to be broken. Today. She would bring the baby back to the farm. She would confront Donald with the necessity of getting someone to look after Aeneas. And then she would leave. It had to be sooner rather than later. Surely even Donald would see that.

When he saw her Aeneas leaned forward from Hetty's arms and held his own out towards her. She took him with the leap of possessive pleasure she always felt, deepened by the way the soft baby arms went round her neck and the little fingers entangled themselves in her hair. He was like part of her. She kissed his soft cheek.

"I'm taking him back to the farm today," she told Hetty without preamble. The large, molasses-dark eyes turned on her questioningly, but Hetty made no answer.

"He can drink fine from a cup," Annie argued. "He eats meat and eggs and it's time his father settled the housekeeper problem, for I'm off to Victoria before the winter sets in. I don't think I'm being unreasonable."

"You fond of that man," said Hetty, in her conclusive manner. "And he fond of you. You got a good farm there, plenty to eat."

"But I'm going to Hector." Hetty knew all about Annie's plans. They had discussed them often enough, looking after the children together and Hetty had never raised a dissenting voice till now.

"What going to happen to little 'Neas?"

"I don't know."

"Ain't like you to be hard."

"You don't know everything, Hetty," said Annie subduedly. She sat down with the baby and he gave her an enquiring, old-fashioned look, patting her face, squirming to stand up on her lap. "You've got my word for it, I've got to leave soon. I would like to do it with your blessing."

Hetty wiped the corner of her eye with her apron. "That poor baby sure going to miss you," was all she said.

Annie began to prepare the baby for going home, sniffing loudly as she got his little mug and other belongings together. Since the men were especially busy at the moment and would soon have to take a day off to load thirty head of cattle for the market in Victoria, Mac had not accompanied her recently to the top of the hill and no arrangements had been made to meet her on the way back. Had Donald known about the return of the baby the arrangements would certainly have been different.

Annie was confident she could manage as well on her own as with Mac. Her eyes and ears were sharp, she had grown fast and fleet of foot on the hillsides. She had the shotgun. And besides, she had never till then seen any Indian activity.

But there he was. Halfway between Hetty's and the farm, she stopped on the top of the hill and saw him, down on the dunes that led to the shoreline where she had first set foot on the island. A shiver ran up her spine. Since her coming, that shoreline and bay had been provided with their own makeshift wooden quay and several hastily-erected cabins were already turning them into quite a busy little port, so great was the demand on Vancouver Island and even on the mainland for the island produce, the butter and lamb in particular.

Positioning herself behind a tree and squinting round it, Annie watched the Indian. He seemed to be carrying out some kind of reconnaisance of the bay. That done, he turned and followed one of the tribal tracks along the shoreline, till he came to the next bay, the one where she often paddled and loved because it was full of wildfowl, especially the Old Squaw ducks who ran gossiping flotillas at the wide mouth of the river that ran into the sea there.

Aeneas squirmed protestingly in her arms but she shushed him, sitting down behind the tree and giving him pine cones to play with. After the tensions of the night before, it was almost a relief to give herself over to the half-scary, half-exciting frissons of curiosity involved in watching the Indian. It was as though by doing so she tuned into the island's history – what it had been before the black and white folk came, when the Indians were its only inhabitants. The man she watched moved with such economy and stealth her feelings of awe and admiration overcame all others.

"Hush, Aeneas," she warned the baby. What was the Indian doing now? He seemed to be making some kind of signal. And then came a sight she was never to forget. Round the little bay came what seemed like canoes by the dozen, paddled so silently they were like a drawing made animate. Two went ahead of the others, up the narrow river mouth, then turned sideways to form a barrier. The rest encroached on the U-shaped bay and river mouth and at last their purpose became clear to Annie: they were massing the ducks together, herding them into a narrow area of water that even as she looked seemed to undulate with the beating of frantic wings.

And then came the arrows. One or two birds rose into the air but fell as the unerring Indian marksmen took aim. The beating of wings gradually ceased and the water where the birds had swum in their earlier terror became a dead, inert mass, through which smaller pick-up canoes moved – were they paddled by the squaws? – and were gradually filled up with wildfowl. Without her knowing it, the tears of protest fell down Annie's cheeks, while the baby watched her bemused. "No," she whispered. "Ah, no." But the canoes were going, as fast and silently as they had come and now over the whole area there was a quietness, a stillness, broken only by the occasional harsh cry of a seagull.

When the tears had stopped, she rose slowly, brushing twigs and dead leaves from her skirts. Only this morning she had thought this island was everything Donald had said about it, a place full of promise and bounty. Now it had just shown its other, more ruthless face and reminded her she and Donald and the rest were the intruders and that the Indians were still very much there, ready to claim what they regarded as theirs.

She shivered. It was suddenly very important to get back to the cabin.

5

"You had no right to bring the chilt back till you consulted me," said Donald again. "And to bring him back, unescorted, when the Indians are active was just plain, bloody stupidity. You could both have been taken."

"Rubbish," she said, shortly. "You've said yourself; they're only interested in fighting each other."

"They've been known to take incomers prisoner. And do you know what the Bella-Bella do so you can't run away? They cut the sinews in your legs."

She turned away with an expression of revulsion. "All the more reason I should leave on the earliest possible sloop."

He ignored her. "You said you saw one near the other bay? I think that means that they've got cattle rustling in mind as well. They're getting stored up for the winter. They know the beeves are in prime condition and they probably know I intend sending some for sale in Victoria. Me and Gump Gallacher and the others."

"Let me take Aeneas away with me!" she burst out. "I can find a safe place for him in Victoria and send for him once I've contacted Hector. Let me have him! You know he's like my own!"

"He stays here."

"You never look at him. You would leave him with Hetty forever."

"I know nothing about infants. Some woman body has to care for him till he's old enough. But he's my ultimate responsibility. You want to look after him, you stay here."

She almost threw his food in front of him.

"Gump Gallacher's daughter Alice says she will come and housekeep for you. She's brought up her brothers and sisters since her mother died.'

"Then let her continue to do so."

She sat down and picked listlessly at her own meat and potatoes, stealing an occasional look at Aeneas who had fallen asleep on the bearskin rug by the hearth.

She said at last, with great deliberation, "Please, Donald, at least let us talk about Aeneas's future. You know it's breaking me in two to leave him. But if I have to, I will. You will then have to get Alice in. Whatever you decide, I want my fee from you now. I have to leave the island."

"No!" He brought his fist crashing down on the table. She looked up disbelievingly and saw his expression was as dark as thunder clouds. "You'll get no fee. I won't be a party to your leaving. The chilt needs you, I need you and I won't let you wander off into the Cariboo where anything could happen to you and probably would."

She stared at him, totally dumbfounded.

"But I *earned* that money." She was remembering Henderson the engine-maker and the day Nana had been up and down the clean steps.

The dark brows glowered. "You will get it. When I see fit."

"I thought whatever else you were, you were an honourable man."

He moved in tired irritability. "Come, mistress," he said, "I've had a hard day in the fields."

She rose and flew round the room, looking in tins, teapots, canisters, under his mattress, anywhere she thought the money could be. When that failed, she tore down the protective sacking and newspaper from the cabin walls, till the cabin looked as though it had been turned upside down by a gale.

At length he grabbed and held her. She rained blows on his chest, she aimed kicks at his shins, but his vice-like grip on her wrists never loosened. She screamed, she bit, she struggled, till with a rare oath he wrestled her towards her bed and threw her down on it, where she lay sobbing as though her heart would break.

When it got dark, he put up the blankets at the windows and lit the candles and brought her some gruel. She threw spoon and porringer on the floor and he cleaned it up. The baby woke and he fed him.

"I will never forgive you," she said, between gritted teeth. "You are keeping me prisoner."

"I have no option."

"Give me my money. It's mine. I want it."

"All in good time. Will you tend the chilt? It's you he seems to hanker after."

She swallowed her tears and took the baby in her arms. Sensing her mood, he grizzled and then gave way to full-chested bawling.

"Is that how he always is?" demanded Donald testily.

"Like his father," she answered, "his temper is filthy."

"Wheesht!" said Donald, his expression suddenly sharpening. "Quieten that bairn somehow. I thought I heard something."

There was a loud rapping at the cabin door and a voice called out urgently, "Let me in, man. It's Gallacher."

Donald gave his Australian neighbour entry and hastily barred the door behind him.

"What brings you here at this time of night?" he demanded.

"Injuns," said Gump Gallacher, on a rasping breath. "You heard about the duck hunt? Alice says she saw two more Injuns down by the quay. Reckon they're after our cattle, too, don't you?"

"I'm sure of it. They know the auctions are coming up soon in Victoria."

"I can't afford it." Gump Gallacher passed his cap across his brow in a weary gesture, half-acknowledging Annie as he did so. "I'm just about breaking even."

"Me too."

"Simpson at Gulch Farm, Harry Ballantyne at the Fork place, they're worried. Just about getting on their feet, like you and me. You reckon we can do something about it?

Time we got some law and order in this place."

"We don't need to take it lying down, that's for sure."

"You got a strategy, then?"

"We got to think of something." Donald gave Annie a look that was half-deferential, half-intimidating. "You get Mr. Gallacher here a tot, will you?"

She looked as though she were about to refuse. But instead she poured Gump Gallacher the required tot and said in a bright, normal voice, to Donald, "What was that you said, about asking Miss Gallacher to come and work for you, look after Aeneas?" To Gump she said, "You ask your girl if she's still interested, Mr. Gallacher. It's a good meat-house here and the baby'd be good company. I've got to go back to Victoria. My term is up here."

Gallacher looked from one set face to the other.

"I can mention to Alice —"

"Leave it for tonight," Donald ordered. "We got other things on our mind." As Annie looked as though she were going to continue the argument, he said to Gallacher, "We'll go out the barn and talk. Can't hear yourself think for the squawking in here."

To Annie he said shortly, "Keep your gun cocked and the windows covered. Bar the door till you hear my knock."

The long evening passed with a maddening slowness, marked by the vigilant ticking of the wag-at-the-wa' clock. Aeneas, soothed by milk and a molasses crust, changed from lusty howling to seductive cooing. She rocked and sang to him till finally he slept and then she surveyed his innocent, cherubic countenance with a wistful longing, willing the image to stay in her mind.

More carefully and deliberately now she began to search the cabin. She stripped the walls of their remnants of newspaper and rags. She trod the floorboards, feeling to see if any were loose. She drew out the rough desk he had made for himself and, behind it, triumphantly found a small tin box with a lock. More rummaging, however, failed to yield up the key and in a temper of frustration she banged the box against the stove. The lock wouldn't yield.

Her anger and resentment grew. It seemed that all the bad memories of Glasgow, its hunger and deprivation, came flooding back. The way she had felt that day, called into the dining-room of Henderson the engine-maker, refused the small sum that meant all the difference between starvation and getting by. She could remember the rotting boots, the feeling of rain, cold and utter hopelessness but more than that the assault on her dignity as a living entity, one of God's creatures, rendered lower than an animal by Henderson's attitude.

Donald was no Henderson. He had been, by and large, kind to her. But by keeping her fee from her, he was mixed up now with the oppressors, those she had sworn would never get the better of her again. It didn't matter that he had a good meat-house, that there, if she stayed, there would be food, clothes, warmth and more. What mattered was recognition of her place, her worth, her stature. He had to be shown he could not get the better of her.

She scarcely knew what she was doing then. She was aware, dimly, somewhere in her mind, that her actions were neither considered nor wise, but she went ahead anyhow. She wrapped a shawl about her and another about the sleeping Aeneas and let herself out of the cabin, easing the loaded shotgun on to her shoulder and closing the door quietly behind her. Her intentions were, as far as she had formed them, to take Aeneas to Alice Gallacher then search for another farm job on the island until she could save again for her passage to Victoria. Or some other opportunity might present itself – she had even got as far as thinking she might be able to hide away on the mail ship. Something. Anything. *To show him*.

She passed the barn and could hear the low rumble of voices, surely more than those of just Donald and Gallacher. She peered through the join of the barn door and saw Simpson, Harry Ballantyne and Joe and Cuthbert Laboucher had joined the other two – no doubt fetched by

Mac who was sitting, exhausted, on a hay bale. There was a sense of desperate urgency about the little group that almost sent her scuttling back to the safety of the cabin. Almost, but not quite.

She strained to hear what they were saying.

"Soon as the moon's up, they'll be here." That was Donald. "They know the beeves are ready."

"Aye, it'll be tonight, I'll swear it." That was Gallacher, sweating, his sharp, acquiline features drawn up with tension, like Mr. Punch.

"We use the trees," Donald was saying. "We run from tree to tree, shooting in the air. Make them think there's dozens of us, a small army. But we draw no blood. For Christ's sake, remember it. If we so much as wound, never mind kill, we draw down a massacre. Are you game to give it a try?"

There was a scuffling of feet, a clearing of throats, a murmur of assent. Annie found the saliva had totally dried up in her mouth. Automatically, she looked up. The moon was still hidden behind clouds. She could still get to the Gallacher farm. She padded off into the night, listening for every sound, unconsciously copying the Indian she had seen earlier in her careful, stealthy track. Presently the fog of fear cleared in her mind and she was aware that a glimmer from the sea meant she no longer had to strain so hard to see where she was going. But the moon must be coming up. She must hurry.

When she hammered on the Gallacher door Alice's frightened voice demanded to know who was there.

"Annie. Annie McIlvanney, from the Arrochar farm."

Alice's relieved buck-toothed smile was welcoming. The other teenaged and younger children gathered round, noisy and curious.

"I want to leave the baby with you," Annie explained. "I think you will be getting the job of looking after him, so you might as well get your hand in." She handed the sleeping Aeneas over. "Take care of him." It was more of a stern order than an entreaty, but as Alice looked down at the baby, she knew why she'd picked her: she was one of those natural mothers, tender and gentle. Not blessed with great good looks, in fact, plain, thin and homely, with a lisp. Maybe she'd picked her for that, too, so that Donald Arrochar would not get too fond of her, but that was by the by. Of little consequence, now.

"Why are you here?" Alice demanded. "You must be out of your mind. The Injuns are coming."

"It's a long story," said Annie, brusquely, "but you needn't concern yourself with it."

Alice looked offended, but it dawned on her there must have been a row between Annie and her employer. That didn't altogether displease her. Donald Arrochar was the best-looking prospect on Salt Spring.

"Come and have a warm," she invited. 'You can tell me what transpired. I can keep a secret."

"I'm moving on." Annie looked for a moment at the inviting rocking-chair, vacated for her by a young Gallacher, but all her nerves were jumping, she wanted to be out in the frightening but adventurous night, she wanted some sort of resolution of the conflict inside her and she knew she would not find it here. "I'm going. Just mind Aeneas." The baby was the one thing that would make her stay, so she did not look at him. Before Alice had time for any further entreaties, she was outside the cabin door, listening again for the sounds that would betray human rather than animal tracks. Looking up at the moon, which now had sailed completely from behind the veil of clouds.

Afterwards, she tried to define what drew her back towards the hill, the quay and the bay where it was all to happen. Curiosity, perhaps. That trait in her character that was stronger than all others. The need to know. But it might also have been irresolution, not knowing where next to go. It might have been a faltering, something in her drawn back at the last to the farm where she had known, at times, a rare, uncomplicated happiness and fulfilment.

It might have been a mixture of all these things, but it was also a late-discovered feeling of loyalty towards the farmers, to Joe and Cuthbert Laboucher who had worked so hard to establish a living since the year of the shooting stars, to Gump Gallacher and his motherless brood, even towards Simpson and Ballantyne because she had seen them labour seven days a week, had seen the pride in Ballantyne's face when he got his first herd of Texas Longhorns and seen Simpson's wife weep when a casual Indian raider had emptied her kitchen garden of its soft fruit and vegetables. The island wasn't letting her go yet. She wouldn't think of Donald Arrochar, who deserved nothing of her loyalty. But what was suddenly uppermost in her mind was the look on his face in the barn, the look of a man whose tenuous livelihood was at stake. And she remembered, reluctantly, what Effie had told her about the Highland croft and the sheep that were sacrificed for greedy men. It shouldn't happen twice to any man, not even Donald Arrochar.

Keeping her back bent and her head low, she crept up the hill towards the trees where she knew the men would be deployed. She came on Mac first. He was on the point of loosing off a shot when he recognised her. Flopping down beside him, she asked him where Donald was. He was next in the line behind the trees, already looking towards them. She stood up and waved her arms and he beckoned her urgently towards him.

"What in hell's name are you doing here?"

"I can help."

"You can get scalped for your trouble." He shook her by the arm. "Where have you left Aeneas?"

"With Alice Gallacher. She'll be looking after him from now on. I've leaving. I told you."

"Get back to the cabin."

"No. I'm staying to help."

She could hear the furious purchase of his breath, and went on quickly: "I know what the plan is. We run from tree to tree, yelling and shouting, loosing off shot, but we don't aim to kill. I don't want to kill Indians, anyhow. I don't want to kill anybody. But I can screech enough for a dozen men."

She saw the tension go out of his shoulders a little but still he argued. "This is no place for a woman. Go back into the trees and stay there. You don't want an arrow in the chest."

At that moment there was a low, urgent shout from Gallacher, next up the line. "Canoes! Mother of Mary, they're coming! Dozens of 'em!"

She watched them again, stunned into silence, as Donald was. It was like a replay of the duck hunt, only this time the image of the canoes gliding into the bay, limned by moonlight was a sight so strangely beautiful and mesmerising the breath snared in their chests.

"Go back," Donald ordered, thickly. She picked up her shotgun and stumbled back into the thicket, about twenty yards, then turned to watch. The canoes drew up on the beach one by one and with silent, cat-like grace their occupants leapt ashore. What was happening? She realised Donald had ordered the others to hold their fire till the Indians were well up the beach. But would it never begin? So quiet were the Indians the chirping of crickets and croaking of frogs could still be heard in the woodland behind her. And then it was as though all hell was let loose. Shooting and yelling the men ran from tree to tree. She saw Joe Laboucher re-load and jump from his lair, screeching like a demon. She saw Mac, fleet as a deer and Donald, yelling like a madman. A kind of crazy, releasing energy seemed to flood through her own body and she found herself racing towards the front line of trees, letting off shots, screeching, yelling, passing the racing figure of Harry Ballantyne and registering the furious surprise on his face as he saw who it was.

Something pinged through the air and landed on the ground beside her. An arrow. Still quivering. She gave a yelp of terror and raced back to the sheltering trees, reloading her gun with trembling fingers, but still forcing shouts and yells from her bursting lungs. Dear God, they were still coming. She thought then of her mother, of her childhood. Images raced through her mind like a torrent, as though some kind of summation were necessary before the candle of her life blew out.

And then, suddenly, uncertainty and fear seemed to spread through the oncoming Indians like a pandemic. First one, then two, turned and made for the shore, then all of them began to race for the canoes, noisily egging each other on. One by one the canoes were paddled out of the bay, as swiftly and expertly as they had come.

One last canoe waited for a slow-moving Indian; Annie guessed he must be their leader. This last man turned and in a gesture of defiance loosed an arrow in the direction of his harassers. Annie heard a shout to her left and saw Donald go down.

"No!" she screamed. Her feet seemed to skim the ground as she raced towards him. As she reached him he was already on his feet, drawing the arrow away from the clothing on his right shoulder.

"Are you hurt?"

"It's a flesh wound." She could see the blood running copiously from it and her stomach turned over. The other men came running up. "We've got to get him home," she ordered them, "and get this wound washed and bound up."

Mac and Joe Laboucher eased him between them and led him home.

"You done it," said Joe. "Them Indians must have thought there were hundreds of us."

Annie was fearful what she would see when they got Donald back inside, but Donald's stoic demeanour reassured her. The arrow had torn the flesh raggedly but fortunately had not gone deep. She set her lips together and bathed the area, then bound the wound as best she could with a bandage from an old, clean petticoat.

Mac had made toddies while she was busy and now they sat around drinking them and reliving the moment when the

Indian nerve had broken – or, more likely, Indian cunning dictated the wisdom of leaving the rustling till another day.

"I guess," said Gump Gallacher, "that we've taught those sons o' guns a lesson once and for all."

"We eventually have to live in peace with them," said Donald, measuredly. His face was pale but there was no mistaking the gleam of satisfaction in his eyes. "Steea was theirs for a long time, after all. Apart from my shoulder, it was a bloodless battle. Those are the kind I like."

He saw Annie look at him appraisingly and volunteered, "You were brave, for a lassie." She was about to argue being a lassie had nothing to do with it, you were either brave or you were not, but the praise muffled up the protest in her throat.

One by one the men left for their homes. Mac, who had drunk too much whisky, could be heard having one of his roaring fits outside his cabin.

Donald cocked his gun on his knee. "I will sit up," he offered. "It will be easier for me, because of the shoulder. You should get some rest."

There was nothing she could say. She lay down on her truckle bed with all her clothes on, not even taking off her boots. With Donald a few feet away on the other side of the blanket, she felt curiously warm and secure. The unaccustomed toddy did its work and soon she slept.

"And so, mistress, it is final. You are leaving me," he said the next morning. She had made his breakfast, changed the dressing on his shoulder, tidied the cabin, fed the stove.

He brought a key forth from his waistcoat pocket and indicated she should bring the tin box to him from behind his desk.

"Open it," he said, giving her the key.

Inside she saw a pocket Bible and a pen and ink drawing of Effie, as well as two small canvas bags containing money. He rifled in one of the bags and handed her some cash. "Your fee," he said, without expression.

She took it in the same manner.

"Why give it to me now?"

"I can see you're determined to go, whatever I do. Is there a sloop soon for Victoria?"

"Day after tomorrow. I'd *better* go," she said, awkwardly. "No point in prolonging the agony."

"Then today," he said, "we'll go fishing. It's a fine bright day and the heavy work will have to wait a day or two, till this shoulder eases. We'll get a trout for the laddie's tea."

"We'll take Aeneas? Alice should be arriving with him soon."

"We'll take Aeneas."

She brushed Aeneas's dark crop up in its cockscomb and dressed him in his best robes. He laughed and chuckled at her, lively as a cricket. She wore the pink gingham frock Hetty had made her, although she normally kept it for Sundays. She tied some sour-milk scones and cheese, four hard-boiled eggs and a wedge of seed cake up in a cloth, for eating when Donald had tired of the fishing.

There was something about him today. A kind of resolution. It was as though the incident at the beach had released some brooding vapour from his mind. Maybe man-like he was rejoicing in his powers of strategy and leadership. Certainly it seemed the local community looked to him more and more, sensing in him a kind of moral superiority. Annie felt mildly deflated. Some display of sadness at her going would not, she felt, have been out of place, instead of the positively pleasurable delight he took in the day, the sunshine and the river.

"You'll have to take the oars," he challenged her, as they climbed into the punt. "I'll see to Aeneas and the fishing." Aeneas was tucked snugly between his father's knees and she thought, with a lift of her spirits, that at least he was taking more to the child, now he could sit up and articulate, even if it was just crowing and gurgling. How anyone could not dote on Aeneas was totally incomprehensible to Annie and to see incipient signs of it, at last, in Donald, was balm to her heart.

She was clumsy at first with the oars but soon got the hang of it. Maybe Donald's joking good humour was just a little too febrile, but she went along with it. As the trout rose to the bait she joined him in singing Highland airs and even taught him some of the plantation songs she'd learned from Hetty.

She hadn't been sure whether he would permit talk of her departure and itinerary, but he led into it quite naturally, discussing where she should stay in Victoria – she aimed to look up her friend Pheemie – how soon she should set out for Barkerville, what the conditions would be like on the Cariboo Trail. He spoke as an elder brother might speak, guiding her, supporting her and eventually handing over a gift he had purchased from the island store. The one with the notice that said "No cussing when ladies present."

"What is this?" she demanded, flustered. It was a secure little waist purse and inside were three gold coins. "It is too much," she protested, tears welling.

"It is not enough for what you've done," he answered. "I have had it at the ready, with your fee. But I always hoped against hope I would not need to give you it."

When they had caught some trout they tied the punt to a tree-trunk and clambered on to the river bank to play with the baby, eat and rest. An otter poked a curious nose in their direction and wild pigs kept a respectful distance on the marshy reaches.

"Donald," she vouchsafed at last, "I hope I will be able to come back one day and see Aeneas. Don't let him forget me. Or his mother Effie. Tell him about us. How we loved him."

A steady looked passed between them. "You *will* come back," he said, evenly. "I know it."

"How can you *know* it?" She was suddenly, irrationally, furious with him.

"I *know*."

"From a dream?"

He nodded.

"You and your Highland foreseeings! I do not believe in them."

Muckle Annie

"Come here. Put your foot on mine." He put his good arm around her. "Close your eyes. Now do you see it? The day of your return? This way you can share my second sight. No, do not take your foot away."

A shiver went through her. For a brief moment, she thought she saw the island, shrouded in mist, and rain, and herself stepping off a schooner – a self older and more elegant, but sad of face. As her mind filled up with questions, the vision – if that was what it had been – faded. She gazed at Donald in alarm – but he merely smiled and nodded, as though to reassure.

"I will tell Aeneas, anyhow. It will be easy. You will not be far from my mind."

Her eyes were suddenly brimful of tears.

"Don't distress yourself." He kissed her cheek. "When there has been a loving between two people, such as between you and me, it doesn't go away. It's there to remember when you go about your work. It doesn't take away from your life, it adds to it."

"Has there been a loving?"

"You know there has. There would have been a bedding, too, but for the vows you took. I wish you never had, Annie. Taken those vows."

"Well, I did. And I meant them." But she moved nearer him and kissed his cheek, then leaned against him, with a barely perceptible sigh.

He tightened his good arm around her and she leaned her head on his shoulder. Comfortable and comforted, for a little while, till she thought again of the Cariboo and its trackless, challenging snows, where Hector waited.

Then as they rowed back, his face bore the sadness she had wanted and expected. And now she would have given everything, anything, to remove it. But it was too late, her plans had become too remorseless, her commitment was too great, she had to move on. The sloop *Harriet* was coming the day after tomorrow.

The notice in the Victoria shop window proclaimed boldly:
ENOCH ALBERT SAMPSON, THE ORIGINAL PIEMAN
DELICIOUS PIES DELIVERED TO YOUR RESIDENCE
TWENTY-FIVE CENTS PER PIE
BOOTS AND SHOES REPAIRED FOR CASH
SHOES SHINED   HAIR CUT

Annie moved to the window on the other side of the shop entrance and studied a further, fancily-executed notice:
MR. SAMPSON BEGS LEAVE TO INFORM HIS CLIENTS HE IS PREPARED TO FILL TEETH WITH GOLD, SILVER OR TINFOIL, SET TEETH ON PIVOTS AND EXTRACT SAME.

She fancied her jaw had begun to ache in sympathy with the notice. Without further ado, she pushed open the shop door and in answer to the energetic jingling of its bell, a smart fair-haired young woman in a black dress, with a white apron, appeared from the back shop with a brisk, "Good morning. Is it pies, then? They're all fresh and –"

"Pheemie!"

The woman stared, blushed, then her mouth fell open. "Annie! Annie McIlvanney! I never thought to see you this day!" They embraced each other warmly.

"Come in the back," said Pheemie, hospitably. "Enoch is out with the deliveries. I'll put the kettle on. We'll have a cup of tea. And a pie."

"Of course. But what's all this about Enoch? And pies? I thought you were to wed that old farmer with all the money!"

"And no intention of parting with any of it!"

Pheemie laughed and looked coy and embarrassed all at the same time. "I'm afraid Enoch made up his mind to speak for me, the first time I came into the shop."

"And you married him?"

"Within a two-month. And there's a little Enoch on the way!"

"You've done all right for yourself!" said Annie warmly.

"And what about you? I've thought of you often. I want to hear everything you've been up to."

It took the best part of the afternoon for the friends to catch up with their news. Annie enquired after Lizzie and was told she had run away from the family with its marriageable sons, one of whom had wanted the privileges of marriage without the responsibilities. She had got a poor sort of job assisting a tailoress but found comfort in religion. Pheemie doubted if she would ever marry.

"So you are still set on looking for your Hector?" Pheemie sat back in her rocking-chair and surveyed her friend, her animated face now clouded with doubt.

"On *finding* him," Annie corrected her.

Pheemie rocked furiously. "I wish you wouldn't," she burst out at last. "My Enoch's been to Barkerville and I've heard some tales of the gambling and drinking that goes on."

"There's something else worrying you."

"Well, at Richfield last year – that's near Barkerville – there was this girl they called the Scotch Lassie –"

"Go on."

"And she was murdered in her cabin." Pheemie had put a hand to her mouth and her saucer-like eyes gazed at her friend. "They never found who did it."

"Well, I'm used to carrying a shotgun. You don't need to worry about me."

"Promise me you'll not take to the drink –"

"As if I would!"

"That was what happened to the poor Scotch Lassie. She married a drunkard and he led her down the murky path to ruin."

"You're letting your imagination run away with you," said Annie firmly.

Pheemie regarded her young friend with a soft, affectionate eye.

"You're that headstrong," she said. "I can see your headstrong nature leading you into all kinds of trouble, if you're not careful. You'll not be counselled."

"I only want to find Hector."

"And if you don't? Or if he's changed, got himself a hurdy-gurdy dancer or something like that, what then?"

"I'll survive."

Pheemie shook her head and rocked furiously. "Stay here," she burst out at last. "There's a big attic room you could have and I need all the help I can get with the pies. I can easily talk Enoch round."

"I'm booked on the steamship to Yale. Will you come and see me off?"

"We've got to get back to the pie shop," Enoch Sampson told his wife. He was a neat, portly man with dark, button-bright eyes. He did not like to see Pheemie weep.

"Whatever will happen to her?" she demanded of him. The steamship was setting off up the Frazer river purposeful as a dowager and she could no longer see the lace-trimmed handkerchief that Annie had been waving. "What if she never finds him, this Hector?"

"I've twelve pound of cow steak to cut up," her husband reminded her.

"I'll never see her again," wailed Pheemie. "I should never have let her go."

"There was no way you could have stopped her. Come on. Where was that shop we passed with the necklace you liked? Let's go and buy it."

Part Two

6

The woman sitting opposite her in the stage-coach wore a bonnet of considerable grandeur, small silk flowers of mauve and pink piled under the brim and the wide silk ties resplendent purple. If it looked, the bonnet, as though it had seen its owner through a number of doubtful adventures and grown just a little tired, a little jaded, in the process, then this impression was counteracted by the magnificent silk frogging on her green velvet coat and the glossy, deep sealskin collar and cuffs. Lace cascaded from the woman's wrists, blonde ringlets around her neck, and from her ample bosom came the rich smell of wood violets and lavender, compounded by camphor and brandy. Annie stared. Everything she wore suddenly felt threadbare by comparison.

"Goin' all the way to Barkerville?" The voice was richly American, the smile wide and open.

Annie nodded.

"You'd think we must be out of our minds." The woman laughed. "Four blessed days and nights. Mountains, gulches, rivers, the lot. Reckon we'll be shook to a jelly 'fore we get there!"

"I don't care." Suddenly Annie felt quite at home with the big, pink face opposite. If they were travelling together they might as well pass the time in talk and confidence. "I'm going to see my man. Four days and nights are nothing. I can't wait to get there."

"Made his fortune, in the goldfields, has he?" asked the woman, with a look at the other occupants of the coach.

"He may have," said Annie defensively. "That's why he came here. We aim to buy a farm."

"The big fortune days is over," said a slight, bearded man huddled into a tatty fur coat and hat, dismissively. He wore rings on his fingers and a convincing-looking tiepin with a glittering stone. His dark eyes darted hither and thither restlessly, making Annie feel uneasy.

"Don't mean to say the good times is leaving just as Maybelle Macbride is arriving!" The blonde woman gave a full-bosomed roar of laughter. "Ain't that just like the thing. Same thing happened back in '58. That was the start of it all. They couldn't get out of 'Frisco fast enough. California just emptied, like magic and some of the ships — well, you should have seen 'em. We got here and the Fraser went into flood. Wouldn't give up her gold. I stayed a while, but I saw that river wash too many men to pieces 'gainst the canyon. What the river didn't take, Injuns did. I got sickened and went home. But I was given to understand that things were quite convivial up Barkerville way now. Goodness me, the place has only just got started, now we got a proper road there at last."

"My hopes, too, Ma'am," said the man with the glittering tie-pin. "It's just that the shallow diggings up Richfield way, they're more or less worked out now and the deeper claims, below the canyon, well, they ain't so easy, see."

"You'll make a living," said Maybelle Macbride, convincedly, looking at the man's neat, small, card-sharper's hands. "What's your game? Sinch? Euchre?"

"You name it. What's yours?"

"I aim to get up some dancing in one of the saloons. High-class dancin' girls is my specialty." As the level of interest rose noticeably and a certain sneering expression crossed the card-sharper's face, she said emphatically, "My girls are good clean girls. I only train the best." She gave the card-sharp a hard look. "At least I don't rob some poor sap of the gold it's taken him months to mine. Ain't my notion of fair play."

The man's eyes snapped in anger but he said no more and devoted his attention to looking outside the coach. The other men – she and Maybelle Macbride were the only women – did not offer much in the way of interest to Annie. They were mainly interested in sleeping and drinking. They looked to Annie like hardened diggers, men who had perhaps in their time struck gold, spent it, then returned to look for more, perhaps with little success. She was glad she had Maybelle Macbride for company – the woman's robust, combative feminity was reassuring and no doubt a better safeguard than the company of a female of more conventional mien.

They were heading into wild, desolate land now, bounced up and down on the leather-strap springs. The steamship trip up the river to Yale had been uneventful and as she'd landed and sought out the stage-coach the first few flakes of snow had trimmed her bonnet and settled on her shoulders. Then it had held off, but the sky was full of the threat of it. Grey, loaded. She looked out on tracks of country of a vastness she felt she could never totally comprehend; at pines, mountains, rivers, rugged terrain of awesome, empty, inhospitable grandeur. Someone on the steamship had told her they'd used camels at one point to help lay this trail the stage-coach now rumbled over. Poor camels! What must they have felt! The legend had grown round them – how one had been shot by a drunken digger in mistake for a grizzly bear, for example. She was learning you had to take a lot of Cariboo yarns with the proverbial pinch of salt.

She shared some food with Maybelle Macbride, accepted a small tot of whisky from the other to warm her and fell into a sleepy kind of daze as night began to fall, thinking back to Donald and Aeneas and forward to seeing Hector again. There was an ache of regret and at the same time a trembling of expectation in her, that was not altogether without fear. The face that she had not been able to picture clearly for months was suddenly back in her mind's eye – the tall fairness of him, the blue eyes with all that whiteness around them, the way he'd looked at her when they said farewell.

She felt guilty now of the feelings that had been engendered during her stay on Salt Spring Island for Donald Arrochar. But they had surely only arisen from loneliness, from the peculiar circumstances forced upon them. Now, as she had always known, she had to put them firmly behind her. No harm in remembering him kindly, as the father of dear wee Aeneas. But her duty lay with Hector. And it wasn't just duty she felt. Emotions of such intensity were rising in her, such joy and expectation and yet such nagging, relentless fear that this huge land called Cariboo might have swallowed him up, that there would be no Hector or no message when she reached the *Last Chance Saloon*, that she could scarcely keep still on her seat.

The sleepy state that had overcome her earlier was dissipated by cold and anxiety. She opened an eye and saw Maybelle had sunk into slumber, deep in her sealskin collar. The men had started a card school and she listened to their desultory chatter. One, it seemed, was not a digger but a contractor who had worked under the supervision of a detachment of Royal Engineers from Britain, laying the very Cariboo Trail they rode on. She gathered the part that clung to the walls of the Fraser Canyon was a quite exceptional piece of construction. The card player had been a pathmaster, laying out part of the course by marking trees with slashes or 'blazes' as he called them, so that the axemen who came afterwards could fell the trees which were then laid in a strip. Other methods had been used, too, to take the Trail its 385 miles into the heart of the Goldfields. She got tired of listening. How had Hector got to the interior? she wondered. The road could not have been finished when he arrived. The stage-coach was not exactly the acme of comfort, but how much more desirable than pack mules, or trudging part of the way on foot, or using the steamboats zig-zag fashion on some of the lakes. The journey must have taken an eternity.

The second day dawned hard and cold as granite. Annie began to take almost for granted the sickening leap of blood as they lumbered over rivers and ravines or wound round some precipitous mountain pass. Surely they would all end up dead in a gulch. But a fresh coachman drove his 'peerless six,' as they were advertised, with relentless expertise. It was so bitter the snow was still held at bay, but the occupants of the stage-coach suffered abominably. When she could no longer feel hands or feet Annie began a soft helpless weeping she could not contain. She realised her clothes were hopelessly inadequate for the kind of weather they were going to encounter. Presumably the coachmen were in the same state for they drew up unscheduled at a lumber camp and the lumberjacks extended hospitality in one of their big, warm cabins. The cook gave the two women stone jars filled with boiling water and tins of hot sand when they once again embarked on their journey and a young axeman gave Annie a dusty fur rug to tuck around her. The period of warmth had restored everybody's spirits and the atmosphere for the next few hours inside the coach was commendably more cheerful and friendly, even the card-sharp urging Annie to think of what lay ahead. Barkerville, according to him, now boasted every amenity known to man.

"But for you bad eye, you could be a hurdy girl," he said, meaning to be encouraging and perhaps find favour with Maybelle.

"What bad eye would that be?" demanded Annie's new friend, with a dangerous glint in hers. Before the abashed man could reply, she took Annie's hand and rubbed it, reassuringly. "I've known plenty of dancing girls with little imperfections. That's all your eye is: a little imperfection, my dear. You stick with Maybelle, if you like. I'll make a dancing girl out of you. Teach you what to do with your hair and your figure – you could use a little more weight. Those with *many* imperfections," she went on, with a blood-congealing glance at her adversary, "have no cause to seek out the small, the very small, the minor, faults in others. We are all perfect in the sight of God."

"I've come out here to be a wife," said Annie shortly. "I won't be looking for work." But she put her hand unconsciously to her eye and rubbed it, as though to smooth away the squint. Most of the time it did not matter. Hector had said he liked it. Donald had never mentioned it at all. But it was strange how the cruel and unfeeling could bring up the one thing that sapped your confidence in yourself and which then reminded you of all the other areas in which you were at a disadvantage. There was her lack of decent clothes, the sapping poverty in which she and her mother had lived for so long and the many time, such as with the engine-maker in Glasgow – and, it had to be admitted, when Donald had withheld her fee – when she had felt her innate dignity as a human being eroded. Oh, how she longed for a sealskin cape and muff, for good boots, for rings and a necklace such as Maybelle wore and, there was no denying it, for some way of mitigating the squint. As she sat, cold and morose, she remembered Alec Comrie's words: 'I could mend that eye for you." The determination grew in her to find a doctor who would treat her. She wanted to be perfect for Hector. And not just for Hector. She wanted to take on the tough, the wounding adult world she was just entering and give as good as she got. She wanted to acquire learning, poise, stature, stylishness. No doubt when people like the card-sharp looked at her, they saw only a smallish, scruffy person in well-worn hodden grey, someone of the servant class, to at best be patronised and at worst ignored. But she had tasted learning, independence and, on the night of the Indian raid, courage she had not known she possessed. So there was no way she was going to be put down by anybody. The card-sharp refused to meet her scowl.

On the third day when they stopped to refresh the horses Maybelle disappeared off the edge of the highway to be sick. It was Annie's turn now to bolster her companion's spirits as best she could. She tried to take Maybelle's mind off her nausea by urging her to talk about herself.

"They said I was mad, coming all this way," owned Maybelle wretchedly.

"Then why did you?"

"The usual. For a man. The only man who ever treated me right. He wanted to marry me."

"Where is he now?"

"Dead and buried in Richfield Town. He caught the mountain fever and died before he could get back to me. Jamie. Jamie Waterson. I want to see his grave. I want to put up a stone to his memory. The best stone there is. With figures of angels at the side. I want to be buried with him."

Annie stared. "But I thought you wanted to set up a dancing school."

"I do. I shall. But nothing will be the same without my Jamie."

Annie felt the big, soft-padded hand convulse in hers and held on tightly. Another lesson learned. That people's motives were not always what they seemed. And that the desperation of grief found expression in unexpected forms.

"We'll go together to Jamie's grave," she said gently. "We'll take some flowers." Maybelle wept into a damp handkerchief. The brandy flask passed more frequently from her reticule to her lips. She looked desperately pale, almost green.

Now it came at last, the snow. The horses, as though they realised time was getting short, fairly flew over the Trail, the coach swaying rhythmically, Maybelle pleading incessantly for it to stop and let her off to die. The cold was perhaps now a little less intense but it was as though frozen bladders had relaxed and there was a constant exigency in the emptying of them.

Annie tried to muffle herself into oblivion in the dusty animal skin rug as the coach plunged between tall firs and into snowy darkness. She jerked in and out of sleep, waking once to find the engineer's head on her lap and on another occasion to witness them pass some freight wagons pulled by leaden-footed, weary oxen. At last they drove into an orange dawn and the last stage of the journey began. The coach occupants now seemed past anything – eating, drinking or talking. They drove in and out of light snowstorms, passing trains of pack mules, broken freight wagons, the Trail still miraculously passable although the coach wheels threw up slush and mud. As they neared their destination, they increasingly saw signs of gold-mining – sometimes little more than workings, broken machinery, sometimes groups of houses, perhaps a store or two, that could be the beginning of a township.

And then, sheltering in the valley, small and doll-like somehow after the vastness they'd covered, it was Barkerville.

Annie hadn't known what to expect. Not Glasgow, of course, with its fine buildings and churches. Not even Victoria, sprouting like a magic garden, falling over itself to get established. But not this, either. A huddle of timber buildings, raised above the muddy road, each with its own sidewalk. Signs of all sorts advertising stables, bakery, hotel, brewery. A general air of having sprung up overnight, of improvisation and making-do. Were there really ten thousand people living here, as she'd been told? It felt like the back of beyond, the end of the world.

She got out on shaking legs and felt a weakened Maybelle grab her arm for support.

"San Francisco, it ain't," said Maybelle. "That's for sure." She managed a lop-sided grin. "But what I say, girl, is you make your bed, you got to lie on it."

Annie was watching the steaming horses. She felt stunned by the cold clean air after the fug of the stage-coach, stiff and aching and dirty. She helped Maybelle with her luggage to the *New Scotia Hotel and Saloon*, where she would be working and then, then her own belongings tied up in a shawl, made for the *Last Chance Saloon*. You had to be careful

Muckle Annie

of the uneven sidewalks, but as she passed each building she began to sense the liveliness, the activity the card-sharp had spoken of.

Here was one saloon offering a boxing match – between Peerless Joe Sanders and Hooly Underwood, the Fighting Savage – and another an evening of Delectable Magic and Legerdemain from Monsieur Albert Couchman and his Fair Assistant, La Belle Elaine. Yet another invited its 'esteemed clientèle' to 'come and enjoy the light fantastic.' Invitations to sample wine, ale and 'liquors' were everywhere, interspersed with offers of baths, haircuts, shoe-shine, dentistry, a Chinese laundry.

Annie decided she would try out the Wake-Up Jake Restaurant and Bakery before presenting herself to Hector's second cousin, Hamish Maclennan, at the *Last Chance Saloon*, which was obviously at the end of the street. She ordered coffee and a slice of pie and after consuming it unobtrusively tidied her hair and set straight her bonnet. Now had come the moment of the trembling stomach and the shaking legs, but she stuck her chin up and marched determinedly up the wooden stairs towards the saloon's swing doors. Outside, it was unremarkable. Inside, the floor was laid with clean sawdust, a cheerful warmth emanated from the stove and behind a high bar gleaming with well-polished brass and sparkling glass a thin, fair, fifty-ish man with a pince-nez and a white apron raised his head to appraise the visitor.

"Are you Mr. Hamish Maclennan?" Annie had not meant to sound nervous, but she did.

"The same."

"I am Miss Annie McIlvanney and there should be a message here for me from your second cousin, Hector Mennock."

The thin man went on polishing the glass he held. Annie could feel her teeth begin to chatter. She held on to the brass rail in front of her. All the sounds of the saloon interior came to her with abnormal clarity – the cracking of burning wood in the stove, the ticking of the clock advertising the

Finest Ale in the Cariboo.

At last the man put down the glass with a decisive gesture.

"It's the shame it is you came here, Miss McIlvanney, for the news I have is not good. Tell the truth, I never thought to see you. Are you telling me you came all the way from Glasgow on your own? That's little short of a miracle, one I never thought to see."

"Please!" He looked at her in some alarm. Her face had gone deathly pale. Moving quickly now, he lifted the flap on the bar counter and, taking her arm, led her over to the table and chairs nearest the stove. "Please!" She got the word out again between chittering lips. "Tell me he's all right. Tell me he's not dead."

"Not dead. I can tell you that." Hamish Maclennan moved back to the bar, poured brandy in a glass and offered it. Annie looked at him, ignoring the brandy, the colour slowly returning to her face.

"Not dead." She repeated the words, managing even a small, apologetic smile. "Oh, Mr. Maclennan, so long as he's alive, it's all I want to hear. Where is he? What's happened to him? What's the bad news you speak of?"

"One thing at a time." Hamish Maclennan had a wheeze, like an old concertina. She saw that his need to conserve breath was the reason for the pauses in his speech. "You look all in. Would you not like to retire for a wash and some refreshment? Since you've come such a long way, I feel it's the least I can offer you."

"I will be glad of it." Her eyes never left his face. "But I have to know, before I move from this chair, what has happened. Tell me. I must know."

Hamish Maclennan rose and from a shelf beneath the bar counter produced a letter which he handed to her.

"He left this for you. But I don't think it contains the message you are hoping for." He sat down, his earnest face only a few inches away from hers, his hand on her arm as though he would detain her from opening and reading the missive. "You see, he's changed out of all recognition from the man you know. I've seen it happen to plenty, God knows. Gold fever. He struck gold almost as soon as he left here, but on the way back from the goldfields he was set upon and robbed. At least, that was his story. My belief is he got caught up in some gambling den, or began to drink more than was good for him, or both. Whatever it was, I think it half-scrambled his brains. Something happened to change him, that's for sure. He's shaping up for a good-for-nothing, a wastrel. He hung about here, waiting for you to come, saying he had something to tell you, explain to you, then one morning he just took off, leaving the letter for you." He removed his hand from her arm. "Now you'd better read it." He rose and left her.

The two sheets of paper were rubbed, stained. The letter began: "To my dear Annie, if you ever get here." Suddenly she could scarcely follow the lines for tears. "It seems such a long time since we lay among the bluebells together. I look back on that day we stood over the burn and exchanged vows and I wonder sometimes if it ever happened. Then at other times I can see you so clearly in my mind's eye, wearing those bonnie blue ribbons in your hair and I can hear your laugh and imagine your head half-turned towards me.

"I hope you will never get this letter. But if you do, if you come as you said you would, then I am going to ask you one thing: *forget me*. The reason is it has all come home to me, why I came here. I killed a man. I ran away. I can't get away from that. There is no point in trying. My conscience is with me, wherever I go. You were like something out of time for me. For a brief spell I breathed fresh air. I was back in the Paradise I think we must have known before we came to this earth.

"I will tell you, Annie, something I've never told another living soul. I saw the face of the man I killed, staring back at me from a schooner in Victoria, a mad hallucination. From that moment I knew it was all up. They try to tell me it was the result of near-drowning as we came round Cape Horn. I know differently. That face, haggard, pale, follows me everywhere, is always in my mind. Yet I can't face going back to Scotland and bringing the disgrace of a hanging on the family name, which is what it would come to.

"So you see the kind of man you have innocently caught up with. I release you from all your vows and ask you to release me from mine.

"I am off now. I don't know what I'm looking for. We call it gold, but that is only a name. Maybe it's absolution for our sins. Forget me. Stay with Hamish a while. Know that I love you. May God guard you for I can write no more. Hector."

She slid from the chair unconscious and came to, to find sawdust on her palms, her skirt, her hair. Hamish's concerned hatchet face looked down at her and beside him a scrawny slant-eyed girl, who did not look more than ten or eleven (she was to learn later she was 14), gazed at her, fingers in her mouth, eyes wide in a kind of terror.

"There, there! I told Soo Lin here you were going to be all right." Hamish shifted her head on his lap. "Take a sip of this and then see if you can stand up." The brandy stung and made her cough but she rose slowly, palely, brushing the sawdust from her skirt as though her life depended on it.

"Take Miss Annie upstairs," Hamish bade Soo Lin relievedly. The girl scrabbled up bare stairs behind Annie like a little scurrying mouse and opened the door on a big airy room, bearing little else but a brass bedstead, a chair and a table with a candle on it.

Annie sat on the chair and presently, feeling more in command, said to the child: "Who are you? Do you live here?"

"Please miss, I'm Soo Lin Wong."

"You *American*, Soo Lin?" She was, from the sound of her, if not the look.

"My Da came from 'Frisco, so they tell me. My Ma was a dancin' girl there. She's dead."

"You didn't take your Da's name, then?"

"They wasn't married." The girl turned her head away evasively.

Annie could see she was poorly dressed, in a coarse, heavy-skirted sort of garment, with boots that looked a size too big. Those boots! Memory made her heart swell in empathy. She said, "Do you work here, Soo Lin?"

"Sometimes. I work various places."

"And where do you sleep?"

"They let me sleep in the kitchen, when it's cold."

"And at other times?"

"Don't rightly know. Anywheres."

Maybe the indignation was what she needed. She sent Soo Lin downstairs and freshened her own face and hair. She looked at Hector's letter once more then folded it with tender care and placed it underneath the pillow on the big bed. She had a lot of thinking to do, but for the moment she intended to take Hector's advice and stay with his cousin, if he would have her.

As she entered the saloon once more she could see evening business was beginning to pick up. She waited till the clients had been served before presenting a meek, submissive front to Hamish.

"Mr. Maclennan, if I can stay a little while with you I can make myself useful."

Hamish pressed his lips together regretfully. "Can't afford nobody, Miss Annie. 'Fraid after tonight you got to make your own arrangements. There's work to be got in the town if you're an honest girl. No fear of that." He wouldn't look her in the face.

"But I don't know anybody. Save Miss Maybelle at the *New Scotia*."

"That whore-house. You'd do well to keep away from there."

Her pale face had gone a shade paler. "You mean they're – that Miss Maybelle is …"

"Did you think dancin' girls meant what it says? Well, some is and some isn't."

"Don't the same thing apply here, in your saloon?"

"What do you mean?"

"Some of the men are bigger sinners than the rest."

He glared at her. "My lamented cousin never indicated you took a loose line in morals."

Furiously she grabbed his arm, all caution about a roof over her head thrown to the wind. "Listen here, Mr. Hamish McLennan, you watch what you say. I only know it isn't up to me to judge who's a sinner and who isn't. But I won't stand to see women judged harder than men."

He looked a shade abashed. "Well, maybe I spoke a shade hasty."

"No maybe about it." She shook a little now, more shocked than she cared to admit to realise that what she had landed in here in this frontier town wasn't exactly a Sunday School picnic. Yet neither had it been back home in Glasgow so it wasn't as though she didn't know the pitfalls. A sense of her own worth, her unassailability, lifted her head resolutely. "Hector said in his letter you might help me," she persisted. "I eat very little. I work very hard."

Almost as though it were against his better judgment he gave in. "All right. You can stay a week or two, I suppose. Bed and board only. Don't mess up the customers. This is a quiet drinking house."

"Thank you." She moved as if by instinct towards the kitchen. One glance told there was plenty that needed doing there. In a scullery beyond, the girl loitered, scraping a heavy iron pan free of what looked like burned porridge.

"Soo Lin, let me look at you," she commanded. The girl turned a woebegone face towards her. The skin was like parchment and there were red sores on it. Her arms were as thin as the spurtle used to stir the porridge. "How did you get in this state?"

"Don't know. Been sick."

"Well, we're going to get you a bath. Then I'll see if I can find you something better to wear." Desperately Annie thought of her own meagre wardrobe and wondered if her old calico working dress for the farm could be made over. The gingham that Hetty Laboucher had made for her would have to be sacrificed for aprons for the pair of them. She lifted Soo Lin's stringy tangled hair. "You ever brush it? I got a brush. Go upstairs to my room and fetch it."

She had to admit her ministrations didn't make a lot of difference. The poor creature still looked half-starved and half-terrified. It became clear she was regarded as no one's liability in Barkerville, falling somewhere between the whites and the considerable number of Celestials, as the Chinese community were called. In a more rigorous society she would have been put in an orphanage. Here, where no other help was available, she did the pots, ran errands and slept where a dog might sleep.

Annie's sense of outrage on the girl's behalf sent her running to Maybelle to see what could be done. Uncharacteristically for her, Maybelle hummed and ha-ed, before admitting she shared the general dislike for the Celestials, who, she alleged, gambled and fought when they weren't smoking opium from Victoria, and fed their pigs in the street. (When Annie read in the local paper that nobody was killed in a local mining accident 'except a couple of Chinamen' her sense of fair play asserted itself and she resolved not to join in the general condemnation too readily.)

"Maybe some male relative was trying to sell her to a man she didn't like," Maybelle suggested. "That's why she broke away."

"*Sell* her?"

"It happens in the Flowery Kingdom," said Maybelle with a fine irony. "I heard of one with charms above the rest who went for 700 dollars."

"That's slavery!"

Maybelle shrugged her shoulders. "Women are slaves, anyhow, of one sort or another."

"Not like poor Soo Lin. Anyway, she's half-American. From 'Frisco."

"That won't get her into no academy for young ladies," said Maybelle, succinctly.

"She said her mother was a dancing girl."

"A waterfront whore, more likely!"

But what about you, Maybelle? she wanted to ask. She had thought a lot about what Hamish had said. If girls sold their bodies under Maybelle's surveillance, even complicity, what did that make them? And her? She decided not to think too much about it. She could not afford to give up her sole friend so far. And besides, she felt she knew the real Maybelle, the heart-broken mourner of Jamie Waterson. No doubt, if you wished to survive, life forced some tough options on you.

Annie decided to keep Soo Lin under some kind of surveillance. Soo wouldn't sleep on people's porches if she could help it. She also tried to make sure the girl was given decent food. Hamish Maclennan pretended not to see the warm straw mattress Annie arranged for the girl in the corner of the kitchen. It was in his interest not to complain, for food was being cooked to his liking, even pies for the customers. The bannocks and skirl-in-the-pan were greatly to his taste. He was a cautious man and if an arrangement worked he allowed himself to go along with it.

Annie soon began to get the measure of Barkerville. Much of its population moved and shifted. New homes and enterprises seemed to spring up daily. There was a strong gambling element (not just in Chinatown), with horse races and stone-throwing for bets in the muddy main street and card games like euchre and sinch played nightly in the saloons. Music and laughter rang out into the street each time a dancing saloon door flapped open. Tradespeople worked hard to provide goods and services for those with the money to spend. Sometimes a digger would arrive back with his pockets full of gold and there were plenty eager to relieve him of it by any means available to them. Drinking could be heavy but fights were few and well controlled by the saloon keepers. It surprised Annie that someone of such mild disposition as Hamish Maclennan could run a saloon, but his very mildness seemed to work for rather than against him and the 'serious' drinkers in search of a good card game tended to gravitate towards the *Last Chance* rather than the flightier places which brought in entertainment or dancing girls to entice the customers.

She had no plan of campaign to begin with, except to hang on in Barkerville and make herself so indispensable to Hamish that he would not want to get rid of her. Some day, someone might come in with word of Hector. Some day, despite everything he had written, Hector himself would return to see if she was there. Some day, she might pick up a clue as to his whereabouts. That was all she thought about at first.

She listened to everything that was said by the men who came back from the goldfields. She began to know where this seam was being mined, where that mine had hit the jackpot. Carefully she stored away ideas of where she might look for Hector, how she might get there. But it was not going to be easy. She would have to try and save a little money, for a start, and Hamish's careful streak made that difficult.

She decided that she would not make any more pies unless she got a cut of the proceeds. Hamish demurred at first but there was no mistaking the enthusiasm of his customers for the food Annie cooked and he eventually gave in. Annie saved that little she made like a miser. She also began to do a little dress-making on the side – she had always been good at making something out of nothing and Maybelle taught her how to trim hats. Every little helped. That was the frontier philosophy and people in outpost towns like Barkerville learned to turn their hands to anything. She even began to cut hair and dole out simple medicines for upset stomachs and hangovers. He didn't say it, but she knew Hamish Maclennan soon forgot all about her going elsewhere. What would happen to the business if she did? The brass rails and name-plate had never been burnished so brightly. The good, homely smell of cooking would vanish and the brisk, female friendliness could not be matched by masculine gruffness. Annie and her little sidekick Soo Lin were certainly safe for the time being.

Hard work prevented Annie from fretting in the day, but when she retired to her room, Hector filled her thoughts. Every night she took out his letter till she knew it word for word, and then she still held it, like some kind of talisman that linked them, drawing comfort from its curling pages. Over and over in her mind she tried to work out what had happened to him. 'Nearly drowned' at Cape Horn? That meant his journey had been even worse than hers, and that had been bad enough. He must have suffered some fever that had sent him into a kind of delirium. Possibly all the time he had been making his way to the goldfields, he had been sick. And then to have been robbed and attacked ... She felt Hamish had not been as sympathetic as he might have been to his cousin. She tried to get him to talk about Hector, but it was clear he had had no patience, had dismissed Hector's conscience-striken attitude as weakness. The fight with the man back in Scotland had not been of Hector's seeking. What he had done was in self-defence. That, as far as Hamish was concerned, was the end of it.

But no two human beings were alike. The sensitivity in Hector, which was what had attracted Annie to him, was obviously what made him feel the guilt another man might have been able to shrug off or ignore. If only she had been here to comfort him, to care for him in his sickness and rally him after the robbery. She should never have gone to Salt Spring Island. Yet one part of her could still not admit it.

One thing she never gave up was hope. If on the day of her arrival Hamish had said Hector was dead, she knew it would have been insupportable. But he was still alive somewhere and she would find some way of getting to him. She waited for the moment, for the inspiration. If it did not come, she knew one day she would simply track off into the Cariboo, taking her life in her hands. For that she would need warm clothing, shotgun, maps. She would go round the digging grounds, the workings, the beginnings of townships, till she found him. It was as simple as that. She was not prepared to give up.

But meantime she had to be practical and save. Life with Soo Lin and Hamish was companionable enough and when she needed cheering she dropped in on Maybelle and her little team of girls.

Maybelle tried to get Annie interested in dancing, saying that if it was money she was after, she could make more as a dancing girl than as old Maclennan's slave. But although Annie had no puritanical feelings about the dancing girls, who were not all what Hamish thought they were, she was reluctant to give up the security of her own room at the *Last Chance*. She simply tapped her feet to the music, practised the dancing with Soo Lin in the kitchen while they waited for the pies to cook and fended off Maybelle's entreaties with as good a grace as possible.

It was a young customer, a mining engineer, who planted in Hamish's mind the idea for extending the saloon and having a restaurant as well. There was room to build out at the back – not sideways, for the buildings were jammed close together, something of a fire hazard, said some doom merchants – and when he saw Annie favoured the project Hamish went ahead. Annie pleaded for a little wash-house as well and soon she and Soo Lin were taking in laundry on top of their other duties in rivalry with Wa Lee the Chinaman. For some reason known only to himself, Hamish allowed Annie to keep the earnings from the 'Laundry.' These days, with business booming, he was in a good temper. On Sundays he would spruce himself up and attend church with Annie and Soo Lin, and if the weather permitted they would walk round the perimeter of the town and stop for an exchange of news with others doing the same. Afterwards there was Annie's seed-cake for tea and Hamish entertained his staff with tales of his rovings all over the world before he settled in Barkerville.

One such evening, when Soo Lin had been sent on an errand to Maybelle, Hamish filled a pipe and with much humming and ha-ing broached the subject of marriage.

"You would get all this when I kick the bucket," he told Annie. "I've never thought of holy matrimony in my life, till now, but I think it would be a beneficial arrangement all round."

Annie gazed at him in amazement. Now so many things fell into place – his insistence on carrying heavy buckets for her when his chest wasn't bad, his munificence over the 'laundry,' even the way he put up with Soo Lin and her sometimes unhappy, resentful moods. And the ruminative look she had caught sometimes, passing the bar, when he gazed at her over his spectacles.

"But I'm waiting for Hector," she said. "You've always known that."

He said, with a patience that was almost kindly, "You could wait till the end of your days. I don't think Barkerville will ever see him again."

"But I will." The tears rose to her eyes.

"I wouldn't put demands on you. At least, none you didn't want. After a space of time."

"You know I like you, Hamish. I'll never be able to show you how thankful I am you took me in and gave me work. But can you not just look on me as a cousin?"

"If I have to." She caught sight, for a moment, in his embarrassment, of what the young Hamish must have looked like, fresh-faced and shy. He took his pince-nez off and rubbed them industriously. "I'll leave it with you," he said, with a false heartiness. "To think about. You'll come in for all this anyhow. I want you to know that. You've brought a bit of life and sparkle to the place."

She went over, impulsively, and hugged him. "I'm Hector's woman," she said quietly, "but for just now, you're all the family I've got. You and Soo Lin."

"Aye, well," he said. "I could take a shade more of that seed-cake."

Muckle Annie

Being loved, Annie thought in the weeks to come, made a difference. Hamish's loving wasn't a young man's loving, importunate and selfish, but thoughtful and considerate. She did her best to make clear to him the hopelessness of his cause but she knew very well there was no way of stopping how someone felt about you. Gradually she felt he realised the truth of the situation and accepted her hard-working devotion for what it was, that of someone grateful for the chance to earn an honest living. But being loved, approved, needed, all these made a difference. She went about her work with a buoyant step, humming the dance tunes the fiddlers played in the saloons.

She and Barkerville might have been made for each other. The winter was passing in a twinkling. They didn't lack for entertainment, despite the cold and snow: boxing matches for the men, magic shows, plays that brought you to your knees with laughter or tore at your heart with tear-jerking sorrows. And dances. And soirées. The fact that she was young, open to new experiences, with what she was coming to realise was a great and natural ability to make friends, to enjoy life, did not alter for one moment the silent threnody playing itself over and over in her mind and heart – the need to find Hector, the desperation of not knowing where to start looking. Every night she remembered him in her prayers. (Donald Arrochar, too, and wee Aeneas.) But meantime she was Miss Annie, in charge of her own restaurant, and that was balm on the nights she looked at young lovers dancing or a fiddler's tune set up some kind of unbearable resonance in her mind.

The hard winter brought its own train of troubles, however. Hamish was often chesty and ill and had to be nursed and pampered. And stepping from the snow-covered sidewalk one day, a truculent Soo Lin, sent on an errand she didn't fancy, fell in frost-hardened snow and broke her arm. It was set by a layman who ran a local stables but had a good reputation with human as well as animal fractures. It did not mend, however, and when Soo Lin had passed two whole nights moaning in agony, Annie determined to take her to a proper doctor.

Questioning around the town elicited the information that there was a good new one living in somewhat rough and undignified circumstances in a miner's cabin somewhere between Barkerville and Richfield. Some sixth sense made Annie think of Alec Comrie even before the name was mentioned. Her old friend from the *Maggie Love Campbell*! He had said he might make for the Cariboo if he did not find Victoria to his liking.

She dressed with some care for the visit, in her new brown velvet cloak trimmed with sealskin she'd bought from a trapper down on his luck, with its matching muff and bonnet. The stables provided her with a horse-drawn sledge which she felt sure she could drive, although she had never done so before. They set out early in the day with Soo Lin pale-faced and subdued and wrapped in the same moth-eaten fur rug that had saved Annie from freezing on her way to Barkerville. To take Soo Lin's mind off the pain of her arm, Annie told her all about the clever young doctor she had met on board ship.

The cabin was everything rumour had painted it, rough, neglected, with the undergrowth knee-high around all of it save the front door, and everything bowed down under the snow. A brass plate, however, announced the occupant's profession and fees clearly enough. Annie pulled a cord and a bell rang loudly inside somewhere.

The boyish face and air of abstraction had not changed. After a first incredulous look, Alec Comrie said composedly, "I thought I'd bump into you again some time," but then he gave Annie a huge, heart-warming smile and ushered the two into the bachelor untidiness of his country lair. Books lay open everywhere: Annie recognised some of the medical paraphernalia from their shipboard days. On a table various instruments and vessels were set up and beside them lay, typically, notes of immaculate neatness. He sat the visitors down near the stove and, carefully adjudging Soo Lin's strained and set features, said immediately to Annie: "What service can I do your young friend? I take it she is the patient."

"Yes. This is Soo Lin, Alec. She's broken her arm. It isn't mending and she's in constant pain."

"I can see that. Please remove your mantle." Alec gently lifted the broken limb, examining it closely and with immense delicacy of touch. Even so, Soo Lin moaned and looked as though she were about to faint.

"First things first. We'll see to your young friend." Alec nodded at Annie. "Then we'll have time for conversation. Agreed?"

"Agreed." Annie felt caught up in the old familiar dedication to matters medical. Set in her white, pain-wracked face, Soo Lin's huge dark eyes never left the doctor's face. He began talking to her soothingly, hypnotically, as if to a small child or animal: "Now what I am going to do is give you a little whiff of chloroform. You've heard of that, haven't you? Used by the Queen of England, no less. So when I set your arm, you'll not feel a thing." He motioned to Annie to help the girl on to a horse-hair couch by the cabin window. Swiftly and expertly he worked while the chloroform took effect. To Annie he kept up a stream of chatter.

"What a godsend this chloroform is! The anguish people suffered before it! I remember reading about Robert Chambers, the man who wrote Vestiges of Creation, one of my scientific mentors. Poor bugger was born with an extra finger on each hand and an extra toe on each foot and the amputations were execrable. *He* would have welcomed chloroform!"

"Indeed," said Annie. She looked down anxiously at Soo Lin's white unconscious face.

"This one's had a hard life. Not much on her frail bones, is there?"

"She's everybody's scodgie," said Annie.

"She reminds me of the little maid in 'Bleak House.' The

one who got the dregs of everybody's tea and the heel of everybody's bread."

"That's her. Or was. Till I came on the scene."

"Good for you, McIlvanney. They don't call you Muckle for nothing! I'll lend you 'Bleak House.' Do you still enjoy your reading?"

"When I have the time."

"Do I take it you found your man in Barkerville?"

"You do not."

He turned momentarily from his task to give her a swift, probing but unguarded, look. "What happened?"

"He's still out there. It's a long story."

"But you look prosperous."

"I'm in work."

Soo Lin was coming round. Alec went to great pains making her arm comfortable in a sling, then he gave Annie some medicine to take away, to administer at night so that Soo Lin should get some sleep.

To the girl he said, "It will be all right now. You must not use it for several weeks. You must eat up all the nourishing food Miss Annie puts your way."

How good he is, Annie thought. Amusedly she watched Soo Lin's gaze change from timid trust to open adoration. She made some tea, tidied up the cabin as best she could and they spent a further hour while Soo Lin recovered going over old times to their hearts' content.

"Where is Soo Lin?"

Hamish came into the dining-room looking angry and put out. "Her arm's better. She could put it to good use polishing these mirrors."

Annie looked up from her baking. "I don't know where she is. She's not been easy to manage these days," she admitted. "Something's making her terrible unhappy. But she'll not tell me what it is."

They looked for her by lantern, in the dancing saloons and down by the stables, everywhere, likely or unlikely, she could be. Annie passed a sleepless night, picturing the small angry figure in all manner of predicaments.

Next morning, Alec Comrie rode into Barkerville with the girl seated on the horse in front of him.

"She wanted to come and look after the house for me," he told an outraged Annie and Hamish. "I found her this morning asleep on the porch."

"I wouldn't have been any trouble," protested Soo Lin. Thereafter, when she was missing, they knew where she would be. At first Alec was halfway between amusement and exasperation. Despite what Annie had taught her, her housecraft still left much to be desired. But it seemed she cooked him a tolerable sort of meal on occasions. She cleared the garden and scrubbed the cabin steps.

7

Annie climbed the stairs to Hamish's room with a dish of fresh porridge and some cream in another porringer. This was what he favoured above all else when he wasn't well and for days now he had been confined to his room, feverish and ill.

She sponged his hands and face gently and settled him up on his pillows.

"Aye, you're a good lass," he said, labouring for breath. "It was God's blessing you came here when you did. Else what would have happened to the saloon?"

"Now you're not to worry about it," she soothed. "I can take care of it. Just you concentrate on getting well. Dr. Comrie will be back to see you later."

"Annie."

"Yes?"

"You're not to think me foolish."

"What is it?"

"Doctor's don't know everything. My mother knew how to cure me with the silvered water when I was sick as a child – water from under a bridge where a silvery coin had been dropped. Or they passed me through an iron hoop with burning straw tied to it."

"Hamish," she said patiently, for she'd heard it all before, "it's Highland superstition, no more."

"I've taken parings from my nails. Listen, cut a rag from my old shirt and wrap them in it, then bury it but don't tell me where …"

She sighed, but carried out the first part of his bizarre instructions there and then. Later, when she had done the morning's baking, she walked to a field on the edge of town and, feeling strange and foolish, buried the pathetic shirt rag and its contents.

She did not disclose any of this to Alec Comrie when he called later. As always, he was noncommittal when she sought for reassurance.

"He's a delicate man," he said, "but he has a great will to go on living. It never fails to amaze me how the frail can often outlive their sturdier brothers."

"Of course he'll go on living," she retorted, angrily. "Barkerville wouldn't be the same without Hamish Maclennan. Ask anybody."

"Well, see he rests and eats. But you have to face the fact; he's not a young man and there's not a lot I can do for him now, except ameliorate the symptoms."

When Alec had gone she stoked up the saloon stove and savagely polished the advertisement mirrors behind the bar. Then she went into the restaurant to make sure Soo Lin had laid the tables properly. Covertly she studied the girl's face as she went about her duties.

Soo Lin was not of a mood to talk. The old, easy relationship had gone between them in any case and where in the past Soo Lin had been eager to please, now she was sullen and resentful, answering back cheekily when Annie reprimanded her. She would never admit it, but the good food Annie made sure she got had filled out her wretched little frame; the ugly red spots had faded from her skin, her bosom was rounding out, she was half-way to being pretty. Annie could never be wholly angry with her. Thinking back to her own hardest times, the dire days of starvation and indignity, she remembered the resentments she too had felt against nearly everybody, even those who had tried to be kind. Charity might be praised in the Bible, but it was a hard thing to take.

She looked up from cutting up a pie and saw Soo Lin eyeing her with a stormy expression.

"What's the matter?"

"Did he say 'Where's Soo Lin?' 'How's Soo Lin?' 'Tell Soo Lin that was a good meat stew she made me.' I don't suppose he even made a mention of me –"

"Who? Who are we talking about?"

"The doctor, of course. He was here this morning. Did he ask how my arm was?" Soo Lin threw down the knives and forks she was setting and hurled her fists to her eyes. "He doesn't give a tinker's cuss for me, does he? Nobody does."

Annie went over and gently drew the girl's hands away from her eyes. "He was here to see Mr. Maclennan. That was professional business. You don't mix professional with private."

Soo Lin gave her a furious glare. "He'll take me for granted once too often. See if I care! He can dig his own garden, do his own crocks. Soo Lin Wong's finished with him. Tell him that when you see him, Miss Annie!"

Annie hid a smile. It would no doubt be something of a relief to Alec if Soo Lin put an end to her excursions – excursions which got her into trouble with Hamish and Annie.

"I'll crimp your hair for you after dinner," she promised.

"What's that about dinner?" Annie spun round at the sound of Hamish's voice. He stood, fully dressed, shaved, in the doorway. "I've had enough of doctors. I'm better." She helped him to a chair, pretending she did not see his narrow chest heave like bellows in its quest for air. "If you say so, Hamish," she agreed. That evening he was back behind the bar. Annie thought of the buried rag and wondered.

Soo Lin's excursions to Alec's cabin still did not cease, however. The next time she was brought back by Alec and seen to be wearing Annie's second-best bonnet and fur tippet.

"Apologise to Miss Annie," Alec commanded her.

"Why should I?" spat out Soo Lin. "I only borrowed her things. I was going to put them back."

Annie did not make a fuss while Alec was present. Later she said calmly to Soo Lin, "It was an underhand thing to do. Next time, ask me."

Soo Lin glowered at her from under the curly bangs that Annie had lately engineered for her. "He told me about the two of you. How he wanted to marry you. Why didn't you want him? He's the best man God ever put breath into."

Annie felt the breath pounded from her own body. "I love Hector."

"But he's never coming back. You shouldn't let the doctor hope. It's a cruel thing to do. I hate you for it."

Annie found her own voice rising. "That will do, you young madam, you! I'll put up with no more of your tantrums. Who are you to say whether my Hector will come back or not? He will, you know. He will. Oh, Hector!"

To her horror she found she was weeping, not weakly, helplessly, but with a stormy abandon that frightened her and, from the look of her, Soo Lin. "Leave Alec Comrie alone," she shouted, her control snapping. "You'll get yourself into trouble, going over there. You'll hurt his good name, you little trollop. You'd better mind your ways or it'll be back to the gutter for you. I'm beginning to think that's where you belong."

By the time she had calmed down, regretted most of this outburst and washed her face, Soo Lin had disappeared. She felt resigned, pushed to the end of her tether over the girl. The small age difference between them prevented any mother-daughter relationship, but she had done what she could to guide Soo Lin, to be a kind elder sister to her as well as her mistress. If all the gratitude she was to be shown was to be this inclination to bolt, well, so be it. Alec Comrie would have to cope with his visiting 'housekeeper' as best he could.

When Soo Lin did not return that evening, Annie checked and found that this time she had taken her few belongings with her. Next day, she closed the restaurant and took a buggy to Alec's cabin. Soo Lin was hanging some clothes out on a line.

Marching up to her, Annie said her name. She was not prepared for the venomous face turned towards her.

"You get outa here, you hear?" Soo Lin screeched. "I can stay where I like. He's made a little room for me. He needs me. He ain't got nobody. Neither have I. You go back to your *Last Chance Saloon* and stay there, hear me?" She took pegs from a canvas bag and began to throw them. Annie retreated. She could see Alec watching the tableau from the cabin window. He beckoned her inside.

"You can't let her stay." She was uncompromising.

"Where's the harm in it?"

"The harm's in what people will say."

"Who cares? I left that sort of concern for small minds behind me, in Scotland."

"You'll regret it, Alec."

"I regret many things. You among them."

Her voice rose. "In some ways I *like* you better than anybody I've ever known. Don't you want my respect, Alec?"

"Never mind what I wanted."

"Send her back to the *Last Chance*."

"She won't go."

"What do you mean, won't go? Make her."

He grinned at her a little foolishly. "I don't think I can do that."

"Well," said Maybelle, drawing Annie into her tiny cluttered parlour at the back of the *New Scotia Hotel and Saloon*, "I hear the little filly has run true to form."

"She's only gone to housekeep for him," said Annie, a little stiffly. She wasn't quite sure how to stifle the gossip, but mainly she emphasised the doctor's need to work and write and the fact that when he was caught up in his research he would scarcely notice who was around him, who fed him or kept his home tidy. Maybelle, however, raised a thinly-arched eyebrow at all this and merely said, "I've been told her mother was an old tail. Died out in a trapper's cabin, drunk out of her skin."

"Soo Lin is only a child," said Annie, unhappily.

"Well, a bit more than that," amended Maybelle. "And she doubtless took in a trick or two with her mother's milk."

Annie stared moodily at Maybelle's crowded chiffonier. Had anyone ever so many gee-gaws? "You wanted to see me about something else," she reminded her friend.

"Could you take a touch of gin?" offered Maybelle.

Annie shook her head. "Nothing, thank you."

"A cup of tea, at the least, and a ginger cookie."

Annie assented. She knew hospitality would be pressed on her till she accepted something, but she really wanted to get on with the purpose of the meeting. Maybelle had sent the potboy from the hotel with a hastily scribbled note: "Something to discuss with you." Was it the fire and brimstone evangelist who was trying to clean up gambling in the saloons? Or the defection of two of Maybelle's dancing girls to a new saloon in Richfield? Maybelle could go on forever when a grievance occupied her mind and Annie was worried about leaving the still-convalescent Hamish for too long on his own.

"I may have word about your Hector's whereabouts," said Maybelle at last. The words seemed to reverberate round the tiny room, sending Annie's head spinning like a din of bells.

"What did you say?" The question came out in a pitiful croak.

"Drink your tea," Maybelle commanded, creaking back importantly in her rocking-chair. "A digger came into the saloon last night and he'd been 'way up beyond the Quesnel River, to a really wild place where they'd just struck gold. Word had got about there about a man they called the Highlander. Seems this man's gone native, fraternises with the Indians. His hair is grown nearly to his waist, he lives in a cabin of sorts in the woods and he shoots first and asks questions afterwards."

"Why do they think it might be Hector?" She could not stop the quaking in her voice.

"From all accounts, he is handsome, talks in an educated voice. He has friends among the trappers and lumberjacks, not that there's so many of *them* left. Seems he's all right if he keeps off the firewater. When he takes that you got to look out."

"Firewater?"

"Whisky. Drink."

"But Hector doesn't take drink."

"Does now," said Maybelle succinctly. "If Hector it is."

Annie held on to the arms of her chair. She was trying to visualise this wilderness where until recently only the fur-trapper had gone. Trying the visualise the rough cabin in the wood, the 'Highlander' with the hair to his waist and the unpredictable temper. Trying to listen to the intuitive voice which Donald Arrochar had taught her to trust, to *feel* whether this possibility was the right one.

It was coming through to her, it was making all kinds of sense. Hector would side with the underdog, in this case both trapper and Indian. In his disillusioned and disorientated state, he would not pan for the gold that could have set them up in the farm they'd dreamed about. He had shown the loner's instinct before, even back in Scotland when he'd holed up in the bothy for days. In that makeshift cabin he would be conducting a daily dialogue with his conscience and when it all got too much for him, indulging in the drinking that was surely understandable if not excusable. Oh, it was Hector all right. She *knew*. She began to tremble so much Maybelle looked at her in some alarm.

"I'm going to him," she said.

"Now hang on," said Maybelle, "Ain't no country up there for a woman."

"If men can take it, women can." Annie dismissed the doubts. "I am not going to wait about, Maybelle. I must get away as soon as I can. Snow's gone. It's good travelling weather."

"Snow could still come."

"Unlikely. Anyhow, I don't care. You'll have to keep an eye on Hamish for me, though. Can you spare one of the girls part of the day – the German girl, Gerda, she's kind and willing – to go down to the saloon and help out?"

Maybelle nodded. "I'll keep an eye on the old cuss myself." Despite herself, she was caught up in Annie's excitement. "Listen. He's going back beyond Quesnel soon, the case I told you about. They sent him to Barkerville for some piece of equipment they need for the cabin. T'ain't all that heavy – he's hoping the horse can take it, as well as him."

"Could he take me back with him?"

"I don't think he'd be all that keen. Anyhow, you'd need a horse, too, and you can't ride."

"I can stay up on one. Time of the horse-races, I had a go."

"I can't vouch for this digger."

"I'll have my shotgun. He won't try any nonsense with me. 'Sides, I'm going to wear men's breeches and put my hair up under a fur cap. I'll aim to be mistaken for a man. Till I get to Hector."

"You've thought it all out?"

"Nights I've thought of nothing else."

"I don't like it at all." Maybelle's anxiety was patent. "I wish now I hadn't told you. But I've always fell for that tale of yours. The vows you took over running water. The two halves of the same coin, you each wear round your neck."

"My life will never be complete, if I don't find him." Annie put her hands, reassuringly, on her friend's shoulders. "Say to yourself you've done a friend the best turn ever." She kissed Maybelle's rouged cheek. "I hope I can bring him back with me, Maybelle. You'll like him when you see him. He's wonderful!"

She did not know how to break the news of her departure to Hamish, but she could not put off telling him in case he heard about 'the Highlander' from someone else. He had a habit of withdrawing into silences that hurt more than argument.

"I'll be back in no time," she reassured him. "You said yourself, things have been quiet. Maybelle is going to send a girl down to do the cooking and cleaning –"

"Seems you've got it all arranged." The cold hurt on his face brought her to the edge of tears. "You don't seem to realise the dangers."

"I do." She wasn't aware she had drawn herself up, so that for once she looked almost tall, and formidable. "You told me once you followed your star. All I'm doing is following mine."

"Then there's no help for it." He retreated to polishing his glasses behind the bar. Thereafter he put no obstacles in her way, but was formally polite with her.

The man who was going back to Quesnel was named Jed. He was dark, taciturn, a Californian. Something of an unknown quantity, he never once expressed either pleasure or reservation about having Annie's company, but behaved rather as though the whole thing were happening without any connection with him. He was helpful in one respect only. He found her a horse, a quiet mare named Peg. In the end she simply had to forget whatever scruples she had about leaving; Jed had acquired the piece of equipment he needed for the winding engine in his claim and was anxious to be off.

It had been one thing fooling around on a mount the day of the horse-racing in the main street: it was another thing staying up on the saddle while they followed rough paths and sometimes took off over rocky, hilly ground. She ached with the terrible necessity of not falling off and after a couple of hours begged her companion to stop so that she could get off and relax her arm and back and leg muscles for a little while.

The mare Peg rolled her eyes at her as if to say, "I'm doing my best for you." "I know, old girl," Annie said to her, as if she had in fact spoken, "it's me that's at fault." But some kind of rapport did seem established between horse and rider and as Annie learned to trust the mare and her own sense of balance, the journey became easier. They rode till it was dark and then stopped near a forest and built a crackling huge fire, over which they heated soup which Annie had brought in a canister.

"What about wolves?" Annie asked her companion nervously. He gave a laconic shrug and lay down with his gun at the ready. She had been prepared to read him a lecture about respecting her privacy. In the event it proved unnecessary. He was asleep long before she was, snoring loudly. She lay awake under her blanket, feeling the beautiful, ecstatic warmth from the fire receding and the cold gradually creep into her bones. Far away she thought she heard wolves howl. It made her think of Salt Spring and brought a hard, fierce need to see Donald and Aeneas again, as though the prospect of finding Hector had awakened other emotions in its train.

She was glad when morning came: she was stiff and frozen to the marrow and wanted to hunt for fresh wood to rekindle the fire. The animals stamped nervously, cold also. Jed refused to engage in any kind of conversation till they had heated beans and made tea and he had performed some kind of rough ablutions in a nearby stream. Then they rode hard, he making no allowance for her greenness as a rider, the horses sensing and even enjoying the relentless purpose of the journey.

Beyond the Quesnel River he pointed to terrain as bare and lonely as any she ever seen.

"You should make the forest yonder in about an hour," he instructed her.

"You're not coming with me?"

"Time's money, down there." He jerked his head towards the claim in the bend of the creak just below them. She could see men moving about, tiny, busy, animated figures. "I should be able to keep track on you from there. There's a lumber camp up where you're going – it ain't totally uninhabited."

"And the Highlander?"

"You go past the camp. 'Bout a mile or so. You'll come to the prettiest little creek you ever did see. There's an old hut there, belonged to some old digger who struck gold, years back. Empty now. Strike into the forest – there's a kind of clearance, where they made a false start on cutting the trees down – and you'll come on it quite soon, the cabin. Ain't scared, are you?" The jibing irony of this last wasn't lost on Annie. She said, with a little less confidence than she'd intended, "Of course not." Jed smiled for the first time, showing a mixture of gold-filled and blackened teeth. "Didn't think you scared easy," he relented.

"Come on, Peg." That big, bursting beat was her heart against her ribs, but as she rode away from Jed's protection she realised it was better she was on her own. She had to prepare herself for seeing Hector, for after all, she did not know what kind of state he would be in, whether his welcome would be warm, ecstatic or non-existent. Now at this late point the demons of uncertainty at last assailed her. What if he had changed out of all recognition? What if she alone had been keeping their love alive? What if despite her intuition it turned out not to be Hector at all, but someone else entirely? No wonder Hamish had almost refused to speak to her. Barkerville with its cosy saloons suddenly seemed a very desirable place to be. Not this great wide world where the sky was a canopy that went on forever, where nature painted everything big except the puny humans who hacked at trees or panned the rivers for gold. Or rode in search of long-lost, maybe irretrievable loves. Why did she never listen to people? Why did she always think she knew best?

Despite her anxiety, the beauty of her surroundings as she rode along touched her and heartened her. Winter was giving way to the softer airs and gentle colours of spring. It was almost as though she felt the earth softening under Peg's steady clip-clopping feet and once she entered the forest, spring's green-shooting immanence was evewhere palpable. In the soft, cool, green light Peg raised her head questioningly as if to say, "It's different here." "Steady, old girl," Annie advised her. Her own fright and expectation were communicated to the animal.

There it was. The cabin. Smaller, neater than she had imagined it. Two goats tethered in front. A hundred yards away she dismounted and tied the whinnying mare to a tree. Chickens clucked into the forest in alarm at her presence. She forbore from looking through the window but went straight to the door and knocked. There was a long silence that seemed to stretch away endlessly into the trees. She knocked again and kept on knocking. And then she heard movement. The door creaked open.

She stared at him for what seemed like an eternity, a terrible joy and gladness suffusing her, scattering her wits and turning her legs to water. The hair was long, certainly, but not as long as she'd been led to expect. Unkempt and dirty, yes. The shoulders had filled out, the face was thin, bearded and a curious papery white colour. The eyes gave no show of recognition. But it was Hector. She took a step forward and said in a broad Glasgow accent, "It's me, Hector. It's your Annie. I've come to you as I said I would. Aren't you going to ask me in?"

He turned and walked back into the cabin without saying anything and she followed him, closing the door behind her. The joy was ebbing fast and in its place there was fear, which she pushed down resolutely. This was Hector. No matter what had happened to him, he was still her husband and she would not desert him. Wood crackled in an ancient, ramshackle stove and he lay down on a makeshift bed next to it and closed his eyes, as though he were very tired. She felt this action like a blow on the face and staggered where she stood, as though hurt or wounded. She felt the light, sweet odour of whisky permeating the cabin and looking briefly round decided the interior was like nothing so much as a nest, an animal place made of spruce twigs and dusty furs, dun-coloured but warm. Empty tins and food-encrusted pots, egg shells and discarded food lay on the floor. She gave a shudder of revulsion and dragged her gaze back to the figure on the bed. His mouth had fallen slightly open and his breathing came fast and light.

"Hector?" She knelt beside him, her voice soft and tremulous. "Are you ill? Why didn't you wait for me at Barkerville? I told you I would come. You should have believed me."

He didn't appear to hear her and she put the back of her hand to his brow. It was clammy and damp. She took his pulse as Alec Comrie had shown her and could feel it gallop away like a racing burn under her fingers. Now that she was close, she could hear a rough, clattering wheeze emanating from his chest. Dear God, was she going to lose him just as she had found him again? She had not expected this.

She got stiffly to her feet, momentary despair filling her legs with lead. But then she threw off her coat and began to talk to him, to fill the dusty cabin with some evidence of existence even if it were only the sound of her own voice.

"We'll get you mended! They don't call me Muckle Annie for nothing, you know." She gazed wildly round and saw a bearskin on the floor and gently laid it over his legs. She had noticed some logs outside the door and she brought some in now and fed the stove, clattering an iron poker about its innards to clear away ash and then, as the logs took, placing a pan of water from the nearby stream to heat.

"You've got the congestion, that's what it seems like to me. If I just had some oil to rub on your chest." There was something like dripping lying on an apology of a table and she parted the edges of his grubby shirt and rubbed it on his chest. He burned to her touch. When the water boiled she held the steaming vessel so that he breathed in the vapour, tirelessly reboiling and bringing it back to his bed again and again. She saw some hectic colour come into his cheeks and he began to move restlessly.

"We'll have to sit you up somehow. When my grannie had a hoast on her chest, we sat her up with pillows." She put her own coat behind his head and when that was not enough rushed out and gathered an armful of soft spruce branches to put under the coat. She found a piece of rag on the deplorable floor, washed it as best she could and then with water from the stove sponged his hands and wrists and forehead. All the time she talked gently, sometimes nonsensical babble, anything, and all the time watched his face for some sign that he knew she was there. She could not give in totally to the panic that was flooding her. She had to keep her head, think what to do next. Get help from the lumber camp? But it was getting dark. And if she left him, she had the terror he would slip away from her irrevocably.

"Naw! Get back! I'll fight the lot of you! I'll cut your bloody heads off!" He had suddenly sat bolt upright and with his eyes wide and brilliant with fever he cast his arms about him like flails. She caught the arms and held them, making soothing noises, urging him to lie back. But he began to cough, great racking coughs that seemed to shake the very cabin, never mind his skinny body. She made a toddy from the dregs of whisky in several bottles and held it to his lips till a little went down.

"Where's Annie?" he demanded, looking straight at her. "Where's Annie? She'll never come. Annie will not come, I tell you."

"Annie's here. Annie will look after you. Try to rest." She went through all the procedures as before – sponging his hands and face, rubbing his chest, bringing the steaming pot so he could inhale the vapour, keeping his thrashing limbs covered, moistening his lips with toddy and when that ran out a concoction made from hot water and molasses. All she had to go by was the light from the front of the stove and what little moonlight could filter through the dusty windows. It was the longest night of her life and there were times through tiredness and terror it seemed it was her lungs that fought for air, her roasting limbs that sought coolness from their fever. She prayed intermittently, begging her bearded stern-faced Scottish God to spare his servant, to forgive him his trespasses and sometimes reverting to childish entreaty of the gentle Jesus of her baby prayers, to 'look upon a little child.' When the dawn came the figure on the bed was still, inert, so that she had to keep touching and listening to make sure life was still there.

She must have nodded off at that point, her head resting on the foot of his bed, for she woke to full daylight and the touch of morning frost. She got up stiffly, saw that Hector slept still and dragged herself out for more logs. She had never milked an animal before, but she was determined to get something from the nanny goat and after a tussle succeeded. She found oatmeal in a sack and put some on the top of the stove, with water, for porridge.

"It is you," said a weak conclusive voice from the bed.

She turned as though scalded, rooted where she stood.

"Annie," said the voice, "Is it Annie?"

Almost shyly then she went towards him. "Aye. I'm here. How are you feeling?"

"Very sick. Far away." He looked at her piteously.

"You've had the congestion," she said, "from neglecting yourself. You needn't worry now I'm here. I'll take care of you. Could you try a little porridge?" Her hands, her legs, her voice shook from the gratification of being identified at last.

The extent of his weakness came home to her when she tried to feed him. He could not raise himself up on the makeshift pillows, he could not wipe the dribbles of goat's milk from his chin. But he took a little nourishment and when she had washed him and made him comfortable she gave serious thought as to what to give him for his dinner.

The hens were clucking about outside the cabin and she

scattered some corn from a sack next to the oatmeal, noticing as she did so there was a rough coop on the edge of the forest. When she examined it she found several eggs of varying sizes. She would coddle him one – that would be nourishing. But she knew she also had to get up the courage to kill a hen for soup and meat. This she did with a kind of cool, passionless despatch born from desperation, refusing to look more than a second at the twitching carcass after she had chopped off the head with the axe leaning against the cabin side. Plucking it was harder but she did that, too, and when the fowl was cooking, she found the juices running into her own mouth in expectation.

He did not want to eat that day. He drifted in and out of hot sleep, groaning and sometimes delirious. He needed a doctor. She could not bear to leave him now they had made some contact, but she knew that he was very ill. Perhaps last night had been some sort of crisis point, but they were by no means out of the wood yet. Supposing she got to the lumber camp or even to Jed at the gold mine, and supposing they agreed to try and locate a doctor, that would take ages. And meantime Hector would have been left on his own. She felt if she removed her physical presence by more than it took to fetch logs or milk the goat, he could easily give up the ghost. Just by gathering up her strength, by willing him not to give in, by being on hand to foresee his every need, his every wish, she could make him better. She had to believe that. So she stayed and ministered to him as best she could, all her instinctive intelligence, her nurturing skill, the little medical knowledge she had got from Alec Comrie, brought into play. For five days and nights there was little change and then imperceptibly he began, she thought, to get better, at least physically. The fever went, his chest became easier, he even evinced a little interest in the food she offered.

When he got up at last on skeletal, tottery legs it was only to gaze out of the door, then fall back on the bed. The next day she installed him in the one rickety chair while she bustled round the cabin, lifting skins to take them out to shake them, cleaning the windows with the one rag, laying fresh spruce on the bed to make it easier on his bones and in the corner where she lay at night.

"Are you really here?" he said. "I don't know whether this is happening or I'm just imagining it." His gauntness gave him an uncharacteristically wolfish air.

"Oh, I'm here all right." She knelt in front of him. "You've been sick, my poor lamb, but Annie will not leave you." She tried to take his hand but he drew it away. She felt the tears well up but by an effort of will held them back, merely gazing at him with a longing, sorrowful, reproachful look.

"Don't look at me like that." His voice was rough and hard. "I want you to go away again. I am not the man you knew."

"Let me stay a little longer," she coaxed. She knew she must not allow him to get upset, but her tears would not be stemmed. She saw with alarm that he was weeping also. Down the pale emaciated face two tears meandered, as though even they did not have the strength to take their course.

"I have to make restitution."

"What for?"

"For my sins."

"They are no more or less than any other man's."

"I have to give up my dear desires. It came to me, when I was ill."

She rose from her knees and put her arms around him. Apart from bathing him, easing him up in his pillow, it was the first physical contact she had had. He was so frail she knew if she squeezed his bones they would break. So she simply held him gently and said with quiet conviction, "It was because you were ill and had such sick fancies. Don't break my heart by talking as you do."

"I want you to go back to Barkerville."

"When you are well, we will talk about it."

She began to think his convalescence would never end. The fever had left him, his chest was clear, but he lay day after day on the foetid bed, staring at the cabin roof, remote and alienated from her, although when she said 'Sit up' he did so and when she said 'Eat' he did so. He would get up for short spells when she urged him and they would repeat the argument about her going. She tried to sing to him, to get him to read, but he would close his eyes and sleep or pretend to do so. When she remonstrated he said he was very tired. Perhaps after all, she thought as the days passed, she would not win the battle. The anxiety took the colour from her cheeks and made her look haggard and careworn.

One morning, when he had taken a better breakfast than usual and turned his head to watch an importunate hen shooed from the cabin threshold, she held on long enough to the little spurt of optimism she felt to suggest she should saddle up Peg that day and ride down to the lumber camp to get some supplies. He had told her he had an arrangement there, either paying in labour or cash. "Whisky," he said. "Ask for whisky." There were other items needed more urgently, but she promised to do what she could and took her own money to pay.

She asked to speak to the foreman when she got to the camp.

"That's a strange one you've got up there," he commented when she had explained her business. "A bit wrong in the head since some robbers near killed him. Tries to fraternise with the Indians. You tell him not to trust them. They ain't all alike, but them round here's a mean strain. You cover your cabin window nights, take my advice."

"I've seen no Indians," she said, with a dry throat.

"Well," the man conceded, "they may have cleared off. But come the winter, they might be back. You get back to Barkerville, 'fore then." She had given him a potted history of her own life since coming to British Columbia, partly to ingratiate herself while he got some stores together and partly out of a genuine desire for human interchange.

"You can pay for this, Mrs —?"

"Mrs. Mennock," said Annie, with a formidable briskness she was far from feeling. "I am the wife of the Highlander, as you call him. He is not wrong in the head, but ill from the trials that have befallen him, so try to be charitable." She softened the injunction with a smile. "And of course I can pay. I would not ask for anything I couldn't pay for."

The big, slow man gave her a respectful look.

"Glad to be of service then, ma'am. Anything you want brought up from the Forks, let me know. We got to keep good supplies here. Felling trees is hungry work."

When she got back, he was sitting up by the stove and she saw, touched, he had made an attempt to draw a brush through his beard and hair.

"Got the whisky?"

She poured a little into a mug. "Go easy. It'll make you light-headed."

"You will be going soon," he said, "and I shall drink as much as I like."

"Do that," she said, angrily, tired from her ride. She threw the rest of the items she had brought on to the sagging table. "You drink any more tonight and I set off in the morning." She was prepared to call his bluff and was not displeased to see he took no more whisky that night.

She was working about outside the cabin next day when he came up behind her. "I'll get the eggs," he offered, and he carried them and the canister back to the cabin when she had milked the nannygoat. The next day he broke a few logs, though he had to give up after a few minutes. But it seemed to her that at last his strength was coming back to him. He ate his food with a new gusto. So long as she kept the talk impersonal, he was prepared to interject the odd sentence, but there were still the long silences, when he walked off into the woods or sat in the cabin, staring into the middle distance.

The time came when she could stand it no longer. He was almost fit. From being the cavern-eyed scarecrow she had first encountered he daily took on more and more of his old appearance, reminding her of how handsome she had thought him all that time ago at their trysting-place by the bridge in Springburn. He had thought her bonnie then, too; had thought even her squint gave her a look of serious purpose. When she looked back now, these two young people seemed like people from another planet, from a book or a song. Nothing to do with the grim-faced man who strode about the clearing with some constraint, some conflict, eating away at his mind and soul. Nothing to do with the woman with the roughened hands and tragic eyes who watched him, like a collie dog watching its master, not sure whether it will be saved or drowned.

She chose one morning when they had both been busy and stopped for a mug of tea, to make the confrontation.

"We must leave here one day, Hector," she postulated.

"Now that you're better –"

"You can leave. I stay."

She looked round the tacky cabin. Despite her best ministrations, it looked still like some animal lair. She gazed into the blackened tin mug she was forced to drink from and the tears blurred her eyes, but she went on with a gritty determination to sort things out: "We have to start building some sort of life and we can't do it here. If we go back to Barkerville, we can both get work. The farm will just have to wait a bit, till we've saved –"

"Annie, leave me." The words burst from him. "You can still make a decent life for yourself. You don't deserve a millstone like me round your neck." She saw the desperate supplication in his eyes and she began to sob. "I'm not going away. You can say what you like. Nothing'll make me leave you."

"Aye, you'll go," he said, with equal determination.

She went over to him and threw her arms round him at last, clinging to him as though she were drowning. "Ah, Hector, don't do this to me," she begged him. She sought his mouth and forced her own on to his. It did not matter that the jerkin he wore smelled of goat. She felt his lips move away then come back and her arms tightened in triumph. She wound her legs round him, she clung like a limpet to a rock. She heard him begin to pant and say her name like a terrible sigh dragged from his depths. "Annie! Annie!" She wouldn't let go. Even when he began to drag at her arms, she wouldn't relax her monkey-like grip. They fell to the floor, rolling over and over, both crying out and sobbing, pummelling at each other and coming back to that desperate embrace until somehow the struggle was over and they were coming together as she had always dreamed they would. As he entered her she gave a great shout of triumphant joy. Even then she would not move away from him. The sea that had carried them towards coitus picked them up mercilessly once again and rolled them towards the rocks of a terrible ecstasy.

She lay on the cabin floor. She could smell earth, dung, trees, animal skins, forest. She lay there, thinking how this was how a squirrel must feel in its lair, a rabbit in its burrow. Animal. It did not matter. She was with him. It had been as terrible and wonderful as she had known it would be.

He got up at last, without speaking, and went out of the cabin into the clearing. She could hear him chopping wood and presently she went out and stood by him, feeling strangely shy.

Then she put her hand on his arm to stop him chopping the wood and pleaded, "Tell me everything that has happened to you. I want to know it all."

He put an arm about her shoulders. "How can I tell you? What has happened has all been inside here." He tapped his forehead. "I should never have run away from Scotland. I should have stayed and faced the music. Now it's all between me and God."

"You had a terrible sea journey."

"First I had the fever and then I was thrown out of my bunk and half-drowned at Cape Horn, striking my head when I fell."

"Do you want to talk about it?" She could see he was becoming distressed and his recent weakness beginning to make itself once more apparent. She led him towards the tree trunk outside the cabin where they could both sit down.

"I want to forget it all. It was a nightmare. I told you I thought I saw the man I had killed in a sloop at Victoria? How could that be anything but God's punishment?"

"It was a sick fancy," she said positively. She held his hand, tightly. "You were ill. Can I remind you of something? You only thought you'd killed that man."

"He looked at me with such sad, reproachful eyes! I'll never forget it. It must have been a phantom, Annie."

"It must have been your delirium. The fever does strange things. I have seen it."

"You think so?"

"I know so."

"I got to the goldfields. You know I can scarcely remember any of it? My memory is still affected. It's a kind of white blur. I drank too much in order to make it possible. I drink too much now. I struck gold on the Quesnel and had it all taken from me. How could I face you?"

"Hamish told me you were set upon and robbed."

"I had a great wound here." He touched the top of his head.

"Show me." She touched the deep rivulet of a scar.

"It was an Indian half-breed who found me. He carried me to this cabin and used some herbal medicine on my injury – some cure he'd learned from his mother. I've tried to befriend the Indians because of what he did – you know there are three of them to every white incomer. It's *their* land. When I was better he went away. They found his body at the bottom of a gulch – he'd been in a fight over a claim with some trapper or other."

He got up abruptly and produced the whisky bottle from under his bed.

"You don't know what gold does to people. I need a drink now. Do you want one?" When she shook her head sombrely he said, "Don't try and stop me. If you stay here, that's a condition. You don't say to me stop drinking and you don't ask me to tell you everything that happened. I don't want to talk about it. The past is the past. Learn that and you can stay for a while. You'll go, eventually. I know that already. I'm willing it. But stay for a while, if you like."

"I am going to stay forever. I am never going to leave you."

"You are taking on a loser."

"I'll be the judge of that."

As she lay beside him on the narrow bed that night, sickened by the fumes of whisky on his breath, she determined that she would lose no time in trying to wean him off "John Barleycorn" as her mother had referred to it back in Glasgow.

At first she tried persuasion and then matched his cunning with her own. If she could distract him, she did. But she realised it was going to be a long, difficult, perhaps impossible task. Her main hope lay in restoring his self-esteem, in trying to get him to come to terms with his conscience, in trying to ease his guilt by reiterating over and over again that he had not meant to kill Colin Macandrew, that he could not have known the man would hit a stone as he went down. She pointed out he had not got into the fight on his own behalf, but to save his brother Rab from another drubbing which might have finished *him* off.

She let him talk about it interminably. She began to notice the lightening of his mood. Sometimes when she sang or did a few dancing steps, he looked at her with the slow, sweet smile of the old Hector. But he was still for a large part of the time abstracted, absorbed in his own thoughts, touchy, unwilling to talk about any rational plans for the future. When she tried to pin him down he simply said, "I'm not leaving here." It gave her no option. She sent a letter back to Hamish, via the lumber camp, telling him she would not be returning and asking him, as a great favour, to settle with the man from whom she'd hired the mare.

She found it hard to analyse her own feelings after the first week or so. Her joy at finding Hector had been tempered by so many things. When they made love in the narrow bed it was still as wonderful as it had ever been. Divested of its rough clothes, his hard slender body, his loving lips, told her things his speech never did. Yet all their joint ambitions, about farming and a family, had gone by the board.

She was used to company: she missed the busy life of the *Last Chance Saloon* and the troops of friends she had made in Barkerville. She liked nice clothes, looking trim, and here it did not matter, which was just as well, for it was difficult to look fresh, uncrumpled, anything other than half-tamed, wild almost. In the mornings she wept over the tangles in her hair, the lack of a looking-glass. It was so lonely in the clearing. It was possible to think at times there was no other life on the planet, except occasionally for the chunk of axe on wood, the noise carried up from the lumber camp. In the absence of people, the few fowls and animals took on character and importance. She spoke to Katie the pig and Peg the mare and praised the hens extravagantly when they produced their pale-yoked eggs. The goats, Billy and Susan, followed her like dogs. She made cheese of sorts from Susan's milk.

She was, she decided, of a very resilient nature, for although she found the quiet strange and bewildering, she began to plan order and productivity in their lives. The cabin did not possess a clock but at least she was determined they should not lose track of the days. She drew up a calendar. When the cock crew each morning, she rose and after a time, Hector began to do the same.

She set the broody hen on a clutch of eggs and soon had a scattering of yellow chicks. Hector laboured to produce shelter and fencing for the animals. Although there was not much she could do about making the inside of the cabin more attractive, she got Hector to improve the table, which helped her in her baking, and she hung curtains torn from an old petticoat and tied them back with old hair ribbons.

She had to bide her time. Her mother's phrase, that. Whatever sickness, whatever uncertainty had gripped Hector, would only loosen, would only leave him when its force was spent.

If only she had scissors, she could cut his hair and beard. If only she had a cow, she could make butter and cheese. If only she had seed, she'd grow something. If only she had a decent stove and pots, the food would taste better. The list grew.

But bide her time she must. There was a look she could only describe as sanity coming back into Hector's eyes. Sometimes when he went to the camp to work for whisky he would bring back some treat – molasses, a tin of candy, a cheap vase for flowers, a needle and some thread. On the day he finally brought back rusty scissors she felt for the first time the stirrings of confidence about her new life. She cut his hair and trimmed his beard and saw the handsome man she had fallen in love with almost restored to her. Everything else that had happened to her began to fade from her consciousness, even little Aeneas, Donald Arrochar and Hamish. The Cariboo had laid hold.

8

The summer weather made living easier. The lumber camp had taken on extra labour and on warm, sunny mornings they could hear the thud of axe on tree trunk, the shouted order and exchanges. The sounds rose and reverberated in the bowl of the valley. It made them feel less remote and cut off.

He was not drinking so much. She had made up her mind she would not nag him about it. He was anxious to lay up his own stock of logs for the winter and the back-breaking work seemed to exorcise some of his demons. As for her, she had her work cut out trying to feed them, to vary the meals as much as was possible, and in looking after the animals. But they were both out in the open all day, browned and hardened by fresh air and sun.

She had grown used to the luxury of an occasional bath in Barkerville, taken at the ladies' bath house which was an adjunct of Maybelle's saloon. And now she suggested they bathe in the stream from which they got their water for domestic use. It felt freezing cold at first but then it was gloriously invigorating. They rubbed each other dry and after lay in the sun wearing the minimum of clothing. His lovemaking became tender and fanciful in the open-air, but she waited to hear him talk about the future. A future together. Certainly there had been less discussion recently of her leaving him, though he still came back to it from time to time, like picking over an old scab.

She could feel the delicious warmth strike up through her body from the big streamside boulder they shared and moved languorously in his arms. "How can you ever say you want me to go away, Hector? Tell me you don't mean it."

He gazed into her eyes, not answering her at first. Covering her face with kisses. Then he lay back, feeling her lack of response and said, almost roughly, "You put me on too much of a pedestal. I don't know if I can live up to it."

"Live up to what? What do I ask you to live up to?"

"You know."

"I don't."

"The farm you want. The family."

"I'll do without all that," she said instantly. "As long as I have you."

"You don't know me," he said, moodily. "I'm not all you set me up to be. I don't know me. Things I've done have made me a stranger to myself. It's this country. It's too big. Too demanding."

She leaned up on one arm. "Hector," she demanded, "is there something you haven't told me? Something you want to talk about, that's come back to you now your memory's better?"

He didn't answer.

"There is, isn't there?" When he was still silent, she said, "Well, it doesn't matter. You'll tell me when you're ready."

"I've never told you about how I struck gold." There was something in his look now that struck a cold chord of apprehension in her mind. She pushed her head into his shoulder so that she would not have to look at him.

"I hit pay-dirt enough to keep us in comfort for the rest of our life and I let it all go. I lost it. That's the kind of idiot you've got yourself hitched to –"

"Tell me about it." Her voice was muffled and tentative.

"All of it?"

"Yes. All of it."

"We came up here – further up." He pointed in the direction of the mountains. "The canyon Indians knew there was gold up there for the taking. They'd fought off the whites as long as they could, but by the time we arrived a lot had been killed, some had followed trails elsewhere and we made peace with the few that were left.

"Long and short of it, there was this young half-breed I told you about, I gave him my pocket watch. He seemed to want it: the one who later saved my life." She looked swiftly at him, hearing emotion roughen his narrative. "Go on," she said, gently. "Something he said one day, when we were having a conversation. He let drop where there might still be gold. When I asked him why he didn't go after it, he said he couldn't convince his brothers it would be worthwhile. He was just working on a kind of hunch, I guess. Or maybe they were sick of gold then, what it stood for, the fighting and the killing.

"Anyhow, I got my three friends to come with me up Cottonmill Creek. We found prospects on the east side, then sunk a hole on the north-west side and got a good result there, too. About ten to thirty cents to the pan."

"That's good?"

"Well, fair. Promising."

"And then?"

"We were tired by then. Walking on snow shoes, which is what we did, takes it out of you. We lit a fire beside the stream and we cooked supper. Sitting there speculating what we might hit the next day.

"I couldn't settle. I was thinking of you, getting you out here. I left the others dozing and talking and wandered up the stream a bit further, till I saw the bare bedrock sticking out. I had a job separating the frozen gravel from the rock, but I thawed and panned it in the stream and I got – what do you think? a dollar to the pan."

She could feel his remembered excitement. "I couldn't get back to the others fast enough. I shouted your name to the mountains. Well, the long and the short of it, we laid a flume – a channel for the stream – 160 foot long, four wide, two deep. We were sawing lumber 16 hours a day. That's *work*! But we'd hit pay dirt. We were rich. We were also tired men and desperate to get back to some kind of civilisation to spend some of it."

She waited in a kind of dread for what came next.

"Have you taken in what I've tried to say, Annie? About the work and the solitude, the hoping and the getting? We were like wild things when we got back to Quesnel, desperate to spend and with not much to spend it on."

"Except gambling and drink."

"It was just a means of celebration."

"And women. Were there women?"

He rose and paddled in the stream. She called after him, "Was there a woman?"

With his back towards her he said, "I slept with a whore and told myself it was you."

She could feel cold pervade her everywhere, cold and terror and screaming. When he came back and looked down at her, she said, "But we were married. You said you would be true to me. You said. You said."

"I was. I was with her, but it was really you. I wanted you then, so badly."

"You were drunk."

"I was drunk and tired and a little out of my mind."

"And then," she said, evenly. "What happened then?"

"What I told you. We'd promised ourselves we wouldn't

let the cat out of the bag but we were all the same when we'd drink taken. I don't know what happened to the others. The robbers got me on my way back to the hotel. The half-breed found me by the roadside, where they'd left me for dead. All I remember is a one-eyed rogue with a pistol and a Cockney accent. *Forgive me.*"

She turned away, thinking how curious it was that the scene she had thought so sun-warmed and beautiful, the mountains, spruce and stream had somehow turned hostile, rejecting. She could not speak to him. She got up and shook out the folds of her petticoat. She wanted her mother. She began to weep, harsh, unlikely sounds, walking always away from him and back towards the cabin as though by instinct. "Forgive me," he called after her. "Forgive me. I did not mean it. I should never have told you."

She sat in the dim cool of the cabin, warring emotions tearing her apart. Uppermost was the hurt of his betrayal. But there was also fury at her own trusting nature, for she had not really thought to get a confession from him when she had mentioned women. She had not been serious. Had there been others when he stayed at Barkerville? Hamish had never said as much, but it was possible. Did it matter? One infidelity was as bad as two or more. She did not want to know, chiefly because she did not want to acknowledge any further weaknesses in the man she had committed herself to so desperately.

She could have slept with Donald Arrochar. She remembered very well the insistent needs of her body at that time, the torture to both of them of keeping apart. If she could fight temptation, why hadn't he? That was what vows were about. When he came into the cabin and looked soberly down at her, she shouted and ranted at him through her tears, "I hate you! I will never speak to you again!" and then as he turned away, the need to know came uppermost and she shouted "What was she like, the whore?" and he turned and said sadly, "I have no mind. We were not particular," and she summoned up all the contempt of which she was capable and said "Judas! Judas! You betrayed me!" and he answered "Do you not think that I know it?"

The days passed and they exchanged no word. He signed to her when he was off down to the lumber camp. She indicated with a lift of her arms when she wanted logs brought in. They ate in silence and slept in silence, he on a bearskin on the floor. She thought of Donald Arrochar and his kindnesses to her, of her happiness when she had looked after little Aeneas. She even thought of Hamish and how he had not allowed his love to curdle when she rejected him. For the sake of her own dignity, she had need of all the affection she could bring to mind. She began to see Hector now in a more realistic fashion. His callowness. His irresolution. How did she know he had not killed the man Colin Macandrew in temper? How did she know, really *know*, anything about him? She had thought her love sealed him off in a kind of perfection, like a jelly. It wasn't true. He had not been a grown man when they exchanged their vows. He had not behaved like a grown man over the gold. He had not behaved like a grown man when he did not remain at Barkerville long enough to face her with his losses. It had been a bewildered boy who had made that awful sea journey, a bewildered boy who fled to the backwoods.

And yet she had vowed to love him forever. She did love him. He had taken over and filled every corner of her life. What had happened back in Glasgow when she was poor, dirty, starving, had been the most miraculous event of her whole life. His love had lifted her out of deprivation and despair, given her a beacon which lit up her days.

She remembered the Hector she had met then, touched with a gentle nobility and she thought that the sea passage, the sickness, whatever it had been, had taken something away from him, shaken him up and reassembled him, the essential Hector, in a way that was strange to her.

Perhaps she should leave him. In some ways it surprised her that she didn't. Living with Hector was not the only option open to her now. She could go back to Barkerville and earn a decent living. If her anger and sense of betrayal did not abate, perhaps that would be the best course of action. Yet she was stopped by a curious lassitude that was almost an acceptance of the status quo and by the fact that by her silence she was punishing him. Oh, yes, she wanted to punish him. She wanted him to feel the agony and pain he had caused her and to feel it over and over again. When he made any tentative advance, pleaded with her to talk to him, to resolve their differences somehow, she walked away, sometimes into the forest, staying there long enough so that he would think she was lost; or shut herself up in the cabin with a log rolled to the door, so that he couldn't get in.

For his part, he took himself off twice or three times a week to the lumber camp, labouring there and coming back with whisky to drink before bedtime. It was as though they were locked in a kind of mutual purgatory and she began to be afraid that they would never break out of it. She was doing something to them both that she did not understand and yet she could not change. She stumbled weeping through the days, her only comfort the animals and exhausted sleep.

"Mistress." She was making goat cheese one day when he entered the cabin soft-footed and startled her. She turned her practised, hardened, silent face towards him and he spread his hands helplessly.

"We have to talk. Well, I will talk, and you shall listen. You've punished me enough. I will make one more effort to get through to you and if that fails, then it is over between us. Do you understand?"

Still she said nothing.

"I want to go back to the Cottonmill claim and try again for gold. The summer has made me strong. If there is nothing left at Cottonmill I know there must be more gold in the hills. I said I would give you a farm and that is what you shall have. I shall prove it to you all over again that I love you. That I am not the despicable weakling you seem to think me. I have prayed to God and this is His answer."

She heard his voice break but still nothing in her softened. He waited and when there was no response he turned on his heel and left. She saw him take the path to the lumber camp and when he had finally disappeared from her sight she broke down and wept as though her heart would break. She wanted then to run after him, but it was too late. She was too practised in coldness. It was as though she were frozen through and through, though the sun was still warm.

She sat outside the cabin, drawing threads from an old sack so that she could push rag strips through the holes and make a rug. The goats came up to her nosily and hens clucked inquisitively near her feet. At one point the tethered Peggy neighed for food. She went through the motions of her day like an automaton. The sun began to sink and he still had not returned. She could not believe that he had gone. He would not do it just like that. Besides, he had taken nothing with him.

When it grew dark and he still had not come back she did not know what to think. Even during their estrangement, he returned from any trips before dark because he knew she was nervous about being alone then. She was torn between nervousness on her own behalf and terror at what might have happened to him. In the same strange dazed way she had behaved all day, she lit the lantern he had acquired on one of his trips to the camp and with a shawl about her shoulders took the track he had taken earlier in the day. In a cracked voice she said his name. "Hector! Hector! Where are you?"

When she reached the banking that rolled down to the camp she heard a cracking of twigs and a moan. She saw him then, half in and half out of a ditch.

She ran and grasped his arm and swore at him. "You blackguard! What's happened to you?" She quickly realised from his useless, floppy attempts to extricate himself from the ditch that he was drunk. She sat down with the lantern between her knees and let him get on with it. When he finally scrambled, swaying, to his feet, she took his arm and led him back towards the cabin.

"You spoke to me!" he said. To the trees on either side of them, he announced in drunken glee, "Annie spoke to me. Did you hear that? She called me a blackguard, but she spoke to me!"

Whether it was from relief, she did not know. The corners of her lips were turning up, irresistibly, and she was actually laughing. He was not so drunk as to miss his advantage. When they reached the goats he made a courtly bow before them and said "The mistress is back with us. See her laugh!" To the bewildered animals he made a solemn promise. "I am going to get her a farm. You can come if you like. Be the chief goats among many. We'll have milk cows and corn and dances in the barn. I've promised her that." Was there anything, she wondered, quite so ridiculous as a man who was 'fou,' as they said back home in Glasgow?

"Come inside," she bade him.

"She spoke to me," he reiterated. He did not trust himself to look at her. She threw logs on to the darkling stove and lit a candle. He poured water from the ewer into the basin and sluiced his face, drying it exhaustively with a sacking towel. They sat down on either side of the stove and at last looked at each other.

"Oh my love," he said, shaking his head, "I've missed you sorely."

"If you go to the Cottonmill claim, I am coming with you."

"You should go to Barkerville and wait for me."

"Never again. I am coming with you."

"So you think we should go?"

"It is what I have waited for. For us to start over again."

"Well, come and bide with me, lass, and we'll talk about it."

He took off his clothes and got into the narrow bed and she followed him. It was strange and somehow formal, lying there in his arms. His body seemed harder, more mature.

"You will need to learn to use snow-shoes," he told her. "By the time we get there, winter may have started."

"Not if we go at once."

"We have to make preparations first. Get rid of the animals."

"Surely we'll take Peg?"

"She might be too much of a liability."

The conversation was punctuated by his kisses and suddenly there was nothing formal between them any more. Only the sweet, singing insistence of skin on skin, lips on lips. How could it be, that she who had been so frozen and sorrowful was alive again, her body a river of joy, her head full of singing birds?

"Say to me," he asked her tenderly, "that you will never turn your face from me again?"

"If you will never give me cause."

"No. Even if I give you cause."

"How can I say that?"

"For that's what love is. Ah, don't look like that, Annie. I want with all my heart to please you."

She spread herself on top of him. "Say your vow. That you will love me forever."

"I have no option. I want to come to you again."

"Say it."

"I say it."

"You love me."

"I love you."

"Forever."

"Forever."

It was blurred. Who was who? Who breathed in, and who out? And they lay thus all night in the cabin in the clearing while the stars gazed down on the pale Cariboo.

"I have a feeling," she said, as they moved slowly up Cottonmill Creek, with the claim still not in sight, "that last night my mother passed from us and went to join her Maker."

"How can you know that?" He turned to gaze at her with a tender look.

"I had a dream. Of swans. And she was on a river and turned and looked at me. And I knew I would not see her again."

"Don't be sad. If it is so."

"I would like to have seen her just once more."

"My mother died when I was three. I can't even remember her face."

It was a strange conversation for them to be having, but ever since leaving the cabin they had been in a state of heightened intimacy and communication that bordered on the freakish. He knew her train of thought and said "I wonder if you will bear me a son one day?"

"Would you like that?"

"We were all boys. I know nothing of girls."

"A girl might look a little like my mother. I had a fair semblance to my own grandmother, it seems. I am told this is how it goes."

When she was serious, pontificating, it made him smile. "It's all a mystery," he postulated.

"For the farm," she admitted, "we could do with sons. But a girl or two will not go amiss. For the fun of it."

"To make me clootie puddings. And kiss my balding head."

"To take care of your soul and go with you to church."

"Do you think my soul will be saved?"

"If you do not become too full of yourself. If you're humble in the sight of the Lord."

"Amen to that."

They climbed. They had taken Peggy with them in the end, because she was useful for transporting the gear. The mare revelled in the travel, the chance to crop fresh grass. The terrain was rough but there were hospitable, sheltering trees under whose branches at night they could pitch their tent. They had been lucky. The snow had held off and the days glittered with a fierce, limned clarity so that they could see for miles.

She was happier than she had ever been in her life.

Although they were both often weary, he insisted on rests whenever he saw her stride become lengthy and plodding and they talked about everything that had ever been important to them. His education had been superior to hers and her delight had no bounds. Latin. Greek. People called Plato, Socrates, Catullus. His knowledge about how things worked – steamboats and railway engines. His understanding of plant life and animals, of science and medicine, Gaeldom. His intimacy with the poets.

Only on theology she gave no ground. Years of Sunday School both as teacher and pupil had given her a thorough grounding in the Bible and she clung to her own interpretation of the Gospels. Sometimes to keep their steps going they sang the hymns they knew, interspersed with somewhat bawdy bothy ballads on his part and the Negro spirituals she had learned from Hetty Laboucher on Salt Spring Island, on hers.

Above all, he was not drinking. She made no comment about this. She simply accepted that total trust had been restored between them, the gap of days closed and that when they met each other's eyes it was like gazing at a mirror image of each other's soul.

A stunning surprise awaited them when they finally reached Cottonmill Creek. Where Hector and his three companions had sunk the flume a small township was now in existence. It was no more than a scattering of cabins, a few essential shops and a couple of saloons but it soon became clear that its presence had been triggered by the original claim and that people were still mining gold there and others getting a living from their efforts.

"No matter." They had booked a sparsely-furnished room for a few nights at one of the saloons. Hector did his best to hide his disappointment.

"It's clear," he said, "the gold is working itself out. I've always thought the richer veins are higher up." Conversations he had with diggers in the saloon confirmed his opinions. There might be more gold in Cottonmill, but capital was needed to sink shafts, to dig deeper, and nobody seemed convinced enough to take the risk at present.

When they eventually left the little township behind, he pointed out that at least its being there removed some of their worries about keeping up supplies. They were concerned now about keeping warm, about survival. He panned the river as they went, but the results were poor. She began to feel the blood running thinner in her veins, to realise how reluctant she was to leave their campfires and face another day of perishing feet and frozen hands as they tried to wrest the secrets from the river.

"I don't think we can go on." They had built a huge fire to warm the horse and themselves and cook supper but snowflakes were falling in ominous silence all around them. "We should go back to Cottonmill."

"Not yet." His face was closed, cold and stubborn. "The gold is there. I know it is. It is just a question of persistence. We have come this far —"

"To perish of the cold."

He looked at her sharply. "You are feeling a bit down, that's all."

"I was sick, this morning, Hector. I think I may be going to have a child." It was out, the frightening, scarifying, exciting secret that had been bothering her for days.

He came to her and held her in his arms, kissing her cold face. "Are you sure?"

"Pretty sure."

"Then we have all the more reason to persist. The gold must come."

"But the snow —"

"Are you willing to give it one more day? Just one, Annie?"

"Just one, then."

"You can stay by the fire, I'll do the prospecting. If nothing comes of it, we'll go back to Cottonmill. Find something to do to keep us —"

He kept awake most of the night, building the fire before

it sank low so that she should not wake from the cold. At first light he roused her and told her he was off. As the day strengthened, she looked along the creek and saw him, bent in the characteristic panning position over the river. Sometimes as the river wound he was hidden by trees. She fed the fire in a kind of panic, waiting for it to snow again. Mid-morning she was sick. She folded her hands across her tender stomach, growing accustomed already to the thought of the baby. Growing pleased and broody despite everything. By mid-afternoon she saw him come staggering back along the creek, waving to her from afar off.

"Good news."

"You've found something!"

"Not gold. But a cabin. Against the trees, on that bend of the river, there." He pointed. "Somebody made it and left it, a time ago. But it's snug enough inside. It even has a stove. Our troubles are over."

She looked at him as though he had taken leave of his senses.

"A cabin? Up there? With the snow coming on?"

"We'll not go if you're against it." He looked at her with a challenge. She saw that his hands and face were frozen to near-purple with the cold, yet he had not complained.

"We'll go." She got their things together, pulled the reluctant horse on her way. "Did you have any luck panning?"

"Nothing. But we'll find it yet."

"Hector."

"Aye?"

"We have to face it. Perhaps we never will."

They set their faces in the teeth of the wind. She wore the britches bought for her journey to Quesnel. On top she wore a sealskin coat and had wrapped a coarse, thick woollen shawl round her head and shoulders. Hector's britches were of soft-tanned animal hide and his coat was bearskin. He wore a trappers's cap with ear-flaps. Yet the wind flayed them; it felt as though it lifted the very skin from their faces.

When they reached the cabin he went out to pan the river again before it got dark, leaving her to take stock. It was even rougher than the one they had recently left, but a little bigger and lighter. The stove was also fairly commodious and after cleaning the top she made some hasty scones to eat with cheese. He would be ravenous when he returned.

There was no bed so she gathered armfuls of spruce and spread it on the floor, covering it with an animal hide from the wall. They would be warm and comfortable enough. Her spirits began to lift. His panning had been fruitless but the lightening of her mood communicated itself to him and they made a banquet of the frugal meal before the roaring stove.

"This time," he said to her, "when I hit gold, nobody takes it away from me." He looked towards his shotgun. "Do you know what I think as I stand with my feet in freezing water? I think of the big homestead we'll have, with proper stables, proper grounds. When I think of it, the sun is always shining and it's always warm."

"We'll have a big brass bedstead with a feather mattress and a patchwork quilt," she said. "Do you know we've never slept together in what you would call a proper bed?"

"I hadn't noticed," he teased her. "I've always paid too much attention to who was beside me."

"We'll need a crib for the baby."

"I'll make it myself."

The next day he rose early and began panning once more. At about three o'clock in the afternoon he came to her, a look of closed excitement on his face.

"I think I'm on to it. It's like the last time. A dollar to the pan." He showed her.

"What do you do now?"

"Start channelling a flume."

"But it's too much for one man."

"I'll do what I can. If the snow but holds off –"

"Let me help."

"You can't saw lumber. Not in your condition."

"I'm not far on. I'm perfectly strong."

"We'll see." He was reluctant. While she started to prepare a meal he returned to the river and she heard the fall of his pick. When he came back his tired muscles could scarcely respond to his will. He fell on the spruce bed and she pulled off his boots. But he was smiling. "I'm going to call it the Springburn Mine. For that's where we first met." She brought the food to him and fed him and before he had finished he had fallen asleep. She sipped her mug of tea and contemplated him, thinking how it could finish him, the work, yet knowing no way of stopping him or even if she should.

"Oh, God," he said next morning, "I ache." Yet he got up, dressed, moved about and departed after breakfast. "I'll bring you down some hot coffee," she promised.

It was as she turned from the stove to pour the boiling water into a canister that she saw the two faces at the window and almost dropped the kettle in her consternation. Both were bearded and both were topped by battered, wide-brimmed hats. One grinned at her, showing rotten teeth and the other, black-eyed, stolid, simply stared. With thumping heart she looked towards the door. Should she bar it and pick up the gun? She did the latter, anyhow, and turned to see the men were already at the threshold and had pushed the cabin door wide open.

"Good morning," she said, carefully.

"Good morning to you, missis," said the larger of the two. "You can put that gun away for a start."

"I'll be the judge of that."

"We're after a word with your man there," said the small man, quickly. "We've come up from Cottonmill, so we have, just to have a word."

"Does he know you?"

"We know him," said the big man. "Least, we've heard tell. We've come to offer our assistance, in the event that he needs it."

"What are your names?" She couldn't think of what else to say, and wished to sound severe and in control.

"I'm Irish Sam, and this here's Big Jim Boulder," said the black-eyed visitor. "Pleased to meet you, Mrs –"

"Mrs. Mennock."

"And that wouldn't be coffee you're making?"

She gave them the hot drink without relinquishing her shotgun and led them thoughtfully down towards the stream where Hector's back was bent. She saw his astonishment as he turned and saw she was accompanied.

"This here's Big Jim Boulder and Irish Sam," she said, by way of introduction. "They want to talk to you."

"Come a long way for the privilege," said Hector, wiping his brow.

"Reckon it's worth it, if you count us in," said Big Jim, levelly.

Annie could feel her body begin to shake with anger.

"This is our claim. We were here first."

"Reckon if we went back to Cottonmill and told 'em about you, you'd have dozens of 'em up here," interjected the smaller man, spitting. "Hundreds, even. We're doing you a good turn, keeping it just among ourselves."

Annie looked hastily at Hector and saw from his face that what Irish Sam had said had gone home. She recollected the many tales she had heard herself of claims contraverted by human locusts falling on a seam after one or two men had done the initial grafting.

Hector laid down his pan and asked, "Do you mind if I have a word with my wife?" To Annie he whispered urgently, "Look, there's going to be enough for the four of us. With their help, we'll get the gold out that much more quickly and I have to think of that, with the snow coming. Don't worry, I'll keep the reins." Turning, he said to the men, "You got picks and shovels? A saw?" They nodded. "Then you're in."

"There's nothing here to share with you," said Annie with last-ditch defiance, and a furious look at her husband.

"Well, we know better," said Big Jim almost apologetically. "We been watching you."

"How did you know we were here?"

"We heard you talking when you was stayin' in that there saloon in Cottonmill. We'd been bumming around since we come up from Victoria, looking for a lead. We jest followed your tracks. Reckoned you might be on to something."

They had no option but to let Irish Sam and Big Jim Boulder share the cabin. With more time in hand, they might have built something of their own. But all three men knew now the heavy snows were on the way and that the flume had to be constructed as top priority. If there was a time for the finer proprieties, Annie acknowledge, it was not now. The men shacked up in the opposite corner, delicately erecting a rough barrier from a tree branch over which they put their day clothes to dry off, and shutting each other up when the talk became too replete with expletives. She was prepared to put up with much out of the genuine fear that the work could have killed Hector on his own. Besides, the men had come well provisioned, with food and tools stacked on a sledge and snow-shoes at the ready for when the snow lay thicker. Their competence was heartening, although she still felt the sharp edge of anger at their presumption and was determined they should treat her with full respect.

They fell into a pattern of days. Jim Boulder, especially, proved himself an invaluable member of the team, for his way with cutting timber and the sheer strength of his amazing shoulders. Annie realised more than ever that Hector's initial aim to set up the flume on his own had been unrealistic. Sam was not as strong as the other two, but quick-witted at solving construction problems and seeing the simpler way to do things. His energy was limited. It was his idea to use spare timber to construct a hasty shelter for Peggy abutting the cabin. They used the mare to drag heavy timbers.

Annie's task was to keep the team fed. She did her best but the food was of necessity monotonous. She washed and dried their clothes and did what mending was needed, sitting by the stove and dreaming of the day when she and

Hector would have their farm and the baby would sleep in its home-made crib.

When the men had eaten in the evening, their talk was mainly of what could be achieved the next day. Everything depended on the diggings being shallow, for then the gold could be secured once the sluice boxes were laid.

Jim Boulder's aim, with his share of the gold, was to set up a saloon in either Barkerville or nearby Cameronton and bring his wife and child out from England. Sam's ambitions varied from grocery store to gambling hotel, possibly in Victoria, but his mate cast doubts on every scheme he came up with, declaring Sam would drink and gamble it away, as he had done in the past. "Not this time," said the little man, furiously. "Not this time." There was some needle between the men over an incident in the past, when Big Jim's money had been needed to bail his friend out of trouble.

Just as the river began to yield up its gold, the snow came. At first the men disregarded it, working on to dropping pitch, but then the frost laid its hard fingers on the gravel and allowed the snow to pile on top of it. Every day snow had to be cleared, a huge fire lit, before the picks rang out on the clamorous river-bed.

And then there was no mistaking the generosity of the claim. The first time Hector staggered home with his cap full of gold and dirt, he and Annie danced round the cabin floor. Then it became commonplace. Their worry was where to keep it. The men took up the floor timbers in the cabin and hid the precious trophy underneath.

On the days when the snow was too relentless they concentrated on keeping it clear of the cabin. They couldn't let the winter beat them, but it was hard going while the snow lasted. When it finally held off, but lay deep, crisp, treacherous, they got to the cabin on snow-shoes. Annie could not get far from the cabin and began to think of the expression cabin-crazy. But it was still coming. They had hit pay-dirt. Farm, saloon and grocery store were suddenly more than just a glorious possibility. They were going to be rich.

9

It was when the men were busy and preoccupied with the claim that she began writing. At first it was to ameliorate the loneliness. She knew her mother was dead – something deep inside her convinced her of this – and yet part of her still wanted to communicate with the person most dear to her, after Hector; and the stories were partly that, an exercise of the imagination, a way of talking to what she thought of as her mother's spirit or her memory, a way of binding the generations, with herself the link between the past and the future. Somehow it was also a way of keeping track of her identity, of saying who she was in the great white wilderness, of keeping her womanhood in a world dominated by men, their purpose and their will.

Getting enough paper to write on was the problem. She saved anything, old envelopes, invoices, wrappers, journals. Once when Jim saw her scrabbling to smooth out some greasy paper he produced a handsome leather-bound diary with a gold clasp from his carpet-bag and said she could have it. He would never write in it, but she knew he must have treasured it to have carried it about with him. Perhaps it had been a present from his wife. She took it, if with many protestations, gloating over its smooth lined pages and in it, in her curly, careful hand, light strokes up, heavy strokes down, wrote the title *Tales of a Cariboo Woman*. They were all in it, Jim and Sam, Maybelle and Hamish, Pheemie and Effie, everyone she knew, re-named and lightly disguised, pawns in the fascinating game of making life over as fiction. "At your scrieving again," Hector would say indulgently, happy she had found a way of passing the dead hours, and shyly she would close the covers on her work, refusing to let him read any of it, in case by the merest breath of criticism he should kill the tender creative urge. It was private, for her eyes only, some kind of statement of self she did not fully understand.

Sometimes in the evenings they made music. Sam had a small, battered concertina, which he called the squeeze-box and Hector made the mouth-music he had been taught at home. He had perfect pitch and Annie loved to listen to him sing the cornkister or bothy songs he had picked up goodness knows where, from his brothers maybe, nearly all about true loves either betrayed, poisoned or left behind in – to say the least – unfortunate circumstances. Jim, too shy to sing, hummed or tapped his feet.

When Annie sang they had all to be shushed into silence while she got into the right key and the right mood. There would be several false starts while she cleared her throat and la-la-ed or protested she could not remember the words; but when she finally performed it was with power and effect, no wither left unwrung if the song was a sad one, or comic nuance missed if it was amusing. Then there was no stopping her and she would dance, too, remembering the steps Maybelle had shown her, improvising others, and sometimes Hector would hold her in his arms and they would move round the uneven cabin floor together in some restricted version of the minuet or polka.

She was aware then of the simple power women had over men, seeing the respect and admiration in the faces of Jim and Sam, the vague sad longing for what she represented, for what these rough, worn men might never possess again, if indeed it had ever been theirs. It made her kinder towards them, more motherly, more forgiving.

In a strange way, as her belly grew bigger, she and Hector became the parental figures of the small ménage, Sam and Jim the deferential ones who sought advice and reassurance about the future.

The farm she and Hector talked about became the farm of all four, or rather, The Farm, a kind of mythological country they would all inhabit together when the gold was mined, the snows gone and the baby born. Jim made sidelong references to 'coming in' as a partner, for he was convinced Hector would need help on the livestock side while Sam's mind was taken up with designing the buildings that would house them, even down to discussing with Annie on occasion the kind of drapes she should have or the pattern on the 'cheeny cups' she was determined to possess. No more tin mugs! They were to live a life of elegance and style. There were fewer references to the setting up of saloons or grocery stores, even to bringing Jim's wife and child out from England (where, it transpired, they would rather remain). The Farm was a communal interest, a mutual dream they all served to construct.

Annie combed her memory for details of the homes of her maternal relatives before the grandeur had evaporated and of the domain of Henderson the locomotive-manufacturer. She would have a breakfast-room, she told her bemused audience, with a hubble-bubbling – well, *thing* – she thought they called it a percolator – that made hot coffee, and fresh rolls and honey and butter every day. She would have a parlour with turkey-red carpets, a big grandfather clock with pictures of rustic scenes on it, a chiffonier bearing all kind of grand ornaments, a what-not with waxed fruit and glass-fronted book-cases stuffed full of books. Books for reading, at that, not just for ornamentation, at which Sam always looked a shade downcast as he had never learned to read or write.

Jim's mind ran to the garden, the plants he would have sent out from England, asters, gloxinias, lavender, marigolds, pansies, conjured up in a glorious tangle from the cottage where he'd spent his infancy in Devon.

"Sure, it'll be awful grand," Sam would insist with a drawing-in of breath between his teeth, when they had run out of furbelows for the parlour and exhausted the permutations of stock for the stables.

"And I shall have a little jaunting-car," he would add, as a kind of codicil, "and a hard hat and a big cigar." They were tolerant of this, seeing no harm in a little vulgar ostentation when it had been so hard-earned.

In November, the little Irishman went down with what, by common consent, was diagnosed as mountain fever. He was fiercely ill, even delirious, for a week, while Hector and Jim continued the back-breaking task of the keeping the claim workable. Annie's nursing skills, by now, were considerable and once Sam was on the mend, though weak and irritable, she was glad of his company in the cabin, even if he did spit and hawk interminably. She got to know his family history (fifteen assorted brothers and sisters, a roistering wild ma and a da who resorted to petty thievery), his own picaresque adventurings, first as trapper, then as digger, in British Columbia. Even to understand a little the lure of the card game and gambling table for one who wanted to wrest back recompense from a world prepared to offer so little. She saw there had been no tenderness, certainly of the female variety, in his existence, little to help him relate in any but aggressive or retaliatory fashion to his fellow-man. Caring for him, offering some human warmth and guarded sympathy, was, she saw, like putting a meagre bandage on a great festering sore, not a great deal of use. She began to understand more of the nature of loving, how the lack of it stunted, soured, retarded, hardened. Yet something remained in Sam's nature that had not been subverted, an innocence, a kind of incontrovertible merriment, riding through and in and out of the hardness, the conniving, the sometime treachery, the selfishness, the male cruelty. And in those days she knew she won an allegiance from Sam that was something like loving.

When he was well enough to go back to work at the claim, Annie's thoughts moved towards Christmas and the turn of the year. It would be good if they could have some kind of celebration, something other than porridge and greased eggs, treacle scones and barley broth. Supplies were adequate but the need for a little variety was borne on them. It was agreed after some argument that Sam should take the sledge and make the journey to Cottonmill Creek to bring back some liquor for New Year and a selection of whatever comestibles were available. Candles, thread, wool, ink were on Annie's list and Hector privately instructed the messenger to bring back a length of material to make Annie a new gown.

With mighty oaths Jim warned his workmate about his behaviour when he reached Cottonmill. He was to talk to no one about the whereabouts of the claim; he was to keep out of the saloons and ignore the card games. He was simply to do what he had been sent to do and return on the instant. Failure to do so would result in disembowelling, beheading, the cutting off of limbs and mighty kicks up the posterior. Jim's language was such that Annie covered up her ears.

"He has a fortune under the floorboards here," Hector pointed out. "Why would he give the game away?"

"I trust him about as far as I could throw him," Jim glowered.

"Then *you* go to Cottonmill," said Annie.

"He's better on the sledge and snowshoes than me," admitted Jim.

With many utterances of reassurance, Sam at last started out. They watched the small, nimble, fur-clad figure disappear over the snowy horizon with mixed feelings. It was not that the journey was all that far. Or dangerous for one so experienced. Yet they quivered with misgivings and Annie for one could settle to nothing till, as the light ebbed, she saw the trudging figure reappear, a well-loaded sledge behind him. As he reached the top of the hill, he mounted the sledge and rode it almost to the cabin door.

He was exhausted but well pleased with himself and as the others unwrapped the packages it was generally agreed the journey had been a good idea. He had picked up a side of ham, molasses, candy, currants, tobacco, an American mail order catalogue, as well as a length of fine blue velvet material for Annie's gown and a number of other items. The cabin took on, willy-nilly, a festive kind of air and

Annie promised a feast for Christmas Day itself, when the men would only work a few hours during the morning.

"Were you asked any questions?" Jim demanded.

"Nope. 'Cept for the Injun."

"What Injun?" All heads came up as one.

"He come up jest as I was pullin' out. Sez had I heard tell of the Highlander finding gold further up. I sez "What Highlander? I never heard tell of no Highlander," and I gets on my way mighty fast."

"There were Indians at Cottonmill?" demanded Hector.

"Just the one, as I could see. He seemed a doped-out, lazy kind of good-for-nothing. Never fear, I never told him nothin'."

Hector had begun to look thoughtful and when pushed by the others admitted to an unease.

"One Injun," scoffed Jim. "What could he do?"

"It's what he might tell others. He might be one of those I knew, made friends with, but then again he might not ..."

"We'll just have to keep our eyes skinned," said Annie, practically. She was so entranced by her treasure hoard she was not prepared to be worried about anything. Already she was cutting out the blue velvet. Swelling figure or not, she would have a new gown for the Christmas feast, and after the baby was born she could take a few darts in the bodice and who would be any the wiser?

Just the same, for the next few days, like the others, she kept her eyes well skinned and took extra care covering the cabin windows when darkness fell and the candles were lit. Things were going so well, they all lived in superstitious dread it could not continue. The riverbed continued to give up its gold, if anything more readily than ever.

On Christmas Eve, she and Hector stood outside the cabin door, looking up at the bright North Star, while Jim and Sam undertook some rudimentary ablutions inside.

"That must be the star followed by the Three Wise Men," said Annie.

"If you like," agreed Hector, with his arm round her. "I

wonder if it was cold for them, too?"

"Must have been. At night." She shivered lightly. "There's something special about *this* night, Hector. Can you feel it? A waiting. An expectation."

He smiled down at her. "If you say so." He gazed at her glimmering, cold face. "Can you feel the old year fading, too? A year I'll never forget. The year you saved my life."

"Did I do that?"

"Aye, you know you did. I wasn't wrong about you, Annie McIlvanney, the first time I saw you. I knew you were my fate."

"You say that soberly."

"It's a sober thing, making yourself over to another human being. I can believe in God, because of what I feel for you. Is that blasphemous?"

"No, I don't think so. I think it's what the Bible means. We find Him through one another."

"But what I feel for you comes before everything else. I would kill for you, I think. I would die for you."

She put her cold, cold fingers to his face. "Better to live for me, my darling, my jo."

"Annie!" He wrapped his arms around her. They kissed as though they had been apart for months, with a passion that ached like the cold and seemed as vaultless, as unassuageable, as the silent, blue and snowy night.

"We're fit. We're decent," came Sam's voice from the interior. "Come in, the pair of you, before you catch your death."

Before they went back in, he gripped her arm.

"Don't make too much of him."

"Of who?" Although she knew.

"Of Sam. He can't take his eyes off you."

"He's been ill."

"But he's better now."

"Poor old Sam!" she said.

They had wrapped small presents for each other. Annie had

stitched tobacco pouches for Sam and Jim and contrived a pair of mocassins for Hector. She had candy from Jim, a hand-carved candle-holder from Sam and from Hector a huge gold nugget, polished to a beautiful dark sheen, and a tortoiseshell comb he'd secretly instructed Sam to bring back from Cottonmill.

Christmas Day dawned bright, clear, flawless, frozen. While the men worked during the morning, she put a clootie dumpling to boil, got a huge fire going and laid the table. First she served them hot barley broth, then boiled ham with omelette from the greased eggs and finally the pudding, rich and sweet with currants and molasses. She moved, resplendant in the newly-made velvet gown that dipped a little more than it should behind, her splendid auburn hair tied up in ribbons, serving them with the formal dignity the occasion demanded.

She had trimmed Hector's hair and beard and as he carved the ham at the 'head' of the ramshackle table she thought how the work on the claim, the success they'd had, the promise of fatherhood and farm, had settled him, taken away that haunted, febrile look and given him an air of self-possession, of serenity, that touched her to the core of her being, for she knew none of it could have been achieved without her and it was indeed, more blessed than anything she knew, to be a giver.

Even Sam and Jim moved her, their hair slicked down unnaturally smooth, their coarse, purpled hands, covered with dark hair, hacks and cuts and calloused skin, resting at ease on the table in front of them. When they cleared the table, fed the stove, poured the whisky, began to make music, she wept a little, and they were tender and solicitous of her, saying she'd worked too hard, praising her cooking and her gown extravagantly.

After tea, with Annie's version of Scotch black bun, they swopped stories and reminiscences. Under the influence of the drink and the warmth, these grew wilder and more fanciful, Jim and Sam determined to cap each other in every direction, till Hector and Annie, refusing to believe the half of it, fell about in helpless, childish mirth each time Sam said "Did you ever hear tell of ...?" or Jim nodded his sage head and began "Wonst when I sailed to the Panama Isthmus ..." Playing to the gallery, the two rogues produced tales that grew more and more far-fetched until Hector was obliged to place a moratorium on any further yarning, on the twin grounds that further hilarity could bring Annie to premature labour and that some of it – most of it – was now going beyond the bounds of common decency.

The two were not easily silenced, but gradually as the soft ash fell through the stove into the ashcan, the windows were covered and the candles lit. Warm, content, more than a little fuddled, the two men fell asleep in their spruce-layered beds, while Annie and Hector read the Christmas story together from the Bible, before snuffing out the candles and retiring behind their makeshift curtains to their own 'room.'

"Feel," she commanded him, in the darkness. She took his hand and held it to her stomach. He felt something kick against his touch, quite strenuously. It was, he thought, companionable. They touched and stroked each other, delicately at first and then swept up again in a heedless, demanding passion heightened by the happiness and intimacy of the day.

Annie did not fall asleep immediately afterwards. There was just enough light from the stove for her to make out vague, amorphous shadows and she fed into them her own images of Hector, right from the day she'd seen him at Springburn, limping, scared, on the run, through the terrible times of his sickness in the forest, up to the day he'd declared his intent to get her the promised farm and they had set out together on the hunt for gold.

What bounteous fate had restored him to her? There was so much to remember, mull over, treasure. The trek here, the discovery of the cabin, the day she knew for certain about the baby, the arrival of the two who now lay snoring gently at the other side of the cabin. And all that gold! She felt for the polished nugget in her bodice – she had wanted to keep it there, because it was his gift, because it represented so much, his dedication, his commitment. She would never let it go. And one day when the farm was finished, down to the last lace curtain and gilt-lettered conch shell, down to pony-trap and dairy, rocking horse and tea-set, she would have it set on a stand with the inscription underneath: Found near Cottonmill. And would tell her children all that had followed from it.

She was submerged in a formless prayer of gratitude when the sound came. *Wolves*! She would know that sound always, from the moment it had struck bleak terror into her heart on Salt Spring. Strange she had never heard it here before. She placed her hand on Hector's back, but he was soundly, peacefully asleep. Maybe she had imagined it. But there it came again! From far away, no doubt, carried on the clear night air. Poor, hungry creatures. What had driven them from their lair?

It was coming closer. Sounding all the more unearthly and terrifying contrasted with the reassuring rise and fall of Hector's breathing. But she shook him this time, atavistic fear hoarsening her voice: "Hector! Wake up! *Wolves*!"

He listened. It came again. It was as though they were making wide circles, but still some distance away from the cabin. It was unsettling, to say the least. But they would move on, he assured her. She did not think so. She wouldn't be reassured. And soon rumbling from the men's corner indicated they, too, had been woken by the cries.

Big Jim stumbled to his feet, needing to relieve his bladder and declaring his intention, as he opened the door, of seeing how near the devils were. After that, it all happened so quickly it was like speeded-up nightmare. She heard a terrible cry from Big Jim, the cabin door was flung wide open and the cabin was full of movement. She did not know at first it was Indians, simply that it was men. And then she became aware they did not speak like white men. And as the snow-reflected moon threw its light into the cabin she was able to see the forms and, dimly, the faces.

She realised that the high, cleaving noise going through her head was her own screaming. She had jumped to her feet, automatically taking with her the shotgun that never left her side, but someone knocked it out of her grasp and then picked it up. She felt a staggering pain in her head as she was struck by the same shotgun and fell to the ground, grasping at Hector's leg as she did so. She was aware of him starting forward, felt his avenging fury and then the cabin seemed to tilt about her in a frenzy of assault and blows.

"Don't let me faint," she begged the Deity, but she could feel her consciousness ebb and flow. She wanted to scream her husband's name but no sound came. No part of her body obeyed her will. In a way the blackness when it came was very ordinary, like sleep, and she had no option but to give in to it.

When she woke up it was daylight. The cabin door was barely open – broken wood had jammed it – but even so a light powdering of snow had blown inside. She was very cold and her head ached explosively, but she forced herself to sit up slowly and take in the scene around her.

The cabin floor had been wrenched up and the gold was gone. Well, that was what they had come for, creeping through the night from Cottonmill like the grey wolves who had followed them.

"Hector!" she screamed. She rose then, swaying and tottering in her distress and certainty. "Hector!" He was gone. The other two men also. She was alone in the wreck that was the cabin, with evidence of the struggle that had taken place all around her. She put a hand to the wall and touched still-wet blood. "My God," she said, "why hast Thou deserted me?" She could feel the need to escape into unconsciousness rise like a great black beast inside her, but with an enormous effort of will forced herself to calmness. Hector might be lying somewhere, still alive. He would not be taken from her now, when her child would soon be born. Would he?

She moved on stalky legs like someone in a dream, towards the cabin door. A few yards away the body of Big Jim Boulder lay spread-eagled in the snow. Or what the wolves had left of him. The sight was indescribable and made her throw up there and then. The Indians had left his scalp on a post. She stood heaving and shuddering until the world steadied about her: a different world, in a way, perceived as though from a great distance, but with enormous clarity. She moved inside the cabin and closed the door. The stove still had some rosy embers. She fed it with wood and wrapped herself in shawls. She would never get warm again. It did not really matter. But she sat close to the stove because its heat was the only kindness left in the world. When that went, she would die.

She must have fallen asleep, for she woke thinking it was morning, that the porridge should be made; and then the pounding sledge-hammering in her head brought everything back and she retched again, although there was nothing left to bring up. Slowly, slowly, as she raised her head, she became aware of the figure sitting on the other side of the stove. Sam. His face a bruised red and purple, like a horrible 'Hunt the Gowk'*, mask, the eyes fixed on her, but vacantly, the mouth spread in a fearful rictus of a smile.

"Hector?"

He did not answer. She went over to him and shook him with a terrible vigour. "Where is Hector? Where *is* he?" She shook him so hard he fell to the ground. He lay there, while spittle ran out of his mouth and his breath came in great, stentorian gasps. "Don't die on me," she ordered, brutally. Then, more gently, raising his poor head till it lay on her lap, "Did they get him, Sam? Tell me." He tried then to speak, but the words would not come. It came to her he must be suffering from exposure. God alone knew at which point he had returned to the cabin, or how he had escaped

---

* Hallowe'en

the fate of Big Jim. But he alone could tell her what had happened to Hector and so she had to keep him alive, had to get him talking.

With a shaking, dry-mouthed attempt at practicality, she put a folded fur jacket under his head and covered him with the skins from her own and Hector's bed. She fed the stove again, from the pile of logs. She made toddy and dribbled it into his mouth, not knowing whether he swallowed or not. He simply lay there with that dreadful glassy-eyed, smiling look. She knew he was more dead than alive. All she could do was leave him. She knew of nothing else she could do. But she spoke to him, in dreadful scolding tones like some low Glasgow tail. "Die on me ye scunner, and the wolves'll have ye. Ye would let them have my Hector, would ye? Crawl back here while they took my man? I'll have my own judgment on ye, if that proves to be the case. Do ye ken how I loved him? I cam' four thousand mile for him. He was my jo, my darling." And then she screamed and sobbed and lamented and beat her fists against her child in her stomach or on the rickety table or the cabin walls.

Before the light went she wrapped herself up, put on some snow shoes and set off on a search. She could not go far, she was too weak, but she scanned the snow for as far as she could see. There was nothing, neither grey wolf, nor Indian, nor body left in the snow that might be Hector. She trudged back to the cabin, her strength spent. She heated some broth and ate a piece of bannock and her stomach kept the food down. She felt Sam's brow. It was hot and dry. She bathed his face and hands with tepid water and moistened his lips once again with the toddy. Then, her strength totally exhausted, she lay down in the corner she had shared with Hector and sank into an uneasy state halfway between sleep and unconsciousness.

When she woke, it was dark and she covered the windows as usual and lit a candle. She raised Sam's head on her lap once again, gently smoothing his temples. "Sam, poor Sam," she said with infinite resignation. "We are done for.

We are all done for."

"Prisoner," he said. "Hector. Alive."

She gazed down at him unbelievingly. His face had altered in the hours she had been asleep, had lost its frozen-mask-like look and softened into a more normal expression. Sam's eyes were still brilliant, his skin was clammy to the touch, but the hope, the conviction, that he might live, swept through her. She did not know she was weeping as she said his name: "Sam! Are you better?"

"Better," he agreed, weakly. "Water."

She laid his head unceremoniously on the makeshift pillow and quickly offered him the weak toddy she had made the night before. He drank thirstily and asked for tea. She did as he wished, holding back the questions she had to ask. Hector a prisoner? How? Where? In the end her anguished face did it for her. Sam struggled to prop himself up on an elbow.

"I'll try to tell you."

She nodded. "Take your time." She had a terrible patience.

"He saved my life." His voice broke. "They knew him. They said they wouldn't kill him, just take him with them, prisoner. But they were going to do to me – what they did to poor Jim." Sam broke down.

"I don't know how he did it. Talked them into taking me prisoner, too. Except, as I say, they seemed to know him. 'The Highlander.' He couldn't get them to take you, too. He threatened them and I thought we were all done for. They told him you were dead, Annie. I thought so, too. He wouldn't believe it. He struggled, so they tied him up.

"They had a sledge and dogs. They bundled us on to it like parcels of meat, me on top of him. They didn't tie me up, just kicked me."

"Which direction did they go?" "North." Her mind was racing, trying to work out ways of pursuit, ways of rescue. No solution came and she said in desperation, "What else? What else? How did you get away?"

"I fell off into the snow."

"Why didn't the wolves get you?"

"I did it deliberately. Near the claim. Near a tree I knew, that we'd stripped of branches for bedding. I knew I could climb it. The wolves circled round for a while then decided the Indians and their dogs were a better bet."

"But *they* never saw you – the Indians, I mean?"

"They were posting on in too much of a hurry. But Hector saw. He must have done. He'd know I would try to get back to you –"

"You were near dead from exposure."

"Near enough."

"Oh, Sam, what are we going to do?"

"Get you back to Cottonmill –"

"No! I won't leave here. Hector might escape and come back –"

"He's trussed up like a chicken. No likelihood of that."

"I can't!"

"You'll have to. We might get some lawman to go after them Indians. It's our only chance. And you'll need a woman body to help when – when the babby comes. So be a good girl. Sam'll get you there."

"Oh, Sam, if anything has happened to Hector –"

He would not meet her eyes.

"What will they do to him?" she persisted.

He didn't answer. She was trembling uncontrollably. He lay where he was, too weak to move, while she sat working her hands over the bump that was the baby, occasionally giving a sob that seemed to wrack her whole body. But eventually she quietened and they both fell into exhausted sleep. When he woke again she was moving about, seeing to the stove, cooking food. He rose on shaky legs. It was daylight. Bright, calm.

The days, several days, merged into one another as they tried to gather their strength. He could see what ailed her, the not-knowing if or when she would see Hector again, but he did his best to rally her spirits. She grew more gaunt-faced despite his efforts, less able to do anything but the lightest chores. When he was strong enough he broke some more logs for the stove and on the fifth day he dragged poor Jim Boulder's bones and rags behind the cabin.

When he came back, she stood swaying in the doorway.

"Sam, this poor baby's coming. He can't wait any longer."

"You hang on," he said, terrified. "Ain't due for a while yet, is it?"

"When it comes," she ordered, "you wait outside, Sam." She lay down in her bed corner and he could hear her moaning. He said, over the rough partition, "Is there anything I can do?" "You wait outside," she repeated angrily. He paced up and down the floor. As it grew dark, she seemed to rest, even sleep, and he was the one to light the candles and feed the stove.

He heard her say her husband's name. "Hector!" and then there were a series of sounds so urgent and primitive and private he found himself outside the cabin door, in such a state of agitation he scarcely knew what he was doing.

When he went back in again, he could hear scrabbling noises, like a mouse in straw. He peered, willy-nilly, over the partition and saw the baby had been born and that, although it was still attached to the afterbirth, she was trying to lift it on to her chest.

All inhibition forgotten, he pushed the curtain aside and knelt beside her. Her pale face was soaked with perspiration and something else, a realisation that filled his own mind with a desperate pity.

"It's not living, is it?" she appealed to him. "It's a little boy, but he's dead."

He had seen babies born before, he realised. As a child. Year after year to the mother who'd not known, in her own words, how to stop. But none like this. They'd all come fighting and screaming into their awful world.

"I knew," said Annie. "It died the night they took Hector. It never moved after, Sam. Poor little cold baby." She held and rubbed the tiny lifeless purple scrap. "It would have been a William. Leave it with me, Sam, and see to yourself, your meal. I have to sleep, I'm very, very tired."

Gently he covered her and the baby and in the morning cut the dead child's cord and wrapped the infant in a cloth. Then he brought Annie water to wash herself and made her some gruel and tea.

"It is all over," she said. "He is with the angels."

"He was *yours*," he said, from an obscure, retaliatory anger. "You should have had him a while."

"I knew," she said again. "It was the night they took Hector, that did it."

She got up the next day and talked about burying the baby. "I want snow cleared, Sam," she pleaded.

"But underneath the ground is rock hard."

"There's the pile of pebbles, from the river bed. And you can make a little coffin, Sam, and a cross to put his name on. "William Mennock, who did not live a day, or hour."

He humoured her. She was so frail, so gaunt, so transparent, and so insistent on what she wanted done. She was easier once the sad little burial had been completed. "I will bring Hector back," she said, "one day. And show him the spot." And she gave Sam the haunted look that more and more filled him with a superstitious dread. He had to get her back to Cottonmill before it was too late. To womenfolk who would somehow know how to comfort her. He couldn't. He had no words to say, except "Eat" and "Rest" and she would do neither.

It occurred to him to leave her. He wasn't used to being alone with a woman and the complexities of the relationship disturbed and frightened him not a little. He'd come this far without getting himself cornered and he wasn't used to looking out for anyone except himself. He didn't know what tied him, but it was something stronger than self-interest.

When, however, after another couple of days, she still demurred about making the journey to Cottonmill, he used straightforward emotional blackmail and said he would travel alone, leaving her behind. At first she coldly invited him to do so, but then she saw signs of preparation for the journey. He nailed two strong posts and a cross-rail to the sledge, and a sturdy sort of platform, so that she could sit on it in reasonable comfort while he pulled it or rode it on the downhill paths. She was not a heavy burden, he thought. They set out early on the day of their journey. They had to make Cottonmill before the daylight went. He had made the journey for the Christmas supplies, there and back, in one day, but he had been fitter then and able to take risky shortcuts he could not undertake now.

She had filled tins with hot sand from the top of the stove to keep her feet warm and had wrapped two furskins around her. She made him stop for nips of whisky, although when he hit his blank, unthinking stride he refused to do so. He did not like the sound of the wind nor the way the sky closed down with a hint of heavy snow to come. He did not like the heaviness that was invading his legs, nor the weight of his snow shoes, nor the fact that for minutes on end his mind functioned only in a white void of nothingness, so that when a kind of consciousness returned to him he was surprised to find his limbs still moving, for it did not seem to be of his bidding.

At last there was a cry from Annie. "Smoke! I can see the smoke from the Cottonmill lums!" And moments later, she made him stop to look. Cottonmill's huddle of cabins was clearly identifiable, about three miles away, she thought. "Nearly there, Sam," she encouraged. He tried to move the sledge, but couldn't. He fell against it, his cap over his eyes.

She poured neat whisky down his throat. "Sam!" she appealed desperately. "Can't," he said. His eyes appeared blurred. She somehow managed on her watery, tottery legs to drag him on to the sledge. She unloosed his snow shoes and put them on her own feet and put the rope loop of the sledge across her own shoulders and under her arms. She pulled him a little way. The sledge gained its own momentum and for about half a mile she struggled, then could move no further. She looked down at him, but he gave no sign of consciousness. She felt it then, the snow, touching her face almost caressingly, the flakes soft and small and thick. She dropped the rope and shook the man. "Sam, it's beginning to snow. It's thick." If he stirred, it was only fractionally.

She knew she could not pull the sledge much further. She was not sure whether it was actually happening, or whether she heard it in her own mind, but she thought she identified wolf cries and at one moment, peering through the curtain of snow, she thought she saw grey shapes on the edge of the trees that ran down towards Cottonmill.

Someone had been working among the trees, cutting them down and there was a recent pile of neat timber, cut into short lengths for some construction job. She stared. The work must only have been abandoned that afternoon, when the light began to go, for it was only this last powdering of snow that lay on it. She shouted, thinking there might still be some workman nearby, but soon realised it was useless. Her mind was not working clearly. It seemed to her the snow and the whiteness were invading it, and would soon overwhelm her.

She saw the smoke rise from a dying bonfire the workmen must have left and instinctively she dragged the sledge towards it. She took wood from the pile of neat timber and threw it on the fire. It looked at first as though it wouldn't take, but suddenly it did and roared and flamed. Somebody was not going to be best pleased but she kept carrying the manageable timber and throwing it on the flames. Wolves hated fire, didn't they? It would keep them away. She couldn't feel the heat from the fire at first, but then she did, and it was wonderful. She drew the sledge as near the flames as she could and looked to see if Sam felt the warmth. But he was lying in a strange kind of huddle, like a broken scarecrow. She sat on the sledge and leaned her own body over him. Oh, God, she was so very tired. She knew she could not pull the sledge any further. Not another inch. Nor could she feed the fire. The wind howled through the trees and in a white maelstrom of fury the snow suddenly whirled and eddied about them, hissing as it hit the fire.

Hector, she thought. And she saw the baby's grave very clearly in her mind's eye. The pebbles would be covered now. Only the little cross would be visible. 'O cruel death; thou waster severe.' She remembered then, as though they were actually round her neck, the arms of little Aeneas. She had lost him, too. Two babies. It was curious. She was beyond the cold. She felt nothing.

10

"Annie! Sit up and take a sup of this. It'll do you good."

She struggled up from a sensation of ineffable softness, thinking she must have fallen in the snow and that this was what it was like, not cold after all, but wonderfully welcoming. And then she realised she was in a huge feather bed and could discern a snug, well-furnished room with a big fire burning. She must be in heaven, then. How strange, how reassuring! No one had told her it would be as homely as this. If she had to remain here forever, she took no exception to that. She felt no pain, no cold. But where was Hector? Images were streaming back into her mind and she struggled to cast off the smothering comfort. "Hector!" Inside she was screaming the name, she was trying to run, but there was no sound, no movement of limbs. Only a terrible inertia pulling her back on the pillows. She was falling back into the snow, that snow that never stopped coming, that covered poor Sam, that would cover her forever ...

"Annie!" The quiet, insistent female voice came again. "Do you know who it is? It's Maybelle. I'm here, your friend, Maybelle. Take a little broth for Maybelle, will you?"

That was better. She could open her eyes without the room going round, the fire going up to the ceiling, the bed sinking through the floor. She grasped something soft and cushiony that held and steadied her. Maybelle's hand. Oh, it was Maybelle all right. She could see the pink, powdery face, the ringlets, the ample bosom. She smiled weakly, knowing she had to stop struggling, to wait for the answers. Anything else and what little strength she possessed would leave her.

Gently Maybelle held the spoonful of broth to her lips. It was delicious. She took several sips before she closed her eyes again and rested. Then the questions marched in more orderly procession into her mind. She opened her eyes. "Where am I? How did I get here? Where's Sam?"

"You're in the minister's house in Cottonmill. The Reverend Darroch, from Glasgow. They saw the bonfire you lit and three men struggled through the snowstorm to reach you. You were almost a goner —"

"And Sam?" She knew the answer already. Maybelle avoided her eyes.

"Sam didn't make it, did he?"

"Sam's dead, Annie." The cushiony grip tightened.

"He —" She wanted to tell Maybelle about Sam, how difficult and sly and lying he could be; how he and Big Jim had moved in on the claim; how he had looked at her sometimes as no man should look at a spoken-for woman; and how noble and sacrificial he had been on the last journey, prepared to lay down his life so that she could get to Cottonmill.

"He was an ordinary little digger," she said. It wasn't how she had meant it to come out at all and yet that was the point. What he had been capable of, despite being ordinary and sometimes wicked. Was meek the same as ordinary? Did God love Sam, in the end? He must have done. He'd said the meek would inherit the earth.

Maybelle gave her head a shake. "They found Hamish's name and address among your things and sent word to him at

Barkerville. He asked me if I would come. And I did. Two days ago. I wouldn't let you slip away. You've a lot more harm to do in the world, my girl. A fighter like you! Why, it's only morning with you yet. Now, a little more broth and then you can sleep."

It was one thing for Maybelle to talk about fighting. There was this terrible lethargy that flowed like a slow river through her consciousness and sometimes, surfacing like nightmares, the memories of what had happened at the cabin. The Reverend Darroch and his wife, recently moved to the Cariboo, sat with her when Maybelle was absent, soothing when her tormented thoughts made her toss and turn, diverting her with talk of home, gently guiding her mind towards the future, to going back to Barkerville.

When she mentioned Hector all their faces assumed the same expression, or lack of it. They told her a law search had been put out for the Indians, but she didn't believe them, she knew the uselessness of it, in a country that belonged to the tribes long before the white man had set foot in it. They thought Hector had been murdered, were convinced of it. Had been thrown to the wolves. She read their eyes, not listening to the words that came out of their mouths. But they were wrong. She did not tell them so, because she didn't want to force them into a corner where they would have to argue their convictions. She simply wanted to tend this tiny, wavering, stubborn flame that was hope, that the merest breath could put out, the merest word extinguish. Without it, she too would be extinguished. Was near enough to it, to know what the word meant.

Nursed with great tenderness and concern by Maybelle and the Darrochs alike, she soon began to regain her physical strength and the day came when the occasional coach arrived to take the two women back to Barkerville over rough and ready tracks. "Dr. Diet. Dr. Quiet and Mr. Merriman," as the whimsical Reverand Darroch had suggested, had done their work.

"I never envisaged coming back to Barkerville as poor as

when I set out," Annie mused.

"They took everything. Overlooked nothing?" asked Maybelle.

"Only this." Annie produced the gold nugget Hector had given her at Christmas, from her reticule. "And I'll never part with it. This is for the mantelshelf on the farm Hector and I will have one day –" Her voice trailed off as she saw the pity in Maybelle's face and hastily she stowed the nugget away again, resolutely turning her gaze towards the landscape.

Hamish had grown thinner and greyer in her absence and his greeting could not be read as other than constrained.

"If you're coming back here, you'll need to work." He laid it on the line. "The saloon went down after you left."

"When have I not worked?" Annie demanded. The tartness in her voice was enough to restore eye contact between them and to her dismay she saw the depth of hurt in his. She said, more gently, "Hamish, I have no place else in the world to go. But if you don't want me back –"

"I never said that." He was more offhand, wary, than before, but she did her best to please him. Restoring the brass, cooking mutton pies, washing the curtains, was good medicine for her. She fell into bed exhausted at night. For two weeks she thought of nothing else but work and bed and making restitution for the wrong Hamish fancied she'd done him by going away in the first place. Perhaps there would never be total trust between them again. It saddened her, but it could not be helped.

She was not eating much. All the curves had left her figure and she was all elbows and angles. She who had always been fussy and a little vain about her clothes did not much care how she looked, so long as she was neat.

The story of her misfortunes had gone round Barkerville and there was no shortage of sympathisers. Even the Celestials gazed at her with concern as she walked past the Freemasons Temple, which served as their community centre, court, medical clinic, you name it – or past Trapper

Dan's cabin, a kind of home or hospital where elderly Chinese came to die. Once she thought she saw Soo Lin come out of the former, but the girl quickly turned her head away and did not appear to wish to make contact.

She thought she might go to Alec Comrie about her general feeling of apathy and listlessness, (no, it was more than that, it was despair), but she could not be bothered. She didn't want to 'come out of it,' as Maybelle kept urging her to do. She wanted to mourn the baby and Sam and to go over and over in her mind, unhindered by the sceptical, the permutations of what might have happened to Hector.

Eventually she went to see the young editor of the *Cariboo Sentinel* to persuade him to run a story:

"The wife of a miner abducted by Indians from his claim, several miles out of Cottonmill, begs readers of this journal for any word that might give her hope that her husband is still alive.

"Hector Mennock, known as 'the Highlander,' was taken prisoner during the attack in which one workmate died. Mrs. Mennock was left for dead and as many readers will know, survived a trek to Cottonmill thanks to the efforts of another miner, Mr. 'Irish Sam' McCleary, who expired in the snowy wastes just before the point of rescue. A child born to Mrs. Mennock gave up its frail breath to the Northern wastes.

"Despite the heavy snows reported north of Cottonmill, the direction in which the Indians are thought to have gone, Mrs. Mennock, who has returned to work for her husband's cousin, Mr. Hamish McLennan, in Barkerville's respected *Last Chance Saloon*, is convinced her husband may still be alive and lives in hope of seeing him again.

"She begs any trapper or other traveller who may have information to get in touch via the editor of this organ."

It wasn't much, but the mere effort of doing something, or the illusion of it, fanned the dying flame of courage in her and that evening she sat down with Hamish and ate her first relished meal for months.

Maybelle was quick to notice the difference next time they met. She had laid out a tray supper in her hopelessly cluttered little parlour and watched with a growing satisfaction as Annie disposed of the food.

"Do I see a return of your old spirit?" she vouchsafed gently.

Annie gazed at her friend unsmilingly.

"Maybelle," she speculated. "I liked it in John McClaren's office at the *Sentinel*. I wish I could have been a journalist. What he does all day is write. I'd like that."

"Maybe you could be one."

"I haven't McLaren's lettering. He was a headmaster before he came here."

"But he might take articles from you."

"Do you think so?"

"I could ask him, next time he comes into the saloon. Matter of fact, he might be over at the *Bella Union Saloon* tonight. Fannie Bendixen is bringing in some hurdy-gurdy girls from 'Frisco. Why don't you get dressed up and come with me? It's high time you took off that long face."

"I have to make some money, in case Hector comes back." She stared at Maybelle's protesting denying face till the other looked away. "Hamish pays me nothing nowadays. Says he can't afford it."

"Miserable old blackguard. Leave him. Come and work here. I'll ask the boss —"

"No." Annie was definite. "The *Last Chance* is where Hector will come looking for me."

"Annie." Maybelle's voice was rough and hard. "It's time you disabused yourself of thoughts that Hector will come back. Tell yourself he's gone. Else it's going to go on eatin' at you and eatin' at you till it eats you all away."

The still-thin, pale face had hardened. "We will *not* speak about it. I'm not *listening* to you —"

"We shouldn't aim to fall out," said Maybelle, at once conciliatory. "Come to the *Bella Union* with me, do. It'll take you out of yourself. And I have to size up the opposition.

These hurdy girls are different from my girls, you know, or the other dancin' girls in town."

"In what way?" Annie was interested in spite of herself.

"They've got a 'Boss Hurdy,' who signs them up and makes a fortune out of 'em before he lets them go. They're mainly Dutch or German and don't speak no English. Still and all, the whole town's talking about them and they'll all be over at the *Bella Union* to see 'em tonight."

"I'll come then," said Annie, decisively. In spite of everything, Barkerville's liveliness and vigour was reaching out to her and she realised how much she had missed its fun and excitements.

As she dressed in her bedroom, she felt as gauche and unprepared as a fifteen-year-old. She could not bear to wear the blue velvet gown and besides, it would need adjustment before she wore it again, but her serviceable grey with its tiny jet buttons was perhaps in any case more suitable. She stared at her face. Could this whey-faced creature be the Annie who had journeyed to the claim beyond Cottonmill, carrying the happy burden of her love in her womb? Or the Annie who had sung on Christmas Day to a rapt audience of three? Well, it was foolish to stare too long. She saw the tears climb up the stalks that were her eyelashes and dashed them away. She was glad then of Maybelle's planned diversion. She clung to that diversion like a drowning woman might cling to a ship's wreckage.

As she came downstairs, Hamish was setting up a card school with a few faithful customers. She had been through an earlier catechism with him when she told him her intentions. "You can't go to the *Bella Union*." He had been adamant. "Why not?" "If you don't see why not, I'm not for telling you." She had known then something had hardened in her. She was not prepared to be dictated to by anybody. She had to live her life. *Her* life. Now Hamish gave her a glowering look. She passed him with studied unconcern. She was no longer any kind of child, looking for approbation.

At the *Bella Union* everything was music and rowdy animation. The hurdy fiddlers were in a class of their own as far as making a noise was concerned, but it was impossible not to rise to the insistent gaiety of their strings. The 'boys,' that was to say the miners, had come in from all over Williams Creek, faces shining with soap and anticipation. Maybelle and Annie gawped at the new girls with honest curiosity.

They had a certain alien attractiveness and as they pointed their toes and arched their insteps made it clear they had been *trained* in the terpsichorean art, as the *Sentinel* grandly called it. Their 'boss hurdy' had put them into uniform, cotton print skirts with red sashes and a half-mourning headdress resembling in shape the top-knot of a male turkey.

Maybelle gave an irrepressible giggle. "Did you ever see anything like them?" But as the evening wore on it became clear the 'boys' were greatly taken with the newcomers and the dancing took off in fine style. The main new feature seemed to be to see how high a girl's partner could hoist her at the end of a 'figure,' which he did with a straightforward lift or by raising her, back to back, while she peddled air. 'Like a ring of bells in motion' was how Barkerville's hawkeyed newssheet was to describe it. Glumly Maybelle admitted by the end of the evening that the newcomers were bound to take away custom from her own more decorous and old-fashioned saloon.

"I wish I could find some new girls with a bit of style. I could train them if I could find them."

"Could you train me?"

Maybelle gave a whoop. "D'you mean it?"

"For pay."

"Of course."

"Then I mean it."

Covertly, Maybelle studied her young friend's face. There was, she thought, a new hardness in it. Annie had changed from the fresh-faced youngster who had come in the coach to Barkerville with her into a steely young woman whose determination to go forward had an edge of desperation to it that frightened Maybelle. It was despicable of Hamish McLennan to pay her nothing, but then she heard he'd been gambling heavily all the time Annie was away and no doubt he spoke the truth when he said he couldn't afford wages. She would have to keep an eye on the girl: place her alongside Gerda, perhaps, who was skilled in gentle flirtation that never went beyond the promise of more, that extricated gifts from the generous, without strings. But Annie had always enjoyed dancing and had a natural aptitude for it. She'd be an asset and the diversion would be good for her, as well as providing her with a little money.

She gave Maybelle her new, glimmering, nervous smile, the one that didn't reach her eyes and said, "And I want to meet the *Sentinel* editor again. You said you'd put in a word for me. He's over there."

"I can't promise anything, but I'm prepared to read. Don't ramble. Keep to the point." Young McLaren was amused at Maybelle's sponsorship and by the sudden flush of animation on Annie's pale face. But then many ladies thought they could write – as did many men – and found when they got down to it inspiration escaped them.

She took the first of her *Tales of a Cariboo Woman* in to the *Sentinel* office a week later. When he'd read it the editor sent for her.

"How did you learn to write like this?"

"By reading."

"What do you read?"

"Anything I can get my hands on."

"I can't use it." He threw it across the desk at her. "But I know someone in San Francisco who publishes a story magazine. I think he might buy it."

"Why won't you?"

"Too long. Too sentimental. Watch out for the truth."

"Feelings are truth."

"Be more detached."

"I'll do it my way, or not at all."

He looked at her flushed face, the sparkle of intelligence in the eyes. Pity about the squint, yet it was endearing enough in its way. It was a face full of challenge and uncertainty and he found himself moved by it.

"I'll give you the publisher's name. Good luck."

"I don't need luck. I'm *determined*. That's enough."

"I hope so," he said, amused again.

The estrangement between herself and Hamish did not lessen in the days to come. He glared at her when she went out in the evenings to Maybelle's, referring to it as "that brothel," hissing that she'd come to no good. When she worked in the *Last Chance* during the day, he passed her without smile or recognition. It was a sore point with her that he wouldn't allow her to take on anyone to replace Soo Lin, because then she could have re-opened the 'laundry,' but he'd never been keen on that, thinking it somehow degraded the saloon's status.

He wouldn't risk another like Soo Lin, he said, uncharitably. Look how she'd turned out. Living with the doctor now, having his bairn and causing the poor man to be ostracised by all the decent folk in the town. Annie hadn't known about the baby and even she was shocked, although she wouldn't let Hamish see it.

The day came when Annie had had enough of his bad temper.

"You're full of criticism of other folk," she challenged him, as she served him what she knew to be a tasty supper and saw him give it a look that was enough to turn the milk sour. "But you've let sinch and euchre take over your life. Sitting up to all hours! A man with your delicate health. Gambling's going to be the death of you, Hamish McLennan."

"Much you care. We had a good business here, before you saw fit to take off into the wilds –"

"I *do* care! I work as hard as ever for you and then in they come every night, Paddy Downey, Pete Anderson, Jock

McAvoy, and you're off again. Can't you see they're practised rogues?"

"They're my business." He turned his back on her. He was getting old and cantankerous, behaving like a spoiled child. She bit back her impatience and served him some fruit pie, the crust the way he liked it, well browned, and watched with wry amusement as he ate the lot.

The potboy at Maybelle's place, a hard-working young Negro called Leroy, usually saw her home on the nights she went dancing, on Maybelle's instructions. The lad was relating some anecdote about a stone-throwing competition – his favourite pastime – as they approached the *Last Chance* one evening, when Annie drew back in alarm, holding the boy's arm. A figure had just come sailing, head first, through the saloon doors, landing face down on the sidewalk, then there was a loud crashing sound and a bottle came through one of the windows. From inside came shouts and oaths and every indication that the saloon furniture was in the process of being broken up, not to mention some of the customers.

Without pausing for thought, Annie tore through the door. Hamish was half-sitting, half-lying against the bar, blood trickling from a cut on his forehead. All around him the battle waged, with men bringing saloon chairs crashing down about each other's heads and shoulders and others swapping punches or wrestling. Glass and broken wood covered the floor and the scene behind the bar was one of indescribable chaos. She knew it had happened in other saloons. Never before in the *Last Chance*.

"Stop it!" she screamed at them. When she wasn't heard, she stood on top of the counter, ringing a big brass ship's bell that Hamish had brought back from his travels till the sound rode over everything else. When they stopped and turned to look, one by one, she shouted, "Do you want to end up in the hoosegow? 'Cos the law is just coming down the street. Get the hell out of here, all of you, 'fore I get my gun."

Something about her stopped them in their tracks. She had picked up a bottle and was brandishing about her head like a knout. They saw a virago who was prepared to stop at nothing. The bit about the gun had the ring of truth, even if the mention of the law hadn't. One by one they relinquished chair legs or bottles or whatever they had found handy, one by one they straightened their clothes and shame-facedly shambled to the door. One or two even murmured apologies. She saw the last one out then turned the lock in the door, her legs suddenly like jelly. She walked over to Hamish, who groaned when she knelt down beside him. The cut was quite deep and the blood had run into one eye, giving him a gruesome appearance.

"What happened?"

He could not answer her. She put her arm under him, wishing Leroy had not high-tailed it back to Maybelle at the first hint of trouble. It was a struggle, getting him to his feet, but she finally managed it and installed him in the luggie chair by the stove. She got water and bathed the cut and the eye. She did not like the look of him. His face was ashen, his breath short and shallow.

All her anger fled and was replaced by concern.

"Hamish, let me get the doctor."

"No. Be all right."

She put his feet up on a footstool and covered him with a blanket. She chafed his hands, gave him sips of water. At last he seemed to feel better and tried to tell her what had happened. It had started out with an accusation of cheating, progressed to arguments about gambling debts.

She shook her head at him. "I've tried to tell you."

She had never seen tears in his eyes before. "Annie, I'm finished."

"Only if you think you are," she scolded.

"The saloon's wrecked. They won't give me any more liquor —"

"I'll talk to them. I'll borrow some chairs. I'll clear up."

In the days to come, she did it all. Hamish retired to his

bedroom, where before her eyes he seemed to shrink into a little, beaten old man, a child who wanted her attention. By offering to pay a little each week, she got the liquor firm to agree to continue limited supplies. Maybelle let her have a few rough chairs and a rickety table. The *Last Chance*, it seemed, was living up to its name. It had a sick and sorry air and only a few customers who did not seem to know the road to any other saloon still foregathered there of an evening.

"It's yours, when I'm gone," said Hamish, daily.

"If I want it," she would return, grimly. "It's fit nowadays for neither man nor beast."

"It's all written down," Hamish persisted. "It's yours. Everything's yours."

She let everything else go, the dancing, the stories (three of which had been sent to San Francisco), the baking, to sit with him. He refused to see the doctor, saying there was nothing he could do.

He seemed to want to talk of nothing but his childhood days in Scotland, remembering with a lyric clarity that drew her into it everything that had happened to him then. She didn't mind: the clan loyalties, the ceilidhs, the tradition of medical knowledge, the love of music and dancing, the hospitality extended to strangers, the whole strange, proud Highland story, had belonged to Hector as much as to Hamish and brought her darling close to her. Now, in their restored intimacy he allowed her to talk about Hector without displays of petty jealousy. She was able to tell him that a party of volunteers sanctioned by the police commissioner had set out to hunt the Indians and bring them to justice, adding "I don't care about justice, Hamish, I just want Hector back." And then her tears had wet the back of his frail but comforting hand. It was the hand that told her his mortal span was ending. When she lifted it, it and the arm were all bone and paper skin. Mortally heavy. Mortally inert. She was with him when he died. She was sitting by the window, sewing, when she heard him sigh.

Then she turned and knew by his look of infinite peace that he had gone to Tir-Nan-Og, back to the land of his childhood, the Land of the Apple Trees.

She sat twisting the fur cap between her hands in the back room of the *Last Chance*, with Maybelle rocking broodily in the old chair that had been Hamish's. It was eight days since the funeral, for which most of Barkerville had turned out. And she had just had a formal visit from the new gold commissioner and magistrate himself, the respected Irishman, Chartres Brew.

At last Maybelle burst out, "A lot of Cariboo men die young. They fall down lift shafts, or get the mountain fever, or die from working in the cold and wet –"

She did not appear to hear Maybelle. Still twisting the cap between her hands, she said, almost musingly, "Hamish called them the Argonauts. Those who come here to search for gold.

"That was the name they gave them, the *Sentinel* still does. Those who searched for the golden fleece. It's Greek mythology."

Maybelle leaned over and put her hands over her friend's restless ones, stilling them. "Whatever Hector was looking for, tell yourself he has found it. Let him rest with his Maker. That was the commissioner's advice. To me he seemed a man who could be trusted. A good man. He took the trouble to come and see you himself."

Again Annie gave the impression that she'd heard nothing. "It's Hector's cap, all right. See here – this is the flap that got burned when he left it near the stove."

Maybelle shifted in her chair. "Annie," she repeated softly, "let him rest."

"The commissioner said they'd found the tracks eventually, of the Indians who took him. But they thought there had been a battle between the abducting Indians and the Bella-Bella and if I know the Bella-Bella, they won, which means they would take over the prisoners."

"Or despatch them."

"Hector had friends among the Bella-Bella. I know they're supposed to be the most warlike. But the time he lived in the woods, before I found him, he told me he saved one of them from being mauled by a bear and they made him some kind of blood brother."

"It sounds like a tale he might have made up."

Annie blushed. "Hector wasn't like that. I know I discounted some of the things he said about that time, because he had been ill and the fever had made him delirious. But he always did have a lot of sympathy for the Indians."

"Well, they have little with the white man. I saw what they did to the whites in the Fraser river and the floods did the rest. I'll never forget it. I don't like to do this to you Annie, but I got to. You got to accept that your man is gone. The Cariboo eats up young men like a bear eats honey."

Annie rose and carefully put the cap away in a drawer of the chiffonier, a strange and tender little smile on her lips.

"You got to think about the future. What you gonna do with the *Last Chance*. At least that miserable old goat did the right thing and left it to you."

"With its debts."

"Sell it and go back to Victoria. Or Salt Spring, to that decent farmer you told me about, who wanted to marry you. Go back to him and give him some sons."

"I would like to see little Aeneas again," Annie admitted. "But you should get one thing straight, Maybelle. I'm staying in Barkerville. I'm staying in the *Last Chance*. And I've got a proposition to make to you. I lay in bed thinking it all out last night and I hope you'll hear me through."

"Fire ahead."

"How much do you like your present position?"

"It's all right. I make a living. You could say I'm comfortable."

"But you're not your own boss."

"True."

"And you could be. You could come in with me here, we could do the place up real nice, make it a proper dancing place, just *dancing* and entertainment, out with the card schools, let them find some place else. We could give the *Bella Union* and the German hurdy girls something to think about. We could be high-class. What do you say?"

"I would say you got a nerve. Who would provide the wherewithal to do it up? To hire the girls?"

"You would have to provide some of it. And maybe the bank would give us a loan. I'm willing to try for it. I can build up the restaurant and baking side —"

"That would take time."

"You could have a free hand with the decorating, the drapes, the furniture, the girls' clothes. You've got taste, coming from 'Frisco, you're a cosmopolitan woman. Between us we could show Barkerville what's what."

"You're talking about a little old mining town, when all's said and done."

"The gold's still there. It still comes in. The boys still want ways to spend it."

Maybelle looked at once pensive and flustered. She sipped the tea Annie made her, then at last placed the cup back in its saucer with a decisive flourish.

"Hamish wouldn't like it."

"Hamish never looked life in the face. I do. I'm not afraid."

"You're on. Just one thing, I ain't so young as I used to be, so you gotta be the one who goes out there at night and makes things go. I'll be right behind you."

"I knew you'd do it!" Annie rose and kissed her friend impulsively.

"I'd do anything to see that fighting light back in your eyes, my girl. I've got real fond of you. You could be a daughter to me. Never had one of my own, though I own I'd have liked it."

"What colour do you think for the dresses?"

"Dainty colours. Real dainty. None of that black and red

stuff they have at the *Bella Union*. I want my girls to look like flowers, in pink and purple and blue. And when we can afford it, I'll bring some new girls in from the Bay City."

"I thought lace cloths for the dining tables. And we could have flowers to match what the girls wear. And a waiter wearing gloves."

"Wait a minute. We gotta walk before we run. There's a saloon out there needs scrubbing out, for a start."

"No harm in dreaming." Annie rose and lit the lamp and the small cosy room flared into life. "More tea?" The wag-at-the-wa' clock ticked its sonorous, even rhythms and the sketch of the late Hamish, executed by an artistic drunk in lieu of payment, stared down bemusedly as the women talked and planned.

At length Maybelle said, with a note of puzzlement, "You seem mighty composed, Annie. Not that I ain't glad to see it. You've taken the commissioner's visit real well."

"He *isn't* dead, Maybelle. Hector isn't dead. Whatever you may say. I had the strangest feeling, handling the cap. As though it was sending me some kind of message."

"If it comforts you to think it, go right ahead," said Maybelle. "But you gonna have to face the truth one day, my girl."

When Maybelle finally rose to go, Annie helped her into her cloak and bonnet and then laid a detaining hand on her arm.

"Are you sure you want to come in with me? That I'm not rushing you?"

"Maybelle Macbride has never been known to go back on a bargain."

"You won't regret it, Maybelle."

"I never regret nothing. One thing I've learned, regrets is useless. I'll be round tomorrow, help you clean up."

Two days later, a letter came from the editor of the magazine in San Francisco, saying he liked Annie's first three *Tales* and offering her forty dollars a time. He also asked for more. Annie could not believe her luck. She showed the letter to Maybelle, who regarded it as a good omen. The bank came up with a loan and the materials for drapes and dresses were soon on their way from Victoria. Even the Celestials found excuse to wander down from Chinatown to have a look at the refurbishing *Last Chance*, painted outside in black and gold, with gold-corded crimson curtains at the windows. *Style*, said Maybelle, with satisfaction, was what it was all about. And she and Annie rubbed ointment on their poor hacked hands nightly, for style was hard work and an infinite capacity for taking pains.

Part Three

11

"Mornin' there, Madam Annie."

"Mornin'." Annie civilly returned the greeting of the man who had tipped his hat to her as she strode down main street to the bank. He had been at the ball last night at the *Last Chance*, the first spring ball and the third they had held since the saloon had reopened. Like the others, it had been a resounding success, with 'boys' coming in from all over the goldfield to see the four new girls Maybelle had imported from the Bay City; with good food, nobody overdoing the drink and passable music from the 'orchestra' of five which Maybelle had insisted on having instead of hurdy fiddlers.

But the girls in their gauzy dresses, carefully schooled by Maybelle and herself, had been the crowning glory of the evening. So loudly enthusiastic had the male onlookers been that often the poor girls had scarcely been able to hear the music, never mind keep to the figures of the dances. But it had all been very good-natured, and only towards the end had some of the 'boys' got a little out of hand, throwing their partners a shade too high and too roughly. It had been a shrewd stroke of Maybelle's to bring on the young female singer then, singing ballads that had the more sensitive of the males crying into their beer. In fact, Annie now thought, they should probably have more entertainers at the *Last Chance* – she herself liked magical turns and dramatic recitations of the works of the Cariboo poets, like James

Anderson, and she had heard of a troupe of Chinese acrobats who would be something of a novelty.

She had every reason to feel well pleased. A pale but welcome sun shone on her new mauve gown and fur tippet, her feet were encased in a splendidly fashionable pair of new boots and her little velvet hat, nestling on top of her massed curls, had veiling falling away behind, giving her, she felt sure, the regal and commanding air befitting a leading business citizen of Barkerville. Besides, she was on her way to pay off the last of the loan from the bank.

"Mrs. Mennock." The manager shook her warmly by the hand, saw that she was comfortably seated and offered her a glass of fine Madeira. "I hear that business is going well."

"You should know so, Mr. Allan," she returned, with a small smile. "Did I not see you among the throng last night, admiring our new girls?"

"You may have done," Mr. Allan conceded. The slightly priggish young married man had gone a bright pink. "And very pleasant it all was, too. I hope you might have a few minutes to spare me, for I have a proposition to put to you."

She sipped the wine composedly and indicated he could go ahead.

"You know there has been a big new strike outside Cameronton. Backed up properly with men and machinery, to go down as far as need be. It involves a number of our fellow countrymen who, I may say, are well taken with the amenities you are providing for the town. The long and short of it is, they would like to invest some of their gold in the hotel business and have put it to me you might wish to build on, expand."

"I would have to consult my partner, Miss Maybelle MacBride."

"Of course. It goes without saying, I have the greatest respect for both of you. But think of it, pray. With proper financial backing, the *Last Chance* could be just the first of a chain of such places, throughout the whole of British

Muckle Annie

Columbia. Throughout Canada, when we join the new self-governing Dominion, as we assuredly will in the next year or two."

Annie expelled a long breath. "It sounds a bit – well, grandiose, Mr. Allan."

The young banker shook his head. "Railway hotels, Mrs. Mennock. You can't begin to think what a future there is there, now that the war's over in America and they can't lay the rails fast enough there – or here. Once we get established in British Columbia, railway hotels would be our concern."

"That's all going a bit too far for me."

"Well, of course, all you need concern yourself about for the moment is whether you wish to expand your business here. But I feel your advice might well be valued in the future, also, in the matter of style, furnishing, the engagement and training of staff in other establishments. In these matters, we men have to bow to your obviously superior wisdom."

Annie blushed. "I'm flattered to be asked."

When she found herself back on the sidewalk, Annie walked back towards the *Last Chance* in something of a mental haze. She trusted young George Allan implicitly. He had always seemed to her to balance sharpness with total probity. If he painted a future of golden opportunities, then she was inclined to believe the picture. Sometimes she herself had felt the *Last Chance* required replanning and extension – and now here was the opportunity to do it handed to her on a plate. It seemed as though Fate, so cruel to her in the matter of Hector, was trying to placate her in every other area of her life. She had sold three stories, she and Maybelle had made a good start to their partnership and now she was being given a gilt-edged chance to make, possibly, a good deal of money. Already she was planning the kind of clientéle they would have once the *Last Chance* had some bedrooms – the kind of men who brought money and machinery to the goldfields in order to take more out. The planners, financiers, those with a vision of what the land could be.

She knew she babbled a bit when she tried to put this over to Maybelle. Her friend was never quite at her best in the mornings, keeping to her room where the little maid brought her a light breakfast, until she appeared around noon, well laced-up, her hair carefully coiffed, a change of gown daily, rings, necklaces, earrings on display. She was then quietly efficient at deploying the small staff, at keeping accounts, at seeing tradespeople.

She was cautious. "We're doing well enough as it is. All we want is an honest crust. And a diamond or two." Her laugh rang out. "Don't you agree?"

Annie turned to face her. "I want the farm," she said quietly. "I want to be back in the position we were in before the Indians took it all from us. The Cariboo owes it to me, one way or another."

"Sometimes," said Maybelle mildly, "you sound – not exactly hard, honey –"

"Determined." Annie said it lightly. She pushed up her sleeves. "Now I've got to do the baking."

"You work too hard. You ought to leave some time for pleasure."

It was not exactly pleasure Annie took out of life in the months to come, but there was satisfaction in making things work, in being so involved that sleep came the moment her head hit the pillow. She met the businessmen George Allan had talked about – Maybelle opted out – and with them agreed on plans for enlarging the *Last Chance*, plans she quickly saw through. They came to her when similar enterprises were undertaken within a radius of some fifty miles and sometimes she would have to leave the *Last Chance* in Maybelle's hands while she supervised the setting up of those new restaurants and hotels.

When she began to earn quite a bit of money, George Allan advised her on her investments. Quickly she learned how money could make money. And for relaxation she wrote her *Tales* when the inspiration took her. Mainly she tried to write about the women of the Cariboo, for the men, the 'Argonauts,' were already celebrated in song and story. But the women had shared in the legend – women like Elizabeth Barker, the merry London widow who married the man who had given Barkerville its name then left him when the saloon keepers had taken all her husband's money. Women like Sophie, wife of 'Cariboo' Cameron. When she died of the mountain fever, 'Cariboo' wanted her coffin transported back to Victoria and his partner undertook the hellish task in 40-below weather, taking 36 days. Cameron had offered money but the partner had done it 'not for gold.' It seemed the world at large were hungry for such tales. The Cariboo, despite the reality which was cold, fever, accident and 'slum,' the oozing mud, had acquired a kind of romantic ambience and the public could not have enough of it.

Maybelle kept up her litany about Annie working too hard. She did not like the way in which flesh refused to settle on her bones. She did not like the febrility with which she sometimes conducted her affairs. Sometimes, because Annie was busy, abstracted, irritable, the two friends fell out. But occasionally they managed to have a quiet evening meal together, when the two women opened their hearts to each other as to no one else. Maybelle would talk of her Jamie – it had given her great pleasure when she had enough money to erect a grand stone to his memory in Richfield Town Cemetery. And Annie, carefully skirting round the actual question of whether Hector could still be alive or not, because it upset them both so much, would recollect the happy days in the cabin, or talk of little Aeneas back in Salt Spring, how fast he must be growing, what he must now be like.

"If only your own little William had lived." Maybelle understood very well then why Annie had to fill her days with activity. The girl's face was luminous with pain. But talking seemed to help a little. That, and the passing of time and the learning of acceptance, as Maybelle well knew. "We must do as things do with us," she would say, but once

Annie had replied with her hands over her stomach as though over an interminable ache, "I want a child, Maybelle. I *still* want Hector's child. You'll never understand."

"But I do."

"How can you?"

"Do you think you are the only one to bring a child to birth, and lose it?"

"You never told me. Jamie's?"

"Jamie's."

"Forgive me." Annie looked deeply contrite. "What worries me –"

"Well, go on!"

"What worries me is I'll never be able to have another, if Hector ... I was kicked – there – and that was why the baby was born dead. I feel pain there every month."

"You should see a doctor, then."

"Who is there to see? I only trust Alec Comrie but from all accounts he doesn't see patients any more."

"You mean, the patient's don't go to him. He scandalised them, taking that Celestial to his bed."

Not long after this conversation, Annie saw Soo Lin come out of the Chinese Freemasons' Lodge. She had a toddler by the hand and appeared to be on the point of having another child. She did not look happy, but wan and downtrodden.

"Soo Lin." Something made her confront the girl. She smiled down at the little boy, who turned his face away in shy confusion.

"Mis' Annie."

"How is the doctor?"

"He is not very well." Soo Lin's face was unsmiling. "He is in a very bad way. Have you any money you can give me? He likes whisky."

Affronted by the direct begging, Annie nonetheless felt in her purse and gave the girl five dollars.

"Tell him I will come and see him."

"Nobody else comes. Why should you?"

Muckle Annie

"Soo Lin —"

But the girl had already turned on her heel and was making for the town's outskirts. Annie guessed she had been in some begging mission to the Lodge — with little sympathy from the whites, she had to fall back on her own kind. But what about Alec? Who could he turn to? It was difficult. She felt Soo Lin's hostility as a palpable presence whenever she was near her. But perhaps that should not let her stop seeing Alec.

"Why have you come?"

Soo Lin's greeting was no less chilly than on their previous meeting. But Annie had made her mind up that she would overcome the girl's intransigence. She smiled at Soo Lin graciously and stepped over the threshold of the cabin. But before she did so, she pointed out how the brass plate bearing Alec's name and qualifications needed cleaning. "I'll show you how, Soo Lin," she promised. "We must get those patients coming back to Dr. Alec."

"He has told me he doesn't want to see you."

"What? An old friend like me? That I can't believe." Alec had obviously erected a surgery-cum-study at the rear of the cabin, joined by a narrow passageway to the main house. Annie traversed this passage now and knocked in a no-nonsense way on the door.

At first there was no response, then a surly voice called out, "If you wish to see me, make an appointment."

"I do wish to see you, Alec. Do I have to make an appointment to see an old friend?"

More hesitancy and then the door opened. She tried to hide her shock. Alec, who had always been clean and dapper, wore a disreputable old striped shirt and baggy trousers. His hair was long and tousled and he had grown a straggly beard. But it was his expression more than anything that profoundly disturbed her. He looked pallid, withdrawn, ill even. She tried to hide her perturbation and said with as much warmth and assurance as she could command,

"Alec! It's been too long. I have been telling myself for weeks I must come to you for advice."

"You haven't been well?" It was there, the note of concern she'd been hoping for.

"I have a great deal to tell you. But you've probably heard most of it."

He gave a brief nod. "You have our condolences. I was remiss not to send them."

"Could Soo Lin make us some tea? Is it not time we wiped the slate clean, and started again?" She walked determinedly back into the main cabin where Soo Lin stood irresolutely, her child at her skirts. Looking directly at the girl, Annie said, "I am not here to make judgments on anybody. I am here to *help*. And to ask for help. But you, Soo Lin, must stop treating me like an enemy. Why have you turned against me, when we used to be friends?"

Soo Lin said nothing, but turned her head away.

"She felt you didn't approve of what she did, coming here." It was Alec who spoke. "But then, you weren't alone. The whole town has made it very clear it approves of neither of us. Which is why we're in the sorry pass we're in today."

"Yes." Annie acknowledged the truth. "But a lot of water has passed under the bridge since Soo Lin came here. She's had your child. And, as I see, there's another on the way." She looked directly at Soo Lin. "You can't imagine how I envy you that."

Soo Lin said gruffly, "I make tea. You can sit down, if you like." Noting the gradual melting of the atmosphere, the little boy shyly approached Annie and touched her lap. Gently she lifted him on to her knee.

She said, briskly, "Don't you think it's time you made it legal?"

Alec looked at her sharply, but she ploughed recklessly on. Or perhaps not recklessly. She had decided on her course of action before coming.

"They will take you at your own face value, you know. If you show Soo Lin the respect of marrying her, they will see you are both in earnest about being together. If you don't give her that respect, how can they?"

"Wait a minute," said Alec angrily. "What is this? The old holier-than-thou attitude? I thought I'd left that behind me in Scotland."

Annie gave an exaggerated sigh. "No, I'm not being holier than thou. Just practical. I don't want to see a good man go to waste. And all his learning."

"He does not need to marry me," said Soo Lin, but her eyes never left Alec's face.

"Stop demeaning yourself," said Annie, abruptly. Now they were both looking at her, unable to believe their ears, wondering where the next attack was coming from. But she relented and smiled at them. "Come on! I'm only talking sense. You must admit it."

"I admit the thought had crossed my mind that we should get the minister in," Alec owned.

"So what stopped you?"

"Money. Or the lack. Soo Lin can't get married in the rags she stands up in."

"Soon remedied." She turned towards the young mother. "Remember how I used to make my dresses down for you? I'm still handy with a needle." To Alec she said, "All you need is a visit to the barber. You must have one decent suit we can press. After that, we must think about getting you premises to rent in the town itself. A surgery, at least. I might even manage to set aside a room at the *Last Chance*, for a month or two anyhow, till you afford something better."

Carefully, she was not looking at Alec, for she saw he was on the point of unmanning tears. She took a proffered cup of tea from Soo Lin. Now none of them could trust themselves to speak. She said brusquely, "I have no family. I don't know whether my man is dead or alive. Let me do this. Let me make you a loan."

It was the baby, little Alec, who broke the constraint between them by demanding to get back up on Annie's knee and to be jiggled some more. And somehow, as the afternoon wore on, it all came out – what had happened the night the Indians came, the birth of the stillborn child, the trek in the snow, the death of Irish Sam. And because these two had gone through their own dark night, she was able to relive hers and to weep without constraint, and to take their offerings of sympathy and friendship.

At last it was out, her worry about her own fecundity and by putting incisive questions to her and giving her an external examination, Alec was able to reassure her. "When these terrors have faded from your mind, your body will lose its hurt," he explained. "There is no physical reason why you shouldn't bear more children."

The next day, Soo Lin turned up shyly at the *Last Chance*, having left the baby with Alec.

"Next time," Annie scolded, "come to the front door." Maybelle had heard the whole story and refused to be left out of things. She produced bolts of materials she had hoarded and they settled on sprigged muslin for Soo Lin's wedding dress. Before the girl left, Annie pressed into her hands the loan she had arranged to give Alec, signalling by putting her forefinger to her lips that she didn't wish to hear another word about it. Maybelle had filled a basket with dainties from the restaurant. When Soo Lin had gone, Annie said, "You've changed your tune about Soo Lin." "I'm giving her benefit of the doubt," said Maybelle, with a magnanimous smile. "For the time being."

In view of the circumstances – Soo Lin being eight months pregnant – the minister was prepared to conduct a quiet ceremony in the parlour at the *Last Chance*. Afterwards, Annie, Maybelle and the newly married couple, with little Alec also in attendance, had a sedate meal, after which Alec inspected the room where he was going to have his surgery – a room to the right of the entrance hall, easily entered off the street. And underneath the hotel bellpull Annie had a discreet brass plaque put up, indicating where the doctor could be found.

She was still secretly worried about Alec's health. He had made prodigious efforts to get back on an even keel, but she suspected he was still drinking to keep his courage up. After the birth of a little daughter, Sarah Ann, to Soo Lin, he came to the surgery five times a week. Visitors were often happy to consult him but the townsfolk still held back.

"They don't know how lucky they are!" Annie fumed. "A doctor *and* a surgeon of your quality in their midst and they'd sooner go to some quack for a bottle of coloured water."

"It will take time."

"But you need the patients now."

They were talking in his surgery before he took the trap back home. She had gone to consult him about a burn on her arm, from water splashed from a boiling pot. Without dissembling, he took a bottle from his desk and poured himself a tot of whisky.

"You don't need that, you know."

He said nothing, but she could see from the tightening of his mouth and his smouldering expression that he was angry with her. Calmly she opened the desk drawer, took the whisky bottle out and, opening the surgery window, poured the liquid out on to the sidewalk.

"You interfering bitch! By God, you've gone too far this time."

"Sit down, Alec," she said, tonelessly.

He did so, though not immediately, defiantly swallowing the tot of whisky in one go.

"You told me once," she said, "how your mother sacrificed to send you to the university. What was it we called clever bairns like you? 'Lads o' pairts,' wasn't it? Even with your bursary, she had to scrimp and save. And you, you had to live off oatmeal and salt herring. But when I first met you, you were *burning* to be a good doctor. You said it came before everything else. Does it still, Alec? Tell me the truth."

He nodded, looking somehow frail and defeated, the raw boy whose brains had taken him too far too soon. "It does."

"Soo Lin understands that. She would sacrifice her life for you. But she does wrong to fetch you whisky. You can't be a good doctor and a servant of John Barleycorn. You know that."

He gave her a look of the most acute misery.

"You don't know how Soo Lin got the whisky. When she went down Chinatown."

"You don't mean –"

She turned away, feeling her stomach heave. But she said in an even tone, "Well, things are different now, now that you're married. Do you love her, Alec?"

He did not answer her directly, but said after a pause, "She is – she is just Soo Lin. I should maybe not have done what I did. But aye. I do have some tender feelings for her."

"I'm sorry," she said, in confusion, "I overstepped the mark. It is no business of mine, what exists between a man and his wife."

"My confidence has gone." He held out his hands, stretching the fingers and she saw that they shook with a fine tremor. "How can I operate, with hands like these?"

She had suddenly caught sight of herself in a small looking-glass hung on the surgery wall. Some trick of the light exposed her face harshly, like a coloured drawing, so that the squint was ruthlessly exposed, making her look, she thought, singularly unprepossessing, even ugly. She gave a small start of denial. And then it came to her, the idea, with a beautiful, fateful clarity.

"Do you remember," she asked Alec, excitedly, "the time you said you could do something for – for this?" She pointed to her eye. "Do you still say that?"

He came forward and examined her eye, from this angle and that.

"I have read up the recent work done on strabismus," he said. "I think I could make a good job of that."

"You would need steady hands." The inference was obvious. He began a slow smile.

"Is it a bargain?" she demanded.

"Is what a bargain?"

"That you stop drinking and I ask you to mend my eye."

Quickly she went on, "You can't think what it would mean to me, Alec. I have to meet a lot of people nowadays, some of them very important people.

"I have put my days of poverty behind me, days when I felt so low and outcast I thought I'd never have the dignity I longed for. Now I have a position, I can afford good clothes, I am respected. But I look in the mirror and I see my poor eye and I somehow associate it, rightly or wrongly, with the days when I had nothing. My downtrodden days."

"You want to be beautiful," he said. "It is no good me telling you you are beautiful. Because I know thoughts can become entrenched and your eye is a symbol of the inferiority you once felt."

"So you think I am vain?" she demanded.

He laughed at her troubled expression. "What woman isn't?" Then, his voice deepening with emotion as he looked at her, "I would like to do this for you, Annie. Give me a few weeks to get on an even keel." He went to a small corner cupboard, took out a still-sealed bottle of whisky and handed it to her. "Take it. Pour it away if you like. To show I mean what I say."

Her fingers closed over his before she gently took the bottle from his hands.

"I trust you," she said, with total commitment. "I trust you implicitly. And don't worry. If it is a success, everyone from here to Victoria will know about it. I shall be your advertisement, Dr. Comrie."

"I am worried," Maybelle confessed the night before the operation. She and Annie were preparing a side table for Alec's surgical instruments in Annie's bedroom, removing all superfluous objects and laying out a supply of freshly laundered towels.

"There is no need to be," Annie repeated for the umpteenth time, though this time with just a hint of irritation. "I have seen Alec at work. I understand what he will be doing. I have every confidence in him. We are talking of the man who was top of his year at Glasgow University."

Maybelle gave a snort of derision. "And who lives in a muck-heap with the whisky bottle for companion."

"He hasn't drunk since we made our pact."

"You only have his word for it."

Annie's temper broke and she turned to her friend. "Do you not believe in giving somebody a second chance? There's more in Alec Comrie's little finger than in all the other doctors in the whole Cariboo."

"I wonder you didn't snap him up for yourself. When you had the chance."

It was eyeball to eyeball confrontation, but Annie's annoyance dissipated as it had come. She simply got on with the careful work of preparation. She couldn't expect Maybelle to understand how long she had waited for this moment, how determined she was not to let it slip away now it was within her grasp. She couldn't say to Maybelle this was for Hector, for the moment they met again and he looked into her eyes and saw there was no flaw. For Maybelle believed with everybody else that she would never see Hector again.

"They just bandaged my cousin's eye," Maybelle said now. "They bandaged the bad eye –"

"And much good it did. You told me so yourself." Annie looked round the room and drew a deep breath. "Come on. Let's go down for supper. I want a good night's rest."

She was up at crack of dawn the next morning and as she moved about the kitchen, Maybelle appeared, sleeping cap over her eyes and joined her.

At ten o'clock, Alec arrived, scrubbed down and laid out the delicately formed instruments he had sent away for – forceps, scissors, dissector and a beautiful little tenotomy hook. He was pale and set but in command.

Annie lay back on the sheeted ottoman settee and while Maybelle held her hand he administered the chloroform.

"You know," he said conversationally to Maybelle, as he worked with great delicacy and concentration, "in its earlier stages this operation used to produce a complete paralysis of the muscle, and a corresponding excessive over-effect. In other words, you got a secondary squint and as cellulitis frequently set in the final result was total disaster."

He permitted himself a minute smile at her aghast reaction. As neatly and delicately as a spinster seamstress at her embroidery he deployed the tenotomy hook. "Now we do a partial cutting of the tendon only – in surgical terms, a subconjunctival myotomy. It's a graceful little operation." He fell silent, working with intense concentration and Maybelle remained like a statue, her eyes drawn despite her feelings of acute nausea towards his meticulous handiwork. At the early stages she had thought she was about to faint – that was perhaps why he had sought to distract her by talk – but now she was like someone spellbound, unable to run away. At last it was finished, and the eye bandaged with tender care.

For the rest of the day, Alec remained in attendance of his patient who came round from the anaesthetic feeling wretched and nauseated. By evening, she was sleeping, but he had arranged with Soo Lin that he would spend the night at the surgery, just in case.

Annie confessed that the days she spent waiting for the bandage to come off were the longest of her life. She suffered some pain but Alec reassured her there was no cause for concern. She knew about the possibility of cellulitis, of things going horribly wrong but her faith in Alec's skill did not really waver.

When the final result of the operation was in evidence it was clear that Alec had done a perfect job. Annie's left eye now functioned as efficiently as her right and its gaze was as limpid and direct.

"I have to confess," said the instigator of this miracle, "that from an aesthetic point of view, where you were once merely beautiful you are now very beautiful." His voice shook a little. "I feel like Pygmalion."

"How can I thank you?"

"The least I deserve is a kiss, don't you think?"

Awkwardly, she put her lips to his warm cheek, aware as she did so of the current of intimacy flowing between them, a current as strong almost as sexual attraction, but compounded of their shared background, of Lowland genes, of imponderables that stretched away back into the mists of Scots time. Shyness, reticence, formality, were a part of that, too, and he blushed after the brief salute and said, brusquely, to hide his feelings, "What I've done for you is nothing to what you've done for me."

"Alec Comrie," she said, gravely, "All I've done is prove what a good doctor and surgeon you are. Don't you ever forget it, or you'll have me to reckon with."

Annie retired to the privacy of her own room to gaze at her features in the mirror. She had, she realised, rather beautiful eyes, a soft, purpley blue set off with long dark lashes. They stared back at her now with astounded pleasure. Her skin was creamy, without blemish and her dark auburn hair curled abundantly. A little pulse of excited conceit beat in her throat. If only you were here to see me, Hector, she thought. She had never thought she matched him physically, with his long, lean body, his fairness, but now ... They should be together, he should be able to see what she had done so that she could be perfect for him. Her whole body and being ached and wanted him, throbbed with the terrible pain of denial. She was like a widow who was not a widow, hungry for the comfort of a man's arms, a man's body, and yet it could not be any body, it had to be Hector's body. It had to be Hector. She threw herself down on the bed and wept for him, allowing her feelings of deprivation to swamp her, take her over, toss her about like a helpless vessel in a stormy sea. And then, curiously light and empty, she rose and bathed her face and combed her hair and put on the semblance of normality.

They stopped her in the street to wonder at the success of her operation, to shake her hand and admire Alec Comrie's handiwork. They came into the saloon on the pretext of a

Muckle Annie

drink or a meal to gaze at her surreptitiously – those who did not know her so well.

The effect on Alec Comrie was no less remarkable. Patients began to beat a path to his surgery door, bringing every kind of ailment and injury for his attention, including squints. In a matter of weeks he moved into his own premises – a large office and surgery with living accommodation above for Soo Lin and the children. Soo Lin had new clothes and Alec a well-cut suit and a gold watch with its own chain.

Annie was still not completely at ease with Alec's little Chinese wife. Certainly, since the upturn in their fortunes, Soo Lin looked happier, like a sleek little cat who had fallen on all four paws. She now employed a maid and had time to go shopping and to the dressmaker. She had become quite regal, almost imperious in her manner and woe betide the tradesman who tried to take advantange of her or did not deliver on time. But Soo Lin obviously wished to keep the friendship between them on a formal footing.

"It's because of the way *he* looks at you," said Maybelle, when Annie broached the subject.

"How does he look at me?" Annie challenged.

"If you don't know, why should I tell you?"

Alec came to the *Last Chance* frequently to eat or meet people, though he never drank. Annie always served him herself and if he was unaccompanied sat at his table to exchange the brief gossip of the day.

She did not intend to give up this privilege because of Soo Lin's unfounded jealousy. It pleased her to see Alec so fulfilled in his work. And she put herself out to try and understand what he was getting at when he spoke of new techniques in surgery or talked about that complex and amorphous area of medicine where it seemed, the mind affected the body and its workings. To Annie, the most fascinating aspect was how Alex always seemed to be trying to see ahead, to divine what development might happen next. She knew Soo Lin would not understand and if he could not talk to her, Annie, who could he talk to, with the same degree of openness? She could not see any danger in this, for her mind was totally shut off from any possibility of a deeper or closer relationship. They were more like brother and sister, she always thought, and if he brought his speculative notions of medicine to her, she liked to use him as a sounding board for her new business ventures. They were friends.

12

"Come on, Leroy," Maybelle bellowed. "We got the brasses to do, the lamps to set up, the tables to see to. And I want you to go down to the *Bella Union*, see if they got half a dozen of them little gilt chairs they can lend us."

"Yessum," said Leroy, calmly. He knew his value. Miss Maybelle wouldn't have asked him to follow her to the *Last Chance* if she hadn't thought it worth while. Tonight he would be wearing livery and white gloves, serving the town bosses at table. He knew there wasn't a smarter waiter in town. But all this running about beforehand, with the women shouting do this, do that, only brought out a defiant lethargy in him. What if he started scuttling around the way they did? Leroy saw it as his task to keep a kind of masculine rein on things.

In the kitchen, Annie's hair escaped from her cap and fell down over her hot cheeks as she made another batch of pastry and put the pies with their various fillings into the oven. Normally she was good at compartmentalising her work, at not letting her mind run on too far ahead sorting out the tasks to be done. But tonight's was no ordinary ball. All the bosses from the Chisholm and Hendry Cariboo Mining and Hotel Company would be there, including the ambitious young banker George Allan who had first roped her into being their hotel adviser. It was important not only that she put on a good show but that she was seen to do it with immaculate ease. One day, who knows, she could be on the company board. Eric Chisholm had hinted as much, last time he had stayed here.

And Eric Chisholm, she knew, was as much responsible as the pastry-making for her sighs of exasperation, her sweating back and rosy face. A big, ruddy-faced Border Scot, he had made no secret from the start of his interest in her. Women were scarce in the Cariboo and a man could not be too reticent. He had made a lot of money, invested it shrewdly and was more than ready to settle down, start a family and spend some of his cash on making the woman of his choice happy.

He had ignored the tacit agreement somehow accepted by most of the other men that she should not be subjected to sexual hassle.

"Do you know what they call you?" he'd challenged her while they were dancing. "The Frozen North."

Appalled, she had looked up into his tantalising smile. There was a rugged, happy-go-lucky yet at the same time dependable air to him that appealed to her greatly. If only he knew! There was nothing frozen about her. When the lamps were lit and the music played and the 'dance ga'ed through the lighted ha',' as Burns had put it, a part of her responded with all the vigour and gaiety in her nature. She loved to dance and there were times when she wanted to fall into an easy dalliance with someone, anyone, who would help her to come to terms with the desperate demands of her body. Did they think it was easy? *The Frozen North*! The unthinking witty cruelty of it had brought tears to her eyes and a hasty, repentant assurance from Chisholm that he had not meant to upset her. Only she should understand that a man had his needs. She should forgive him his crassness. It came from too much masculine company and from the chagrin he felt at making no headway with her. She must know that from here to Victoria, from Victoria to the Bay

City, there was no one to touch her for the beauty of her eyes and figure, or the wistfulness of her smile.

He could wear her down. As Maybelle said in one of her periodic lectures, you could not go on forever living in the past. And yet that piteous fur cap still lay in the drawer, she was still in love with a fair-haired, bookish laird's son or with his ghost that would not lie down. With whom would she be breaking faith if she allowed another man to lie with her? With Hector or with the essence of herself, the rock-hard, basic, unchanging part of her that had vowed over water to be true to one man, and no other?

When the morning's work was finished, she felt weak and spent. For once she did not turn down Maybelle's offer of a glass of Madeira wine. She was vaguely aware that some kind of battle was raging in her, the precepts of her Scottish upbringing ranged on one side, that upbringing that put principle above all else, that said a promise was a promise, a vow a vow; and on the other, the needs of the present, the big, easy, smiling man who wouldn't go away, the tide of energy in her that wished to be caught up in the dance of life, to hear the music, respond to the caress.

She bathed and dressed in a strange kind of languorous haze. Her ball-gown was a delicate shade halfway between pink and blue, its big puffed sleeves caught up on the shoulders with tiny blue forget-me-nots and pink ribbon. When she gazed at herself in the mirror, for a shadowy moment she imagined the little cross-eyed Glasgow urchin she had once been peeking at her unbelievingly from behind. She had worn hodden grey, that one, her split boots had let in the rain and cold. The present-day Annie gave an urchin-like sniff. What a softie she was being! In Glasgow or Barkerville, you didn't get swamped by life. You went out there and lived it.

There was a challenging sparkle in her eyes as she marched down the stairs to inspect the girls, adjusting a ribbon here, a curl there. One or two of them had romances going with 'boys' working in Williams Creek; others were hard-boiled, almost anti-men and took the customers for all they could get.

Leroy stood by the door, looking resplendent in his dark green uniform with silver buttons and Maybelle wore a silver gown with a black lace décolletage. She was busy instructing the musicians that they must adjust the tempo for one particular dance – make it too fast, she warned them, and the stamping of the customers' boots could bring the floor down.

"You are ravishing tonight. My little Polar Star." It was Chisholm, demanding he be the first of her partners, that cheeky tantalising grin not quite concealing the serious purpose, the almost-anxiety, in his eyes.

She let him take her in his arms. Despite his size, he danced gracefully and well. She surrendered to the music, to the rhythmic dipping and swaying, well aware of the interested looks from the rest of the mining company board, from Alec who had brought Soo Lin, from Maybelle and even Leroy. That was the trouble with a little town. Change your mind and the person living next door knew about it. Annie stuck up her chin and looked at Eric Chisholm through her sooty lashes, calculating full well the extent of the devastation she wrought.

It was a splendid ball. Outside the snowy Cariboo night sparkled with frosty stars, the horses ridden into town pawed at their posts, the elderly Celestials dozed over their opium pipes, the gambling saloons took in their quota of dedicated sinch and euchre players, and other dance saloons cursed their poor turn-out, for everyone who was anyone was at the *Last Chance*.

The editor of the *Sentinel* locked his office door and turned to the grubby little fur-trader who was the cause of his late departure from his desk.

Trappers were becoming a rarer breed these days. Once New Caledonia – you had to call it British Columbia now – had been all theirs, but gold and fur didn't go together. The editor was of a naturally sceptical turn of mind and did not know just how much credence to put in the tale just told him by the trader, McGraw. But if there was anything in it, it would make a good lead story for the paper. So he dragged the chubby, bearded, not-altogether-wholesome-smelling little trapper behind him into the noise and hubbub of the *Last Chance*.

Annie was between dances, sipping a cool lemonade, when he touched her elbow and said quietly, "You remember that appeal you put in the paper? For anyone who might have caught sight of your husband? I got Ferdy McGraw here might be able to enlighten you a little."

He saw the light and animation flee her face to be replaced by an alarming pallor. She gripped his arm and led the way from the saloon into the entrance hall. He fancied she swayed a little so insisted she sat down.

"I am all right. What have you got to tell me, Mr. McGraw?"

"I could use a drink."

"Certainly." She summoned Leroy and ordered whisky and glasses to be brought to the little table.

"Tell Mrs. Mennock what you told me," the editor ordered.

"It was like this." McGraw had to indulge in much lip-smacking, beard-wiping, looking round before he got properly started. "I was trapping 'way beyond Quesnel. I don't rightly like to say where. Just east. You got to be careful. Don't want nobody after my traps. Blessed diggers taken away enough of my livin' as it is."

"Get on with it, man," said the journalist irritably. "I've my supper to get."

"Well, I know where their camps are. I've seen them 'fore now, ringed with scalps they've taken. This partic'lar lot was well settled in.

"I don't go too close. I've had dealings with them, when I've had to, but it didn't suit my book this time."

"Please," Annie pleaded, "tell me what you saw."

"I saw this white man walk to the edge of the camp and

look out towards the hills. He was fair, real fair, even if he was dressed like 'em. No mistakin' that. And then I just saw him turn and walk away, real slow. He was kinda crippled, to my way of thinkin'. Like walkin' was hard for him. Kinda stuck in my mind. Things don't get to me that easy, I seen enough bad things, but it kinda stuck in my mind, the look on his face and all."

"Hector! It was my Hector!" Those who saw it were never to forget the revelatory look on Annie's face.

"I saw this old copy of the *Sentinel* when I got back home to Cameronton, the bit where you asked anyone with any information to get in touch. I was laid up sick for a while but when I got better I sez to myself, I sez, you get over to Barkerville, Ferdy, tell that poor woman what you saw. Times being hard, I could use a small reward."

"Yes. I'll see to it," said Annie, impatiently. "You say you've dealt with them, these Indians? You must take me to them. They can have whatever they want. If they release Hector."

"I don't think that's a good idea," McLaren interjected hastily. "Far better to take the information to the commissioner and let him send his men."

Annie scarcely acknowledged him. She looked only at McGraw. "How long would it take us?"

"*No!*" McLaren brought his fist down. "You're talking madness now."

"Madness, is it?" Annie turned a closed, taut face towards him. "The Commissioner's done his best, but he hasn't found Hector. What makes you think a body of lawmen are going to get anywhere near the Indians? Our only chance is to send in somebody they know –"

"Now hold on there, ma'am," said McGraw, in alarm. "I ain't sayin' I'm going to do nothin'."

"You can name your sum." She looked him straight in the eye.

"We don't rightly know it is him. Could 'ave been trick of the light, made me think I saw a white man. Could have been a half-cast from one of the squaws. I know trappers as have had their way with Redskin women."

"That's not what you really think. You said the man's face struck in your mind. Was the hair fair and long?"

Reluctantly McGraw nodded.

"What's going on?" So intense had the conversation been between her and McGraw that Annie had not noticed Eric Chisholm emerge from the saloon and stand behind her. Now she said, her face glowing, "Eric, this man thinks he may have seen my husband."

The big man's face became abruptly wary.

"Where was this?"

"I ain't bein' exact, not to strangers," said McGraw truculently.

"I want to go there." Annie turned appealing eyes to Chisholm. "Eric, you do see? I want to know whether my husband is dead or alive."

He gazed down at her. A hard man accustomed to going after what he wanted. But something moved in him as he looked at the anxious, animated face, a tenderness, a wish to give without quibbling, that took him by surprise.

"We'll arrange it," he said, conclusively and the other two men looked at him, not demurring. When Eric Chisholm spoke, things got done.

When they reached Quesnel Forks on the way to the Indian encampment, matters became suddenly more complicated. Annie was sent for by the commissioner of police.

"I understand you are going after some Indians who you think may be holding your husband." The commissioner's voice was coldly accusing. When Annie said nothing, he demanded sharply. "You must tell me. Is this true?"

"How did you find out?"

"My dear Mrs. Mennock, your adventure is the talk of the Cariboo. We don't go round with our ears stopped up. One of my men was at the *Last Chance* the night McGraw came in with his story."

"What McGraw says is true." Her mouth had begun to tremble.

"He could be a rogue. I'm not saying he is." The commissioner's manner softened slightly. "What I am saying is you would have done best to take McLaren's advice and brought the information to me."

"I didn't want lawmen rushing in. If it is my husband in there, what do you think would happen to him, at the first sight of your volunteers?" She drew her finger across her throat. "They don't stop to argue, do they?" She leaned forward with an urgent face. "Please, commissioner, let me do it my way."

The man threw down the letter-opener he had been fiddling with obsessively. "You tell me your plans." As she demurred, he conceded, "I will go along with them as far as I can."

"Will you let the man McGraw make contact?"

He paced about the room. "Very well," he agreed at last. "But my men will be deployed in the vicinity. Don't worry. They'll sink into the landscape. We've learned a thing or two from the Indians, you know. It's your safety that concerns me."

The next day, on Chisholm's handsome sledge, they moved up-country, accompanied by the commissioner's deputy, Wilson, over snow that hardened as the cold intensified. They came to a small, newish settlement called Humberton and checked into the only guest house. After that, McGraw was on his own. He set off on snow shoes in his trapper's gear, head down against the searing wind.

It was possibly the longest day of Annie's life. In the guest house's bare and spare little front parlour she and Wilson and Eric Chisholm played endless card games, their talk stilted and desultory. At last McGraw returned.

Annie marvelled at her own patience while the little man thawed out and ate and drank.

"Did you see him?" she demanded at last.

He shook his head. "They wouldn't let me."

"But he *is* there?"

"A white man is there."

"Did they tell you his name?"

"They wouldn't do that. They had him hidden away. We can have him, though. They'll trade him for two of theirs being held in the hoosegow here, on rustling charges. And if they can have hides and tallow and some geegaws the squaws been asking after."

"Surely that's posible?" Annie looked pleadingly at Wilson, the commissioner's deputy.

"It may be," he said carefully. When he had gone into the proposition carefully with McGraw, he insisted on seeing the two Indians held in custody. He came back shaking his head. "One of them can go. The other is wanted on other charges but may possibly be released later. You can take this information back to the camp —"

It took another day to get the supplies the Indians demanded. While Annie argued for the release of both men, Wilson remained adamant. Annie insisted on sending beads and blankets as well as the hides and tallow and assembled what trinkets she could to please the womenfolk. This time McGraw took a sledge drawn by dogs. He was back before midday.

"They've gone."

"They can't have done."

She stood, rooted by disbelief, a wild crazy scream running through her head. She felt steadying arms go round her, but threw them off.

"Where is Hector?" She shook the hapless McGraw. "What have they done to him? You lied, you blackguard. He was never there in the first place."

"Calm down." Chisholm stood before her, gripping her by the arms firmly. "Take a deep breath. Let's get the story out of him. All may not yet be lost."

McGraw gave Annie a bruised, angry look. "I staked my life on it," he reminded her savagely. He looked at Wilson, who looked away. "My guess is they got wind of the commissioner's interest. They must have known men with guns were on their way up from the Forks."

"How could they?" It was a question of the utmost desolation and bleakness.

"They survive by being a step ahead." Wilson's admission was wrung from him. "Perhaps the delay while we got the skins disturbed them. Who will ever know? I don't pretend to understand the Indian and I've been in the Cariboo for twenty years."

She shook off detaining arms and ran out of the room and out of the boarding house, standing outside and looking up and down as though she didn't know which road to take. Chisholm followed her and gently brought her back indoors.

"I want to see for myself," she sobbed. "I want to go there and see for myself. How can they just have disappeared? Maybe we can still follow them."

"I will come with you," he said. "We'll take the sledge McGraw had and we'll go and look."

She gave him a look of consummate gratitude.

"But first," he urged, "you have to wrap up in warm clothes and get some food inside you."

She didn't eat. Chisholm, like her, refused to listen to any misgivings uttered by the rest of the party.

"She wants to go, so she's going," he said adamantly. In other circumstances the trip might have been enjoyable. It was a bright day, the sub-Alpine forests in their mantle of snow looked picture-pretty. When they reached the forest-edge where McGraw had described the encampment as being, they went over the ground carefully for any sign that would substantiate his claim. True enough, they found signs of camp fires, skins, feathers and food. Indians had been here and recently at that. She cast her eyes towards the northern horizon. Nothing. A narrow range of hills revealed a landscape devoid of movement. No bird, no animal, no wind. She began to walk towards it.

"Come back. Where are you going?" Chisholm's anxious voice reached her, but she didn't turn her head. He let her be.

Coming from a family of sisters, he had an instinctive understanding of women, when to press them, when to leave them alone. He watched the lone figure trudge over the snow, stopping to hold her hand to her eyes from time to time and scan the country all around her.

Annie pressed on. Somewhere in these hills, Hector survived. She knew his presence had been here. Back in the encampment she had felt it, though she had said nothing to Chisholm. But it had been palpable. She had been able to see his face in her mind's eye, the fresh skin reddened by cold, the blue eyes crinkled from looking at whiteness. She had thought about the crippling of his legs. They must have made an attempt at cutting the sinews on one or both. At the thought of him hirpling the furious tears rose up in her throat. She had been so sure of getting him back, she had planned immediate consultation with Alec about his legs, about possible surgery that would help him. And if, in the end, nothing could have helped, at least she would have had him with her, her love, her darling. She had the money now to care for him, to buy him books to divert him, to provide a room for him to study in.

She turned and looked at Eric Chisholm, gazing after her concernedly. Poor Eric! She was at such a great distance from him, from everybody. She pressed on. She was in a state of abeyance, knowing only her need to find her man. She remembered how they had made love, out-of-doors, on the big flat rocks by the river before they had left the cabin in the wood for Cottonmill Creek. She felt Hector's big yet fine-boned hand move over her skin, felt him touch her *there*, felt him take her, invade her, so that her being spread like sunshine on water. She had waited so long.

She kept on walking, making for her goal, that was Hector. She could not face the prospect of going back to her disappointment. Something stronger than will or sense kept her going and she felt neither cold nor tiredness.

"Annie! Annie! Wait! Wait!" Chisholm's voice came from afar off and then came nearer. He pounded behind her, a big, heavy man panting in perturbation. At last he caught up with her and held her fast by the arm. Still she tried to keep on walking.

"Come on. He isn't there." He gathered her up in his arms, his huge frame damming the impetus of her body. She struggled against him, kicking, scratching, swearing, but he turned her round. She stumbled rather than walked back towards the sledge and the encampment, her sobs wracking her body, the tears freezing on her cheeks. Anxious faces greeted them at Humberton. The next day it was decided to take her back to Barkerville.

"How am I supposed to manage on my own? There's been another new strike, just up the creek and they're pouring into the saloon at night looking for the best that money can buy. Nobody bakes as well as you, nobody runs the dances the way you do."

Maybelle gazed down at Annie, who lay back on her lace-trimmed pillows, her long, curling hair spread out fanwise, in tangles, her hands fine, white and looking almost lifeless on the coverlet. Not the busy, sometimes roughened, sometimes reddened, always competent hands of a working woman. Indifferently Annie turned her face away from her friend, and closed her eyes.

"Where do you hurt?" Maybelle pursued, with a deepening note of anxiety. "If you have a pain, tell me about it."

"No pain," said Annie. She ran her tongue between dry lips. "I just can't get up. I am tired unto death."

"Try a little broth."

Annie didn't bother to shake her head. She closed her eyes once again and said, "Leave me, Maybelle. I just want to sleep."

Maybelle wanted to say, "I know the sickness that ails you. I can put a name to it. It makes you turn away good men like Eric Chisholm, for a shadow." But she turned away from her friend's sick-bed, moving stiffly, suddenly visited by something more than concern. Annie did not want to see anyone. Especially she did not want to see Alec Comrie, the doctor. But Maybelle moved out of the room and downstairs towards Alec's surgery with a renewed sense of fright and urgency. This was more than just reaction to the shock of missing Hector – if it had been Hector. Nearly a week had passed now while Annie refused food and company. She was going into a decline, that was it, and Maybelle confronted Alec now with the worst of her fears.

"But she doesn't want to see me," Alec countered, angrily.

"She's out of her senses," said Maybelle. "It's as though she's lost the will to live. I'm frightened, doctor. It's not like Annie. She's always been a fighter." Maybelle could say no more. The tears were coursing down over the rouge on her cheeks. "Come up. See her whether she agrees to it or not."

He pondered momentarily before he nodded. "All right. But alone."

"If you say so."

When Alec Comrie entered the darkened room, he closed the door gently, then went to the window and pulled the heavy drapes apart to let in the winter light. The figure on the bed didn't stir. He saw with a jolt that she had lost much weight, that her face was as colourless as a sheet. He sat down and took one of the inert-looking hands, feeling it twitch momentarily in response. Still Annie did not open her eyes.

He began to speak softly. "When I was a wee lad, my mother told me I would soon have a brother or sister. Then my father was killed in the pit and my mother was brought to bed but the baby didn't live. I was five at the time. I still remember her face, as pale as yours is now. It was spring, but she didn't want the birds to sing, she who loved the laverock and the linnet. She said it didn't seem right, when she was suffered such sorrow."

The eyes had fluttered open and fastened on him.

"Children are given wisdom sometimes we grown-ups don't possess. I used to pick her flowers, lay them in her lap.

Try my best to let her know I understood. For I did. You can't love somebody and not know how they feel. And that was the first step. I'm telling you now I know how you feel. It's bad. But we share it."

Her face had taken on a listening look. "And the next thing was, time passed, I needed a new pair of boots and we went to the town to buy them. She got herself a ribbon for her bonnet. I saw her prink at herself in the looking glass. One day we went for a walk and I paddled in the burn and she lay back on the grass and got the sun in her face. We ate bannocks and cheese and a wee dog came up and we threw sticks for it. She listened when she heard the laverock climb the sky and she smiled, she couldn't help it. God's gifts were still there, you see. He hadn't turned his back on her."

"He took my bairn."

"Aye. I don't know the reason for that, any more than I know the reason why He took my wee brother or sister."

"And Hector's been taken from *me*." She gave a great wailing cry and turned over in her bed. He could only hear her muffled voice by bending over her. "I've waited and waited and I thought the time had come." She turned towards him once again and held out her arms, like a child. "I want him, Alec. I want him so bad."

"I know." He said it close in her ear. "I have wanted *you*. The time I came with you to Salt Spring – I wanted you. I hoped and hoped to the last you would turn and say you would come with me. But it wasn't to be." He held her off and smiled at her ruefully. "I've survived. So will you."

"I never knew I hurt you." There was a new kind of shock on her face.

"I don't have the kind of face that shows it."

She was silent, laid back again on her pillows. The words were drawn from her: "Do you suppose we're made to suffer to make us understand one another better? Alec, dear Alec, forgive me, if I've pained you."

"There is nothing to forgive." He stood up, fiddled with her hair-brushes on her dressing table. "Do you think now you could do something for me? First, take a little broth. Second, get up for a little in your room, even if it's just to sit in your chair by the window. See, the coach has just come in, F.J. Barnard's Peerless Six, the horses are steaming, a man in a hard hat is getting off with a carpet-bag as big as himself. He's looking round, as if to say, what sort of dump is this. I sometimes think, Annie, we should burn it all down and start again, it's so ramshackle. And it *could* burn down, with all those stove-pipes coming so close through the wooden roofs. I'll feel happier when the snow settles again. Safer.'

"I'll try to get up. If it's just to stop your chatter. But – but thank you – for coming. And talking. I know you mean well."

"I'll come and see you again tomorrow."

When he entered her room the next day, her head was turned to the wall. She did not greet him.

"Annie." He said her name softly, coaxingly.

"Leave me."

"If you wish." But he did not go. She turned her head to see if he was still there. "Ah!" he wagged an admonitory finger. "You didn't mean it, did you?"

His patience with her over the next few days was exemplary. With Maybelle as his confidante, he slowly built up her strength with tonics, good food, a little judicious brandy.

"You know," he told, "you have three physicians looking after you. Dr. Diet, Dr. Quiet –"

"Yes, I remember it from shipboard," she interrupted – "and Mr. Merriman."

"Don't forget the latter."

"And what have I got to laugh at?"

"You haven't noticed the way Tamson the hurdy fiddler tucks the fiddle under his four chins? You'd think he was eating it!" He looked at her hopefully. "Or the way Madam Fanny at the *Grand Union* shooes her girls before her like so many cackling geese?"

Muckle Annie

A vestige of a smile rewarded him. He continued to bring her tales from Barkerville at large, playing up human foibles to divert her, making her look at life with, as he put it, a whimsical eye. It was uphill work, but at last she was wearing her day gowns instead of deshabille, she was combing her hair though she did not bother to arrange it in its former elaborate style.

She began to go downstairs to do a little baking, but she still tired easily. Alec made a call on her daily. Their morning half-hour, which often stretched longer, was something they both began to look forward to and she to miss with a disproportionate ache if he was called away on an emergency.

When Soo Lin came to mind, she did not allow herself to think of her for long, for Alec was, after all, attending her in a medical capacity and she would settle with him generously one of these days, although he shook his head when she mentioned payment. She was resting one morning and did not hear the disturbance in the lobby outside Alec's surgery. It was Maybelle who, red-faced, told her what had happened when she brought up a tray with some Madeira wine.

"Soo Lin was here. She claims she never sees him. Someone's been running to her with tales about his visits to you."

"But he's my doctor."

"That's not what she called him this morning, I can assure you. She says he visits you for other things. I had to bundle her out of the door before the whole neighbourhood heard her. She was threatening to set fire to the place."

"And Alec? Was he upset?"

"No. He kept calm. Says to tell you he'll be up to see you later." Maybelle said, as composedly as she could, "There's no truth in what she says, is there, Annie? I would not believe such things of you."

"What do you take me for?"

"A lonely woman." Maybelle's gaze was direct. "Wasn't it your poet Burns you keep quoting who said it? – 'to step aside is human.'"

"I only want Hector."

"You think you can only love one man in your life? I almost wish it were the doctor. Find someone else, Annie. You're too young to live like a nun."

"What about you and Jamie? You've said many a time no one would replace him."

"Someone might have done, if I'd let him. Learn from my mistake. Keep your heart open."

"I don't want to talk about it." Annie's voice shook. "You all have answers for me. I don't want your answers. Leave me alone."

She was still feeling shaken when a little later Maybelle reappeared, holding a copy of the *Sentinel*. Her face was ashen. Wordlessly Annie took the paper from her and saw the headline: Manager Killed in Blasting Accident. The name Eric Chisholm swam up at her from the rest of the print. She remembered, during that long afternoon at Humberton while they'd waited for news, Chisholm telling her how you drilled a pattern of holes in a hillside and by the scientific placing of explosives blasted ore into fragments. When she'd said ingenuously, "Can't it be dangerous?" he'd nodded, with an odd sort of excitement on his face. "That's part of the charm," he'd said.

"I'm sorry," Maybelle said, inadequately.

"Can I keep the paper?"

"Of course."

"I'm all right." She gave Maybelle a thin, dismissive smile and when she'd gone she sat by the window in her room and read the story again. She felt cold, half alive. She kept imagining Chisholm's ruddy, kindly face, remembering the sensitivity that had been there despite his massive bulk, his desperate and sometimes unfair attempts at seduction, such as when he'd called her the Frozen North.

It came to her now that what she was doing was killing herself by running away from love like that which had been offered by Chisholm. Maybelle was right. Surely it was possible to love more than one man? Surely it was possible to recover from the passionate obsession that was her love for Hector? She would have to struggle free, to live. That was what her recent illness had been all about. She could not put what she felt into words, but the realisation was there, that she was turning away from life itself and though she did not flatter herself that her rejection had somehow made Chisholm careless, she saw how her cold distancing touch, her uncaring, could blight those who felt affection for her.

The tears crept down her cheeks. Then presently she rose and carefully folded and smoothed the newspaper, as though by her tender and sad reflectiveness she could bring back the man who was dead, and ask for his forgiveness.

There was a knock at her door. Recognising it as Alec's, she called "Come in." She saw from his expression that he knew about Chisholm.

"Alec, I must get away from this place," she burst out.

He didn't answer her at first, merely stood as though in a trance, gazing through the window.

"Aye," he owned at last. "Maybe that would be the best thing."

"Hector may never come back, but I have a life to live. Eric Chisholm tried to tell me that. I liked him, you know. I could have lain with him. There, does that shock you? I can only admit now how much I wanted that. There, does that shock you some more?"

"Nothing shocks me."

"I don't know what God wants from me. My loyalty to my vows, I always thought. But does He want me to stop warming my hands at the fire of life? To sicken and turn cold?"

"No, He doesn't want that." She heard his voice roughen. "Any more than I can think He sees me as wicked for loving you the way I do."

"Alec —"

"No. Don't 'Alec' me. I take a long time to learn some things, to define a word like love, for example. I thought what I felt for you would go away, like a cold. I tried to bury what I felt through Soo Lin and the bairns. But she *knows*, you see. She knows where my first loyalty lies. Unlettered she may be, stupid she isn't. We've just been having it out in one hell of a row."

"I know she came to the surgery this morning, Alec. Maybelle told me."

"It isn't any good me telling her I care for her. She knows that too. What she wants is for me to love her the way I love you. To give her everything." His voice rose. "Do you think, if I could, I wouldn't? Aye, gang awa', Annie Mennock. It would be best for everybody."

She moved quickly now and put her arms gently about him, feeling him shake and shudder before his own arms went about her.

"I am frightened, Alec. I don't know where to turn."

There was a long pause while they gazed at each other.

Then he kissed her with a rough and awkward passion. "How I've wanted to do that," He broke away and tore off his coat. "Jesus, woman, we're flesh and blood. Not a set of precepts." He caught her again, bundling her towards the bed, pushing up her skirts, tearing at her bodice. She began to pant, to weep, to laugh. She wanted to push him off but her arms tightened around him, held on. One moved up to stroke his head, to catch it, the crown of his hair, to guide his lips down on hers. They were beyond all caution now. One by one their garments came off, they struggled to get underneath the sheets, he touched and kissed her everywhere, he took her with a wild impatience, he cursed her and showered her with endearments. When it was all over, they lay like two people stunned by hammer blows, almost insensate. She was aware of how different his body was to Hector's, of his harsh, broken breathing and of a stillness, a quiescence in her own breast. "Oh, no," she said softly at last, "we should never have done that." She lay up on an elbows, bent over to kiss him, aware of his happiness and guilt.

"I came here to tell you I wouldn't be your doctor any more. Soo Lin demands it and she is my wife. I never meant *this* to happen. But I'm not sorry it did. I've never been so happy in my life, as I am at this moment." The expression on his face told he did not lie.

The quick tears rose to her eyes and fell on him.

"You have been good to me, Alec Comrie. I'm glad if you're happy." Gently she stroked his brow.

"Let us not analyse and talk. Let us just be like this a few minutes more."

She lay back on the pillows, his arm beneath her. How was it that she, who had been so weak and frail, could feel the beginnings of a valid life in herself once again? She might have sinned, but it did not feel like it yet.

"Do you hear something?" Alec said. He half-sat up.

"Like what?"

"Like – crackling. Like fire!"

Something leapt past the window then. An orange flag. Then another. At the same moment, something acrid reached her nostrils. With the speed of light, it seemed, Alec was already out of the bed and struggling into his clothes. He raced to the window. "The street is on fire!" he yelled. "Get dressed! For God's sake, anything, put on anything. We must get out!" They could hear shouts now, clatter rising up from the street. As they rushed downstairs – she had grabbed a cloak and what jewellery lay on her dressing table – they saw Maybelle stagger out from her parlour, where she had been sleeping, urged on by Leroy, and residents run from their rooms, from the dining-room, fear and disbelief warring in their expressions.

There was something she should remember, she thought, but it was pushed from her in the urgent need to make sure the *Last Chance* was emptied of all its clients, carrying as much as they could in one go, for there would be no coming back. It was impossible to say where the fire had started, but the surgery side and the back of the hotel was burning, so was the building next to it and the steward's house and even as she stood aghast and transfixed on the sidewalk opposite she saw the flames leap the street at the farther end and the

Bank of British Columbia go up like dry tinder.

People were fleeing from every remaining building, making their way from the town to the safety of the middle of the creek where they could watch the fire's remorseless progress. For remorseless it had to be, with the wooden buildings so close to each other and everything so dry. Those whose buildings had not yet caught tore in and out of them like mad ants, removing all they could to relays of helpers.

Annie, Maybelle and Alec stood with the others from the hotel, watching the smoke rise and billow from the back and then drawing back as, with a fierce blast of heat, the whole building was caught up in conflagration and with a deadly progression the saloon and shop next door caught fire.

"Move! Move! There's blasting powder up there!" A saloon keeper raced towards them. "They're trying to get to a dry shaft. But move!" Taking Maybelle's arm, Annie joined the stream of people moving towards mid-creek. She felt she was in a dream and would presently wake up. Her legs moved in a mechanical action and did not seem to belong to her.

"Annie! Annie!" The girl, Teenie, who had worked at the grocery store came rushing behind them. "My wedding dress is back there! My china, my bed!" She grabbed the girl's wrist with her free hand and dragged her on with them. "Leave them be, Teenie." Where did the firmness in her voice come from? "We've got to get away before the blasting powder goes up."

Even as they ran she turned to look and saw men carrying the powder kegs. There must have been fifty barrels and the movement of the men carrying them was accelerated by their terror as if in some half-mad nightmare. People fleeing from Chinatown were joining their exodus now and it was in that moment that her mind clicked back into focus, that she remembered Soo Lin and what she had said that morning about 'burning the place down.'

"Alec!" She turned towards him in a dread of alarm.

"Where is Soo Lin?"

"Thank God," he answered, "she and the children set off in a buggy for Cameronton after – after our row. I suggested it. I thought the outing would calm her nerves –"

"Are you sure? Did you see her go?"

She saw the doubt reach his eyes at the same moment as Teenie screeched, "Soo Lin? She went into the Chinamen's Temple. I saw her. The children were crying –"

"How long ago was that?" Annie's fingers bit into the girl's arm so that she winced and cried out.

"Half an hour, maybe an hour ago –"

With an oath, Alec left the group and ran back towards the burning town. Annie said to Maybelle, "Go on, dear, go on further up the creek. Go with Teenie here." She began to walk after Alec, the unthinkable thought beating in her head like a drum, so that she didn't hear Maybelle's entreaties for her to come back.

It was strange how quickly you adapted, even to disaster. A few hours ago Barkerville had been tranquil and clear in the hard morning frost. She had seen icicles hanging from the sluice boxes two and three yards long. She had smelt snow in the air. What had Alec said the other day? 'I'll feel happier when the snow settles.' Meaning on those tinder roofs. Well, the snow would come too late. Barkerville was burning. Too late for hindsight, too late for plans to store water. Now calm had given way to a landscape of loss and terror and that ultimate horror that could not be acknowledged. Yet you could still live and move and breathe. Just.

She ran after Alec now. It was impossible to go down the main street. Both sides had joined up in a mass of flames, the forestation on part of the hillside, too. But he took the path behind the buildings till he was as near to Chinatown as he could get. It too burned and in the centre was the Temple. He began to run towards it. She screamed his name, fleeing after him like the girl she had been in Springburn, the fleetest when it came to games. She brought him down in a kind of tackle, almost sitting on him, all dignity gone as she tried to restrain him.

"You can't go further." She tore at his struggling form.

"I must. They might be there!"

She brought her hand down on his face in a stinging slap.

"Alec! Listen! They will be with the Chinese. Look!" She pointed up the hill, where people were moving about, already trying to set up makeshift shelter for the coming night. "Come with me. Come away from this heat."

Patches of burned materials that had been floating in the air landed on them, covering them with black smuts.

He staggered behind her, pulled by her hand. As they went there was a thunderous explosion and they turned to see burning furniture, bedding, thrown hundreds of feet in the air. Jagged metal fell only yards away. Alec gazed at the source and muttered "Coal oil tins."

"You could have been killed," she said savagely, "if I'd let you go on."

"She wouldn't have done it, would she?" He turned a pleading, agonised face towards her. "You don't think she did this terrible thing, do you?"

"Of course I don't. No, never."

"She isn't like anybody else I know," he said, in desperation. "The things that were done to her when she was young made her different. Christ in heaven, Soo Lin, tell me you didn't do this."

Celestials stood about in little forlorn groups, separating themselves, as always, from the rest of the Barkerville people. Some cast furtive looks in their direction and Annie thought they might have indulged in looting to augment their own sparse belongings.

One or two were propping up boards or nailing blankets to props to give some kind of miserable shelter from the winds blowing down the canyon and older people huddled into blankets, cocooning grandchildren with them. Fires had been started to heat food and water.

"She's not here." Alec gazed around him, desperately

trying to sort out the individual figures in the shifting groups.

"There!" Annie pointed with a shout of triumph. In the midst of a throng of Chinamen she thought she saw little Alec and then a female figure bearing a baby. She followed behind Alec at a more restrained pace, her heartbeat still sounding loud in her ears.

The Chinese set up an excited babble at their approach and the men made a deliberate screen, hiding the woman and children. Alec tried to strike his way through this but the men would not give way. Annie recognised several of the older men from the Temple, including Chen Lau who ran the laundry.

"Let this man speak to his wife." She spoke sternly to the latter who knew a little English. Chen Lau stared through her, saying nothing.

"By God," cried Alec, "you *will* let me through." And he lunged into the knot of men only to be manhandled away once again from Soo Lin. At this he seemed to lose all control and began to strike out with his fists, bending his head like a battering ram. The barrier dispersed, thinned a little and then one man, smaller than the rest, suddenly produced a knife.

"No!" Soo Lin at last stepped forward. She uttered something in Chinese and the men reluctantly parted to let her through with the children to talk to her husband. The man put away the knife.

"Soo Lin!" Alec could barely speak as he tried to regain breath and composure after his struggle. "Soo Lin," he tried again, "tell me what you have done." The baby, hearing her father's voice, set up a thin wail.

"I am leaving you." Annie watched, mesmerised, as the small, pretty face with its lustrous slanted eyes broke up in venomous fury in which, Annie felt sure, there was also fear. "I am going back to the Bay City where I belong. My uncle at the Temple has arranged it."

He did not seem to hear her.

"Soo Lin, you have to tell me. What have you done?" He had her by the wrist and for a moment the emotion between them vibrated so strongly everyone around fell into inanimation.

"I have done nothing."

"Are you sure, Soo Lin, you have not done a very bad thing?"

Annie held her breath. For an instant, she thought she detected a gleam of sheer animal terror in Soo Lin's eyes. And then with a swift, jerking movement the girl broke away from her husband's grasp and ran back behind the protection of the Chinese men.

"Go away," she cried from there. "Go away and leave me with my people. You have done the bad thing. Go away with her. I have taken money from you. Enough to take us to the Bay City."

"You can't take the children. How would you live?"

"As my mother did."

"Soo Lin, don't do this to me."

She gave him a last look that cleaved like a knife. "It is what you have done to me." She turned and moved to the back of the knot of men till they stood like a solid phalanx in front of her and the children and he could see them no more.

"Alec, come away," said Annie. The words came croakingly. "There is nothing more you can do here."

13

"What else am I fit for?" demanded Maybelle. "I've always run a saloon and I'll still run a saloon. It may not be up to the *New Scotia* or the *Last Chance*. But there will always be a few old boys looking for a game of sinch, that's for sure. And Maybelle here will look after them."

"You've done wonders." Annie's tribute was heartfelt. Less than a week after the fire which had wiped out the town, thirty houses were already standing and Maybelle was occupying one of them. There was a bar, there were tables. No dancing girls, for the saloon was too small, but outside the sign said in bold gilt lettering "Maybelle's" and some of her old customers were already in occupation, swapping tales of what they'd saved in the fire and exchanging gossip about who had left the district for good and who intended to remain and rebuild.

"I can't stay with you." It was one of the most difficult tasks she had ever faced, trying to make Maybelle understand why she was going away. Had she not said she would always remain in Barkerville, so that if Hector ever returned from that ghostly land of lost probabilities she would be there? Had she not enjoyed the good days at the *Last Chance*, when 'the dance ga'ed through the lighted ha' ', the fiddlers' tunes had throbbed out through the saloon windows and the hurdies had kicked for the ceiling? Hadn't she been part of it, the hard work, the excitement of new claims, the thrust to make good, even the accidents, the times when 'slum' or explosives or fever took their toll?

"It isn't," she went on, cursing her lack of articulateness, "that I'm not sure Barkerville will come back again, better than ever."

"Well, then," said Maybelle, hardly, "kindly try and tell me what it is. For I always saw you here for good. That Chinawoman and her antics are the top and bottom of it, aren't they?"

Annie sipped her tea, holding the cup in both hands and gazed at her old friend reflectively. These days, although she still fought the war, there were times when Maybelle and her allies, rouge and powder, lost the battle. Days like today when there had been much to organise. When change presented too harsh a countenance. They had had their spats, but they had trusted each other. She could confide in her old friend, knowing it would go no further.

"I had made up my mind to go away, even before the fire."

"And why was that? Because Alec Comrie was making a fool of himself over you? Because of what happened to poor Eric Chisholm?"

"Partly. But mainly because —"

"Well, go on."

"It's so hard to talk about, Maybelle. When I say I scarcely knew who I was, would you understand? So much of me was tied up with Hector and when I came back from Humberton, after missing him, if it was him, it was like I would never get myself together again. Can I tell you something I will never tell another soul?"

"I'm the soul of discretion. You know that."

"The day I heard about Eric Chisholm's death, I went to bed with Alec Comrie."

"The day of the fire?" Maybelle was doing her best to register a minimum of emotion, but her face was a study.

"Just that once." Guilt had brought a mantle of red up over Annie's neck and face. "I had to feel alive again. I was sick of promises and shadows. I had felt something for Eric Chisholm, he was a good man, I think he might have loved me and when he was near me, my body answered him. I can't put it any other way.

"When Alec came into my room that day, I was desperate for comfort, if you like. What I feel for him — have felt for him — is different again. We're that close in some ways I can tell what he's going to say before he says it. But as for the love a woman should feel for the man she lies with, well, no, I have never felt that for Alec. I went with him that day because he was a man, he was Hector, he was Eric, he was even Donald Arrochar, what I'd felt for *them*. It was a bad thing to do, wasn't it? But it made me feel I belonged to my body again. Once you've lain with a man, and it's been good, your body gives you little rest till it happens again."

"I remember," said Maybelle. "I do remember what it was like. I am glad I am growing older."

"I'm not proud of what I did. It was almost as though Soo Lin made it happen, by going on the way she did about the two of us. Somebody else's suspicion is a terrible thing to live with. But when all's said and done, the blame doesn't lie with her. It lies with me and with him."

"He still thinks she was the one who set fire to Barkerville."

"But they know now what happened. It was a miner knocking over a stove pipe, trying to kiss a hurdy who was pressing her dress at the back of *Adler and Barry's* saloon."

"Try telling him that."

"Don't you think I do try? He isn't seeing straight about Soo Lin yet. The way they got her out of Barkerville without him knowing. He watched every coach, but they must have smuggled her out along the Trail so she could catch it further on. He knows when she gets to 'Frisco, the waterfront Chinese will swallow her up, hide her and the children. He'll never see them again."

"Isn't that what he wants?"

Annie gave Maybelle an angry, hurt glare. "How can you be so cruel, Maybelle? He loves his children, he was a good father, an exemplary father. And it was not as though he felt nothing for Soo Lin. Would he have allowed her to stay in the first place? Would he have married her, if he hadn't had some feeling for her?"

"She was far beneath him."

"In some ways she was far above him. She loved him so much she would have done anything for him. I even see her going away as a way to let him have what he wanted."

"You, you mean?"

"I do mean me. How can I deny it? We must have seemed to poor Soo Lin to have some private language she couldn't understand. We sprang from the same soil, sailed in the same terrible old ship, weathered the same storms –"

Maybelle stretched to pour herself some more tea. She sighed.

"And will he go away with you?"

"We'll travel to 'Frisco together. I have to go there to see my publisher. He wants to bring out my Caribbo Tales in book form. And Alec won't rest till he's tried to find Soo Lin again, seen his children. He talks of working in 'Frisco."

"Will you stay there?" asked Maybelle carefully.

Annie's expression changed and faltered. "I don't know what I might do. Sometimes I think I would like to go back to Salt Spring. I think about little Aeneas. Maybe I could settle there. It's a beautiful island."

"Barkerville won't be the same without you."

"Barkerville will never be the same, in any case. But you must do your best for it, Maybelle. And I will often think of you and be thankful I knew you."

San Francisco was big and bustling, filled with people of all races, its saloons alive with piano music and hurdy-gurdies, its restaurants serving a variety of exotic dishes Annie had never heard of in her life. It reminded her of Glasgow in a way, with its hilly streets, although it was bigger, warmer and more cosmopolitan. She responded to the colour, the lively, sunny bay, the multiplicity of accents. The hotel she and Alec picked – they had separate rooms – was run by a Spanish couple of pious if easy-going nature. They were glad to get back to its quiet, somewhat dusty rooms after a day in town pursuing their various businesses.

She ran up the steps of the magazine company, eager to put a face to Wilbur J. Skeffington, Esq, the signature at the base of letters she had received. He turned out to be a brisk, amusing Yankee, wearing a checked suit, a loud ring and a bristling blonde moustache.

"You got a natural talent, there, Mrs. Mennock," he told her. "Where did you learn to write like this?"

She thought of McLaren of the *Sentinel* who had asked the same question and felt mildly mutinous. Nobody asked editors how they got to be editors. "I worked at it."

"You're Scotch?"

"And proud of it."

"You got a good education system going back there. All the Scotch I know can write and spell."

"We don't live in caves any more, if that's what you mean."

"Touché. But I mean it, I admire your style. Who taught you?"

"There were books in our house. They taught me."

"Good answer. Still doesn't tell me what makes one person a writer and another not."

"A mystery, isn't it?" she teased. She liked him. "It's a kind of presumption. Making life over. I'm not sure the Almighty approves."

"You would have that kind of reservation, being Scotch and strait-laced. All the Scotch I know have that stratum in them. You got a beady eye for human nature, though. I give you that."

"What," said Annie pointedly, "about the book you mentioned in your last letter? Will there be enough in what you've already got to make a volume?"

Skeffington nodded. They got down to business, Annie surprising him by her astuteness over payment. He offered a generous advance there and then. She went back down the steps with the money tucked securely under her arm. It was good to feel in command of her fate, to be told that what she had done was commendable. She looked back at such times on the girl who had been Muckle Annie, the one with the gaping boots and the empty stomach. What makes a writer? Skeffington had asked and she knew the answer was a complex one, to do with pride and deprivation as well as a kind of love for the people you wrote about. But she wasn't one for too much complexity. She wrote to find out who she was, she thought with some astonishment. How was that for an answer? She wrote because she liked it. How was that for another?

Now a week had passed and she had reached the decision that had been lurking in her mind ever since Barkerville. Her manner hovered between the hesitant and determined as she sat down opposite Alec in the dining-room to share a tortilla. First she put the question she had asked him every evening: "Any luck?"

Again he shook his head as he had done each night that week. "San Francisco is swarming with them, running laundries, cook-houses, you name it. But if they've seen Soo Lin, they're not saying."

"Did you go the Freemasons' temple?"

"They were quite helpful there. Asked me to keep in touch. I think they may be my best hope."

She put a hand out impulsively and covered one of his. "Alec, can I say something to you?"

He looked up and into her face, then away again, barely nodding.

"Don't live on hope alone. Try and set up your surgery soon. Do you remember Dr. Diet and Dr. Quiet and Mr. Merriman? There's another, you know, called Dr. Work. I think he would be best in your case." She invited him to smile.

"I hear you," he answered.

"You know what it says in Proverbs – 'Hope deferred maketh the heart sick.' I know the truth of that, Alec. I'm not saying give up hope. Just don't live on it. Turn your hand to what you do best. There are plenty of people here in need of your help – just look in the streets."

He said flatly, "All this is a preliminary to saying you're leaving, isn't it? You've seen your editor. You've got your advance. Where now, Madam Annie?"

"I am going to farm on Salt Spring, if I can. I've cashed in my shares in the mining and hotel company. I hope to get a small bit of land and a hired help. To see Aeneas and Hetty Laboucher –"

"And this Donald Arrochar you've told me about. Does he come into the picture?"

"Of course. He is a friend," she said, steadily.

His apparent calm deserted him then and he said, as though the words were forced out of him. "Why can't you stay here? I'm not suggesting we share a home. But we could meet sometimes, offer each other moral support."

"I don't know what to say to that. Except that if I did stay we could destroy each other."

"I don't see how that could be," he said stiffly.

"Alec, you would want more than I'm able to give."

"Was it so terrible, the one time you let me?"

"You know it wasn't. But if you find Soo Lin, what then?"

He put his head down on his hand and would not look at her.

"Alec," she said gently, "there's still your work. You used to say it was your dearest passion."

"There's also John Barleycorn."

Her expression hardened. "That's blackmail."

He gave an angry laugh. "What if it is?" The expression of anguish on his face tore at her. "He sits there in your heart, doesn't he? The one you vowed to love till death do you part. But he's a chimera. Why can't you care for me like that?"

"Because it wouldn't be right." He had struck where it hurt. "And because you can't choose who you love best. I'll never quite give up hope of seeing him again, whatever anyone says. I'll never stop loving him, either. That's the way it is."

"Go away, then," he said hopelessly. "I hope your prescription works for you, though I think you'll get sick of tending chickens. You'll end up knee-deep in good works and eccentricity."

"I intend to make it work." Her chin lifted. "I intend to take life by the scruff of the neck and make it work. I shall never give in. Never."

He looked at her with grudging admiration. She knew that protestation and pleading were building up in him, that he was looking to her for something perhaps only his adoring mother had ever been able to provide and she wanted to save him from further embarrassment.

"I will send you my address," she promised, "as soon as I have one. We must write to one another and one day I hope you'll be able to tell me Soo Lin has come back and you are seeing your children again. You must never forget how much they will need you."

"If you say so." The words were wrung from him in deepest reluctance.

She stuck her hand out towards him. "Friends?"

He took it and held it as though he could never let it go. He could not reiterate the word, the word that seemed to have the power to wound, but merely nodded.

On her way to Salt Spring, she spent a few days with her old friend Pheemie in Victoria. Pheemie, now the mother of three lusty boys, insisted on giving her the best bedroom and treating her like royalty.

"I remember the day we saw you off on the steamer," said Pheemie, misty-eyed. "I cried all the way home, I was so worried about you. But look at you now! You're – you're beautiful, Annie! And your clothes!" She pointed to the eye that had been operated on. "Your eye – what happened?"

"I had it fixed. Don't go on about me – you'll turn my head! I want to hear all about you."

It was one of the few periods in his life when Pheemie's husband had to wait for his meals and then sit down to meat that was alternately singed or watery in nature. The women scarcely stopped talking, Pheemie incredulous as she listened to Annie's adventures and Annie tenderly, openly envious as Pheemie recounted her life of simple, but blessed, domesticity. The little boys clambered all over their new 'aunt,' damping her lap, mussing her hair, but Annie enjoyed every moment of it.

She was sad when the time came to take the schooner to Salt Spring, silently contrasting Pheemie's busy family life with her own solitariness. But as she stood on the deck watching Victoria recede into the morning mist, she knew she must embrace that loneliness. Just as wider seas had separated her from her earlier life in Glasgow, so these waters were separating her from more recent hardships. She had time at last, after the terror of the fire, after being caught up in the imbroglio that was Alec's life, to think again of Hector. To ponder, quietly, on what his fate might have been, to learn to live again with the imponderability of his existence.

It seemed to her that at last she could feel closer to him again, could remember the good times, the days of loving and laughter. She fed ravenously on these memories, every time she saw a couple together or a child that was the age William might have been.

Coming to Salt Spring, deciding to farm, had been a kind of compromise between sacred memories and promises and the need to find some kind of fulfilment for the solitary Annie. Perhaps she would never have the rolling fields of grain they had visualised together, she and Hector. Perhaps never the huge cattle herds, the sheep, the orchards. But she could have a few pigs, a cow or two, cherry trees to yield a sweet, rich harvest and chickens clucking about the homestead.

She did not go to Donald Arrochar when she landed. Instead, she was seized with a strange kind of agitation and indecision about where to go, where to start. She found herself hiring a dogcart to take her to Hetty Laboucher's place. It brought back vivid memories of the day she had first encountered Hetty, when it had looked as though little Aeneas would die if she could not find someone to wet-nurse him. Hetty had been against her leaving the island. She was not altogether sure of her welcome. But when she knocked on the cabin door of the prosperous well set-up farm, it was Hetty who answered and who immediately held out her arms in welcome.

"Miss Annie! It *is* Miss Annie! I was dreaming 'bout you the other night and here you are. A grand lady now!" She shooed her goggle-eyed children in front of her as she ushered Annie in to the best chair by the stove.

It was the visit to Pheemie all over again. The children were a little more timid at first, but were soon touching Annie's rings, necklace and earrings with inquisitive fingers, until their mother explosively lost her temper and sent them all out into the yard to play.

Annie sat back and sighed. "Can I stay with you a day or two, Hetty?" she begged. "I want to seek your Joe's advice about buying a plot of land. Something with a pretty view."

"You coming back here?" Hetty could not believe her ears. "You alone? What happened to you?" Patiently Annie had to fill in the gaps, while Hetty's eyes grew wider and wider. Absently she made and served tea, refusing to take her attention for one moment from her visitor's face.

"'Course you can stay here," she said at last. "Joe is the best man to tell you about land. He might even sell you off a bit of ours. I know he's been thinking of it. We got more than we need and he could use the money for a fancy plough he's set his heart on."

"And the Arrochar farm?" said Annie tentatively. She could not bring herself to mention Donald or Aeneas by name. "Have there been – developments there?"

Hetty gave a broad and understanding smile.

"He ain't married, if that's what you mean. Not Donald Arrochar. We all thought he had the Gallacher daughter Alice in mind but she's got hitched to the hired man, Mac, and they've built their own cabin, near the farmhouse.

"But Mac – he was –" It was Annie's turn to goggle.

"He's talkin' better, walkin' better. They got a little baby. They're – sort of settled."

"Who cares for Aeneas?" There, it was out.

"Alice still helps out at the farm. 'Neas follows his pa like a little shadow. Wherever one goes, you see the other."

"He must be five now."

Hetty quickly noted the wistfulness in Annie's voice.

"You goin' over there to visit?" She tried to sound casual.

"I don't think so." Annie could not have explained why she gave the answer she did. She only knew she wasn't ready. Ready for what she didn't care to define. She sent one of Hetty's children to fetch a box from her luggage and produced sweetmeats which the little ones took from her shyly. Then she got the conversation on to general lines and when Joe came in from work, astounded by the visitor, she kept coming back to the practicalities: would Joe sell her some land and, if so, how much and where?

Joe was a quiet man, the only man Annie knew who could refuse to answer without giving offence. She soon realised he was not to be rushed, that he was considering the proposition from all possible angles. There was his brother Cuthbert to be consulted. There was the fact that he would have to provide land and work for his own growing brood. But the farm was big and by no means fully worked even now. The section he had in mind to sell off ran down to the bay and was partly of rock and shale, though he would include about two acres of good productive soil. "Ain't it too near the bay? What about Indian raids?" demanded Hetty. "Don't need to build near the water-edge. Y'can build on the hill. Then you look out to sea *and* all over the island," retorted Joe testily. "It sounds perfect." Annie was in no mood for drawbacks.

At last Hetty's impatient sighs and clucks got too much for Joe and he gave in; Annie could have the land and he and Cuthbert with their boys would erect a cabin to her specifications. They would have a building party, get men in from the surrounding area for a couple of days and the work would soon be well under way. For all this, he and Annie worked out a fair price and a delighted Hetty laid plans for a party to celebrate, plans that included such ambitious projects as a cow stuffed with venison, which they'd not had since Cuthbert's building bee. She would have an old friend close by and was more than pleased by the prospect.

"There's one thing." Annie faced Joe diffidently. "I don't want to ask Donald Arrochar for help."

"He never helps at building bees," Hetty interjected. "He's too set on tending his own farm."

"'Tain't that," said Joe. "He ain't got no gift for knocking in nails. Owns it himself. 'Sides, he got the biggest place round here. Takes a lot of looking after."

"Why do you not want to see him?" demanded Hetty.

"I do. But not yet." Hetty gave Annie a look that was almost comical in its bafflement.

While the cabin was being planned, Annie took herself off sometimes to rediscover the plants and the wildlife on the island, or just to fish idly with perhaps Joe junior for company. Despite the depredations of the Indians, there were still wild duck in plenty and she rejoiced at the sight of quail and pheasant and listened for the piping of the bald eagle.

How lovely it was, her island, rich and domestic and comforting after the sub-Arctic austerity of the Cariboo. She was enchanted all over again by glimpses of elk and Black Tail deer, of otter and raccoon on the beach, even by the wild pigs rooting as ever in the marshes. Sometimes she and Hetty just dozed in the sun, in the compound, the children playing around them, and she could not get enough of the warmth penetrating her bones. Soft breezes blew in her face, she paddled in the bay when she felt like it, she skimmed stones across the water's placid surface, she gave up thinking for an existence that was far from mere, that was rich with colour, sensations, sounds, vibrations.

She asked Hetty about Indians, but although they still came on their periodic duck hunts there had not been any raids for some time. It seemed Donald Arrochar had been prominent in trying to get a new deal for those Indians who wanted to settle, who resisted the cattle-thieving ways of some of the tribes. One or two of the island men had taken Indian wives. Hetty was not one of those who thought there would never be any more trouble from the Indians, but if they were active, they were choosing different areas to raid or terrorise. Hetty was insistent just the same that Annie's new cabin should be well fenced round and that Annie should get back into her old habit of keeping her shotgun by her side.

"I know. And cover my windows before I light the candles." Annie smiled strainedly at her old friend. "You once engraved that on my heart. It's still there." This time, the dread was in her that she would shoot first, out of terror, a policy that Donald had always warned could have disastrous consequences. She would not admit to anyone her nightmarish memories of the night Hector had been taken. To admit to hatred would be against all Hector had tried to instil in her about the native inhabitants, those with first claim to these parts – and the Cariboo – the Indians, yet hate them she did for what they had done to her. Her hatred gave her the courage to live alone in the cabin. She would not let them dictate the terms of her life. But she vowed to keep a shotgun in each of the two rooms and one slung over her shoulder whenever she moved about outside.

The building bee was an occasion for feasting and jollification and the relegation of fears. How these farmers had acquired their myriad skills – those of builder, carpenter, glazier, roofer – was a constant source of amazement to Annie. Gump Gallacher came, and Harry Ballantyne, pleased to see her again, innocently curious about her plans and on the last day Mac even turned up from the Arrochar farm with his wife Alice in tow, and their baby.

Annie felt her legs tremble as she walked towards them. Mac, whose beard was neatly trimmed and whose scrawny frame had filled out, gabbled something at her excitedly that she did not understand, but Alice intervened and said Donald Arrochar sent his respects. She could not take her eyes off Annie's handsome golden-brown dress or the brooch at her throat and Annie waited with a small spurt of acknowledgedly worthless vanity for the moment when she would spot the squint had gone. It came. But Alice, being Alice, blushed and said nothing. Taking pity on the girl's embarrassment, Annie picked up the toddling infant and fussed over him, admiring his curly locks and big, ingratiating smile. There was no need to ask if Alice was content. There was a bond between her and Mac that was touching to see.

Had she hoped that Donald Arrochar would come to the building bee himself? The answer to that had to be that her main sensation was relief that he hadn't. She could not explain this to herself except to acknowledge that she wasn't yet ready for a meeting. She contented herself with queries as to Aeneas's progress and was pleased to hear from Alice that he could read and write already, that he was a bright and happy little boy, active from morning till night. It was an almost maternal pride that welled up in her when she heard all this, compounded by a longing that was nearly physical to see the little boy again. Aeneas, whom she had saved from certain death on board the *Maggie Love Campbell*. Aeneas, whom she remembered lying back on his father's knee, that day they had all gone fishing before she had left to start her search for Hector. Her child and yet not her child. Oh, too much soreness of heart lay there. She turned away almost abruptly from the Arrochar trio and went off to help Hetty with the roasting of the cow, her composure threatened by an onrush of nameless emotions, in which Donald Arrochar as well as his child, was involved.

Almost miraculously, the stark structure of the cabin rose against the background of sea and sky. Harry Ballantyne brought over a second-hand stove in his farm wagon. Alice shyly proferred an iron cooking-pot she had inherited from her grandmother and Hetty had made curtains for the windows. Annie knew she had to exercise patience while the furniture and crockery she had ordered came from Victoria by schooner, but meantime so long as there was a roof over her head she wanted to move into her own place. The Labouchers had made her feel at home but she had ousted two of the children from their bed and there were times when the constant stir of a big family, combined with Hetty's uninhibited bawling when the younger ones got out of line, had made her feel she was presuming on friendship and causing strains where none had been before.

Meanwhile, there was the eating, and dancing, and music, and gossip, overlapping with last-minute jobs to be done. She had the feeling they all wanted to ask her more questions about why she had come back but they knew a little of what she had been through and they were considerate, respectful of her privacy. Harry Ballantyne's lad of thirteen, young Fergie, was lined up to come and work for her, though he would sleep at home with his family. She thought she might eventually get a maid who would 'sleep in' but for the moment she was determined to live alone. In some ways it was what she had been waiting for, the moment she closed the door of her cabin and let it all flood back into her consciousness, the love that she had vowed would be for life, that had been snatched from her, had once more seemed as though it would be restored and then had disappeared into the northern snowy wastes of the Cariboo.

She had to summon up memory, relive it all. And as she set her cabin straight, as the bed and the whatnot and the chiffonier and the table and chairs took up their places and the hand-hooked rug lay in front of the stove, she laid out the days she had lived with Hector, in her mind, and the essence of them came back to comfort her.

She had only ever wanted one thing, practically from the moment she saw him and that was to be with him. In their short time together they had known a rare happiness, a state so rich and nourishing to them both that they could have gone on to build a substantial life from it, embracing a family, friends, employees, the world at large. In both of them there had been the wish to work, to give, to transmute the gift of their love into good things for those around them.

And now. After the memories and the tears she came back to it. Now. Where was she now? How was she to make sense of *now*? She had never seen her husband buried. Unlike Maybelle, she had no grave to visit and tend, no headstone to remind her of what once had been. No certainty. Only the whisper of Hector's name in those trees where the encampment had been. Only feathers, stones, firs, to speak their mysteries. Only the word of a trapper who could have been half-crazed from his lonely existence, that he had seen a white man looking to the hills from the inside of an Indian encampment. Only snow upon snow, blank upon blank, hope flickering like a desolate little flame, that nourished nothing.

Had he tried to escape? She liked to think he must have done. But if they had crippled him, how could he have survived? Sometimes she hoped he had made that desperate lunge for freedom, even if it might have cost him his life and at other times she tried to imagine him biding his time, waiting for the right moment, even making friends with his captors so that one day he would be set free, having convinced them of the rightness of his case. But what did captivity do to a man? Did it reduce him to less than himself, eat away courage, sap his mind? She would not allow herself to think too much along these lines. She preferred to think of Hector the plotter, Hector kept alive by the wish to see her again ...

So this was what she had come here to examine, this hope, so pale, so flickering, that sometimes she could scarcely distinguish it, but which never quite went out. She had to find out if she could build her life around it, or if it would some day do her a kindness and go out altogether.

Until she had some answers, she did not want to meet Donald Arrochar face to face. From her cabin she could see as far as the Arrochar farm and it was his lean figure she made out sometimes behind a plough or working in the fields. That was enough.

Her days at first were busy, as she supervised the fencing round the cabin, bought in livestock – a cow, a horse, pigs, chickens – and set young Fergie to work in what she thought of as her Big Field, where she aimed to grow grain. Near the cabin, she planted fruit trees and set up a kitchen garden. It was amazing how quickly her small homestead assumed a settled air, looking as though it belonged in the landscape. It wasn't the farm – or rather, The Farm – as she and Hector and Big Jim and Irish Sam had envisaged it – but it was something that demanded her work, her attention and even her love. One day she brought out the gold nugget that had been meant for The Farm's mantelpiece and set it on the shelf above the second-hand stove, like a sort of affirmation. She had the feeling Hector would be pleased by the gesture.

Often it was as though some message emanated from her memories of him, so strongly it was as though he was there and she half-expected to turn and see that slow, consuming look of his, that had hurled her so often into his arms. *My jo*, she would think, tenderly. *If only you could be here, could see it all.*

It was after she had got a routine established, found out what she could and couldn't do, that grief came back and laid siege to her all over again. By day she remembered every detail of the trip to Humberton, her useless trek off up the hills with Eric Chisholm in pursuit.

And in the dark she woke from nightmares of loss and terror, of invasion, blows, death. In her dreams she wandered over snow that melted under her feet, leaving her in a fathomless wilderness where she could discern no cairn, no cross that marked a baby's grave. She heard grey wolves, she saw feathers, fire, scalps that lay like symbols in the wasteland. Sometimes she struggled to where he was and their hands caught, held, while their lips met and their bodies merged. But the waking was always bitter. At least when she wept nobody saw her. Even her grief was special to her, not to be shared. That was what she had brought to Springburn, named, inevitably, after the claim and the place where she and Hector had met.

One morning, after she had collected the eggs and set a broody hen to hatch some chicks, she was aware of a movement behind her and turned to see a black mongrel dog slinking in her shadow.

She shooed the animal away. "You leave my hens alone!" she warned him angrily. Maybe he had followed Fergie from one of the farms. In any case, she didn't want him around, not with his half-collie look of sly intelligence, as though he were just waiting for her to turn her back before he'd be off with the plumpest fowl in the yard.

The brute went down on its belly, half-wagging an ingratiatory tail.

"You've no business here," she warned him. "Get away." But when she came out of the cabin several hours later, he was still there, lying in a patch of sunlight just outside the door, as though he'd belonged there always, head studiously averted from the hen-run. Fergie thought he might have come from the Gallacher place, where they were always overrun with dogs and cats. When he left for home he dragged the unwilling animal behind him, on the end of a rope.

The next day the dog was waiting for Annie when she went out to feed the hens. Same ingratiating crawl, same careful tail-wagging. She gave him the scraps from her dinner. After that, he was her dog. There was no moving him from her side. She did not bother too much about a name for him. She called him Boy.

14

Fergie Ballantyne was a wiry, inquisitive youngster with button-bright brown eyes. She had brought him in from the savage, driving assault of the rain, to dry off and have some hot soup and because there would be no harvesting today. If the rain did not go soon, no harvest at all.

"Do you like living by yourself?" She tried to avoid his questions usually by treating him briskly, not allowing too much familiarity, but today she answered civilly, because he was after all a willing, hard-working youth and did not complain about the vicissitudes of the weather. "I've got used to it, Fergie. There are worse things than solitude."

"But," he pursued, "living on your own, being a woman —"

She permitted him to go on with a for-once indulgent look.

"I mean," he floundered, "you could turn a bit funny, like Miss Bates at Ardnacher. She talks to herself, they say. They say she's a bit of a witch."

"What do they say about me, Fergie?"

"That it's funny you don't talk to Donald Arrochar, when you used to work for him."

"They could say that he doesn't talk to me."

"My mother says he sent you his respects, and Mac and Alice to help you at the building bee. And that it was up to you after that."

"I'm glad folk keep an eye on me." Her irony was lost on the innocent Fergie. "But my life is my own. If I need advice from other folk, I'll ask for it. And now I think you'd be as well getting off home, for there's no work we can get on with in this weather."

"Did I say something I shouldn't?" enquired Fergie, hopefully.

"Not at all."

"Maybe if you didn't wander about on your own –"

"Boy comes with me." Why should she bother to justify her behaviour to the hired hand, she wondered?

"But it's not like folk, is it?"

"Listen," she said, anger mounting. "*You'll* get a reputation for being a gossiping old woman, if you're not careful. I collect plants and seaweed for their medicinal properties – I don't wander aimlessly. Away home now and learn to avoid tittle-tattle, if you want to keep working for me."

When he had gone and she picked up some sewing, she was troubled to note that her hands were shaking and her stomach churning. It was too much to hope for, that they'd leave her out of their gossip and speculation indefinitely. But then, maybe there was something in what they said. Maybe she did appear unfriendly. Maybe she could have got the meeting with Donald Arrochar over and done with, although she'd half-expected an overture from his direction.

They couldn't be expected to understand how difficult it was for her. To know the battle she waged daily to keep a meaning to her life. To realise her mourning, the mourning that was increasingly exacerbated when she thought how near they had been to securing Hector's safety, that time at

Humberton. *If Hector it had been.* They could not know how the longings and recriminations, the doubts and the cruel, needling hopes did battle in her tired mind. There were times when she thought it had all been a terrible mistake, coming here, thinking she could start all over again, gain peace of mind.

But neither could she have remained in Barkerville. That ghost town. It would rise again, no doubt, but she had lost the stomach for a fight. And as for San Francisco, what could there have been for her there? Muddle and compromise in her relationship with Alec. She thought of him often and dreaded the thought that he might once again be drinking. Although she had written to him twice, there had been no reply. He would still be angry with her, of course, but she had hoped that out of that anger would come the resolve to show her he could go on with his doctoring.

The rain bashed against the cabin window and she rose and looked out, unable even to see the bay. Mesmerised, she watched the streams of water meet up, run, separate on the window pane, widen, vanish.

She could not give him up. That was what they wanted, wasn't it? It was what Maybelle and Alec had wanted, had recommended; it was what Hetty would say, if she gave her the chance. Forget all about him. You have a life to lead. But she could not belong to anyone else, she could not give herself up to anything whole-heartedly, while that pale, miserable little flicker of hope remained, that would not, God damn it, go out.

So she would probably end up as eccentric as they said she would be, a half-mad 'old maid' except of course she could never be that. Half-mad, yes. Old maid, no. A hermit. A solitary. Obliged to live up to their image of her by uttering imprecations at passing children, by gathering plants and seaweed for medicine, sleeping with her clothes on, trusting no one. They'd be accusing her of turning the milk next.

"It isn't so far-fetched," she told Boy, whose dark collie eyes were fastened on her face, trying to read there when the rain would stop and they would be able to take a walk to the shore.

"We'll go, rain or not," she told him abruptly. She didn't want to eat, she felt less and less like eating. It had become a duty, a chore.

Somehow she had to find the will, the resolve, to go on. The rain was not so bad, she was well wrapped up against it, it was good to feel the wind taxing itself against her, it blew away those cobwebs in the mind. Boy danced ahead of her. If the mistress chose to walk in the rain, it was fine by him.

She took the path above the bay, watching the breakers, hearing the mournful sound of a ship's hooter, far off. The sun was struggling out from behind the clouds and suddenly there was a rainbow – a watergaw, her mother had called it. It straddled the bay, like some giant talisman arranged to rout the downpour. The stinging assault lessened, faltered, went. Boy shook himself vigorously and cantered back to her, as if to say 'Now we needn't hurry back.' She took off her coat and laid it to dry on a piece of bleached timber flung high up on the beach, while she sat on a rock and combed her fingers upwards through her hair, feeling the skeins dry by the minute.

"Where did it go?"

She started. The voice had sounded behind her and she turned, knowing who it would be, from a deep unconscious response, before her eyes rested on the child. He wore moleskin breeches and a navy blue jersey, like an infant version of a grown man.

"Where did what go?" She held her breath. He was a sturdy, handsome child.

"The rainbow. Did you see it?" Under her intense gaze he seemed to falter a little. "I shouldn't be here. I'd better get back –"

"Are you Aeneas?" The words were drawn from her, willy-nilly.

"How do you know my name?"

"Never mind that." She looked up. She could see no sign

of Donald, or even Mac, though she was not far, she realised, from the Arrochar farm. "Go back home, Aeneas. They'll be looking for you."

"I can run. I'm a very fast runner. Has the rainbow gone for good, then?"

"I'm afraid so."

"Goodbye, then." And he was off like a whitterick.*

She sat, after he was gone, smiling. He remembered nothing, of course, of the early days of his life when she had virtually been his mother. Even now, there had been a strange feeling of closeness in the encounter. She rose, stiffly, and with the dog walked a little nearer, nearer than she had ever been before, to the Arrochar farm. She made out the orchard, the fields, the outhouses. He had built on to the main building in her absence. The homestead looked substantial, prepossessing. A feeling akin to homesickness swept over her, almost as though it would be natural for her to go up to the front door, and knock and be taken in.

But her home was over the bay. She had her own cottage, with her own things.

"We must get back, Boy," she said. He gave her that look of total complicity that was near to being uncanny and picked his way carefully back over the uneven path, turning from time to time to make sure she was following. Aeneas stayed in her mind all day. His eyes, she thought, had been as dark as his father's. He had the same clever brow. And he seemed full of high spirits and energy. He was everything a little boy should be. It was a good and satisfying thing to know that she had given him his chance of life. It helped to sustain her when the other, darker things loomed, when her loneliness was bitter and palpable and no letters came from Maybelle or Alec.

Donald's visit came, totally unexpectedly, one afternoon when she was trying to settle again to some writing. Somehow, she had not wanted to recollect the Cariboo, had

* A weasel

been unable to reconstruct the lives there, had found too much unacknowledged pain attached to memories of her days and nights at the *Last Chance*, where she had listened to most of the tales that formed the basis for her writing. She had been staring out of the window, pen in hand, when the figure had gradually entered her consciousness, walking with deliberate steps over the tussocky grass leading up from the bay. Donald. She had stood like some semi-tragedienne, with her hands locked over her heart, waiting for his knock, thinking at first she would pretend to be out, then realising this would not work as Fergie was in the orchard nearby and would apprise Donald otherwise.

"Mr Arrochar."

"Mrs. Mennock."

"Won't you come in?"

She had forgotten how Highland-shy he was, the bigness and awkwardness of him, but she was able to take pity on him and it conveniently drove out the other feelings, temporarily at least, the feelings of alarm, defensiveness, funk.

"Please sit down," she said formally. "And can I get you a glass of something, or a cup of tea?"

"Yes," he said, arranging himself on the wicker chair with a decorous care that made her smile momentarily, inwardly, thinking what funny souls men could be, with their inability on such occasions to know what to do with hands and headgear and even facial expressions. This one was doing his best to look at home in a room full of feminine knick-knacks, frilled shelves, china vases and the like and from his uneasy look would much rather be out behind a plough. And then the spasm of amusement went, to be replaced by something more atavistic, more primitive. She had shared a cabin with this man. She had fended him off once with a gun. She had lain back in his arms, the day of the picnic, with the sun in her face. She felt herself blush now, like a schoolgirl, and could only hope he didn't notice.

"How have you been keeping?" he asked her.

"Quite well."

"Aeneas said he met this lady at the beach. I knew it must be you. I wondered whether you'd like to come over to the farm and meet him again."

"He's a grand wee boy."

"I didn't know whether – I mean, I'd heard things, about your husband. I felt I might be intruding."

"No, you don't intrude." She looked up at him and quite involuntarily her eyes swam with tears. She had forgotten how intuitive he could be, how surprisingly considerate, as well as awkward.

"What is it, lass? Should I not have come? I don't want to give them cause for scandal."

She dashed the tears away. "Let them think what they like," she said scornfully. "I am past worrying about that sort of thing. They think me enough of an oddity as it is."

"You have grown into a very fine woman. Aeneas was right. He said you were a beautiful lady."

"He did?" She blushed again.

"He was very taken with you. When I told him you who were, that you had cared for him when he was a babe in arms, he said I should come and talk to you and we should all be friends. He has more sense than you and me put together, has he not?"

"More tea? A scone?"

"But if you would rather I went, I will."

"No, no, please. It is an artificial situation, us not meeting." She met his shy solicitous gaze. "I have had so much to come to terms with. I don't know whether my husband is dead or alive. I waver between the conviction that his bones are bleaching somewhere in the Cariboo and the wish to believe that he is still held prisoner, even after all this time, by the Indians. It is the uncertainty that is killing. At times I do not know how to live with it."

He said nothing at first, merely bowed his head as if in some kind of acknowledgment. Then he said softly, "Live a day at a time. It is what I did when you went away that time."

"You know you shouldn't say these things."

"They are the truth."

"We have to put certain things behind us, if we are genuine about being friends."

"It is better to be honest. Shame the devil."

"I can't take this," she protested. "It's the reason I have kept away."

"Did you think of me, too, then?"

"I won't answer that. Donald, I warn you. You are going too far."

Her head came up and she glared at him in hurt and anger, only to see burning in his eyes an expression of suffering equal to her own. She made a gesture of hopelessness. "Oh, I thought I would find some peace here. I am finding none."

He said, with a steadiness that upbraided her, "I am offering whatever you need. I can't change my feelings for you but I do recognise that you are another man's wife and so what is between us must take the form of friendship. I won't overstep that friendship. You have my guarantee. But say you will come and see Aeneas. A child can be balm to a sore heart. I know that."

She said with a quivering smile of relief, "Oh, it's good to know where we stand at last. Aeneas has never been out of my mind. He's like my own child. I can help him with his letters, I can read to him. I shall order some books from Victoria –" She stopped, aghast at her forwardness. "If you say it is all right."

He nodded. "It *is* all right. Thank God, I have brought a smile to your face at last."

"So shall I come over one day and meet Aeneas?" She was establishing a kind of formality between them by her tone.

"Shall we say Friday? It's Alice's baking day. She makes wheaten scones and pancakes that go well with fresh butter."

"Yes, Friday then."

She saw him to the door, formally shaking hands with him outside for the benefit of Fergie, whose inquisitive head bobbed up and down like a robin's at a worm.

In formal voices they discussed what she was doing with the land. He opined that she was wasting her time growing such a small amount of grain, that it would be more rewarding to have livestock, that she could usefully extend the chicken run. He gave her tips on keeping pests at bay in the orchard and promised to teach her the skills of grafting. Then he set off back towards his farm. She watched him from inside the cabin till he disappeared from view. When she turned to set about her domestic tasks it seemed as though the house had a different, less lonely feeling to it. Maybe that was what it had wanted all the time. People calling. She could have the Ballantynes over to tea. And Pa Gallacher with the daughter who kept house for him. Even poor lonely Miss Bates.

And Aeneas would be coming! She looked around for anything that might amuse a child and was appalled at the paucity of objects. She would get one of those cup and ball things for him. And a cardboard theatre with figures to cut out and colour. She would get him paints. And a ball. No, wait, she mustn't be too generous. It might show his father in a poor light and be bad for his character. She would produce one new item per visit. What would he like to eat? Would he want her to tell him stories? And then she scolded herself, for after all, he was only a child, like her sister's children back home in Glasgow, and when had she found it hard to amuse bairns?

She was reluctant to draw the blinds that night. There was such a beautiful sunset over the bay, gold layered with apricot layered with deepest orange-red. The sea was calm save for the occasional undulating heave, like a sigh from a sleeping child's breast. She was able for the first time in months to give credence to the thought of a beneficent Deity.

Donald had not changed much. His powerful form had become only slightly stooped from labour. There was a tinge of grey on the temples of his thick, dark hair. What a contrast between his darkness and Hector's fair and ruddy looks! Donald *dhu* and Hector *bhan*. She sat musing with her crochet-work lying still on her lap. Boy scratched to go out for his final night inspection of the neighbourhood, then came in and settled on the mat.

"Good old Boy," she said to him and his silly tail thumped out a sleepy pleasure.

She blew out the candles and fell straight off into a dreamless sleep.

The stormy weather had blown itself out and now, with the sun making restitution, it appeared as though the harvest would be saved after all. But it meant hard work from morning till night, on farms all round the island. Fergie, when he had completed his less demanding role at Springburn, (for it had been too late to sow grain this year) went off to give what help he could to his father. Annie had brought Aeneas down to the beach for a picnic.

He was a child full of curiosity about everything that went on around him. When she told him some seaweeds had medicinal qualities – linarich for burns and megrim, for example, and dulse for headaches and skin troubles – he kept bringing new varieties for her inspection. When that topic was exhausted, they went on to plants. She explained how scurvy grass was good for stitches, nettles for nose bleeding, scabious and gentian as tonics and marsh trefoil for colic. The plantains were good for drawing the inflammation from sores.

She showed him the little book that had been Hamish's with the Gaelic names in it – *cuach phadraig* for the greater plantain, *tribhileach* for the marsh trefoil.

"My father says the Gaelic is our true language," he said earnestly gazing into her face. "He says he will teach me some when I am older."

"I've no doubt you'll learn quickly enough," Annie laughed. "You are a glutton, you are, for knowledge."

"I think my father likes you, because you are a Scot, like

us," said Aeneas. "Though not Highland," he temporised.

"Is that bad?" she teased him.

"Oh, not at all," he assured her, kindly. "I am sure it is quite all right to come from Glasgow. Although you don't have the Gaelic, you cannot help that."

There was something of Effie's imperiousness in him, which she found touching, since he had never known his mother. And she tried to coax him out of the introspection which seemed to be part and parcel of the only child by getting him to run races with her, skim stones and play guessing games.

While the harvesting went on he seemed to spend more time at Springburn than at the farm and Annie had to make a conscious effort not to feel too proprietorial about him. He was so trusting and affectionate, so responsive and although she knew she was probably prejudiced, she was certain he was a child of rare mental ability.

When she mentioned this to Donald, he laughed and nodded. "He'll end up a professor of medicine," he admitted. "I don't see him running the farm when I am gone."

"Would you have liked him to do that?" she queried.

"I would have liked one son with a feeling for the land." Their eyes met and as quickly they looked away again. It was dangerous ground and they both knew it.

Her role as 'Aunt Annie,' though she greatly cherished it, was in danger of bringing her too much into contact with Donald and she took steps to prevent this by sending Fergie to bring the child on his visits to Springburn and taking him back afterwards. She hoped Donald would understand. Sometimes there would be constraint in his manner when they did meet, a certain hardness that suggested hurt, but it was better than allowing too much warmth or familiarity. Did he not see that it cost her, too?

She felt that curiosity about her among her neighbours was abating and they were beginning to accept her on her own terms. She attended church service and met them there.

She exchanged produce with them, she undertook to teach one or two of the smaller children their letters and put them through the Catechism.

"You're looking better," Hetty assured her. "But I wish I saw that sadness leave your eyes."

There was nothing she could say to that. All she could do was throw herself into work on the small-holding. There was satisfaction to be gained from growing things and tending animals, and although it was paid for in aching muscles, it guaranteed dreamless sleep at night.

She was planting winter cabbage one afternoon when Boy skittishly led a visitor towards her. The man carried a wooden box on his back and delivered it at her feet.

"Delivery from Victoria," he said, panting heavily.

"For me?" She was expecting nothing.

"Orders was to deliver it personal. I came over on the *Fideliter*, the mail boat."

She made the weary man a mug of tea and spread home-made scone with lavish butter, then slipped some money into his hand as he departed.

She gazed at the box in puzzlement. It was not unduly heavy. For some reason she was in no hurry to open it. But at last she did. On top lay a large envelope addressed in a spidery, copperplate, unknown hand to Mrs. Annie Mennock. She tore it open.

It bore an address in San Francisco and read, "Madam, My late client, Dr. Alexander Comrie, directed that these, his medical books and instruments, be sent to you and directed to such use as may be commendable to you.

"You may not be apprised of the manner of my late client's death. While visiting a wharfside area in search of information about his family, he was attacked and robbed by a Chinaman carrying a knife and received a stab wound from which he died in hospital ten days later.

"It was there that I met him, while visiting a friend in the next bed and was able to pacify him in his dying moments by promising to carry out these instructions in my capacity as lawyer. I have waived any matter of a fee.

"My late client wished to let you know of his undying esteem and affection for you and asked that you make good use of these instruments and text books of his profession or at the least, hold them in memory of him, as being all he possessed at the last."

The letter was signed Ferdinand F. Jones but Annie could barely read it for the tears that gushed to her eyes and throat. With a cry of protest she lifted out the contents of the box – the microscope and slides, the delicate surgical instruments, the books, the notes, the latter in his small, cramped, immaculate hand. From the dates on the latter, she was able to see he had been working until recently and this stabbed her sorrow with something like gratification.

She put everything back into the box, including the lawyer's letter and in a kind of daze took her cloak from the hook behind the door and wandered down the rough path to the shore. She could not help it, she was reliving the last hours she had spent with Alec, hearing his protest, "He sits there in your heart, doesn't he? The one you vowed to love till death do you part. But he's a chimera." And her own voice replying, "I'll never quite give up hope of seeing him again. I'll never stop loving him, either."

"Friends?" she had said and remembered now his look, as though the simple word had had the power to wound and kill.

Somehow she had failed Alec, even as a friend. She had left him to sift through the lower depths of the 'Frisco waterfront, without making him face up to the fact that Soo Lin would be swallowed up there, sealed off from him by sheer weight of numbers, perhaps even carried by her sense of outrage back to China or to some other city in America where he'd never be able to find his children again.

If she had stayed, she could have helped him to come to some kind of terms with his life, to get back to what was his real purpose, his medicine. But could she have kept him away from drink? He would have demanded more and more from her. That had been the crux of it. She had not wished to be compromised, had not wished to change.

It was like a kind of suspended animation, it was like being in a perpetual waiting room, her life. She was not able to move emotionally, one way or another and yet her very stationary-ness seemed in itself destructive. She had been bad for Alec and her guilt was compounded now, by his gifts.

She sent a message to Donald, saying she was unwell and would not be able to have Aeneas for his lessons. She did not want to see anybody. She was abrupt with Fergie and irritable with Boy. She crept inside her skin, neglecting the vegetable garden, doing the minimum of household tasks, sitting by the window, staring out over the bay, sometimes crocheting furiously, sometimes sitting so still she could have been carved out of alabaster. Thrown back into the initial state she had been when she first came to Salt Spring.

When Donald finally called, she would not let him in. She stood shivering, drawing her shawl around her, protesting she was still feeling frail but would be all right and would contact him again when she was ready. Even a message from Aeneas, that he was missing her, did no more than light a momentary gleam of pleasure in her face.

He went away nonplussed and she was glad, or did not care. Her only pleasure for the moment was her solitary walks, when she looked for her medicinal plants or seaweed and brought them back and tried to draw them and write about them. She read avidly through Alec's notes and textbooks, furious because her sketchy education left her unfitted to understand so much.

That had been Alec's real attraction, she began to see. His mind. She had been fascinated by it, jealous of it, even. Her femaleness and her early poverty had cut her off from the higher activities of the mind, yet she knew she had the capability of understanding a great deal. Her brain lay like a rusty, under-used instrument that had never been honed. Well, she would use it now. She would read and study and contemplate and write. She knew she would be the subject of much conjecture and speculation, but she could not allow it to matter.

Alec's jibe had been that she would end up 'knee-deep in good works and eccentricity.' Maybe he had been right. She didn't know about the good works, but if she could understand a little better about how the body worked and particularly its interaction with the mind — which had been Alec's speciality — then perhaps she would be able to help the island people when they were sick.

Alec's box included works on astronomy, astrology and metaphysics. She laboured over these, getting nowhere. She was happiest with his notes, where he had written down the treatment and its outcome of many patients. Through everything he had written ran the need to establish a rapport between doctor and patient, gaining and maintaining confidence. At times it seemed almost as though he were saying it was the doctor's expectation and confidence in recovery which pulled a patient through, or persuaded a nervous one to relinquish his symptoms. Mind over matter.

Daily she struggled to make sense of much that was beyond her, until a kind of defeated lassitude fell on her once again. She was not Alec, nor ever would be. It seemed that wherever she turned, she was unable to find satisfaction. Perhaps eccentricity was all that was left to her. She was back in the world of *if only*. *If only* Hector were alive, restored to her. *If only* her baby had lived. *If only* she had been better educated.

"Annie."

She had come out without bothering to comb her hair or change out of her rough working dress, with an old shawl about her shoulders, and was standing on the seashore, looking out over the bay.

He was right behind her, having come up silently while she mused. She gave him a barely attentive glance.

"Oh, it's you."

"Aye. It's me, Donald. I should be at my desk, seeing to my bills."

"And why aren't you?"

He grabbed her by the shoulders and turned her towards him.

"Because this has gone on long enough."

"What has?" she asked, maddeningly.

"Cutting yourself off. Why won't you even see Aeneas? He doesn't understand what he's done."

"He's done nothing."

"Then is it me?"

"Oh, no." She sighed and looked down. One of his hands had taken hold of one of hers and was gripping it, hard, as they walked. She tried to take it away and couldn't.

"Let me go." He pretended not to hear her. They walked the length of the bay and back again. Saying nothing. Somehow as they walked he moved even closer to her, till his arm was about her waist and she was leaning against his hard bulk. Her hair blew in his face.

"Annie," he said at length, "I have been lonely for you. I have been thinking, all the time I'm working in the fields, and I've come to the conclusion that you are lonely, too. For me."

"What makes you think that?"

"Why did you come back here? I've thought about that, too. Apart from Hetty and Joe, who did you know? Only me and Aeneas."

"I love the island."

"That is natural. It is your home."

She stopped and looked at him with a crumpled face. "I have no home. No rest." She wouldn't take her eyes from him. It was as though she appealed to him, desperately, for an answer.

He gathered her up then and brought his own face close to hers. With great tenderness he kissed her eyes, then her brow, then her mouth. She moved her face, but he brought his lips against hers once again. He felt her sag against him, then her arms went round his neck. They clung wordlessly, unable to break apart.

"Annie," he whispered. "For Christ's sake, let me come to you. Tonight." As she moved away protestingly he pleaded, "Even if it's just to talk."

She did not answer yes or no but began to walk towards the cabin.

"I'll come about seven," he called after her.

She heated water and pouring some into a flowered basin washed all over and changed into a blue gown with a pretty muslin collar. She brushed and dressed her hair. Then she sat down to wait for him and just before seven o'clock he came.

She took a juddering breath and said plaintively, "It will be all over the island. That you've come."

"Well," he answered, hardly, "they don't put the bread in my mouth, so why should I care?"

"I'm a married woman. What about my reputation?"

She had forgotten about his positive, dark, animal presence. Into her mind there flashed a quick image of the night she had fended him off with a shotgun, when she had wept for desire for him but had not given in to it. She could feel these sensations come back to her and fear made her fingers twist in her lap. She gasped as though sobbing.

He came over and knelt beside her, taking her hands and stilling them between his.

"I've never taken a woman against her will and I won't now. Be easy." His dark eyes reassured her. "I've come to get you to talk about Hector." He anticipated her cry of protest and said, "Aye, we must. I should have done it at the beginning. He is a lost cause, I am afraid. It is getting on for three years since he was taken. You have to accept that you are not going to see him. Ever again."

She gave a wordless wail. He went on, despite it, "If it is the formalities you are worried about, I have been to see a Scotch lawyer in Victoria. If you cannot have Hector presumed dead, he says that after four years you can have a divorce, on the grounds of desertion. Being Scotch, he accepted your first, if irregular marriage. I am prepared to wait till things are regularised, if that is what you want. But I would rather put the proposition to you, that you come and live at the farm from this very time, with Aeneas and me. I would regard you in every way as my wife and Aeneas's mother. Later we can have a wedding ceremony, if you wish."

"You went to Victoria?" She gawped. "To see a lawyer about me?"

"I would go anywhere, to get you peace of mind."

"I may never have that."

"Do you remember, the night long ago when I bade you to come to me and at first you did – though you fended me off with a shotgun later?"

"I was just thinking of it."

"What would happen if I asked you to come to me now?"

She sat still for a moment, then rose and stood in front of him. He pulled her down on to his hard knee and she raised her face for his kiss. When she drew away at last he said in a broken, tender voice, "Your home is on the island. Your home is with me. Haven't you always known that, my Annie?"

15

"Look!" cried Aeneas. "This one's the fastest. He must be the strongest. He's ahead of all the rest."

"Stand back," Annie ordered nervously. She had always thought the method of decanting new cattle into the sea and letting them swim for shore alarming and primitive, but Donald assured her the waters were warm and he and Aeneas were certainly enjoying the sight. Donald had ordered fifty of this new hardy strain from Victoria, which promised to make him the biggest cattle farmer on the island. Since she had said she would sell Springburn and come and live with him, he had been brimming with new schemes and ideas, his evident happiness humbling to her and restorative in a way that daily surprised her. Aeneas was as blissful as a puppy. He came up now and hugged her skirts. "Don't worry," he said, stoutly. "I'll protect you. But they won't hurt you."

The bullock which had made the shoreline first shook himself, bellowed and made off at a fine lick along the beach. Mac tore after him, with Boy skirting the dunes, ready to nip and tuck. They would be all day getting the cattle into the requisite field, then branding them. She had come at Aeneas's insistence to watch the action, but now she had to get back to the cabin and finish packing. Tomorrow the farm carts would transport her things to the farm. Her solitary life at Springburn would be over. Joe had agreed to buy back the smallholding for his son Charlie, who was talking about getting married. Maybe he had regretted selling the land in the first place and had only done it on Hetty's insistence. At any rate, it seemed providential that there had been no problem of getting rid of the place.

Seeing her make a move, Donald came over to her and, putting an arm round her, hugged her reassuringly.

"Don't do too much," he appealed to her. "You'll have all the help you need tomorrow." He looked down into her face and smiled the widest smile she had ever seen. "I feel my life is due to begin tomorrow. I must be the luckiest man alive. The farm is thriving, I have a fine, healthy son and the only woman I have ever loved is going to share my life. I ask myself if I deserve it."

"You do deserve it," she assured him, softly.

"Are you happy, too?"

She nodded tremulously, her face clouding only momentarily.

"No regrets? About what people might say?"

"When the lawyers sort things out, I will be your wife in the eyes of the law. But when I come tomorrow, I will be your wife in spirit and in fact. I will take your name. I am coming to you of my own free will."

"That's my Annie talking. Do you remember what you used to say to me, when you first came to the island? 'They don't call me Muckle Annie for nothing.' I thought you were a headstrong little piece, even then."

She laughed. "I'd almost forgotten the nickname. But you might find me headstrong still. Not your conventional wife at all."

"I'll take you at any price," he said. He was like a passionate boy. She laughed again as she put her hand out and touched his face.

"I don't know what there is about you," he said. "You little witch. You put a spell on a man. You turn every day to gold."

She left him and climbed the easy hill to the house. The bellowing of cattle, Aeneas's uninhibited shouts, the low rumble of the men's voices, followed her. Torn between two loyalties, Boy had elected to stay with his work and his sharp, authoritative bark made her smile. He had made no secret of the fact that he would like it at the farm, that, while she was still first, someone like Aeneas was an unexpected bonus in a dog's life.

She could not afford regrets, she thought, harking back to the conversation with Donald. Regret lay in the past but now she was being pulled into the future. Recently she had felt a return of her old stamina, her old determination to take life by the scruff of the neck, as she had once told Alec, and make it work. To have continued along the old paths would have been a negation of life and she could not think her Maker would approve of that. Surely he would overlook the minor transgressions such as not waiting for the marriage licence, when her intentions were to be a good wife to Donald and a perfect mother to Aeneas. Having more or less settled the moral argument in her own mind, she did not greatly care what any of the neighbours said. It was up to her and Donald to carry the situation off with all the bravura they could muster.

She felt a sharp pang as she came upon Springburn bathed in the golden glow of the island sunshine. She had laboured hard over it, but it had never become the live, rewarding place she had wanted it to be. Here were too many sad memories. Here Hector's ghost had been almost palpable in the beginning and still was as she opened the door. She stopped, momentarily, on the threshold, knowing it was only memory playing its tricks. But in her mind's eye she saw him, her golden boy, laughing as they bathed in the stream near Cottonmill; looking up at the stars the Christmas before the attack, saying she was his Fate. Her love for Hector was there, would always be there. She made a gathering gesture with both hands, as though she took him into herself.

There was a lot to accomplish. She left the curtains by the windows and the hooked mat by the stove as presents for Charlie Laboucher and his bride, but she gathered up everything else, wrapped what needed wrapping and packed everything into baskets and boxes. Last of all she took down the gold nugget Hector had given her and put it in her reticule for safe keeping. If she could make Donald understand what it stood for, one day she might place it on the kitchen mantelpiece at the farm.

Boy arrived home at sunset, worn out by his day's cattle-minding. She fed him and pottered about near the doorway, unwilling to go in on such a perfect evening. The island was so peaceful. She could see a light wink at the farm and then disappear as a blind was drawn. That would be the parlour light. Tomorrow night she would draw that blind and take her chair on the other side of the stove from Donald. Smiling, she remembered touching his face earlier that day, seeing his expression kindle. She would have his bairns. She could feel this expectation inside her, fluttering like a bird in its nest. A son to carry on the farm. For Aeneas would never get his hands dirty, if she could help it. Aeneas was special. The first.

Sometimes when she lay in bed it seemed to her that the island sang to her. It was only the susurration of the surf, carried on the breeze and the intermingling of sounds, animal and insect, but it was like a lullabye. The fancy suited her mood tonight. She sank into the feather mattress of her narrow bed, listening, then not listening, drifting like a snowflake towards the airy realms of sleep ...

'ANNIE.'

She sat bolt upright, sure she had been dreaming. But it came again. A thundering on the door and Donald's voice frantically shouting her name. "ANNIE! For God's sake come quickly."

She flew to lift the bar back and let him in.

"Is it Aeneas?" she demanded fearfully.

"Get something on your feet. Where's your cloak?" He stood, painfully drawing breath, while she raced around doing as she was bade.

"It's Indians. They're in the neighbourhood. I think they're after the new cattle. I couldn't leave you here on your own."

He pulled the door of Springburn behind them and they stole with furtive speed back towards the farm.

"Some were spotted by Ballantyne, coming in by canoe. He thinks they're in cahoots with the Cowichans who live on the island. The incomers have shotguns."

"I thought all this was over. That they didn't do this kind of thing any more." She was panting from fear and exertion.

"No. It still goes on. We've just been lucky. If they'd got you –"

"Well, they didn't," she said stoutly.

"I'll never let you out of my sight again."

They dodged along the shelter of hedge and tree as far as possible, then, convinced they had not been seen, slipped carefully into the farmyard, sticking to where there were shadows. The door opened on the instant of Donald's knock.

"They're up the field behind the cattle," said Ballantyne, who stood in the kitchen with his shotgun at the ready. "Must be a hundred of them. Reckon they'll take my beeves while they're about it. My field comes down to yours, after all. They've worked this one out."

"What do we do?" demanded Annie.

"Don't go out there," said Alice. She stood shivering in her nightgown with a shawl about her shoulders, Mac by her side. Fergie was posted upstairs, keeping watch from a darkened bedroom window. A sleepy-eyed Aeneas had been brought downstairs and listened to all that was said from the depths of his father's big rocking chair.

"They've got the better of us this time," Donald admitted. "We can't deploy ourselves among the trees the way we did that last time they came. We're outnumbered."

"I hate to let them get away with it," said Ballantyne. "The thieving bastards. Ain't in my nature to stand here doin' nothin'."

"We could loose a few shots."

"Not when they've got guns too."

"They won't get away with it," said Donald, slowly, "because I'm going to follow them, see where they end up. And if I have to get the law in from Victoria, we'll get the cattle back in the end."

"Where the Cowichans are, back of the island, it's real primitive," Ballantyne demurred. "You got cougar there. You got wolf."

"Please don't go," Annie pleaded, whey-faced.

"I think it was the Haidas who came in by canoe," said Ballantyne. "They ain't noted for their civility. I ain't ever known them hitch up with the Cowichans on the island before. Must be 'cos the Cowichans got horses. Mostly they scalp each other." Annie's hand flew to her throat.

"They must need the beef and leather."

"Whatever pact they've made, it's bound to be short-lived. Maybe the Cowichans have been forced into it, 'cos the Haida got the shotguns."

"Don't ask me to read the Indian mind." There was a shout from upstairs, from Fergie, and Donald raced up the stairs with Ballantyne behind him.

"They got the cattle moving," Fergie cried. "They got

ours too, Pa. They got the lot."

"Mac." Donald looked directly at his hired man. "You game to come with me?"

Mac nodded immediately. Annie and Alice looked at each other and their joint protest seemed to come from one throat.

Donald took Annie's arm and shook it in gentle reprimand.

"You stay here and take care of the others. We'll come to no harm. I don't aim to tangle with the Indians, just keep track of them. We got to get the beasts back, my capital's tied up with them. Bar the door when we've gone and keep those windows darkened. Right?"

She nodded, her mouth drained of saliva. She found her hand clasped in Alice's boney, dry one.

"Mac," said Alice. "You watch out, then. Hear me?"

"Get us some bread and cheese," Donald commanded Annie. He stuffed his pockets with home-made lead shot and bullets and slung a second shotgun over his shoulder. When the two men had gone, Annie made hot drinks for those left and Alice put more wood on the stove. The two women could not settle at first, but as the night passed they dozed fitfully by the table. By the time dawn came, Aeneas was curled up like a kitten, dreamlessly asleep, Ballantyne and Fergie slept on the floor and the two women, stretching aching bones and muscles, quietly went about the business of stoking the fire, heating water and preparing porridge, whispering their estimates to each other of when Donald and Mac might return, trying to reassure each other everything would be all right.

As the day strengthened and the familiar farmyard sounds began, these reassurances became more strained. Leaving Fergie behind, Ballantyne returned to his own farm and Annie and Alice carried out the necessary duties with one eye cocked towards the hillside for the men's return. There were a few milk cows to be seen to, hens and pigs to feed and baking to be done. To keep Aeneas gainfully occupied,

Annie set him to churning butter, then to cutting out scones. She was finding it more and more difficult to keep down a sensation of sick panic.

Then when the late afternoon light was beginning to fade the men reappeared. They were pale and exhausted, saying nothing as they peeled off outer clothing and laid down their guns. Donald claimed his chair by the stove and lay back with a look of total fatigue.

Mac gabbled something at his wife but Annie could make nothing of it. She saw Alice start back with an expression of horror, and with a growing agitation shook Donald's arm and demanded: "What happened? For God's sake, Donald, tell me."

"There was a bloody massacre. They got to the Cowichan camp and something set them off against each other. I don't want to talk about it. It was too horrible. I'd heard about Indians' killings before. I never thought to see them. I think the Cowichans won. The Haida cleared off in the end."

He looked at Annie so long and hard she felt her pulse foundering. "What is it? You have something else to tell me."

"The Haida had a white man with them. We saw him, Mac and I. He dragged one leg behind the other. At the height of the fighting we saw him make off into the trees. You can't imagine what it's like back there. A wilderness. There was no way we could follow him."

"Hector." She said the name and staggered a little, as though she were about to fall. She did indeed sink to her knees, so that her face was on a level with Donald's. "It must have been Hector." Her teeth began to chatter and her limbs go into a kind of convulsion of shivering. She made a high, keening sound that was almost animal in its pain. "He's come back for me! He's come back!" She beat Donald's knees with her fists. "Where is he? Where can I find him? I must find him!"

"Wait a minute." Donald's voice was uncompromisingly harsh. "We don't know it's him. It could be another white man they've taken prisoner."

"What was he like? Did you see his face?"

"He wore Indian hides. His hair was long and fair. He loped rather than ran, dragging one leg behind him. He was too far away for me to see his face."

"Oh, my poor Hector. What have they done to him?"

"Annie, do you hear me? You have to realise. It might not be Hector. The odds are it can't be him. He was taken prisoner a long way from here, and a long time ago."

"Even if it only *could* be him," she said, "we must find him. Let's saddle the horses. Let's go."

He put out a detaining hand. "It's almost dark. We could see nothing tonight."

"If we leave it till morning, they might come back for him. The Haida never give up, you know. They'll find him before we do. Why are you hesitating?"

He said nothing. With a detached part of her mind, she registered how his face seemed to have lined and aged since the day before. He stood up, almost swaying in his fatigue. "Annie," he said at last inarticulately. "Annie –"

She ran and buried her face against his chest. He could feel her wild trembling agitation. She looked up into his face, her eyes full of a desperate pleading. "I'll come with you," he said. "Let me wash and eat something."

She let her arms fall away from him then. "No, you're right. We'd see nothing tonight. And if we took lanterns we'd give the game away. You need to rest. We'll leave at daylight."

"That makes more sense. I'll tell Mac to get the horses ready for dawn. He can come, too. He's a better woods-man than I am and can pick up tracks."

"You rest," she ordered. "I'll see to everything else."

They had ridden across the island, protected by the morning mist and now they stared down on vegetation and forestation so thick and impenetrable it seemed any life would be stifled there. Mac had made them lead their horses into a screen of trees. From there, in a kind of horseshoe indentation of the jungle-like forest, they saw the tepees of the Indian encampment. The stolen cattle had been herded into a makeshift corral at the far end. They could hear their restless lowing. Smoke was rising from camp fires and there was movement which indicated the preparation of food.

"Are those —?" Annie began, when her eyes discerned objects on poles around the encampment.

"Don't look," said Donald. "Yes, they're heads. Scalps. I told you. It was bloody murder."

She turned away, sickened and afraid. "What do we do now?"

"As far as the cattle are concerned," said Donald, with a low note of anger in his voice, "we do nothing till I get a posse from the mainland."

Mac interjected with his gabble of difficult speech. Donald nodded. "Mac says the white man has probably tried to work his way through to the shoreline. We could do the same. We can ride back inland in a kind of arc, come back to the other side of the forest shore and work our way along it. There might be tracks there. It would be hopeless to penetrate the forest."

"But if he's in there —"

He said "Let's go along with Mac. I trust his hunches."

She cast another look towards the lush tangle of greenwood then reluctantly conceded. They rode their horses thankfully away from the witness of the previous day's carnage. At one point when it was well behind them, Annie dismounted to be sick but, whey-faced, was soon back in the saddle. When they got to the shoreline she began to feel a sense of relating to the island once more. Round the lazy curve of the bay she could even see Springburn, far in the distance, on its little knoll, and its familiarity was somehow reassuring.

They dismounted and Donald handed round the water bottle.

"What now?" said Annie helplessly. "Where do we begin?"

Mac indicated that Donald should take the shoreline path in one direction while he took the other. Annie was to keep a lookout, stay with the tethered horses and use a whistle if anything untoward occurred.

She watched them go, fighting back an almost uncontrollable impulse to plead with them not to be left on her own. But she had instigated this search; she could not opt out of it now. She looked fearfully back towards the forest, almost as though she expected Hector to spring forth from it with a loud cry. She scanned the horizon out to sea, fearful of catching sight of Haida canoes. Would they come back for their prisoner? And where was he? She felt a terrible empathy for whoever it might be, Hector or otherwise; prey to the unknown terrors of that dark green interior and the unaccountable atrocities of his savage captors. "Please God, deliver him," she prayed. Her legs were as weak as water.

A long, low, piercing whistle reached her. She looked to the left and saw Mac windmilling his arms excitedly. Like someone in a dream she began to walk towards him. Although he was not more than half a mile away, it seemed to take her an eternity to reach him. Before she did, Donald had caught up with her. She felt his hand go under her arm, supporting her.

A figure lay in the centre of a small sand dune, spread-eagled on his back, his hair blown over his face. She ran now, flying out of Donald's grasp and moved the hair away from the face. The hair and the sand.

"Hector. It's Hector."

Donald knelt beside her, lifting the man's arm to feel his pulse. "He's still alive," he nodded. "But, my God, what a state he's in."

Branches had torn his clothes, his arms, his legs, his face. There was a deep gash above the right eye, oozing blood. He lay deathly pale and still. Annie moved his head on to her lap and looked up at the two men. Something dragged her gaze back to Mac's face. "What is it?" she demanded fearfully.

"I know him." For once she could make out the mangled words. "He's Hector Mennock."

"Hector," she affirmed. "Hector Mennock. Get me water, Mac. Back at the horses."

She saw protestation rise up in Mac, who turned towards Donald, gabbling again.

"Do as she says, Mac," ordered Donald, quietly. "Quick. And bring a blanket, too." As Mac hesitated, then strode off, he took a flask of whisky from his hip pocket and handed it to Annie. "Try moistening his lips with it."

She took the object, though she scarcely seemed to hear him, and with great tenderness moistened the tips of her fingers and then Hector's lips. Still he remained unconscious, totally inert.

"He can't die," she said. She picked the grains of sand from his face, careful not to touch the wound and deep scratches. A string round his neck caught her attention. She pulled at it gently and saw it went through the half-coin she'd given him when they first met.

"Why doesn't he move?" she asked Donald. "Why doesn't Mac hurry? What was he trying to say?"

"This is the man he had a fight with, back home, Mac was left for dead. His brothers let the Mennocks believe they'd killed him. It was their form of revenge. When Mac recovered he was palsied, he couldn't speak properly. The injury to the head did it, where he'd hit a stone. To compound their story, they shipped him out to me. I'm a distant cousin."

"I've only ever known him as Mac," she said, unbelievingly. "I never knew he was MacAndrew. Colin MacAndrew." She gave a grating laugh. "They got their own back, all right. The guilt they put on Hector nearly killed him. Did you know that?"

Donald shook his head. "Look," he said, excitedly, "he moved his head. His eyes are opening!"

She held her breath. Beaded by grains by sand, Hector's lids fluttered open once, then closed again. She took up one of his hands and rubbed it almost dementedly. "Hector! My dear, my jo! I'm here. It's your Annie."

Muckle Annie

Again the eyelids fluttered. The eyes remained open this time, but stared blankly skywards. Mac came back and wordlessly handed Annie the water bottle. She took the edge of her petticoat and, moistening it, wiped Hector's brow and then his wrists. Then she held the bottle to his lips and saw him gulp. His head moved again. "Where?" he said. "Where is this?"

"Salt Spring." She could scarcely get the words out. "And it's Annie you're with. Your Annie!"

His smile seemed to touch her everywhere, so that when she looked up Donald could feel his own constraints desert him at her radiant face. He reached out involuntarily and touched her as though to bring her back to him. "He knows me," she said. "He knows me."

"Annie," said Hector, so faintly she had to put her head down to his face to hear the words, "Stay with me. I'm dying."

"No," she said, her voice cracking, "no, Hector. We'll save you."

"Annie," he said, in a stronger voice, "I am seeing him again." His eyes had fastened in anguish on Mac. "The face, the face."

She said, with great and tender deliberation, "It is Colin MacAndrew, Hector. He came to Canada and is alive and well. When you saw him that time on the schooner, out of Victoria, he was coming here to Salt Spring. He was no dream, no hallucination. He was flesh and blood. Do you understand, my darling, my jo? He is alive. He forgives you." She looked up at Mac pleadingly and after a brief pause, he nodded.

"Annie." It was Donald who spoke, in a voice carefully ironed of all emotion. He indicated she should look at Hector's left leg, which he had begun to move restlessly. The hideskin had moved to show a gaping wound, possibly made by an arrow or bullet, that had begun to bleed again profusely. Donald shook his head hopelessly.

She laid Hector's head back on the sand and stood up.

Lifting her skirts, she precipitately tore a great band of material from her white petticoat and quickly and meticulously bound up the wound. All the while she gave orders in a low, controlled voice.

"Mac, bring my horse, will you? Donald, your jacket." She tucked it under Hector's head. "Donald, when the horse comes, you and Mac must seat Hector up behind me, so that he can lean against me. We have to get him home quickly." She looked down at her husband's face. It was almost without colour. His eyes had closed again. She moistened his lips and tongue again with the whisky.

"I don't think we should move him," said Donald.

"We must," she insisted. "We can't leave him here."

"Annie." It was Hector who spoke her name again, in the merest whisper. She put her head down so that her ear was almost against his mouth. "I found you at last."

She put her lips to his. "Hector," she said, "I waited so long. Don't leave me now."

"Annie!"

"What is it, my love?"

"I – want – you. I – always –"

She held his face in her hands, his scarred and weather-beaten face. "Don't talk," she said gently. "Save your strength. We aim to get you home."

When the horse was brought, Donald picked up the injured man as though he were a child and did as Annie bade, sitting him behind her so that his head lay forward on her shoulder. Donald then mounted his own beast and walked it alongside Annie, his hand ready to go out and steady her burden if it seemed as though she might slide off. Mac came close behind.

Annie could feel Hector's hands lay a feeble grasp to the top of her skirts. She could feel his breath on her neck and the clammy moisture from his skin. His head lay heavily against her, a dead weight she could scarcely support, yet must. As though it knew the nature of its burden, the big mare picked her way forward with a delicate tread.

They were almost at the bay below Springburn when the canoes appeared. As ever, it was as though they came out of nowhere and moved of their own volition. There were only three of them and perhaps a dozen Indians. Even as Donald saw them and shouted a warning the Indians saw the riders. They sprang from their canoes immediately they were beached. This time they appeared to have no shotguns, but they quickly unleashed a brief volley of arrows in the direction of the horses.

"Ride for the farm," Donald shouted. He pointed his shotgun at the air above the Indians and pulled the trigger. Mac did the same. Annie pulled on the reins of her now madly galloping mare and even as she did so felt something thud with tremendous impact against the poor beast's side. The horse stopped with calamitous suddenness and Annie felt the world tilt as the animal fell over, taking her and Hector with her.

"Run! Run for cover!" Donald shouted. He rode forward toward the Indians, still shooting above their heads. Some had turned for the canoes, but about half the number were running fleetly behind rocks, shooting arrows with a certain wildness of aim that indicated they were doing what Donald and Mac attempted – to scare without killing.

Annie scrambled to her feet and turned towards Hector. He lay inertly where he had fallen. She put her arms under his shoulders and tried to heave him to his feet. She saw Mac wheel his horse towards them and then dismount to try and help her.

"Try to stand," she ordered Hector desperately. "Stand, my darling." She felt him make a superhuman effort to do as she bade. At the same moment she raised her head and saw the Indian take aim at Mac as he came towards them. Hector seemed to follow her gaze and then before she could do anything he had somehow stretched, stood and pitched himself between Mac and the arrow. The arrow went into his side and he fell like a stone.

"Hector!" Her cry seemed to freeze the very air. She felt

Mac tug at her arm, mumble some order. She saw Donald wheel and turn to ride back towards her. She shook Mac off and threw herself down on Hector's body, screaming his name. Even as she did so, the Indian who had shot the arrow came forward and tugged Hector's body away from her, dragging it as though it were some animal towards the canoes.

She would not let go. The Indian made angry threatening sounds but she held on. She felt herself stumble into water and then her arm almost pulled out of its socket as the Indians already in the canoe helped their comrade to pull Hector aboard. Still she held on.

"He dead." The Indians pushed at her. "Leave him," she screamed at them. She knew he was dead. She had known the moment the breath left his body, when the arrow hit his side. He was dead matter. But she held on. The canoe moved off and she grasped its side with both hands, feeling herself propelled through the water until some hard instrument struck her hands and she had to let go. She went down, down and then something halted her descent and pulled her up out of the watery element and into air. She screamed and screamed again. It was Donald who held her but she fought at him with her ebbing strength, trying to get out of his arms, to catch a sight of the canoe that was Hector's bier.

Arrows lay around on the sand. Everything had been churned up by horses' hooves and running feet. Panting, Donald lay beside her, just at the water's edge, so that their feet were still lapped, touched by waves.

"No," she wailed, "let me go with him. Hector! Hector!"

Donald lay over her, pinning her arms. "No," he said. His chest heaved with the exertion of the rescue. "You must understand, Annie. It is finished."

"Why did they come back for him?"

"He was their prisoner. Dead or alive, he belonged to them. It was a question of honour."

"He belonged to me."

They were walking slowly along the beach. It was the first time she had walked any distance from the farmhouse. The day was wearing away, with a light, warm breeze stirring the grass, lifting the ends of her auburn hair. She leaned on his arm, feeling her frailty, stopping for breath.

"He saved Mac's life. He was what you said he was. A man worth loving. But he belonged, as we all do, to God," said Donald.

She disengaged her arm and walked forward to the water's edge. From round her neck she took something and held it in the palm of her hand, looking at it for a long time. He joined her, looking down also at the object.

"I gave him the other half, the day we took our vows," she said. She threw the half-coin, with all the strength she could muster, into the water. "Now mine must wear away on the sea bed." So softly that Donald barely heard she whispered, "Goodbye, Hector. Till the day breaks and the shadows flee."

She felt his comforting arm go about her, his lips pressed to her brow. Gently he turned her away from the sea's edge and led her back towards the farm. In the distance, they could see Boy and Aeneas, coming zigzag down the fields towards them.

"Look," Donald pointed. "Can you see the elk on the hills?"

She looked and saw and nodded. He felt her hand tighten in his, the first lightening of her step. Always on the instant he would know her mood, wait for the rarity of her grave smile. As now.

"Let us go home and trim the candles," she said.

... And After

"So this is the place?"

"The very place. There are the steps that got me into all the trouble. And here's the gate I ran through, with the angry tears tripping me."

The man leaned forward and read the brass plaque on the gate. "It seems it's a children's home now."

"I dare say Henderson the engine-maker's been dead a long time." She rubbed her fine kid glove against the iron railings, bemused by the sudden, sharp image of a scraggy girl in ragged clothes, with gaping boots. "I always wanted to come back in a grand carriage with feathers in my hat and pass him with a haughty look."

"You have the feathers in your hat," said Aeneas, "but you'll have to make do with a But-and-Ben car back to town."

The handsome, richly-dressed woman, her auburn hair lightly tinged with grey, drew the spotted veiling back down over her face and smiled at her companion.

"Electric tram cars! Who'd have thought it!"

"I have to describe them when I get back to Chicago. Chicago wants them, too. It's Chicago's declared intent to become America's Glasgow."

She sat musingly as the tramcar snaked its way back towards Mitchell Street and the centre of the city. They had chosen to sit in an open compartment, without glass, so that Aeneas could smoke his pipe. The day was in any case mild and the air sweet.

"I never thought," she said to Aeneas, "when I gave you Alec Comrie's instruments, the day you went to medical school, that one day you'd bring me back to Glasgow because you had to attend a medical convention."

"That little tenotomy hook! I still use it. You encouraged me so much, you know. I'll always be grateful."

She gave him a look compounded of deep, quiet pride and affection. She would rather he had been bringing a bride on his first trip to Europe. Ever since he'd gone to work in Chicago, she'd waited and hoped for news that he'd found a wife to share his life and work. Maybe there had been something, that hadn't worked out. You could not enquire too deeply. And there was still time ...

"Are you missing the farm?" he asked her.

"I'm missing your father. I must get some fine tweed to take back. It's time he had a new suit for Sundays."

"Katie'll be spoiling him."

"More likely, he'll be spoiling her." She knew her youngest child, the Katie who had come after Malcolm, John and Ritchie, was the apple of her husband's eye. Donald would not leave the farm, or the island, but had urged her to take this trip back home.

It had been lovely to make the sea voyage in a fine new ship, with Aeneas an ever-solicitous, ever-informative companion. Perhaps she *had* encouraged him, but she had been given so much back from that clever, lively mind. Even so, Salt Spring was pushing its way back into her consciousness, more and more each day.

Aeneas offered her a hand as she alighted from the tramcar.

"You'll soon be back with them all, you know," he teased. "Back with the boys bickering over the new plough and whether Colina MacAndrew will choose John or Ritchie, or neither of them in the end!"

She laughed. Glasgow was all they said it was, prosperous, bustling, exciting and there were still things she wanted to see and do.

But Aeneas, intuitive as always, like his father, divined her thoughts aright. She could not wait to go back there. To Salt Spring. Steea. Her island of fire.

HEYWOOD BOOKS

TODAY'S PAPERBACKS
– AT YESTERDAY'S PRICES!

Heywood Books is a new list of paperback books which will be published every month at unbelievably low prices. It will range from up-to-date contemporary women's novels to exciting romantic thrillers and the best in historical romance, from classic crime to nerve-tingling horror and big adventure thrillers, presenting a superb list of highly readable and top value popular fiction.

Look for this month's new titles:

HAMMERSTRIKE	*Walter Winward*	£1.75
GOD OF A THOUSAND FACES	*Michael Falconer Anderson*	£1.50
MUCKLE ANNIE	*Jan Webster*	£1.75
THE WINDMILL YEARS	*Vicky Martin*	£1.75
QUICKSILVER LADY	*Barbara Whitehead*	£1.50
THE WINNOWING WINDS	*Ann Marlowe*	£1.50

QUICKSILVER LADY
Sequel to THE CARETAKER WIFE
Would she make a 'good' marriage or marry for love?

Barbara Whitehead

Arabella was eager to go to London to taste the delights of fashionable society. Disappointed in love, she hoped that the distractions of the city would sooth her aching heart. At the advanced age of twenty-one, she hoped to find at last the man of her dreams.
London welcomed her with balls, masquerades, theatres, eligible young men – and trickery. Seeking fashion, wealth and the advantages of a great match, she found instead that she too must follow the dictates of her own heart.

THE WINNOWING WINDS
Death and danger lurk in the snow-clad mountains

Ann Marlowe

Deirdre Sheridan hoped that a teaching post at an expensive school in glamorous jet-setting Gstaad would help her forget a recent tragedy. But there is danger and the threat of death even in the idyllic peace of the Swiss mountains. Among her pupils is the heir to the oil-rich sheikhdom of Qaiman, an obvious target for kidnappers and assassins.

But Deirdre is captivated by Prince Haroun and his two motherless young sisters and when one near-fatal accident follows another, she becomes increasingly worried about their safety. In her anxiety, there are only two people she can turn to: Sadiq, the children's enigmatic but attractive uncle; and the father of another pupil, who has gone out of his way to befriend her. But as the peaceful Alpine resort becomes a setting for violence and conspiracy, she realises she cannot trust even them . . .

THE WINDMILL YEARS
Two sisters, with the world before them
A dazzling saga of contemporary love

Vicky Martin

They were sisters, but no-one would have guessed it. Anna was tall, overweight and terribly shy, a talented artist who was terrified of men. Her sister Linden was a superb professional cook, coolly beautiful, poised, and ruthlessly pursuing her ambition to marry a rich man.
But both Anna and Linden find that life – and love – are infinitely more complicated than they had ever imagined. Anna becomes obsessed with Freddie Munroe, an ambitious art dealer who thinks that she too can be moulded according to his wishes. And Linden chooses James Carroll, cold, successful and rich, ignoring her passionate feelings for a penniless art student . . .

HEYWOOD BOOKS

FICTION
One Little Room	*Jan Webster*	£1.50
The Winnowing Winds	*Ann Marlowe*	£1.50

SAGA
Daneclere	*Pamela Hill*	£1.75
Making Friends	*Cornelia Hale*	£1.75
Muckle Annie	*Jan Webster*	£1.75
The Windmill Years	*Vicky Martin*	£1.75

HISTORICAL ROMANCE
The Caretaker Wife	*Barbara Whitehead*	£1.50
Quicksilver Lady	*Barbara Whitehead*	£1.50

THRILLER
KG 200	*J. D. Gilman & John Clive*	£1.75
Hammerstrike	*Walter Winward*	£1.75

HORROR
The Unholy	*Michael Falconer Anderson*	£1.50
God of a Thousand Faces	*Michael Falconer Anderson*	£1.50

NAME ....

ADDRESS ....

....

Write to Heywood Books Cash Sales, PO Box 11, Falmouth, Cornwall TR10 9EN.
Please indicate order and enclose remittance to the value of the cover price plus:
UK: Please allow 60p for the first book, 25p for the second book and 15p for each additional book ordered, to a maximum charge of £1.90.

B.F.P.O. & EIRE: Please allow 60p for the first book, 25p for the second book, 15p per copy for the next 7 books and thereafter 9p per book.

OVERSEAS: Please allow £1.25 for the first book, 75p for the second book and 28p per copy for each additional book.

Whilst every effort is made to keep prices low it is sometimes necessary to increase cover prices and also postage and packing rates at short notice. Heywood Books reserve the right to show new retail prices on covers which may differ from those previously advertised in the text or elsewhere.